# THE SECRET JOURNAL
# OF BRETT COLTON

# THE SECRET JOURNAL
## OF BRETT COLTON

—

*Kay Lynn Mangum*

DESERET
BOOK

SALT LAKE CITY, UTAH

Visit us at DeseretBook.com

**Library of Congress Cataloging-in-Publication Data**

Mangum, Kay Lynn.
  The secret journal of Brett Colton / Kay Lynn Mangum.
      p.   cm.
  ISBN  978-1-59038-399-5 (pbk.)
  1. Tutors and tutoring—Fiction. 2. Brothers—Death—Fiction. 3. Teenage girls—Fiction. 4. Mormons—Fiction. I. Title.
  PS3613.A538S43 2005
  813'.6—dc22                                                     2004024079

Printed in the United States of America
Malloy Lithographing Incorporated, Ann Arbor, MI

10   9   8   7   6   5   4

*To my parents*
*H. Ben and Janet M. Mangum*

*And in memory of my twin brothers*
*Bret and Bart Mangum*
*who were the inspirations for this book*

# ACKNOWLEDGMENTS

Special acknowledgments to my wonderful family and so many friends who have always given me such great support with my writing. Thank you so much for all of your help in the writing of this book.

And to the people at Deseret Book, especially Lisa Mangum, Chris Schoebinger, and my editor, Suzanne Brady. I can't thank you enough for believing in my story and working so hard to get it into print.

A special big thank you to my good friend, Cheryl Lynn Navas, a great writer and editor, without whose amazing help, support, and encouragement this book would never have made its way out of the back of my closet and over to Deseret Book.

# CHAPTER ONE

I must have stared at that picture a thousand times. The picture rested in the same spot where it had for years, on the top shelf of our living room bookcase. Like countless times before, I was drawn to it, my feet moving me slowly towards its oval frame. As I'd done a thousand times before, I lifted it from the shelf and curled up on the couch to study it. The boy in the picture was fifteen years old at the time it was taken—a boy with dark black hair and soft blue eyes. He'd always been big for his age, but in this picture, he looked thin. Too thin. I knew it had been taken when it was first discovered how sick he truly was, and that at the same time, his little sister was born. His little sister who was me.

My eyes narrowed as I stared at his face. Because of him and his sickness, my babyhood was pretty neglected. Next to no pictures existed of me as a baby, or even as a little kid. In fact, my family remembered hardly any cute things I did when I was little. No one knew for sure when I started to crawl, walk, or cut my first tooth—or even my first spoken word—because at the time this picture was taken, the boy in the picture—my brother Brett—found out he had leukemia. According to my family, Brett put up a huge fight for two years, but the disease eventually won, and at the age of seventeen, he died.

It was completely self-centered of me to feel like I had a neglected

1

babyhood, but since I *was* the youngest in my family—and a surprise baby at that—I didn't think it was a stretch for anyone to believe that I must have been the center of attention. However, this obviously didn't happen. Nothing I did was as important as anything that was going on with Brett.

I carefully brushed the thin film of dust off the glass covering Brett's picture. It was puzzling. More than just puzzling. Confusing. Strange. I'd never known him at all, because he'd died when I was two. And yet, somehow, there was something there—something just out of reach that I couldn't quite touch about him. Almost a—*connection* of some sort.

It was too crazy, of course. Any connection I might have thought I could feel was likely due to the fact that my family talked about Brett nonstop. It was a rare moment when my family spoke about anything or anyone else. Especially whenever my brother Alex and my sister, Samantha, and their families came to visit. Both of them lived close by, so my parents and I saw them pretty often, whether I wanted to or not, mostly thanks to our weekly Colton Family Sunday Dinner. There weren't two people on earth I had less in common with, although I did get along with Alex better than I did with Samantha. Sam. The gigantic age gap I had with Sam had to account for some of the issues I had with my sister—me being fifteen and Sam in her early thirties. But even without the gap, I think she'd still get on my nerves.

Whenever Alex and Sam and their families came over to visit, our family's unique, mind-boggling event would occur. No matter what subject was discussed, the conversation would work its way back to long, drawn-out memories of times with Brett and all of the amazing things my family claimed he did basically every other second of his life. Competing with perfect live brothers or sisters is difficult enough. Try competing with a brother who because he's not around anymore has reached Martyr Status. My family always forgot there was a reason I didn't enjoy the Brett Memory Sessions. Maybe to them Brett was a superstar, but to me, he was nothing but a stranger.

2

I frowned, studying the picture closer. Although my family loved to go on and on forever and ever about Brett, no one ever talked much about the struggle he had with his illness, except to say that it was, of course, heroic and that he'd successfully made it into remission once. Other than that, no one liked to get into that period of Colton Family drama.

"Kathy, honey—are you finished straightening the living room yet?" Mom's voice. I'd almost forgotten why I'd come into the living room in the first place.

"Is there some reason it has to be cleaned up this very second?" I griped.

"Because Sam and Stephen and Alex and Julie will be here any minute for dinner, and they'll need somewhere to sit down before we eat," Mom called back irritably.

I sighed. "Do they have to come over for dinner tonight?"

Mom stuck her head in the living room doorway with a hurt look on her face. "You know they want to come over and wish you well on your big day!"

I rolled my eyes. "I'm just starting high school—it's not that big of a deal!"

"Off the couch, Kathy—I need some help in the kitchen!"

I turned my head towards Mom's voice, ready with one last retort, but instead of looking at her, my eyes were drawn to the sparkle around her neck. It was always there and had been as long as I could remember. I couldn't speak as I watched Mom absently twirl the gold heart on the chain around her neck while she looked at the picture of Brett. Once Mom had stepped back into the kitchen, still clutching her necklace, I looked back down at the picture in my hands and shook my head wryly. *It figured.* The heart necklace my mother always wore was a locket that held a picture of a baby—Brett—along with a picture of him before he died. Big surprise for us all that the only pictures she'd want inside a locket would be of Brett.

3

I couldn't make my fingers loosen their grip on Brett's picture as I pushed myself off the couch, and while I walked back to the bookshelves, my eyes roamed over the other pictures.

The first was held delicately in a large, shiny gold frame. My sister, Sam. She's the oldest in the family and was a high school senior when it was taken, dressed in her maroon and gold Central High drill team uniform. At that time, Sam's hair was long and glossy black. With her body turned to the side, only her face smiled teasingly at the camera. Whatever else my sister might be, one thing I had to admit was that she's beautiful. Placed by Sam's picture was a black, heart-shaped framed picture of her in her wedding gown with my brother-in-law, Stephen. A small, 3 x 5 picture of my nephew, Curtis, rested inside the bottom of the frame, angled to fit inside the heart.

My eyes moved to the pictures taken at Alex and Julie's wedding before pausing to linger on a 5 x 7 frame filled with three faces: my oldest brother, Alex; my brother Brett, who was a year younger than Alex; and Kelly, Brett's best friend in high school—a real handsome guy with blond hair, big blue eyes, and a smile guaranteed to turn any girl into a quivering glob of Jell-O. All three were in their football uniforms, laughing, with their arms around each other, looking all hot and sweaty, right after our high school took state in football. In this picture, Brett looked a lot like my father, with his wide grin, blue-black hair, and eyes that slightly turned up at the corners, but Alex looked like me. We both had Mom's sandy blonde hair, greenish blue eyes, and skin that refused to do anything but burn and turn white again in the summertime.

I studied Alex's face for a moment and felt my eyebrows draw together. Alex didn't play football anymore after high school. I asked him why once, out of idle curiosity, but all he said was, "It's just a game, Kathy. That's all. It's not important."

I frowned as I stared at Kelly's face. I knew little about him beyond the fact that he was Brett's best friend and had played football with Brett and Alex. No one in my family talked about him. Not only had I never met him but I couldn't remember him visiting even once. Or seeing just a Christmas card from him. But Kelly was part of Brett's life, not mine. There was no reason for me to care about anything to do with him, so I didn't bother to ask questions. It would only have led to questions about why I was asking, or worse—more Brett stories.

A gold 8 x 11 frame sat next to the picture of the three football heroes. In it was a nice studio portrait of my parents all dressed up in their Sunday best, so to speak, since we weren't exactly a church-going type of family. Even so, our family was pretty close, whether I liked it or not. My parents loved family get-togethers. They couldn't get enough of my nephew or of having everyone around every second possible. And of course, they loved to encourage every conversation about Brett that they could.

I sighed and looked at another shelf. Both of my brothers and my sister loved drama when they were in high school. Besides the yearly class pictures, a lot of the pictures on our bookshelves were from plays they had performed in. The year Sam, Alex, and Brett were in high school at the same time, they were actually in the musical *Once upon a Mattress* together—a comic version of "The Princess and the Pea" fairy-tale. In this version, the king is silent throughout the play because of a witch's curse, and because Brett couldn't sing, he got the role of the king. The king acts as crazy as Brett supposedly did, so apparently the part was perfect for him. Alex and Sam had large roles in the play, too, and from the way my family talked about it, this play was the funniest and the best play Central had ever done or ever will do.

I stared long and hard at all of the pictures of my family's famous high school moments. Unfortunately for me, because my brothers and sister were major athletes and drama stars during high school, knew how to dress right, eat right, and breathe right, and were popular in every way, my family assumed that I'd follow suit. Right down to forcing me to enroll in Drama 101 instead of a literature class, which I really would have liked to take instead.

"You keep your nose buried in books too much as it is. The last thing you need is another *English* class!" Sam had said that as if the word itself was poison. "What you need is something that will force you to be social. Drama is a great place to do that."

Drama had been shoved down my throat after that. I fought hard for my literature class, but Alex and Sam worked on Mom and Dad and convinced them to force me to enroll in drama.

"Good—that'll yank her out of her shell a little." Sam had grinned in an obnoxious, triumphant way. "We'll work on your hair and wardrobe next."

I sighed again resignedly and looked down at the framed picture still gripped in my hands, searching Brett's haunting, grinning face for I wasn't sure what before I put it back in the center of the top shelf where it belonged.

———

In honor of the big moment when I would enter the hallowed halls of Central High School for the first time as a sophomore, Mom had made my favorite dinner: cheese-stuffed tortellini noodles. Not that anyone noticed either of these two amazing events for long.

"I remember when I started Central High," Sam sighed dreamily before taking even one bite. "I really do envy you, Kathy. I would just love to live it all over again!"

I rolled my eyes and dug into my tortellini. It was going to be more than enough for me to have to live through the whole experience once.

"I'd give anything to relive a week. Man, I had some good times then!" Alex agreed.

"It's hard to believe our little Kathy is about to start high school!" Dad shook his head. "Remember when Brett started Central?" I stopped in mid-chew. Our family's unique, mind-boggling event was obviously about to occur yet again. "He wasn't anything like the rest of you. He had to be the class clown and make everyone laugh." Dad was smiling absently at basically nothing.

"And yet he always managed to get wonderful grades," Mom chimed in.

"Yeah, and don't forget what he did for Central High," Alex continued. "He helped the football team go to region his sophomore year and state his junior year."

"And he always insisted that he never chased girls. *They* chased *him.*" Annoying uproarious laughter followed from everyone but me after that remark from Sam.

"He was wonderful about tending Kathy while I was at work," Mom sighed. "It still amazes me that a teenage boy would be willing to spend so much time babysitting. Most girls wouldn't have put up with it as much as Brett did."

"I know *I* surely couldn't have stood it back then," Sam said, shaking her head.

"What a surprise," I stated dryly, digging fiercely into my tortellini. I was actually amazed at the angry-slash-hurt looks I received from everyone at the table. Except for Julie and Stephen. At least they seemed to find my attempt at dry sarcasm slightly amusing.

"Really, Kathy," Mom began.

"Well, anyway—Brett was definitely one in a million," Alex cut in with a broad grin.

I stared at my half-eaten plate of food. I couldn't help the familiar, hollow feeling that was growing in my stomach just as it always did whenever my family got sentimental about Brett and times forever over and gone. Unfortunately, my family couldn't seem to help themselves. The well-worn rut down memory lane would be traveled yet again. Everyone was so enthralled with Brett's amazing feats that no one seemed to notice the mess Curtis was making. I watched with dull, glazed eyes while Curtis smashed bits of tortellini Sam had carefully arranged on his plate before happily smearing the mess into his hair and onto his face.

"You know what we haven't done in forever that I've been dying to do?"

I shook myself free from my trance to look hopefully at Alex. *Please let it be something that's at least slightly exciting!* I begged inside my head.

Alex was grinning at everyone's expectant looks. "Let's get out our old home movies! And not the ones transferred to DVD—the ones on the old reels!"

I sat stiffly in my chair through all the hustle and bustle while Dad, Alex, and Stephen set up the old projector and movie screen. Julie and Sam followed them with Julie holding Curtis, listening patiently to Sam's babbling about our amazing old home movies. Mom had begun to follow them but turned back to look at me expectantly.

"Kathy, you're going to come watch the home movies, aren't you?"

I hesitated before quickly standing to snatch and stack the dirty dinner plates as I moved around the table. "Someone's got to clean up."

"Oh, honey, that can wait. We'll clean up the kitchen together later."

I wasn't in many of our old home movies, and I really wasn't in the mood for more nostalgia tonight. "You know the kitchen will start to reek if all of this food is left out for long. I'll join you in a few, okay?" But Mom wouldn't take no for an answer, so I was forced to relent and follow her into the living room.

We turned out the lights, and in a few seconds the familiar hum and click of the old projector began. A blurry green with shiny colored splotches flared into view before Dad focused it into its true Christmas tree form. The first couple of reels were filled with Halloweens, birthdays, and Christmases when Sam, Alex, and Brett were little. I watched the silent images before me with only the projector's hums and clicks for background music. Everyone else laughed and interrupted each other with bits and pieces of half-remembered old memories. I wasn't sure what I was feeling, but I couldn't pull my eyes away from Brett's impishly grinning face, racing Alex along beaches during the summer-time—flying over our front driveway doing wheelies on his midnight blue bicycle—tripping Sam (something he truly enjoyed doing on film)—and ripping open red-and-green-wrapped Christmas presents under the tree. My eyes were stinging from staring so long and hard. Why is it that in old home movies everyone always looks so much happier than they are now?

I was glued to the screen, but at the same time, I could feel myself fading, drowning, wanting to yell, scream, say something—and each reel was pushing me forward through the next year and the next until the images swam in a blur and I couldn't see anymore. My familiar hollow feeling was in full force, and I knew I wouldn't be able to take much more.

"Honey, are you all right? What's wrong? Don't you want to—"

I didn't think I'd made that much noise when I decided I'd had enough, but a second later, Mom joined me in the kitchen. I tried to pretend I was fine and made my voice as flippant and uncaring as I possibly could. "Mom, just out of curiosity, why don't we use the old movie camera anymore? Or better yet, why haven't we bought a camcorder? Doesn't anyone think we've done anything noteworthy in the past, oh, say, thirteen to fourteen years?" Mom opened her mouth to speak, but I was on a roll and didn't pause long enough to let her answer. "I mean, since everyone only talks about stuff that happened when Brett was alive, then I guess it's safe to say that no one thinks we've done anything interesting since Brett died. Right?"

Mom slowly walked towards me and reached out to touch my hair. "Honey, you know that's not true. We've had some wonderful, special times together since Brett died." Her voice was low and soft. "I know it's hard for you to have to listen about times you weren't a part of—"

But I didn't want to hear anymore. "I just wish everyone would forget the past and just—move on. Why can't we all just *do* that?" I demanded. "Brett's gone. Why can't this family just move on?" I could feel a lump rising in my throat, and as I swallowed hard, Mom's hand dropped from my hair. I knew I'd said enough. Probably too much.

"Kathy, honey—" Mom whispered.

I stepped away from her and faced the sink, leaving her to stare at my back. "Please, Mom. Just forget it. I don't want to talk about it anymore."

I spent the rest of the evening hibernating in my bedroom until Alex and Sam finally left. That wasn't unusual for me to do when they came for a visit. After locking myself in my room, I always turned to an ancient record player balanced on a little rolling table with two small, square speakers on either side of it. It was an old family dinosaur bone and had been kept in my room for just about forever. I had a nice CD player, but since I'd never gotten around to buying CDs of my favorite record albums that had also been in the family for eons, I had to spin the turntable if I wanted to hear my favorite old LP. Ever since I could remember, I'd put on an old, scratched-up Beatles album—*Rubber Soul*—to relax and sleep after an especially trying moment in my life. Nothing else cured the dark for me like that album could.

After lying flat on my back for a few minutes, I forced myself off my bed and flipped on the ancient record player before setting the *Rubber Soul* album on the turntable. I sank back onto my bed as Paul McCartney's voice softly crooned, filling up every empty space in the room.

I was forced back into reality when the last song ended. Although our home movies ended abruptly with Brett's death, leaving only a few glances of myself as a baby, my family's lives weren't as completely over as the movies might lead an outsider to believe. At least, mine wasn't. I had other concerns in life besides listening to times long gone. I could go for days—even weeks—at a time without thinking about Brett. But I couldn't avoid our living room forever, and then I'd see that picture of him on the top shelf, and as unavoidable as day, I'd feel that strange connection again.

# CHAPTER TWO

True to her threat, Sam took me clothes shopping and insisted on buying me a cashmere sweater. A lavender-colored one with a square neckline and long sleeves, which she claimed was "just meant for me." I had to admit, it *did* look good on me, so I grudgingly let her buy it.

"Now promise me you'll wear it your first day of school," Sam demanded before we'd even left the L'Armoire clothes shop.

I rolled my eyes. "It's still August. It'll be too hot for sweaters!"

"It's your first day of school! It'll bring you good luck. Besides—you'll need something to take the attention off your hair."

I could've smacked Sam for that remark. "Just because your idea of a cute haircut isn't mine doesn't mean there's anything wrong with my hair."

"Whatever." Sam smiled too big and broadly. "We don't have time for anything else anyway. I need to get home to Curtis and Stephen."

There really wasn't time for anything else. Before I knew it, the first day of high school, whether I liked it or not—and I was more and more sure I didn't like it—was here. Luckily, I didn't have to make my official grand entrance alone. My two best friends, Mistie and Crystal, were with me. And I was indeed wearing that lavender cashmere sweater Sam had bought for me. For luck, of course. I had a feeling I would need all I could get.

My home room class was sophomore Honors English. I slid into a seat near the back of the room and watched students enter the class. *So far, so good.* Most of them were calm, normal people like myself—not loud, obnoxiously popular people who would constantly be drawing attention to themselves and make my favorite class miserable for me. I flipped my notebook open and scanned my schedule for the millionth time. Honors English: No real friends were in the class so far, but that was okay, since I loved this subject. Driver's Ed: Crystal had that class with me, so that would be bearable. Tutor/Study Hall: That class was being held in the library and was one every student in the school was required to take. I wasn't sure what the "tutoring" part was all about. Supposedly, it had something to do with a new program that would be explained that day. I looked down my schedule for my next class. Drama 101. I sighed. That was going to be interesting. I was dreading drama worst of all. And then—

The bell rang. I looked up, surprised to see the classroom was almost filled. Mrs. Dubois—the Honors English teacher for about the past century—walked in and stood in front of her desk. "Welcome, everyone. I'm Mrs. Dubois, the sophomore Honors English teacher, which means if sophomore Honors English isn't printed on your class schedule, you're in the wrong room." Mrs. Dubois got a couple of courtesy laughs for that. "Let's get started on the necessary reading of the roll, and then I'll pass out the course syllabus. James Adams?"

"Here."

"Tiffany Allen?"

"Here."

And so on until my own name was called. After I stated the required "here," I picked up my pen and absently doodled flowers in the corners of the first page of my notebook.

"Jason West?" Silence answered. "Jason West?" Mrs. Dubois called again. Silence again. Then faintly, I could hear something that sounded like a minor earthquake outside the classroom. In another second, I realized it was feet pounding down the hall before screeching to a halt at the doorway to my Honors English class.

"Here!" a loud voice bellowed. Like everyone else in the room, I jumped and stretched my neck to see who had insisted on making such a dramatic entrance. My heart dropped when I looked at the person standing there, breathing hard, with a backpack slung over one shoulder.

He was tall and lean, but not skinny. It was easy to see he indulged in regular—probably obsessive—weight-lifting sessions every day.

"You're Mr. West, I presume?" Mrs. Dubois said dryly.

"Yes, that would be me," he—"Mr. West"—said, smiling and hurrying to take one of the only seats left in the room on the front row.

I watched him, my eyes narrowing slightly, as he dug through his backpack for a notebook and pen. There was something familiar about him. Oddly familiar. *Jason West.* Where in the world had I heard that name before? Jason turned around to set his backpack on the floor. My eyes caught a quick glance of the words "Central High Football" in gold lettering on the front of his maroon T-shirt—and the next second, my mind flew back to one Saturday afternoon in the middle of summer when Sam and Alex had dropped by for lunch.

"Hey, did you see this article in the paper?" Alex had waved our local county paper as if he'd found some amazing discovery that would change all of our lives forever.

"What article?" I'd asked, hurrying over to Alex's side to look over his shoulder. I'd rolled my eyes once I'd realized he was looking at the sports page.

"This one," Alex had said excitedly, pointing to one towards the bottom of the page. "I thought Brett would be the only kid at Central to make the Varsity football team as a sophomore—and as a quarterback, no less—but it looks like there's another guy in town who's accomplished the same feat!"

"What's the boy's name?" Dad had asked.

"Jason. Jason West," Sam had read over Alex's shoulder. "Look, Alex—look what else it says!" Sam had pointed excitedly to a place further down in the article.

"Read it to us, won't you, Sam?" Mom had said, clutching her locket.

"It says, 'The last time Central High discovered such raw, remarkable talent in a new sophomore occurred nearly sixteen years ago when Brett Colton entered Central High. Colton was also recruited as a sophomore to the Varsity team, and like West, was recruited as a quarterback. West is currently in training to start the for the Varsity team in the fall.'"

"Isn't that amazing! All these years later, Brett is still remembered," Alex had said with a proud smile.

"I think the article is really more about this Jason West kid than about Brett," I'd said irritably and sarcastically. Before Alex or Sam could retort, Mom and Dad had shushed me to look at the paper themselves, and I'd been quickly forgotten . . .

I shook my head wryly. A football player? In Honors English? He had to be the walking oxymoron of the year. Of all the classes I was taking, I'd thought I'd at least be safe from sports hero wannabes in Honors English, for crying out loud!

"You know what else you are, don't you, Mr. West?" I jumped at the sound of Mrs. Dubois's voice jerking me back to my present reality.

"Uh—not exactly," he questioned, obviously confused.

"You're late. Please don't let it happen again."

"I won't, Mrs. Dubois. I'm sorry. Really."

I lifted my eyebrows in surprise. A jock with a few manners around adults. Amazing.

"Mr. West, would you please assist me in passing out the course books to each student? They're those big, thick blue books stacked in the corner of the room on my right."

I watched while Jason quickly scrambled out of his seat to pick up a huge pile of books. I was expecting a sarcastic remark, or at least to see him move slowly, rolling his eyes, but "Mr. West" moved cheerfully up and down each row, handing out the course books. I didn't look up from my notebook as he set my copy on the corner of my desk.

"Now—as you can see, we're going to be studying American authors and poets this year. One of the best ways to learn the mechanics of the English language is to study and write papers on the works of our country's great writers. As I'm sure Mr. West can attest, you can't learn the game of football unless you practice it regularly. The same is true in English. We will have weekly vocabulary words to be tested on each week—spellings and definitions—as well as some grammar. However, most of your grade will depend upon your weekly response papers to your weekly reading assignments. Your response papers will contain your answer to one of the weekly reading assignment essay questions."

I could hear moans and groans from all corners of the classroom during Mrs. Dubois's speech, but as I looked over the syllabus, I felt nothing but excitement and relief, mostly because I knew I was going to do well in this class. It was going to be hard, though. Challenging, actually. But I was up for it. Definitely.

I was smugly thinking this over during lunch while Mistie and Crystal babbled across from me at a table in the lunchroom about their morning adventures.

" . . . my brother, Dennis, had Mr. Johnson last year for driver's ed. I remember the horror stories he used to tell about him. A total perfectionist about everything—" In midsentence Crystal stopped, her eyes bulging, before she gasped and grabbed Mistie's arm. "Look at that face!" Crystal gushed, straining to look over my shoulder. "I've seen a lot of cute guys today, but that guy is *gorgeous!* Look at those blue eyes—and those long, dark eyelashes! Wow!"

Mistie wrinkled her nose. "His nose is crooked."

"Just slightly!" Crystal said, shoving Mistie with her shoulder. "And who cares about that? He's got the straightest, whitest teeth I've ever seen on a guy! And look how perfect his lips are—not too thick or too thin—"

"Hey, I'm trying to eat here!" I groaned, kicking Crystal under the table with my foot.

She ignored me, of course. " . . . and he's got perfect hair. Slightly wavy, dark, brown hair—I'll bet it looks black when it's wet!"

I couldn't stand it anymore. I casually and slowly swiveled to see what Crystal's fuss was all about before whirling back around. "Him again!" I muttered, crumpling a napkin tightly in my fist.

"Him who? You *know* that guy?" Both Crystal and Mistie were practically in my lap, dying for more.

I rolled my eyes. "It's just Jason West. You know, the amazing sophomore football hero? He's in my Honors English class. Can you believe it? A major jock in my English class."

"Jason West! Wow!" Crystal sighed. "So—*he's* the sophomore on the Varsity team? You are *so* lucky to have a class with him!"

Before I had a chance to attack that remark, Mistie pointed with her fork behind me.

"See that sickeningly gorgeous blonde practically sitting on Jason? That's Angela Barnett. Drill team dancer extraordinaire. And a junior. She's going to be Jason's girlfriend. You'll see."

Crystal shrugged. "I don't care. I'm going to fantasize about him anyway."

"Can we leave now?" I said irritably, throwing my crumpled napkin on my tray.

"Wait," Crystal said, her eyes bugging out again. "Something's going on over at his table. Something—*messy!*"

More than just the expected loud, dull roar was taking place over at the table where Jason and all his football-playing cohorts sat. It had been growing increasingly louder, with high pitched squeals from the girls and loud guffaws from the guys, and even loud clangings and bangings of silverware and plastic trays.

"Looks like a food fight!" Mistie gasped, laughing and pointing in Jason's direction.

I took a quick look over my shoulder at the loud, messy war going on several tables behind me before hurriedly gathering up my tray and book bag. "I'm getting out of here. This sweater cost way too much money to take any chances. I'll meet you in the hall." I turned to leave and silently moaned an *oh no* when I realized the only way to the tray disposal and garbage cans was to pass by Jason's table. I took a deep breath and started to move—fast—taking a roundabout way to avoid getting caught up in the tide of the most immature brawling fray of flying food I'd seen in years. I finally made it to the garbage cans and tossed my tray in the disposal window. "Home free!" I muttered under my breath and turned to quickly slide out the exit door.

It all happened pretty fast. One second, I was turning around from getting rid of my lunch tray, and the next, my sweater had connected perfectly with a wild, powerful squirting of ketchup. All over the front. Some even hit me in the face. *Can I die now?* was all I could think. That is, until I saw his face. Jason's, to be exact. By the surprised look on his face, it was easy for me to surmise that he was the guilty ketchup shooter. Of course, the fact that he was standing up, gripping the ketchup bottle in both hands helped a little.

After a few brief seconds of shocked, silent staring from Jason's whole table, Jason pointed accusingly at the guy sitting a foot away from me and said in mock anger, "You weren't supposed to move! And *you*—" He actually had the gall to point at *me*—"you weren't supposed to be there!" With that, the whole table erupted into huge, annoying guffaws of laughter.

I stood there, glaring at Jason, who tried to keep a stupid, embarrassed smile on his face. "Hey, I really am sorry about that—"

"And I'm sorry you're such a bad aim. I fear for the entire football season this year!" I shot back angrily. Jason stared at me in shock while his cohorts hooted loudly. "And thanks. Thanks a lot," I continued hotly. "I mean, this was only a brand-new, expensive cashmere sweater. From L'Armoire, no less. So thanks. Thanks for making my first day of high school so—*memorable.*" With that, I flew out the exit door to find a bathroom as quickly as I could.

Of course, the sweater was ruined. Trying to "enjoy" the rest of my first day of high school with ketchup stains all over my new sweater was going to be impossible to do, but somehow I had to survive the rest of the day. Luckily for me, tutor/study hall was right after lunch, so I could spend the first part of it in the girls' bathroom trying to clean up my sweater. But of course, ketchup all over me wasn't enough torture. I was forced to an abrupt halt due to the scene in the library when I finally arrived. Instead of seeing students scattered around studying quietly at tables, and wandering up and down the aisles looking for books, I was in for an unwelcome surprise. All of the tables and chairs were pushed together in neat, classroom-type rows facing the opened double doors to the library, filled with students listening intently to Mr. Madsen, the mediaologist and apparent study hall teacher, who was calling the roll.

*Great, just great.*

I tried to quietly sneak around Mr. Madsen, who was barking out names, but he quickly reached out an arm to block my path, his eyes never lifting from the clipboard in front of him.

"—Waddington—hold it there for a second, please."

I stopped.

"Jason West?" Mr. Madsen continued. I jerked my head up. *Please, no—not again—*

"Here!" I heard Jason West's booming voice somewhere to my left. *Could this day get any worse?* I thought miserably to myself. I looked up and locked eyes with him for a second as I gripped my notebook tighter to my chest, hiding the horrific stains there.

Apparently, it could.

After the torture of standing like an idiot in front of the whole study hall class, which *would* have to include Jason West, Mr. Madsen finally turned to me with a glare. "And you are . . . ?"

"Kathy," I began.

"Kathy what?"

"Colton. That is, Kathryn Colton. With a K."

"Hmmm—I'm not seeing any 'Colton' spelled with a K."

"No—it's with a C."

"You just said your name was spelled with a K—"

"Well, it is—"

"Then you're in the wrong class. There is no Colton with a K on the roll."

"No—you don't understand. My *last* name is spelled with a C, but my—"

"Then why did you say it started with a K?"

The more the class giggled at the ridiculous exchange I was forced to endure, the more irritable and short-tempered Mr. Madsen became. It was astounding how long it took for me to explain to a grown man and college graduate that my first name started with a K and my last name started with a C.

"That's enough—enough from all of you! Especially *you*, Miss Colton. Please take your seat." Another glare followed his last words for me.

My heart pounded as I stumbled around looking for a seat, doing my best to avoid Jason's stare. Mr. Madsen wasted a good fifteen minutes droning on about the do's and don't's of having study hall in the library. "You're probably wondering why your study hall period includes the word 'tutoring.' Central High did extensive research concerning other high schools who consistently crank out large percentages of graduates with high grade point averages. What was their secret? It seems the majority of these high schools were successfully using a student-to-student tutoring program, wherein students help other students who struggle in the subjects they do well in . . ."

Mr. Madsen droned on and on about the tutoring program, but what it basically came down to was that study hall was going to become a tutor-slash-study hall after Labor Day. The first two weeks of school would be finished by then, giving students a chance to figure out which subjects they were having trouble with and which ones they excelled in. I would likely be expected to put my name on a list as a potential English tutor. If someone signed his name up by mine, then I would be obligated to help that person in English studies.

"Keep in mind that this is a program for students to help each other succeed. It's not a social dating time. The teachers will review the lists of tutoring partnerships for the particular subject they teach and will give the final approval as to whether or not the partnerships have a chance for success, based on the grades of each member of the partnership, as well as whether both members are currently signed up for a class in that subject. So if you're not taking a computer class, but someone you're romantically interested in is signed up to be a tutor, your partnership will not be approved. Also, if both members of the partnership are doing fine, or both members need help, those partnerships will not be approved, either. Also, if performance in class by either member of the partnership is not satisfactory, the partnership will be dissolved. Also, if I see that productive work is not being accomplished during tutor/study hall, that partnership will be reported and dissolved . . ."

Mr. Madsen had about a million other "Also's" that he had to drone on about, even though everything was in the handout. All I knew was that I hoped no one would sign up by my name so I could use study hall as a study hall. And that I just wanted to get home and change.

When I got home from school, I hurried to my bedroom before Mom saw my ruined sweater. I balled it up and threw it in my closet before reaching for the old Beatles album to spin. So much for hoping for all the luck I could get on my first day of high school.

# CHAPTER THREE

Villiam Carlos Williams's poem "The Red Wheelbarrow," written in 1923, was our first Honors English writing assignment, due on Friday of the first week of school. "Write a two- to three-page paper on your thoughts concerning the poem." That was all Mrs. Dubois had offered in the way of instruction. When Friday arrived, before letting us hand in our papers, Mrs. Dubois had one last, horrible surprise. "We will spend the duration of class today listening to students read their papers on Mr. Williams's poem."

As if the daily dose of humiliation or improvisation numbers in drama wasn't enough! My heart pounded as I stared at "Mr. West's" back several rows in front of me. He *would* have to be in this class with me. To his credit and my surprise, he *had* tried to apologize to me in class on Tuesday for destroying my sweater, but I'd made it clear it'd be best if he just left me alone. For the sake of the rest of my wardrobe. I couldn't decide if that was going to make it easier or even more horrific to have to stand up in front of the class, mere inches from him, to read my paper.

The first mass of readings were the typical boring fare. Lots of strange, mumbo jumbo was thrown around that was impossible to follow, from the incredibly stupid to the incredibly bizarre, until "Mr. West's" turn. He stood up, grinning broadly, as if he actually enjoyed the chance to stand in front of the class.

"I decided to write my 'thoughts' on the poem in a style like Mr. Williams's." With that stupid grin still on his face, he held out his paper for all to see that he had indeed written it in Mr. Williams's style of three words per line followed by one word per line—three horrific pages worth. Then, he cleared his throat loudly and read his "poem" in a deep, booming voice. A "poem" that was nothing more than an embarrassing mockery of Mr. Williams's amazing poem. He even threw in some lines about the chicken crossing the road joke—and stated that the chickens were wheeled across the road in the red wheelbarrow instead.

The nauseatingly flirtatious gigglings from the girls and the admiring guffaws from the guys throughout Jason's "paper" reading made it obvious that I was the only student who was stunned at what he had done. Mrs. Dubois stared without blinking an eye at him until the laughter in class died away and the grin left Jason's face.

"Very interesting interpretation, Mr. West." Mrs. Dubois walked slowly to where Jason stood and took the paper out of his hand. "Actual poem lines and stanzas. Very creative, indeed." She looked up from his paper and smiled icily. "Your peers may enjoy such antics, but I do not. You will need to be serious about your papers in the future if you hope to pass Honors English. Or even to remain in this class. Is that understood, Mr. West?"

I didn't get to enjoy his embarrassed response because I was next and far too nervous to worry about Jason anymore. I was hoping a week in Drama 101 with all the improv work I'd been forced to endure would make this moment easier, but it didn't. My heart pounded so loudly I could hardly hear my voice above it, and my hands were shaking badly.

And then, I saw Jason looking at me with that annoying grin back on his face. Knowing that my paper was pretty great and would knock his flat and wipe that smug grin right off, I gave him a cold stare before turning to face the class with a pretended degree of confidence.

"Although 'The Red Wheelbarrow' is a poem of few words, it is rich with many layers of meaning. The fact that from the beginning, one is forced to stop and take another look at the poem is enough to prove the poem itself is something above and beyond the ordinary and one that will not be forgotten. That the poem is still dissected years since it was written proves that it has transcended time and will outlast us all."

Oh, my paper was amazing, and I knew it. I'd researched the poem and Mr. Williams's life nearly to death. I'd detailed each layer of the poem from the initial layer of what is going on in the poem, at the moment *of* the poem, all the way through to the universal layer—the layer all people can relate to, whether they'd lived on a farm or not. That was the best, most powerful part of my paper. A great finish to a greater than great paper.

"The red wheelbarrow can represent any seemingly ordinary object often taken for granted on a farm. Many chores are accomplished on a farm with the help of a wheelbarrow, yet it is quickly and easily forgotten, even though it is an immensely necessary tool on a farm. The poem could easily have been about a shovel, a rake, or a watering can. Ordinary objects, forgotten and left out in the rain, yet incredibly important to the welfare of the farm.

"The same can be said of ordinary items in everyone's lives. For a student, the poem could have been written about a ballpoint pen—an ordinary object 'so much depends on' in a student's life—for taking notes, completing a written test, or writing down a phone number. Such a poem could have been written about an alarm clock, a set of keys—any ordinary object that is easily ignored and forgotten, yet again, is immensely important in keeping our lives running smoothly. Therefore, in a universal sense, the poem cries out to pay attention to the ordinary—the seemingly unimportant things in our lives, and not take them so much for granted.

"Taking time to discover the opening layers of a poem followed by the universal layers not only shows us how remarkable and rich with meaning the poem is, it also has the wonderful effect of enriching our lives with the powerful truths conveyed in its few, well-placed words."

With that, I ended my paper by reading the poem with some nice, dramatic emphasis courtesy of what I'd been learning in Drama 101.

It was pin-dropping quiet after I finished. Jason was looking down, hunched over his desk, his eyebrows drawn together. *Ha—take that much-deserved kick in the pants, Mr. West! Your ability to throw a football means nothing in here!*

Mrs. Dubois took my paper from me and smiled. "Very good, Kathryn. I very much enjoyed your view of Mr. Williams's poem. You may take your seat."

I was more than happy to do just that.

"I hope you've learned how important reading out loud is in helping you sharpen your writing skills. Reading aloud should show you whether or not you're arguing your point of view clearly and coherently." Mrs. Dubois straightened her stack of papers against the top of her desk. "You'll receive these back on Monday with your grade. Next week we will read some of Edgar Allen Poe's work. It wouldn't hurt to get a head start on it over the weekend. Congratulations on making it through your first week of high school. Have a wonderful and safe weekend."

# CHAPTER FOUR

Y ou haven't heard a word I've said, have you, Kathy? Kathy??"
I jumped as Crystal practically screamed my name in my
face, while Mistie nearly spewed a mouthful of cola laughing at
us. I'd been absently twirling spaghetti strands on my fork, oblivious to
the noise around me. Which included Mistie and Crystal's nonstop
talking.

"What? I mean, yeah. Sure. Whatever."

Crystal rolled her eyes. "Wrong answer. I asked you how your Labor
Day weekend went, since neither of us saw you at all. Did you do anything fun?"

I shrugged. "Just had a barbecue with my brother and sister and their
families." The expected, of course, had happened. After five minutes of
Alex and Sam questioning me about my first two weeks of high school,
they'd quickly launched off into memories of their own. Which, of
course, caused the inevitable story upon story upon memory of Brett.
The perfect depressing preview for today.

"So what's up?" Mistie said, raising her eyebrows. "You're obviously
annoyed about something. What's going on?"

I sighed. They'd find out soon enough anyway. "You know how I
have tutor/study hall right after lunch?" Mistie and Crystal nodded.

"Well, I checked the English tutoring board this morning, and guess who's signed up wanting me for his English tutor?"

They both screamed when I told them.

———

I had to check the English tutoring board in the library as soon as lunch was over just to make sure I hadn't made a mistake. After all, the name I'd seen might have been written next to the name above or below mine. I'd probably read the board completely wrong.

I stared until my eyebrows drew into a scowl at the two names unmistakably together.

Tenth-Grade Honors English Tutoring

Tutor: Kathryn Colton. Prospective Student: Jason West.

He'd scrawled his name in big, bold capitals by my computer-printed name. I still couldn't believe it. *What have I done to deserve this?* I thought miserably.

A moment later, Mr. Jason West himself with his famous backpack sauntered into the library and dropped the pack noisily by my feet where I stood. He grinned broadly and tapped his finger on our names before leaning against the wall by the board to face me.

"Hey, Kathryn. With a 'K.' Looks like we're going to be study partners!"

I gave him the iciest glare I could muster. "Nothing's carved in stone yet. Mrs. Dubois will need to approve this, and I doubt—"

"Yeah, I agree—I doubt she'll have any problem with it," he finished.

I purposely moved away from him with fast steps to slam my notebook and books on a nearby table before sitting down in a chair with my back to him and the tutoring board. Jason easily glided into the seat in front of me, casually tossing his backpack to the ground by his chair. "Isn't there someone else you can torture in here?" I asked. "I mean— why me? There are tons of smart Honors English students in this school. Why do you want *me* to be your tutor?"

"Maybe this will help you guess why," he said, clearing his throat for dramatic effect. A second later, Jason perfectly imitated my dramatic reading of Williams's "The Red Wheelbarrow," word for memorized word.

I stared in disbelief. "You mean—"

Jason grinned. "That's right. By your successfully showing up everyone in class—including myself, I admit—I knew *you* were the only tutor for me. I can handle the vocabulary tests and all the reading we have to do, but I could use some help in the paper writing department."

"I'm not about to write any papers for anybody," I said coldly.

"I'm not asking you to," Jason said evenly. "I just need some help thinking through ideas, making sure I haven't missed any important 'layers.' And another pair of eyes to make sure my papers are half-decent so Mrs. Dubois won't throw me out of her class or flunk me. With your help, I know I'll be fine and I'll pass. So—I hope you'll be willing to help me. Will you?" He'd been looking me in the eye too closely. Too hopefully. I could hardly stand it.

"I—I don't know if I can—" I tried to begin, but again, I was cut off.

Jason laughed and shook his head. "Are you really that modest? Come on—everyone knows you're the top brain in that class."

"You're forgetting one important detail," I said, keeping the ice in my voice.

Jason raised an eyebrow. "Oh? What's that?"

"Maybe I really don't want to tutor you."

He actually had the gall to look surprised. "Why not?"

I grinned evilly. "Maybe this will help you guess why: one completely ruined, expensive cashmere sweater from L'Armoire—"

At least he had the decency to squirm a little. "Hey, I tried to tell you I was sorry—"

"I'm not finished yet," I said sharply, silencing him. "Besides. We're so . . . different. You're an . . . athlete. And I'm . . . not." I didn't have the stomach to use the word *popular*. "I can't begin to relate to you, or you to me. This just wouldn't work."

Jason shrugged his shoulders. "Well, let's just wait and see what Mrs. Dubois says." Before I could say another word, he reached down for his backpack and eased out of his chair to saunter away to another table at the other end of the library.

As if that wasn't bad enough, Drama 101 dropped another bomb on me for the day.

"So, you have to act out Shakespeare plays in front of the whole school?" Mistie asked, snapping open a can of soda after school was over for the day.

"Not exactly. I mean, not the whole plays themselves. Just one scene."

"Do you get to pick which play?"

"Sort of. As long as it's been approved by the teacher." My drama teacher, Miss Goforth, was determined that her idea was going to get everyone excited about Shakespeare. The drama classroom was outfitted with a mini stage, so instead of performing in front of the school in one big whack in the auditorium, each English class would get a chance to come to the drama room to watch our mini Shakespeare festival in November. It was supposed to make the event more "personable" and "intimate." I'd tried to explain to Miss Goforth this wasn't going to work for me and that I'd rather do anything but try to act out Shakespeare in front of the school at such close, point-blank range, but she made me an offer I truly could not refuse.

"You have a choice, Kathy. Either participate in at least two different pieces, or get an F for the class."

How could I refuse when Miss Goforth put it that way?

Mistie shook her head. "Well, at least it won't be in front of the whole school at once." Mistie turned to squint out one of our school's huge windows in the front of the building. Any minute, her mom was due to come pick us up from school. Before I could respond, Mistie jumped as if she'd been bitten. "Oh no—I forgot my history book. Stay and watch for my mom while I get it, okay, Kathy?" I nodded and watched her sprint down the hall to her locker.

" . . . I really hope you can make it. Please say you'll come, Jason!"

I was torn between freezing and whirling around. In a moment, I heard Jason's booming voice answering Angela's high-pitched, nasal one. *Why did they have to come down this hall right now?* It was bad enough to be standing alone in the hallway like an idiot, but to have Jason West and Angela Barnett come around made it ten thousand times worse.

I had to do something—I couldn't just stand there. Now it felt incredibly dumb to be waiting for a mom to come and give me a ride. I turned my back to them and realized I was standing near one of our school's many trophy cases, so it seemed appropriate to fake interest in it. Too interested to notice that Jason and Angela were coming down the hall.

I walked slowly towards the trophy case, dragging my overstuffed bag of books off my shoulder. I started at the top shelf, and as my eyes traveled downwards past an assortment of shiny gold trophies and colorful ribbons, my breath drew in sharply as if I'd been punched in the stomach. I peered harder at the face grinning at me. *Brett.* He was in his football uniform, kneeling on one knee with his football helmet held securely by his hand on his raised knee. His uniform was clean and pressed, and his dark hair was combed. Number nine. Quarterback. For the Varsity team. *And he'd only been a sophomore.* I could feel that strange connection pulling at me and reached out and lightly touched the glass that separated him from me—

"Come *on*, Kathy. How long has my mom been sitting there?" I jumped, pulling my hand back sharply as if I'd been burned. My fingers were trembling so badly I could barely lift my bag to my shoulder as I mumbled an apology. It wasn't until after climbing into the car that I remembered I knew another sophomore quarterback who was on the Varsity team. *Jason.* I squinted hard, trying to see through the school's huge front windows from inside the car, but Jason and Angela were long gone.

## CHAPTER FIVE

A s if on cue, Jason came flying at a dead run into Honors English the next morning while the last bell rang. Nearly late as usual. But I grudgingly had to acknowledge the fact that he'd been true to his word: He'd never been late again. *Barely* not late, but not late, just the same.

I'd planned on talking to Mrs. Dubois alone before class about the tutoring situation, but I was scarcely able to say, "Jason West signed up for me to be his English tutor—" before she cut me off without even looking up from the mass of paperwork on her desk.

"Oh, yes. I noticed that, too. We'll have to speak about it after class, though. I don't have time to discuss it right now."

I sighed in relief. *Good.* At least she agreed that it was a problem.

Once class was over, of course Jason just had to take forever to pack up a mere notebook, pen, and literature book into his backpack, but as soon as he stood up and started for the door, I hurried up the aisle between desks to where Mrs. Dubois was seated behind her desk.

"Mrs. Dubois?"

"Yes, Kathryn?" She didn't look up from thumbing through stacks and stacks of papers.

"About the tutoring schedule for this class—" I began.

Thankfully, she quickly looked up. "Oh, yes—thank you for

reminding me. I almost forgot." With that, she nearly sprang over her desk to hurry to the doorway Jason had disappeared through a second before. "Mr. West, can you please come back inside?"

I shifted my book bag nervously to my other shoulder. I'd hoped she'd tell Jason alone that he'd have to choose someone else to tutor him.

"Yes, Mrs. Dubois?" Jason quickly stepped back into the classroom before raising an eyebrow at me.

"Kathryn has just reminded me that I needed to speak to you both about the Honors English tutoring board and the fact that you signed up to have Miss Colton as your tutor."

I faced Jason with triumph. "I'm glad you agree this is going to be a problem."

Mrs. Dubois turned to look at me with raised eyebrows. "Problem? I don't foresee any problem. What problem are you referring to, Miss Colton?"

I gasped, trying to get my tongue in gear. "I—I assumed you wanted to talk about the tutoring because you agreed that we—Jason and I—are a bad matchup. Wasn't I right about that?"

Jason did nothing but grin broadly as the debate continued between Mrs. Dubois and myself. In the end, I was forced to grudgingly agree to a trial tutoring session.

"I think you both need a trial session before any decision is made to terminate this particular tutoring partnership. You may be surprised at how it works out, Miss Colton."

I gave my locker door a nice, hard slam after lunch period was over before I stalked down the hall to the library for my first tutoring session. *Why hurry? He'll probably be late.* Not only that, I knew—I just *knew*—he was going to make a joke of this. His way of getting me back for making him look bad in English. Another way of squirting ketchup all over me again. But I stopped short in surprise to see Jason sitting at attention at a table near the library door, notebook, pen, and literature book neatly arranged in front of him. He looked up when I came in, grinned, and had the nerve to wave. My heart was pounding as I marched up to him and dropped my book bag to the ground by the table. "You're on time. I'm impressed," I said, sliding into a chair.

"What's so impressive about that?"

I shrugged. "You're late to English every morning. I figured you must be a constantly late type of person."

Jason laughed. "Hey, I get to my seat before the last bell stops ring-ing every day! Besides, *you* try getting from the seminary building all the way to the other end of school every morning and see if *you're* on time."

I looked up from digging into my book bag and frowned at Jason. "Seminary building?"

Jason raised an eyebrow. "The one kitty corner from the football field. My first class of the day is there."

"What class is that?"

"Seminary. Early-morning seminary, no less. Every morning at seven in the A.M."

I shook my head, still frowning. "Seminary? That can't be a required class. I've never even heard of it."

Jason shook his head back. "No, no, it's not required. Totally elec-tive. It's a religion class for LDS kids. Mormons."

"You're an LDS Mormon kid, then?"

Jason grinned. "Exactly."

"Well, I'm not one. Is that going to be a problem for you?" In a way, I hoped it would be. It would make a great excuse to get out of what I was sure would end up being a fiasco.

Jason looked surprised. Almost offended. Or hurt. "No, why would it be?"

I shrugged uncomfortably and looked away. "I don't know. No rea-son, I guess. It shouldn't make any difference at all, right? I mean, we're not going to be studying religion, right?" I was babbling like an idiot, and I knew it.

"Exactly," Jason said. For the second time.

"Well, let's get on with it." I quickly reached down and snatched my English book out of my bag. "It looks like we'll be studying Ambrose Bierce this week. Have you read 'The Boarded Window' or 'An Occurrence at Owl Creek Bridge' yet?"

Jason looked at me in surprise. Again. "Actually, I haven't. Not yet, anyway—"

Why hadn't I guessed as much? I could feel my blood pressure rising. "How am I supposed to help you if you haven't even read the material?"

"I'm sorry—I had football practice and a game this weekend, and we had some family stuff going on—"

*Great. Just great.* "It's going to be impossible for me to help you if you haven't read the assignment. I've got too much studying and reading and papers to write myself to do all of yours, too." I stood up and started packing my bag while I practically yelled at him. Jason stood up, too, and at least had the decency to look worried.

"I'm not asking you to do my papers for me. Wait—please don't leave." I glanced up, my English book in one hand, and forced myself to look at him. Jason sighed. "Look, I'm sorry. From now on, at the very least, I'll have my reading done before I meet you. This won't happen again, okay?"

"And I should believe you because . . . ?"

"Because I promised Mrs. Dubois I wouldn't be late again, and I've kept my promise to her, haven't I?"

I didn't know what to say to that, because that fact was true. Barely, but still true.

But Jason wasn't done yet. "I'm going to be honest with you, okay? My grades aren't the best, and English is my worst subject. If I fall below a 'B,' it'll lower my grade point too much, and I won't be able to stay on the Varsity football team." I must have looked annoyed, because he hurried on before I could interrupt. "I realize that football means nothing to you, but it's important to me. If there was something I could do in return, I'd do it in a second."

I wasn't sure I believed that, and I wasn't about to let it soften me up. "How'd you get into Honors English if you're not good at English?"

Jason shrugged. "I'm too smart for Sophomore English, I guess." I rolled my eyes, but before I could say anything, Jason hurried on. "Okay, okay—actually, I did have some strings pulled so I could be in the class. I want to take AP English when I'm a senior, but I can't get into that class without going through sophomore and junior Honors English first."

"Why do you want to take AP English?"

Jason looked at me as if I was a complete idiot. "So I can take the AP test and hopefully pass and get some college credit in high school— why else?" I opened my mouth to say something cutting, but Jason wasn't finished yet. "Besides—getting rid of a few English classes in college will give me more time to practice football, study, or whatever. And, it won't hurt to have a few more classes out of the way before I go on a mission."

"A mission?"

Jason grinned. "For my church, for two years. Most guys leave at nineteen, and that's when I plan to go. I figured taking AP English as a senior would be a good idea, but I didn't count on massive amounts of reading and paper writing. But if I have someone help me who can show me how to find all the cool stuff in stories and poetry, I know I'll be able to handle this."

I said nothing while he stared hopefully at me. How was I supposed to react to that? I folded my arms across my chest and looked hard at him. "Three times."

"What?" The confusion on his face was priceless.

"Read the story we're assigned each week at least three times. The first time, read just to enjoy the story. The second time, read it with the paper's thesis in mind. The third time, read it to underline passages that will support your thesis. Then you're ready to discuss the story with me, and then you can write your paper. After that, we'll work on editing and proofing."

Jason grinned. "Sounds good."

"And if you turn this into a big joke and try to act all 'too cool for school' with me, like you think English literature is stupid and boring and a waste of your time, then we're done."

He nodded and kept grinning. "Okay."

I nodded and sat back down in my seat. "Good. Open your book and start reading."

Jason quickly slid into his chair and obediently opened his book with that annoying grin still on his face and started to read. I busied myself with the beginnings of my own paper, but I couldn't help sneaking looks at him out of the corner of my eye. It was strange—this feeling of power I had. Here he was, this big, tall football player allowing himself to be ordered around by *me*. How strange, I grinned. No wonder so many people went to college to become teachers!

When the bell rang, I quickly gathered my books and papers together and leaned down to stuff them in my book bag. When I sat up to grab my pen, I jumped. A large, flat, white box with a small pink bow sat on the table just under my nose. I looked up at Jason questioningly and nudged the box suspiciously. "What's this for?"

"For you, of course." He tried to act all casual, but he seemed— *nervous*. Definitely.

I frowned, still looking at the box. "Why?"

"So that you'll consider staying on as my English tutor."

I looked up blandly at Jason. "So this is a bribe, then?"

"I prefer to think of it as a gift."

Before I could say anything else, Jason tossed his backpack over one shoulder with a "see ya" and sauntered out the library door. I stared at the box for I didn't know how long before finally reaching out to tug the ribbon off and open it.

I couldn't help gasping. Inside a bed of pink tissue paper with

L'Armoire's unmistakable gold sticker lay a sweater—a light blue, cashmere sweater. With a square neckline and long sleeves. A small note card was tucked inside the sweater. "They were all out of purple ones. Hope you'll like this one anyway. Thanks for being my teacher.—Jason."

# CHAPTER SIX

S o, how did you like 'Desiree's Baby'?"

Jason waited until he had pulled his literature book out of his backpack and settled himself at our usual table in the back corner of the library for tutor/study hall before answering. I'd been tutoring Jason for about three weeks now, but I hadn't let myself decide whether he preferred to sit at practically the farthest reaches of the universe because he really wanted to focus on studying literature, or if he didn't want any of his friends to know he needed tutoring. Or, the fact had to be faced, no matter how much it hurt—if it had something to do with me.

"Pretty crazy ending, don't you think?"

I snapped out of my thoughts and glanced at Jason before I shrugged. "Yes and no. Kate Chopin loved to end her stories with ironic twists."

Jason shook his head. "I thought it was sad he didn't find out the truth—that *he* was the one 'born under the brand of slavery,' not his wife—until it was too late."

I raised my eyebrows. "How can you be so sure he didn't know all along?"

Jason looked at me with surprise. "You don't really believe he knew all along, do you? I mean, she was his wife, and he loved her."

37

I grinned. Tutoring Jason was turning out to be a lot more fun than I had ever imagined. I loved bringing up opposite ways of looking at the stories and watching him stumble around, trying to mull over a new way of looking at something. "The great thing about literature is that it's like arguing a case in court. As long as you can find evidence to support your theory, you have a chance of winning, so to speak." I tapped Jason's text-book with my pen. "You go ahead and write your paper with your belief that he didn't know until it was too late. Just be sure to support your opinion with examples from the story. I'm writing my paper to the opposite effect."

"Yeah, well, we'll see who gets the A this time!" Jason grinned.

I rolled my eyes. "I love Kate Chopin's stories, because things are never what they seem to be. Reminds me not to make a judgment call until I know all the facts."

Jason nodded seriously. "Funny how you can learn that kind of stuff from stories. I mean, we talk about things like this in seminary and church. And we read about it in the scriptures all the time."

I wasn't sure what irked me more: his actual statement or the annoying way he had of working a religious comment into every tutoring session. Without fail. Sometimes he actually dared to throw one of his religious comments around in Honors English. As a result, I was unwillingly learning more about the Mormon church than I ever wanted to. He was studying his religion's bible—the Book of Mormon—this year in his seminary class, and he got a gigantic kick out of "casually" tossing out stories and statements by the characters in his scripture book with bizarre names like Nephi, Moroni, and Zerahemnah during our tutor/study hour. Sometimes I left his religious comments and stories alone with a shrug, and other times I just couldn't. This time, I couldn't.

"Great literature should always instruct as it entertains. Why is it a shock to you that you can learn moral truths in some place other than the Bible and somewhere other than a seminary class or church?"

Jason looked surprised. "I didn't mean for it to come out sounding like that. It's just that these are just stories—"

"And the Bible isn't full of 'just stories' that are meant to teach? Since you seem to read your scriptures so much, you should know how powerful stories are and how well they can get a message across. Sometimes better than straight preaching on a topic, don't you think?" I had to really fight to keep myself from smiling at the flustered look on his face while he stuttered, trying to think of something to say.

"Yes, I guess, at times." I could feel my heart starting to pound weird and fast like it always did when Jason looked at me too long, so I looked away and thumbed through the pages of my literature book for "Desiree's Baby." Bigger irony for me than any of Kate Chopin's endings was that I had to admit that the tutoring sessions with Jason had been going surprisingly well. He was always on time, had read the material, and had interesting comments and questions ready to discuss. He didn't act at all like a stereotypical high school football star. It almost shocked me how much he got into studying stories and poems. I was seeing more and more every day why Honors English was the best place for him. I would never have admitted this to anyone, but I could secretly admit to myself that I looked forward to tutor/study hall. The time had gone by so fast it was hard to believe we'd been working together for a few weeks now and that October was almost here.

"Can you believe we've been studying together for—what—about three weeks now?" Jason said casually. Too casually.

"Hard to believe it's actually been working out okay," I said dryly.

"Then you agree that it's going okay?"

"Sure," I said without looking up from my literature book. "Why?"

"Don't you remember what tomorrow is?" Something about the tone in Jason's voice made me look up from my book. His mouth and eyes had a funny tenseness about the edges, and he seemed almost *nervous*. Very un-Jason-like. So of course, I had to take advantage of such a moment as this and have some fun with him.

"Let's see. Oh yeah, that's right." He relaxed back into his chair and seemed to visually unwind. I nodded seriously before saying, "It's Friday!" Jason rolled his eyes and chucked a wadded-up piece of paper at my head. "Wait, don't tell me. It's the big game against—now, who is it against again?"

I got another wad of paper chucked at my head for that. "Yeah, you're really funny, Kathy." The grin left his face, and his eyebrows drew together. "You seriously don't remember what tomorrow is, do you?"

I shrugged. "Sorry. What's tomorrow?"

"I guess it figures it would be a day I'd worry about more than you." Jason sighed and continued. "Tomorrow we have to tell Mrs. Dubois whether we should keep studying together or not."

I couldn't believe I'd forgotten, but I had. I thought I'd be counting down the days until I could be released from this punishment, but shockingly enough, it hadn't turned out to be punishment after all. I couldn't deny that tutoring Jason had helped my own papers to improve. The only part about the whole arrangement that was really annoying usually happened right about—

"Jas! Jason!"

—now. Right on cue, Angela, with her bouncy blonde hair and bouncy trim body, came bouncing down the hall to our study table. And then, the only other annoying part about the tutoring arrangement happened. Almost like a mask slipping into place, Jason would turn back into football hero stud mode and quickly start to act Cool while he'd casually scoop up his literature book, papers, and pens, give me a quick "thanks" and "see ya," and leave with her hanging all over him.

This time, though, while we were all standing up, getting ready to part ways, Jason surprised me by using his normal tone, with only a hint of Coolness in it, while he said, "So—are we staying on as study partners?"

Angela gawked at me, for once acknowledging my presence on the same planet as herself. After a second, she turned back to Jason and had the gall to laugh. "You mean, this isn't over for good now? You can't seriously mean you're going to keep studying with her?"

Something about the way Angela said the word *her*—as if she'd swallowed a bug—made my stomach churn. I knew my face was red, but before Jason could say anything, I put a huge smile on my face and said, "I think our tutoring arrangement is going great." At that point, I turned and looked at Angela purposefully. "I have no problem staying on as your English tutor." With that, I turned smoothly on my heel and left them both, with Angela gaping angrily and unattractively at me and Jason trying hard not to grin.

I was still grinning to myself about tutor/study hall during dinner that night—yet another family dinner with Sam, Stephen, and Curtis, and Alex and Julie—and smugly replayed in my head the look on Angela's face. I had successfully zoned myself out of the dinner conversation, which, as usual, had turned eventually to a subject that reminded someone of a story about Brett. Shortly before dessert, I vaguely tuned in to the fact that everyone was discussing some fantastic event that had happened on the high school football field when Brett was doing his magical role of quarterback, amazing the crowd with his supernatural abilities.

"Just having fall around the corner brings back all kinds of high school football memories," Alex said in a dreamy voice. "Have you gone to any of the games, Kathy?"

I shook my head, too busy grinning over today to respond.

"I can't believe you haven't seen a game yet, Kathy. They're such a lot of fun. You are really missing out!" Sam sighed, shaking her head.

"I have no interest in football or in football players," I said with a shrug.

"No?" Sam said. I should've realized by the sparkle that was dancing wickedly in her eyes that trouble was coming. "Then what about this

Jason you've been 'tutoring'?" Sam gave me a huge, exaggerated wink. "Isn't it true that he's *the* Jason West? The new Central High Football Wonder?"

Just saying Jason's name in the house in front of everyone as if I had a *crush* on him, as if the tutoring wasn't for real, shot through me in a way that made me want to slap Sam. "What—what—how did—I'm not—" I was stuttering idiotically, but I was in shock that Sam knew anything about my life I hadn't carefully chosen to tell her myself. Jason was *not* a subject that was open for discussion by her. Or anyone else, for that matter.

"Don't try to deny anything, Kathy. Mom's already filled us all in."

I glared at Mom, who only looked surprised. "Oh, come now, Kathy. It's not like I told the six o'clock news! I didn't think you'd mind if I told your own sister and brother."

"Glad to know I'm not allowed a speck of a private life in this house," I grumbled angrily. "You know, if I'd wanted them to know, I would've told them myself."

"So tell us the truth, Kathy. Are you really an English tutor for Central High's most valuable football player?" I knew Alex was just trying to tease me out of my grumpiness, but nothing anyone could say was going to stop the foul mood that was coming on fast.

"Who would've known being a bookworm could help a girl rope a Varsity quarterback! Guess those English classes are worth something after all," Sam said, more to Alex than to me.

"It's amazing what you can accomplish when you spend some time developing what's in your head instead of just messing with the hair on top of it," I blurted.

"Ouch! Did little Kathy basically just call me stupid?"

"Well, if the five-inch, spiked, tacky heels fit . . ."

"Kathy!" I jumped at Dad's bellowing. "That's enough! Tell your sister you're sorry."

I turned to face Sam. "I'm sorry you're stupid, Sam."

Both Mom and Dad erupted over that comment. Sam babbled in a high-pitched voice about how snotty I was acting while Julie and Stephen coughed into their napkins. Even Curtis got into it by clapping and doing his own baby shrieks.

"Maybe you ought to go to your room if you can't behave yourself," Dad threatened.

"Good grief! Sam set herself up for that. If I'm going to be punished for anything, I ought to be punished for actually *saying* that old line. It's the oldest joke there is," I griped.

Mom shook her head at me, making the locket around her neck swing back and forth. "All I wanted to do was share a bit of what's been going on with you at school with your brother and sister, and Alex and Sam were just trying to show some interest in your life, Kathy. Is that so wrong?"

"Wrong?" I shot back. "No, that's not wrong. What's wrong is that neither of them really cares about what's going on with *me*. They just want to hear about The Amazing Jason West—someone they don't even know. But why should that surprise me? The only person anyone here is interested in is the one person who's not even around anymore!" I knew that comment would get me grounded for sure, so I pushed my chair out from under the table with a good hard, loud scrape and stomped off into my room. Tonight required listening to the Beatles album twice before I could stop grinding my teeth and clenching my hands into fists.

## CHAPTER SEVEN

Thanks to an inspiring talking-to from my parents after Alex and Sam left, I was still feeling moody the next day at school, so I wasn't much use to anyone. Even Miss Goforth had to get after me for removing myself to my own planet instead of being a part of the class. I'd half-heartedly agreed to work with six other students to act out the opening scene from *King Lear* as part of the dreaded Shakespeare festival. They'd even asked me to play Cordelia, King Lear's youngest daughter, but apparently thanks to me, our group was getting nowhere fast.

It was our turn to work on the stage while Miss Goforth watched and critiqued. I could handle the glares from the others in my group when I messed up a line or had to be prodded that it was my turn to speak, but having Miss Goforth get into the act was a unique brand of torture.

"Kathy, I don't mean to keep picking on you, but you've had to be prompted for every one of your lines today." Something about Miss Goforth's tone got the ball rolling today—straight for my head.

"Yeah, we've *all* noticed." This from the guy playing King Lear. "By the way, are all of us going to get a bad grade if Kathy can't pull herself together?"

"Yeah—*we* shouldn't get an F just because *she* obviously doesn't care." And I'd thought Cindy—Goneril—actually liked me!

"Who cares about the grade? We have to do this in front of the whole school! I don't want to look like an idiot in front of everyone because of her!" That figured. Rob—who played Kent—worried too much about what everyone else was thinking about him.

"Speaking of which, whose bright idea was it anyway to let her in our group?" So I was a nameless "her" now! Mike—Gloucester—had no idea what the word *tact* meant.

"Well, excuse me for asking her, but everyone knows how great her brothers and sister were in drama when they were at Central. I mistakenly thought she'd be a natural." By bringing up my family, Michelle had proven herself to be evil enough to play the part of Regan.

"Hey, Miss Goforth, is it too late for us to get somebody else to play Cordelia?" The guy playing Edmund—I couldn't remember his real name and didn't care—was the biggest whiner that ever lived. But I'd had enough and was all set to whale on everyone when Miss Goforth interrupted.

"Enough! That's enough, everyone. I'm sure Kathy will be just fine. Especially since she knows how much her grade depends on her performance in our Shakespeare festival." Miss Goforth gave me one of her meaningful, over-the-top-of-her-glasses looks.

I sighed and mumbled my apologies. Not because those losers deserved apologies, but because I really didn't want to have to force myself on another group and learn new lines. So I pulled deeper into myself and pretended as best I could to be Cordelia for the rest of the hour.

---

Long before the last bell rang, I decided to stay at school late to work on a paper. I couldn't deny that the excuse to stay after school appealed to me because it meant I could put off dealing with my parents. The longer we avoided each other, the faster they'd get over my melodramatic fit, as my sister, Sam, had so insultingly called my outburst the night before. All too soon, though, it was time to gear up for the walk home.

I'd nearly forgotten the only way to the main doors was past the trophy case. A moment later I was there, staring again at that picture of Brett, all spiffed up in his brand-clean football uniform. Behind Brett's picture was a large, framed, maroon football jersey with the number nine on it. Brett's number. Most likely the one he'd worn in the picture. And next to that was the trophy from the year Central took region in football—Brett's sophomore year. On the other side of the jersey was the huge trophy from the year Central took state in football—Brett's junior year. And above that trophy was a shiny plaque with fancy words about how great Brett was.

I felt shivers go up my spine because I could swear Brett was looking back at me. I touched the glass lightly with one hand and felt that strange connection pulling me towards him. But that was crazy. I'd never even known him, and yet . . .

"Hey, you."

I jumped at the gentle punch on my upper arm. *Jason.* In shorts and a T-shirt. My heart was pounding like it always did when Jason was around, but surely this time it was only because he'd startled me.

"Hey, yourself," I said, punching him back not so gently in the arm. "What are you doing here? Shouldn't you be throwing a football around or something with all your cohorts?"

Jason laughed. "I'm on my way to go lift some weights." He gave me an appraising look that made me feel like a bug pinned to a wall. "I can see you're still out of it."

I frowned. "Out of it?"

Jason nodded. "You were somewhere else all through tutor/study hall today. Again. Completely zoned out." I opened my mouth to protest, but he pointed accusingly at me and grinned. "Don't even try to deny it! I purposely asked you questions today that made no sense, and you just nodded and said, 'yeah, uh huh' every time."

And I thought I'd just been a complete idiot in drama. "I'm sorry— I'll be better next time. I promise." I was sure he'd take off then, but instead he turned to face the trophy case, too. Luckily, there were a ton of trophies and awards behind the glass. There was no way he could know.

"Looking at your brother Brett again, I see." For the second time, he made me jump.

I turned to Jason in surprise. "What do you mean—'again'?"

Jason shrugged and looked back at Brett's picture. "I've seen you here before. I know this is one of your haunts." I must've looked irked at that remark, because he quickly moved on with, "I don't blame you. I mean, the guy's a legend. You have every right to be incredibly proud of him. I can't imagine what it must be like to have him for a brother."

I could feel myself burning cold all over. "No, you can't. You don't have any idea what it's like at all." My voice sounded so flat and unemotional I surprised even myself.

Jason looked at me with that appraising look again. "Hmmm. That sounds serious—with all kinds of 'layers' and 'hidden meanings.'"

"Mocking me, as usual," I said dryly. I couldn't help grinning at him a little for poking fun at the things I constantly droned on about in our tutoring sessions. But at least he was paying attention and was maybe even learning something.

Besides the erratic change in my heartbeat that happened whenever Jason came around, another thing I couldn't stop being aware of was that Jason was *different* when he was with me, whether it was studying with me during tutor/study hall or running into each other when no one else was around to see. Even though he was genuinely nice to me and teased me in a definitely pleasant kind of way, I couldn't stop being wary of him. I knew if Angela bounced around the corner, or if any of his football buddies appeared, the mask would slip back into place and he'd become Mr. Cool and pretend I was just his tutor. Nothing more. I didn't want to think about how much it stung to walk past him in the halls when he was with his friends, knowing he'd seen me, only to have him pretend he hadn't. Or to quickly become so engrossed in talking or laughing with his friends that to the unobservant viewer, it would appear he couldn't possibly have seen me walking by at all. It took all my self-control sometimes not to fake a seizure or scream or something just to see if he'd notice I was within ten feet of him. But why I even cared whether he noticed me or not was beyond me. Especially since I was sure I didn't like him at all—I was sure I didn't—

"So—what's it like?" Jason prompted, snapping me back out of my thoughts.

"What's what like?"

"Having Brett Colton for a brother."

I should've known better than to think Jason would let the subject drop. When he was in the mood to probe, nothing could stop him. It was an irritating quality he had that I'd had the misfortune to discover due to our tutoring sessions. I slung my book bag from my shoulder to rest on the floor between my feet. "Believe me, you don't want to know."

"You say that as if having him for a brother is a bad thing."

"You said it, not me."

Jason raised one eyebrow. "Interesting."

I didn't say anything back. Something about the way he was looking from me to Brett's picture was—unnerving.

"Want to know something?" Jason said softly.

I glanced questioningly at him. "What?"

"I find my way over to this trophy case a lot, too. Mainly to look at your brother."

That really surprised me. "Why?"

Jason tapped the glass with his finger. "I've heard stories about his amazing talent for the game my whole life. He's had a huge impact on me since Little League football." Jason turned away from Brett's picture to look at me again. "Strange, huh? I mean, since I never even met him. He's given me a nearly impossible standard to beat. Ever since people figured out I could throw a football, I've been compared to him. Here at

Central, I feel like I'm living in his shadow." Jason abruptly stopped and eyed me narrowly before saying, "What's so funny?"

Had I really been smiling? Grinning? "And here I thought you couldn't possibly have any idea what it's like to have Brett for a brother." Jason raised an eyebrow again at that remark. "You're not the only one who has to beat an impossible standard he left."

"I said 'nearly impossible.' There's a difference. Which means that maybe I'll have a shot at breaking some of his records. If nothing else, he's given me some goals to shoot for." Then Jason probed me again with those blue eyes of his, making my heart pound strangely. "But what about you? What 'impossible standard' of his do you think you need to beat?"

I looked away from Jason's eyes. "Doesn't matter. It's impossible to 'beat' Brett in any way. In fact, it's impossible just to forget him, *period*. For even two seconds together. Now that's a feat my family will never be able to master."

"Forget? Why would you want to forget your own brother?"

"What's there for me to remember? I wasn't even two when he died. I couldn't have meant anything to him anyway."

"I don't believe that. I have a little sister—Emily—who's eight now, and I was crazy about her when she was born. Still am, in fact."

I couldn't help looking at him curiously. "You have a little sister, too?"

"Yep. Just like Brett. I'm sure you meant a lot to him, too."

I turned away from Jason. "Well, it doesn't really matter how he felt. He's over. Dead and gone forever."

"Do you really believe that? That he's 'over' and 'gone forever?'"

I shrugged. "Not entirely. I mean, my family talks about him as if he never left."

"Well, he *is* still part of your family, you know. He's always going to be your brother."

"Doesn't matter. I'll never know him, and he'll never know me."

"Sure you will. Someday."

"You mean in 'heaven'?"

Jason grinned and lightly shoved my shoulder. "Now who's mocking? Don't you believe your life will go on after you die and that you'll see your family again?"

I shrugged again. "I don't know. I haven't really thought much about it."

"Well, I do. I believe everyone keeps on living after they die. And that you can be together with the people you love again. Forever." Jason's blue eyes probed me again. "My family's awesome. I can't imagine not being with them forever. Don't you want to be with your family after this life is over?"

"Let's just say I wouldn't mind some distance from them," I said dryly. I raised both eyebrows at Jason. "Is this what they teach you in that seminary class of yours?"

Jason grinned. "That and more. You ought to come check it out."

"Or not," I said lightly.

"Why not?"

I sighed. "I'm not sure I can deal with some of the crazy things you get fed in there."

Jason shook his head. "Is it so crazy to believe that we'll keep on living after we die? And that you can be with your family again? What's wrong with believing in a religion filled with hope? And so much other amazing stuff, too—you just don't even know—"

"Hey, Jas!"

We both jumped a mile at the booming voice not far from our ears. Jeff and Brad, senior Varsity football players who liked to interrupt our study hour as much as Angela did, were standing five feet from us. I couldn't believe we hadn't heard them tromp over to the trophy case.

Jason clumsily tried to put his Cool mask on fast. "Hey—what's up?"

"You coming or what?" Brad refused to acknowledge my presence, but Jeff was giving me one of his own appraising looks. One that looked me up and down and found me to be seriously lacking, as if I was a problem that needed to be solved. I nervously gripped the handles of my book bag tight with both hands and stared back at Jeff without blinking.

"Yeah, I am." Jason turned briefly to me with a flat, "See ya later, Kathy."

I watched Jason strut down the hall with his football buddies. Then I turned to look at Brett through the glass once more and waited for my heart to stop pounding before finally heading for home.

———

" . . . and that about sums up my day at work. So how was your day at school, Kathy?"

"Yes, dear, how was school? And how is your tutoring of that football player coming?"

"Yes, how is Mr. Jason West doing in English these days?" Dad teased.

Mom and Dad had exchanged boring work stories over dinner, and now both turned expectantly towards me. At least they'd gotten over the Incident with Sam and Alex at our last family dinner. Neither had returned since that Unfortunate Event, but I wasn't complaining.

"Fine," I said and put another forkful of salad in my mouth. Both continued to stare at me. "What?" I demanded, looking from one to the other.

"Well, we'd hoped for a little more than that," Mom answered with a frown.

I sighed. "School's fine. I'm still working on the Shakespeare drama skit, driver's ed is going okay, English is great, and the tutoring's okay, too."

"He's being nice to you, isn't he? That Jason West, I mean."

I grinned at Mom. "Of course. He's a good little Mormon boy."

Mom had been drinking water out of her glass and nearly choked, gagging and coughing while Dad reached over to slap her on the back.

"You okay, honey?" Dad said worriedly.

"I'm fine—fine." Mom shoved his arm away irritably and then turned back to me. "Mormon?" she gasped out, still coughing like crazy. "You never said he was a Mormon!"

I frowned. "So? What difference does it make?"

"How do you know he's a Mormon?" Dad said curiously.

"He told me so. But I would've figured it out eventually. He loves to bring up religious stuff that goes with our reading assignments. It's kind of funny, actually."

"He's not pushing his religion on you, is he?" Mom broke in. "Because if he is, then I think a talk with your English teacher would be in order."

I shook my head quickly. "No, no, Mom. It's nothing like that. He's just really into his religion and likes to find a religious slant in our reading assignments. That's all." I tried to explain, but Mom was already getting into a tailspin over the whole Mormon thing.

"He wouldn't be 'sharing' his 'religious slants' with you if he wasn't hoping to talk you into his religion. I know how much Mormons like to convert other people." Mom was angry. Upset, even.

I tried my best to calm her down. "He's not doing that, Mom. We always talk over whatever we're assigned to read. He usually finds something that relates to his religion. It's just the way he is—the way he reads stories and things. I don't think he's trying to convert me. Besides, sometimes what he comes up with is sort of interesting."

Mom shook her head and stood up, loudly stacking our dirty plates together and snatching up the silverware. "I still don't like it. I don't think it's appropriate for him to be discussing religion with you in any way during your study hour. I thought you were just making sure he understood your assignments. I had no idea he was preaching to you as well—"

"He's not!" I yelled.

"—thinly disguised as sharing his opinions and views of the stories," Mom finished.

"Good grief. And you wonder why I don't like to share anything with you two!"

Mom's mouth dropped open in angry surprise, but Dad came to her rescue and grabbed my arm. "Don't talk to your mother that way, Kathy." I glared at Dad, and after a second he let go of my arm with a sigh. "Just be careful. Don't let him talk you into anything. If I were you, I'd make him stay focused on the work at hand and not let him get off onto any religious tangents."

I stared hard at both of them for the next few silent, uncomfortable seconds, before clearing my throat and trying again. "So *anyway*, about my driver's ed class—I need more practice behind the wheel. Neither of you has taken me out driving lately, and my birthday's coming up in a few weeks. I'd really like to be ready to take the driving exam and not flunk."

"Changing the subject, I see—" Mom began, but Dad chuckled and shook his head.

"I get the hint. Both of them. Want to go practice tonight, Kathy?"

Was *my* dad actually being *cool*? "You mean, you'd take me driving?"

"Grab your shoes and let's go."

———

"So how'd I do?" I asked, easing my mom's old Buick gracefully into our driveway. At least, in my opinion.

Dad finally released his death grip on the dashboard. "Not too bad. Just don't lean on the brake so hard every time you come to a stoplight. And no tricycle turns. Just slow down and make the turn. You don't need to jerk the car in the opposite direction before turning the wheel. Otherwise, you're doing okay. For a nearly sixteen-year-old beginning driver."

I grinned. "I'll work on that. Does that mean you'll take me out again—tomorrow?"

Dad raised his eyebrows. "Well, if I can't, then your mom can. Or maybe Alex or Sam could, if they dare come over again."

I rolled my eyes. As *if*. "Don't worry, Dad. They'll come back. They always do."

"Just promise me you'll behave yourself next time. That is, if you want to get your driver's license."

"You and Miss Goforth must've been twins separated at birth," I muttered, handing Dad the car keys. I reached for the door handle, but Dad put his hand on my arm.

"Wait, Kathy—one more thing." I pursed my lips before facing him, since I knew what was coming. Dad looked at me hard before speaking. "I think it's great that you're willing to help Jason West, but I have to agree with your mother. I'm worried he may be pressuring you."

"Dad, please! He's not—" Throwing up my hands in despair seemed appropriate. "I wish I hadn't said anything about it. I had no idea it would put you and Mom into orbit." Like a thunderbolt to my brain, a thought erupted in my head that was really making wheels turn, so I stopped my own rampage to look curiously at Dad. "Why exactly *is* it bothering both of you so much? Why do you care that Jason's bringing up religion, and that he's a Mormon?"

I couldn't believe it, but Dad definitely looked trapped. "We just don't want to see you go through anything upsetting because of Mormons, too," Dad started, "and—"

"'Too'? Who else in this family has known Mormons before?"

Unfortunately, nothing was going to make Dad say more. "Kathy, it's really late—after eleven o'clock. You need to get to bed, and so do I." I tried to interrupt again, but Dad wouldn't budge. "If you want to go driving again, then go in the house and get off to bed. Now."

# CHAPTER EIGHT

I'd been making Jason read out loud *The Love Song of J. Alfred Prufrock,* by T. S. Eliot, during our tutoring session. Watching Jason struggle, I realized that lately I'd truly been enjoying our tutoring sessions. Jason's focus had been better, he'd been studying harder, and we'd been able to get a lot of work done. In a word, it'd been great. Absolutely. There was no way anyone would ever get me to admit it out loud, but to myself, I could admit I didn't mind helping a jock with English so much anymore. It definitely wasn't so bad to have a popular, handsome, high school football star need my help. Especially when that someone was Jason. It was embarrassing to realize how much I looked forward to tutoring every day and how much I enjoyed every second of attention he gave me during that hour. In fact, I was almost sure that he liked the tutoring sessions, too. He always had a big smile when he'd see me come around the corner to our table, and the way he'd look at me always made me wonder what was going on behind those blue eyes of his.

"'To roll it towards some overwhelming question, / To say: "I am Lazarus, come from the dead—"'"

"Lazarus? Isn't that some guy from the Bible?"

Jason looked like a dog being offered a cookie. "Yeah, he's in the New Testament. Lazarus was a good friend of Jesus Christ. He raised him from the dead four days after Lazarus had died and was already buried in a tomb."

"Really? How did He raise him from the dead?"

"He went with Lazarus's two sisters and a bunch of other people to the tomb where Lazarus was buried, said a prayer to Heavenly Father, and then He said, 'Lazarus, come forth!'"

I listened with a grin on my face while Jason went on and on with the story, obviously thrilled that I was the one to encourage a religious discussion this time. Besides the fact that Jason was just plain fun to watch get all excited talking about anything of a religious nature with me (since I knew he thought I was basically a heathen), just knowing how disgruntled my parents would be about it pleased me. Immensely. Once Jason wrapped up his speech-slash-sermon on Lazarus, I yanked him back to the present with, "So, Jason, have you figured out what the question is?"

"Question?" Jason gave me a blank look. He'd obviously forgotten Prufrock even existed.

"Yes, the question. Poor Mr. Prufrock's question. The one he's afraid to rock the universe with."

Jason bumbled around, running his finger down the stanzas of the poem, mumbling, "Well, let's see. He keeps trying to rethink how to ask, and he's really worried about the outcome, and he also doesn't know if he's cool enough to ask. And he keeps putting it off—"

"Hmmm—like someone else we both know," I said dryly.

Jason sighed, gave his book a frustrated shove, and leaned back in his chair. "Fine. You win. I'm not sure what this Prufrock guy's problem is."

I shook my head and shoved his literature book back. "Think it through, Jason. What's the most important question a man can ask a woman? A woman he's become so attracted to he's basically afraid of her? A woman whose opinion is so important to him that it would kill him if she didn't respond well to his question. In other words, *rejection.*

So we're back to what the question is. And try to think bigger than the question of asking a girl to homecoming, although I'm sure that question wasn't a hard one for you to ask."

I could see the wheels in Jason's head spinning, trying to keep up with me, but my last words made him look up sharply and eye me narrowly. "What's that supposed to mean?"

I rolled my eyes. "Well, the word *Angela* comes to mind."

"What makes you think I'm going with her?"

"I guess the fact that she usually makes an appearance right about now every day gave me the first clue." And then, like another one of my thunderbolts, I realized another reason why I'd been enjoying our study sessions lately. I hadn't seen Angela bounce into our space in days. *Days!*

"I don't know that I'm going to ask her," Jason said casually. Too casually. "Maybe I'm thinking of asking someone else. I don't know. I haven't really thought too much about it—"

I laughed out loud. "What? *You* not think about the homecoming dance? Impossible." I quickly assumed an exaggerated, deep thinking look. "Wait—hold on a second! I haven't seen Angela in days . . . could I be smelling trouble in paradise? How tragic. The most perfect couple in school at odds. And the dance only a week away! How will Central go on? Maybe the dance ought to be cancelled!"

Jason wadded up a piece of paper and chucked it at my head. "Yeah, laugh it up, but I don't remember saying I'm in a fight with anyone. You're the one who's thinking that, not me."

I laughed and snatched the wad of paper and chucked it back at his head. "Well, if you're not going to make up with Angela, then who *are* you going to go with? After all, it just wouldn't *do* to have the Varsity quarterback not go to homecoming! You're probably supposed to be crowned king of the dance!"

Jason rolled his eyes. "Whatever!"

"Come on, Jason—this is serious!" I taunted. "Who are you going to ask, if Angela's out? Who, who, I wonder?" Watching Jason squirm was fun. Almost *too* much fun.

"I don't know. I guess if I get really desperate, I'll just have to drag you along," Jason announced calmly, looking straight into my eyes.

That was the last thing in the world I had expected Jason to say. To me. Ever. I could feel the color draining out of my face. "Me?" I said stupidly. I tried to recover with a nervous laugh and a "yeah, right," but it was too late. An evil grin was spreading all over Jason's face.

"Well, hey, now there's an idea! Maybe *we* ought to go together!"

"What—" I gasped.

Jason scraped his chair loudly to move in close to me. Way too close to me. "I get it now. You're trying to squeeze an invite out of me, aren't you?"

"What makes you think I'd want to go to a stupid dance with you and your big head?"

Jason's smile faded. "You mean, you wouldn't?"

For a second, I felt bad. Confused. "No—I—I didn't say that!"

"So you *do* want to go with me." His evil grin had returned, the big faker.

"I didn't say that, either! Stop it! You're putting words in my mouth!"

Jason smirked and leaned in close to me again. "I think I ought to take you to homecoming, just so—"

"So you can torture me more? Isn't an hour a day enough for you?" I interrupted angrily.

"Like *you* don't enjoy torturing *me*? Please! I think you deserve to have to suffer through an actual school dance. With me."

"Like you'd really take me to a dance," I scoffed, still scrambling to recover from the shock of his even talking about a dance with me.

"You don't think I would?" Jason had a challenging, dangerous look in his eyes that made me scrape my chair a few inches away from him. "Come on, Kathy," he teased. "I'll be fun! Just you and me and—"

"And the entire school in scary colors and styles of tuxedos and ugly homemade prom dresses? No thanks." I snatched my literature stuff up and jumped to my feet, ready to bolt for the door. But Jason was faster and sprang from his own chair to block my way, laughing. He wasn't an annoying, fast, football playing quarterback for nothing.

"You're killing me, Kathy. But I'm serious. You better go home and break out the sewing machine, because I'll be coming by for you next Saturday night. You just wait."

"I won't be the one who'll be waiting," I said irritably, trying to move past him, only to be blocked at every try. I gave him a hard push with my book bag, but Jason was as solid and immovable as a wall. And my heart was pounding away. *Irritating!*

Jason grinned. "You're not leaving until you agree to be my homecoming date!"

"You can't make me agree to anything," I sputtered.

Jason raised an eyebrow. "I can't? Well, then, I guess maybe I need some help here!"

In one incredibly swift movement, Jason leaped onto our study table, and while my mouth hung open and my eyes bulged, he cleared his throat and raised his arms. "'Scuse me—'scuse me—hey, everyone! I'm trying to ask someone to the dance—"

"Stop it! Jason, stop!" In sheer panic, I found that my grip and pull on his leg had become Hulk-like, and somehow I managed to yank him off the table. Jason regained his balance as easy as a cat and stood there laughing, continuing to block my way.

"You know there's only one thing that's going to make me stop. So how 'bout it?"

I couldn't make my mouth do much more than gasp. Jason shrugged and took a step towards the table again—

"Fine—whatever. Can I leave now?" I yelled as loudly as I dared in the library. And finally, thankfully, Jason stepped away from the table and moved to let me pass with a sweeping, old-world bow and a far too victorious grin, but as I quickly moved past him, my eyes caught sight of two maroon and gold letterman jackets. Brad. And Jeff. Neither of them was smiling. I felt like a bug about to be squashed as they glanced at each other before brushing past me to move towards Jason.

"I'll be picking you up Saturday—don't be dogging me!" Jason bellowed, interrupting my thoughts, still laughing his stupid head off.

"Whatever!" I threw over my shoulder. I didn't turn to look back at him as I hurried down the aisle. It wasn't until I'd turned the corner that I realized I was smiling—grinning broadly—and that my heart was pounding away. Excitedly.

---

Crystal and Mistie both screamed in unison that night at Mistie's during a Friday sleepover.

"I can't believe Jason West asked you to homecoming!" Crystal gushed.

I punched Crystal in the arm. "Thanks a lot! Is it really that much of a shock?"

Crystal rubbed her arm. "It's just that I'm sure everyone thought he'd take Angela."

"So did I. I still can't believe what happened." In fact, I *still* couldn't. The invitation had been so strange and unusual I wasn't completely convinced that it *had* happened.

"He definitely picked a bizarre way to ask you, but at least you got asked." Mistie had a wistful smile on her face that made me feel guilty I'd been asked at all.

"Yeah, I wish someone would ask me," Crystal agreed. "What bugs me even more, though, are the guys like my brother, Dennis, who'll let the dance go by and won't feel the urge to ask anyone. It just makes me so mad!"

"Well, you have to admit, Crystal, that Kathy deserves to go more than we do," Mistie said, reaching for a slice of pizza.

"Why is that?" Crystal demanded.

"Don't tell me you don't remember what Saturday is?"

Crystal looked thoughtful for a second, took a swig of cola, and nearly choked on it before giving me a shove. "I can't believe I forgot your birthday!"

"The big Sweet Sixteen!" Mistie grinned before giving me a huge wink.

But I hadn't forgotten. It was part of the reason my heart had pounded so fast and loud when Jason had forced me—*tricked* me—into going to the dance with him. Me, of all people!

"Wow! Not only can you get your driver's license now, but you get to go to homecoming. With Jason West! On your sixteenth birthday!" Crystal sighed melodramatically. "If only we could be so lucky!"

"I still can't believe it's really true," I said. I still couldn't. I dug into the pizza until Mistie turned to me expectantly.

"You've got a dress, don't you?"

A *dress?* "I hadn't really thought that far ahead yet."

Crystal laughed. "Well, you better! The dance is a week from tomorrow!"

"Well, then, I guess we'll be hitting the malls tomorrow!" Mistie said eagerly while Crystal nodded and grinned. "We can grab a bus and hit all the best stores." So without even an okay from me, Mistie and Crystal planned our big shopping trip to hunt for my dress. I called home in the morning to let Mom know what our plans were and got Dad on the phone instead.

"Well, don't leave until I come by Mistie's house, okay?"

"Okay, Dad." I wasn't sure what he was up to, but I was truly surprised—touched, really—when Dad showed up fifteen minutes later with one of his credit cards.

"Pick yourself out something nice, honey. You deserve it," Dad said, pressing the card into my hand.

"Dad—are you sure?" I couldn't believe my dad was being so cool!

"Of course I am. I want you to get something nice that you'll really like. Consider it an early birthday present from your mom and me."

"Well, wow—thanks. Thanks, Dad." I probably should've hugged him, but I hadn't done that in forever and wasn't sure how to propel myself into one.

"Just don't stay out too late. Be back home before dark, okay?"

I raised my eyebrows. "Do you really think it'll take me that long to find a dress?"

Dad grinned. "All I know is that it took weeks for Sam to find something for these dances. But something tells me you'll make up your mind a little quicker than she ever did."

Dad was right, but I was still pretty surprised at how fast I found the dress I wanted. I knew it was the one for me before I even tried it on. The dress was a deep blue in a shimmering, shiny material—straight cut to the floor, coming in sharp and tight at the waist with a walking slit, no sleeves, and a high choker neck that fastened in the back with a vertical row of little pearl buttons. The kicker was the open back. It didn't expose my entire back, but it showed off enough skin to guarantee a few raised eyebrows.

I loved it. Absolutely.

Both Mistie and Crystal oohed and ahhed over it, and before I knew it, I was back home with a fancy dress bag over my arm with a fancy dress in it. And a fancy pair of black high heels that I hoped wouldn't cause me to break an ankle.

———

I'd been home maybe seconds when Sam and Alex and their families arrived.

"Well, don't keep us in suspense. Let's see it!"

I rolled my eyes and handed the dress bag over to Sam while Alex nudged me in the ribs.

"Snagged a date with that football player, eh? Guess you won't be 'sweet sixteen and never been kissed' for long!" Alex laughed and grabbed me in a headlock, but I wrestled free of him to glare at Dad.

"I guess I have *you* to thank for telling everyone all the details of my life."

Dad shrugged and grinned. "So sue me. Sam and Alex both called today asking what we were doing for your birthday. I thought they ought to know what you're going to be doing."

Sam had my dress out of the bag and was scrutinizing it, both front and back. "Mom, come in here and take a look at the dress Kathy bought," Sam yelled before turning to eye me with raised eyebrows. "Don't you think this dress is a little too grown up for you, Kathy? I don't even want to know how much you wasted on it."

*Too grown up? Wasted?* I could feel the fumes rising in me that Sam was so good at setting off. "I'm going to be sixteen, and I'm going to homecoming. And I didn't 'waste' a cent on this dress. I think it's perfect, and so do Crystal and Mistie."

"Crystal and Mistie?" Sam had the nerve to laugh. "Far be it from me to challenge their notable fashion sense." She shook her head while she critically eyed my beautiful new dress as if it were a dead rat. "This is what happens when you take your friends shopping instead of someone who really knows how to shop for an appropriate dress for a high school dance."

The fumes were rising higher—so much higher that Alex and Dad were starting to back away from us. "You mean, someone like *you?* No, thanks. You're too old to know what's in style and what's not!" Sam audibly gasped. I took a step towards her and felt my hands tensing into fists. "You just don't think I could look good in a dress like this, do you?"

Sam faced me and folded her arms before looking me up and down with narrowed eyes. "I'm not sure you've got the figure to pull it off."

I was aching to yank every carefully placed hair out of Sam's head but settled for yelling, "Well, then, it's a good thing your opinion doesn't mean squat to me!"

Mom was now in the living room, eyeing the open back of the dress, as was Alex, who let out a loud wolf whistle. "Well, at least Jason West will like it. I guess his opinion is the only one that really matters, right, Kathy?" Kudos to Alex for trying to lighten the mood, but Sam and I were too busy trading insults to notice. Mom was all ready to say something about the dress and my rude words to Sam, but when Alex said Jason's name, Mom froze and dropped her hold on the dress, causing Sam to scramble to catch it before it fell in a wrinkled heap on the floor.

"*Jason West?*" No girl wants to hear her mom say the name of her date that way.

"Yes, Jason West." I repeated his name nice and loud and slow.

Mom looked hard at me. "You're not really going to go with that boy, are you?"

*That boy?* "Yes, I am," I said as firmly as I could. Mom was about to loudly protest, but I cut her off. "Good grief, Mom—he's just a football player. He's not a hardened criminal!"

Mom turned to Dad with a disbelieving look on her face. "Did you know it was Jason who had asked Kathy to the dance when she called this morning?"

Dad's grin was gone now. "Yes, I did—"

"And you told her she could go with that boy?"

Alex tried to calm Mom down. "Don't worry, Mom. It's just a school dance."

"That's right, Mom," Sam agreed. "Besides, your own two sons were football players, and you didn't worry about them taking girls to school dances."

"Well, you can't count Brett, Sam. He never really went to any dances," Alex stated.

"He didn't?"

"No—remember? He was too sick to go—"

*A Brett Moment? Right now?* I'd been forced to deal with a lot of irritants tonight, but that was one I just couldn't handle. "This is *so* not about Brett!" I yelled at the top of my lungs.

Alex and Sam jumped, but Mom cut us all off. "You two don't understand. It's not the football playing and everything that goes with it I'm worried about. That boy's a *Mormon*." Mom reached up to finger the ever-present locket around her neck while I rolled my eyes and said "Good grief." But the really weird thing was that Sam and Alex looked surprised.

"Kathy," Alex said, turning to me with the same concerned look Sam was wearing, "why didn't you tell us Jason's a Mormon?"

"I don't see why it matters," I said angrily.

"It *does* matter, because he's wasting time during their study sessions to preach at her—"

"Mom!"

"—and now he's asked her to this dance. I just don't like it—I don't like it at all!"

Everyone started babbling, so I stalked over to Sam and snatched the dress out of her hands. "You're all freaks. I'm sorry, but you are. Dad already said I could go, so I'm going. With Jason. And I'm not even going to try and explain anything about how Jason's not trying to convert me, because none of you will listen. Besides, you have no idea how offensive it is to realize my own family thinks the only reason a hot looking football player would ask me to a dance is because he must be trying to convert me over to his religion. I mean, why else would a cool, popular athlete ask a geek like me?" I jumped off my soapbox, leaving everyone with their mouths hanging open, and stomped off to my room, slamming the door threateningly behind me. I even blasted the Beatles album so I wouldn't have to hear any of their voices. Or acknowledge the twinge of doubt I'd had since Friday about why Jason had really asked me to the dance—a doubt I couldn't believe I'd screamed at my family before shutting myself away inside my room.

# CHAPTER NINE

Homecoming became a taboo subject with my family. I was actually grateful to have Monday arrive so I could escape them. Not long after I'd slid into my seat in Honors English, my heart pounded as fast as Jason's sneakers running at breakneck speed down the hall, screeching into his front row desk just as the eight o'clock bell rang. As usual.

"Good morning, Mr. West," Mrs. Dubois said dryly without looking up from the stack of papers she was thumbing through.

"Good morning, Mrs. Dubois." I waited to see if Jason would turn around and grin, wink, or wave, but he didn't. Not that he ever did, but since he *had* invited me to homecoming on Friday, I'd hoped he'd do—something. But he didn't. I couldn't help feeling disappointed.

Mrs. Dubois droned on and on about our reading assignment for the week while she walked up and down the rows, handing out our papers from last week. I was so busy looking over my A paper that I didn't pay attention to the sound of feet marching in unison, straight into our classroom, until the singing started. A bunch of drill team girls in their shiny, maroon miniskirts, sequined tops, and go-go boots had marched into a half-circle around Jason's desk and were now chanting with their arms tight behind their backs: "Roses are red, violets are blue, Does Angela want to go to homecoming? She does—with you!"

I couldn't move or breathe. I could only stare in shock while the drill team girls all turned their backs, only to twirl back to face him one at a time in mind-numbing, fast succession, each one holding up a large card with a letter on it until they'd spelled out, "Angela says yes!"

Unbelievable. My heart had been pounding—and now had dropped into my shoes. I couldn't speak—I didn't know what to say. Jason blushed and grinned and acted embarrassed as he received some nice hearty slaps on the back from a few stud boys. While Mrs. Dubois tried to shush the class back to order, Jason finally dared to make eye contact with me. I looked away when he did and didn't look at him again. The second the bell rang, I darted out in a clump of students before he could grab me. I heard him say my name, but I couldn't deal with him right then. I was too close to tears, and the fact was truly annoying.

---

I was dreading tutor/study hall, but at the same time, I was glad Jason would have to face me. I was determined to keep my emotions focused on calm anger. Otherwise, I was sure the tears I'd been holding back all day would come out in an embarrassing rush. I didn't look up when I heard him coming down the aisle or when I heard his footsteps slow and come to a halt. He didn't sit down but tentatively said, "Hey, Kathy." I didn't answer, and after a second he set his backpack down and slid quietly into his chair.

"Pretty exciting morning in English, wouldn't you say?" I said as unemotionally as I possibly could, still without looking up from my book.

"Yeah, I was pretty surprised."

"You can't imagine how surprised I was." I finally looked up. Jason actually looked somewhat—ashamed. Uneasy, at least. I couldn't decide if that made me feel better or worse.

"Kathy—about that. You know—last Friday? We were just joking around. About homecoming and everything, right? It was just a stupid joke."

I looked at Jason evenly. "Oh, sure. I see. Going to the dance with me would be just a stupid joke."

"I didn't say that. Now who's putting words into someone's mouth!" Jason tried to smile, but my cold look stopped him.

"Whatever. All I know is that it's pretty obvious you went ahead and asked Angela over the weekend, even though you asked *me* to the dance on Friday."

Jason floundered. "It wasn't like that. You—you don't understand, Kathy—"

"I don't understand what?" I interrupted calmly.

"The kind of—pressure—I'm under."

I raised my eyebrows. "I don't understand 'pressure'?"

"Not like the kind I'm under—because I'm—you know—" Jason was really looking uncomfortable now. Truly squirming in his seat.

I could feel myself starting to boil. It was like having Saturday night reheated. "I see. I don't understand pressure because I'm not a big popular athlete. Or on the drill team. Or something equally as stupid and ridiculous. This must be the same 'pressure' that makes it impossible for you to acknowledge my presence in front of your friends."

"What are you talking about?"

I fought hard to keep my voice down to a strangled whisper while I gave Jason a good verbal kick in the pants. "You think I can't see you're embarrassed—*ashamed*—to admit you know me in front of all your friends? I've passed you a million times in the halls, waiting to see if you'll condescend to nod your head at me, but you always pretend you either don't know me or haven't seen me. You just *ignore* me. You wouldn't *dare* lower yourself in front of your friends by actually saying 'hi' to me anywhere."

Jason's mouth dropped open. "Well, you don't exactly look excited to see me, either! I've seen you roll your eyes at your friends when you see me. 'Oh look, here comes the big, dumb jock who's too stupid to write an English paper on his own.' I guess it's only rude for me to ignore you, but it's okay for *you* to ignore *me?*"

Boiling-over time was coming. And fast. "I don't know why I'm wasting my time on you. You're too worried about your stupid place in this stupid school and what all your stupid friends think to be a decent human being to anyone. So go ahead and go to the dance with Angela. You two deserve each other, and I deserve better."

Jason's eyes narrowed as he studied my angry face. "You can't just— look, Kathy, I'm sorry. I know I have no idea what it's like for you, but you have no idea what it's really like for me. How could you?" He leaned closer to my face. "Besides the obvious fact that I need help in Honors English, do you know why I decided to take tutoring?" I shook my head, returning his glare with a cold one of my own. "My other choice was conditioning with my friends, but I chose tutoring over getting an easy A with them, and do you know why?" he asked again. Again, I shook my head. "Because I'm sick and tired of listening to my friends and everyone on the team tell me what to say, what to wear—even who to ask out. You don't know what it's like to start talking about some girl, only to be cut off with, 'Her? Why do you want to waste your time on her?'" He scowled and slouched deeper into his chair. "I'm just sick of it all. This class offers me one hour a day of relief from—everything."

If Jason was hoping for sympathy or understanding, he wasn't going to get either from me. Not after I'd spent a ton of money on a dress I wasn't going to be wearing on Saturday night after all. "It's okay, Jason. I understand. Really. Now I can see how stupid I was to think you would have the guts to ask me to a dance. You may look like a big, tough football player who's not afraid of anything, but you're just a—a—Prufrock." *Prufrock?* Had I just said Prufrock?

Jason looked baffled as he stared blankly at me. "A 'Prufrock'?"

My mind raced. "Yeah, a Prufrock. Too worried about your friends— and I use the term *extremely* loosely—to just go ahead and do and say and be what you want. You're too afraid to dare and disturb Central's universe. Even though you know Central High's universe is in desperate need of being disturbed. I'm sorry you're such a coward."

Before Jason could smack back with anything, Brad and Jeff came strutting down the hall, ready to interrupt as usual.

"Jas!" Jeff yelled. And as usual, Brad ignored me completely.

"Hey, Brad—Jeff." Jason slipped his Cool mask on so quickly I would've been impressed if I hadn't wanted to slap him as badly as I did.

"Has Angela answered you yet?" Jeff looked at me. Meaningfully. With an appraising look that found me to be not only seriously lacking but irritatingly in the way.

"Yeah, in first period." Jason scowled down at his book and flipped its pages.

"I thought she would. You're coming with us to the dance, right?" Brad asked. I almost wanted to laugh. I was less than thin air to him.

"Yeah, I guess. Can we talk about this later?" Jason at least had the decency to sound embarrassed and annoyed. As for me, I'd had enough of all three of them.

"It's okay, Jason. I'd say we're pretty much done here, wouldn't you?" I stood up, threw my literature stuff in my book bag, and left before Jason could say or do anything back.

———

I slumped behind my desk in the empty drama classroom, fuming to myself over the past hour. Hours. Days—

"You're here early today, Kathy." Miss Goforth stood by my desk with her hands on her hips, looking down at me over the rims of her glasses. "Hoping to get some extra practicing in?"

"Is that supposed to be a hint?" I grumbled.

"It certainly wouldn't hurt you to spend more time rehearsing your lines." Miss Goforth slipped into the desk by mine. "I noticed you haven't signed up for any play but *King Lear* for our fall Shakespeare festival. And you know every student needs to participate in at least two. Otherwise, your grade definitely will not be an A for the term."

I sighed. Of course, this day couldn't get any better, but it could always get worse. "Okay, Miss Goforth. I'll sign up with another group today." The problem with that, as I discovered after the rest of the students filtered in, was that there *was* no other group to join that was in need of more actors. Although based on everyone's nervous or cold looks when I asked if they had any more parts in their groups available, I had a feeling I was purposely being left out. Was I really doing that bad as Cordelia? But considering that I had to be shoved hard again during class to remind me it was my turn to speak, I started to believe I really *was* doing that bad.

———

I was thinking about drama class and wondering how I was going to avoid flunking as I trudged to the front doors of the building after school. My stumbling through *King Lear* had turned me into drama poison to the rest of the class. I sighed. Who could blame them? "I guess I'll just have to find some scene I can do by myself," I said. Out loud. I stopped in horror when I heard my voice. Looking around casually to see if anyone had heard me talking to myself, I locked eyes with—*Brett*. Smiling up at me, like he always did behind the glass in the trophy case, where my feet had taken me. Again.

I stepped closer to focus on Brett's grinning face. I reached out and touched the glass carefully with my hand. My heart pounded, because it was there again—that connection I always felt with him. But that was crazy. I knew it was crazy. Or I was. I yanked my hand away as if I'd been burned and ran out of the building.

———

"Okay, Kathy. Out with it. What the heck happened today?" Crystal kept her mouth shut until all three of us were in my bedroom with the door closed.

"What do you mean?" I did my best to shrug innocently.

Crystal rolled her eyes. "Well, let's just say it was a good thing we were driving the simulators in driver's ed instead of real cars." Crystal turned to Mistie. "She knocked over everything in sight and set a new class record for the worst simulated driving in years."

"So? What happened?" Mistie demanded.

I sighed and shook my head.

"What?" Both Mistie and Crystal were pleading now.

I paced the room while the two of them sat on the edge of my bed. "I thought he was different. Jason, I mean. But you know what? He never had any intention of taking me to homecoming. It was all just a big joke. He asked Angela to the dance over the weekend."

"Angela?" Crystal gasped.

I glanced at Crystal. "Of course, Angela. And she answered him during Honors English in front of me. On purpose, I'm sure."

"I can't believe it," Mistie said softly, shaking her head.

I laughed bitterly. "You can't? I can! Going to a dance with me would spoil the image he's worked hard to achieve." I stopped my ranting and pacing to sigh and rake my fingers through my hair. "You know what really sucks?" Both Mistie and Crystal shook their heads silently. My voice trembled. "I actually wanted to go with him." But it was more than just that. I didn't quite know what it was about Jason. After all, we were complete opposites in every possible way. Maybe it was his similarities with Brett. I'd be lying if I said I hadn't noticed that he'd given me a possible window into a little bit about my brother. Or maybe it was just because he was the first guy—and a cute, popular football player at that—who'd ever really noticed me before and paid some attention to me. Maybe it had something to do with the fact that he needed help in Honors English and had specifically picked me to help him. Or maybe it was a combination of everything balled up and combined with something else Sam would simply call "chemistry." All I knew was that my heart never pounded around any guy but Jason, and sometimes, I could swear by the way he looked at me that he could feel electricity starting to hum in the air between us, too. At times I hated feeling anything regarding Jason, because he wasn't the type of guy I wanted to like, and yet he *was*—. It was all just too confusing. The only thing I knew for sure came out of my mouth before I could stop it. "I don't think this would hurt so much if I didn't like him. I never meant to like him at all, but now I know that I do. Probably too much."

Before I could say another word, Mistie and Crystal rushed to throw their arms around me in a huge group hug that made me bawl. No one said a word until we were all sitting cross-legged in a circle on my bed.

Mistie finally broke the silence. "So what are you going to do now?"

I shrugged, wiping at my eyes. "Take the dress and shoes back, I guess. I won't be needing them now."

"Over my dead body!" Crystal was so loud with her angry announcement that both Mistie and I jumped. "It's your sixteenth birthday! I'm not going to let him ruin it! I can get you a new date with a *junior* so you can flaunt that hot dress in front of Jason and everyone else!"

My mouth fell open. "A new date? Who?"

Crystal grinned. "My brother Dennis, of course! And don't say no, because this is my birthday present to you, and I'll be incredibly offended if you reject it!"

My heart started to pound funny. "No way—I'm not—"

But Crystal definitely was not going to take no from me. "Considering the fact that the dance is on your birthday, you *have* to go! Otherwise, you'll mope around all Saturday night and you'll never forget this birthday, but for wrong, bad reasons. You don't deserve to spend your sixteenth birthday moping! And that dress doesn't deserve to go back to the store!"

I couldn't deny that it was pretty great of Crystal to offer her brother on a platter this way, but saying Dennis would take me to the dance and actually convincing him to do so were two entirely different things.

"Don't worry. He'll go. I guarantee it!"

Knowing how paranoid I am, Crystal made her brother call me that night to confirm that he really would take me to homecoming. Especially since Crystal and Mistie were paying for it, both using the excuse of my upcoming sixteenth birthday and saying it was their gift to me, of course.

# CHAPTER TEN

D
ue to the excitement of everything that had happened, I lay awake in bed that night for hours after listening to *Rubber Soul*, just thinking and mulling over lots of things, and by morning I'd made a few important decisions.

The first decision I made was accomplished in the morning with a phone call to Dennis, telling him again that I appreciated his willingness to take me to homecoming on such short notice and that yes, I would definitely go with him to the dance on Saturday.

The second decision I'd made took place following Honors English. After presenting my case thoroughly to Mrs. Dubois, she eventually agreed to my request. Part two of that decision took place during tutor/study hall. I purposely came late, waiting to walk to the table in the back corner until after I'd checked out a book I'd been thinking about the night before and after making sure Jason was already waiting for me. Then, without giving Jason a chance to say anything, I coldly announced that it was obvious this study/tutoring thing wasn't such a hot idea after all. After all, he was pulling an above average grade in Honors English now. Plus, I needed more time to prepare my Shakespeare scenes for the festival.

I quickly finished with, "I've already spoken to Mrs. Dubois about it, and she agreed to let me out of tutoring. She said you can talk to her about getting a new tutor."

Jason's mouth opened, but he didn't say anything. With that, I gave him a farewell salute, turned sharply on my heel, and moved as fast as I could down the hall and out of the library.

———

I accomplished my third and last decision when I entered the drama classroom. I fought through my trembling nerves and strode as confidently as I could to Miss Goforth's desk.

"Miss Goforth?" Even my voice almost sounded confident!

Miss Goforth looked up from her textbook. "Kathy. Early again. This is a surprise."

"It's no surprise. Totally on purpose."

"Really? Why is that?"

I gripped the handle of my book bag and crossed my fingers for luck. "Because I need your help. I mean, I'm hoping you'll help me. That you'll want to."

Now Miss Goforth raised both eyebrows at me. "What seems to be the problem?"

"No actual problem—except for my grade. You know the Shakespeare festival?"

"I do."

I took a deep breath and went on. "If I do a scene by myself, can it count as my second required scene? I mean—can I even *do* one by myself?"

Miss Goforth folded her arms and leaned forward to study me consideringly. "If you can find an actual substantial Shakespeare scene. And it would have to be a scene performed by a female. And I would have to approve it, of course."

"Good. Great!" I threw my book bag to the ground and scrounged around inside it for the book I'd found in the library before flipping to

76

the section in question and thrusting the book at Miss Goforth's face. "What do you think about this one? About me performing it, I mean."

Miss Goforth pulled her head back sharply to avoid being smacked in the face by the book before gingerly taking it out of my hands to glance over the pages in question.

"Well? What do you think?"

Miss Goforth nodded over the book a few times before lifting her head to look at me thoughtfully. "I'm impressed. I think you've found something here. Something that could be quite wonderful. The real question is whether you can really do it justice."

And now for the kicker part of my third and last decision. "Well, that's where you come in. Do you think you can help me? I mean—*will* you help me?"

Miss Goforth raised both eyebrows at me again. "During class, you mean?"

I shook my head and shifted my weight nervously from foot to foot. "No—I mean now. During this hour. It's my study hour. And you don't have a class this hour," I pointed out.

"So of course I must have nothing to do?" I opened my mouth to respond, but she cut me off. "Never mind. Let's see if you're worth my time. Go up there and read a few lines." Miss Goforth handed me the book and motioned me towards the mini stage.

My mouth fell open. "Right now?"

"Why not?"

"Because I just hit on the idea of doing this scene. I haven't read any of the lines yet!"

"Well, there's no time like the present. You've only got a few weeks to pull this together, so give it a try. Forget who you are, and just be your character."

So I did. Not horribly well, but at least I'd given it the best I had at that moment in time. And under Miss Goforth's piercing eye, no less.

"So—what do you think? Am I worth your best efforts?"

Miss Goforth rose from her desk and walked slowly to where I stood. "This is going to take some work. A lot of work. But it appears you have some raw talent moldering away inside of you. Study the scene tonight, and we'll work on it some more tomorrow."

———

I'd spent some time at the library after school on Friday looking up a few books for my next Honors English paper, and as I'd been doing a lot lately, after I left the library, I turned down the hall that would lead me to the trophy case. Brett's trophy case. This week had been rough, and I'd felt a strange amount of comfort just looking at Brett's grinning face behind the glass. Today, however, I was brought to an abrupt halt, clutching the handle of my book bag over my shoulder as I rounded the last turn to the trophy case.

"I knew if I waited around here long enough you'd eventually show up."

*Jason.* I'd successfully avoided him all week, and seeing him now—. Against my will, my heart pounded and my legs felt shaky. He had his backpack over one shoulder, and although he was trying to seem Cool, it wasn't working. It was definitely satisfying to see that he wasn't comfortable, either.

I lifted my chin and glared at him. "And now I'm leaving." I whirled on my heel to get away from him fast, but Jason was faster. He tossed his backpack aside and in two quick strides grabbed my upper arm.

"Wait—hold on a second, Kathy—"

I twisted frantically and shoved at his hand. "Let go!" Jason dropped his hold, and I eyed him warily as I adjusted my now-wrinkled sleeve. "Why are you here?"

Jason sighed and ran a hand through his hair before making eye contact again. "I guess you could say I'm daring to disturb the universe."

I stared at him. "What?"

Jason tried to smile, but his eyes were pleading. "I need to talk to you, Kathy."

"Well, I don't need to talk to you. And I don't *want* to talk to you."

I tried to move away from him, but Jason quickly stepped in my path. "I'm sure you don't need to, or want to—after everything that's happened, I don't blame you for not wanting to tutor me anymore. In fact, I wouldn't blame you if you didn't want to talk to me or see me ever again. But I really need to talk to you. And I really *want* to talk to you. I need to explain—"

I slowly backed a few steps away from him. "I don't—"

Jason stepped forward the same number of steps. "Sixty seconds. That's all I'm asking for. After that, if you want me to stay away from you, I promise I will."

My heart was pounding weird and fast, and I could feel myself wanting to cry again. "Look, I've got to get home—" I tried to push my way around him, but Jason wouldn't budge. After a few more seconds of me trying to get around him, he sighed and threw up his hands.

"Fine. I can't make you talk, or listen, or anything. But before you go—here—take this." Jason had grabbed his backpack, fished inside of it, and now thrust a small white box tied with a pink ribbon towards me. I stared at the box but didn't move to take it from him.

"You think a present is going to make everything all better?"

Jason shook his head. "It's not a present."

"What is it?"

"Open it and find out." Jason continued to hold the box out towards me, so finally I snatched it from him and yanked off the ribbon. I frowned as I looked at the two small white roses nestled on stiff green leaves inside the box. "A corsage?"

Jason shook his head again. "Not 'a' corsage. *Your* corsage. I ordered it for you on Friday after school." I stared at part of a receipt taped across the side of the box, which indeed noted that the corsage had been ordered on Friday afternoon. "I went by the flower shop during lunch today, and it was ready."

"Why didn't you save this for Angela?"

Jason looked at me as if he thought I was crazy. "I wouldn't give her *your* corsage!"

Still staring at the beautiful white roses nestled inside the box, I slowly turned from Jason to sling my book bag to the ground against the wall. A moment later, Jason leaned against the wall beside me.

"Kathy," Jason said softly. "I'm sorry. Really sorry. What I did was— unforgivable." I wholeheartedly agreed, but I couldn't respond because of the stupid tears trying to work their way free. Jason carefully continued. "I honestly wanted to go to the dance with you. Friday night, after the game, Brad and Jeff—they invited me to come with them and their dates and some other guys on the team with their dates to the dance as a group. I wasn't sure what you'd think about that, but I thought it could be cool. The only problem was . . ."

"Me," I stated dully.

Jason sighed and nervously raked his fingers through his hair. "It sounds so stupid—I guess it *is* stupid. They expected me to ask Angela, and, well—you don't know what it's like being on the team, Kathy. They're seniors, and they can make life pretty ugly for me—for anyone on the team. I thought it was cool being friends with all of the Varsity seniors and juniors at first, but it's hard. I mean, they demand one thing, while inside my head, I know I've been taught better. But if I push against them, well, it's just me against a lot of guys older and bigger than me."

I still didn't respond, which seemed to make Jason even more nervous, a fact I guiltily had to admit I liked. It made up for the fact that I knew I was going to start bawling any second.

Jason sighed. "The only thing I could hold onto after Jeff and Brad cornered me into asking Angela was the hope that maybe you hadn't taken my invite seriously." He attempted a nervous sounding laugh. "After all, why would you want to go out with a dumb jock like me?"

Somehow I managed to make my voice work. "Sorry I had to disappoint you."

Jason frowned and shook his head. "Don't say that."

I wasn't sure what to make of Jason's moment of soul-baring. I was surprised that he'd done it. In fact, I was grudgingly impressed. It had raised him a notch out of the deep sludge I'd mentally sunk him into, but it didn't change the fact that he'd hurt me. "What do you want me to say?"

"I don't know—maybe that you'll forgive me, eventually?" Jason asked, looking at me hopefully.

I looked away from him while I reached down for my book bag with one hand and slung it over my shoulder. I walked the few remaining steps to the school's front doors before turning back to look at him. He was watching me closely. My heart hadn't stopped pounding the whole time he'd been near me.

"Maybe," I said softly. Before Jason could say anything else, I pushed the heavy doors open and headed for home.

## CHAPTER ELEVEN

H appy birthday to you! Happy birthday to you! Happy birthday, dear Kathy, happy birthday to you!"

Alex and Julie, and Sam, Stephen, and Curtis came over for a late birthday lunch on Saturday because I was, of course, going to the homecoming dance. Everyone was so overjoyed that I was going with Dennis instead of Jason, it was almost sick. But because I was going to the dance in a new dress, it was impossible for me to be in anything but a good mood.

"Okay, Kathy, make a wish," Mom said while lighting the last of the candles.

"Make it a good one!" Dad winked.

"And keep it clean!" Alex threw in, just to get everyone laughing.

*I wish Jason—*

I looked up for a second above all sixteen glowing candles on my chocolate cake, my eye catching the shiny glints off Mom's heart locket around her neck.

*I wish Brett—*

"Come on, Kathy! We're going to be eating wax if you don't hurry!" Alex complained.

"And Curtis will dive in if you don't hustle!" Sam was wrestling with

Curtis in her arms, who was reaching his little arms for my cake and grunting in protest at being kept away.

I closed my eyes tight and blew. Hard. Everyone clapped and cheered, and after eating a small sliver of cake, I was attacked with presents. Lots of good stuff, too—music CDs, books, clothes—all kinds of things I'd been wanting for a while now.

"I have one more thing for Kathy. Something really special—"

I looked up when I heard Mom mention another gift, but my eyes found the kitchen clock. "Dennis is going to be here in less than two hours! I've got to get ready!"

"Oh, I didn't realize it was so late." Disappointment was in Mom's voice, and an anxious tone, too, which was strange to hear during a birthday cake-and-presents moment.

"Well, I guess I can spare a couple of minutes." I rose from the table and gathered all my birthday loot. "So what's this last thing, Mom?" There had to be time for one last present.

Mom shook her head sadly. "It can wait. I'll give it to you after the dance."

"Are you sure?"

"I'm sure. You hurry and get in the shower. You don't want to keep Dennis waiting. Don't you have dinner reservations?"

———

After yanking on my bathrobe and wrapping my wet hair up turban style in a towel following a record-breaking shower, I hurried into my bedroom—

"Hi, Kathy!"

—and nearly jumped out of my skin. Sam was sitting on my bed, her legs crossed, grinning away, as if she had every right to be there.

"Sam! What are you doing in here?"

Sam shrugged and slid off the bed. "I'm going to help you get ready for your big homecoming dance, what else?"

I was dumbfounded. Truly. "You are?"

Sam laughed. "Yes, I am. Just think of it as an extra birthday present from me."

I wasn't sure I really wanted Sam's help, but after seeing myself in my full-length mirror in my hot blue dress and heels, with my hair in an expertly done French twist and makeup that could rival a fashion model's, I was glad Sam had been there to help.

I turned to face Sam nervously. "Well? Do I have what it takes to pull this off?"

Sam stepped back to slowly and critically look me up and down before meeting my eyes. And then she smiled. At me! "I believe I'm going to be forced to retract my earlier statement. I think you're going to pull off wearing this gown just fine."

———

After Dennis arrived, embarrassing photo snapping occurred, followed by bad jokes from my entire family, who had insisted on hanging around until poor Dennis made an appearance. We'd been standing around in the living room, so while everyone else babbled at Dennis, I turned to catch one last, quick look in a mirror that hung in our living room. My gaze skimmed my hair and makeup, and then, over my shoulder, I saw a pair of eyes watching me. A familiar, laughing pair of eyes. I whirled around, my heart pounding—and was eye to eye with the picture that rested in the same spot where it had for years, on the top shelf of our living room bookcase. I reached out with trembling fingers and touched the frame before hurrying out the front door with Dennis while my family grinned and waved good-bye.

———

Homecoming was held in Central High's gymnasium. Maroon and gold balloons and streamers were everywhere, music was blaring, and couples in all colors of dresses and suits were out in the middle of the floor dancing. A punch bowl and treat table were set up to my right, and a few couples were lounging around it, munching cookies and sipping punch. My heart pounded fast when I saw that Jason and Angela were one of those few couples.

"Want to dance?" Dennis grinned and tried to pretend he was totally comfortable going to a dance in a suit with me in my hot blue dress.

I forced a smile. "Actually, I'm feeling kind of thirsty. Would you mind getting me a drink first?"

"No problem. I'll grab us some punch, okay?" Dennis walked over to the punch bowl and stopped to chat with a girl in a green dress standing with a guy in a gray suit.

I stared at Jason. He hadn't rented a tuxedo but wore a nice Sunday type of suit and tie. Angela, of course, looked gorgeous in a pink dress that looked as if it had been made for her. He and Angela were talking with Brad and Jeff and their dates, but when Jason turned to set his punch cup down on the treat table and saw me, he didn't look away. His face held a mixture of happy surprise and nervous fear, as if he was unsure exactly what to do now that he'd seen me. Against my will, I could feel my lips curving upwards into an actual smile. A small smile, but a smile, nonetheless. Jason's face immediately relaxed. He smiled back at me, which only made my heart pound harder and faster. I watched, hardly daring to breathe, while he leaned down to whisper in Angela's ear before turning to move in my general direction. Purposefully. Behind Jason, I could see Brad and Jeff craning their thick necks to see what Jason was leaving them for. When they both saw me, their stunned reactions, whether over me and my dress or the fact that Jason had abandoned them for me, was truly satisfying.

"Hey, Kathy." Jason tried to call up some casual bravado and coolness. I kept the tiny smile on my face, but I didn't respond. He shook his head and raised an eyebrow as he took a look at my dress. "Wow, look at you!" And then he lifted his hand into position for a high five. *What kind of a stupid joke was this?* I frowned at his hand before grudgingly obliging, only our hands didn't come apart once the high-fiving was done. Instead, before I could pull my hand away, he shocked me by casually intertwining his fingers with mine until our hands came back down to our sides. Even then, he didn't let go. "That's an interesting dress," he grinned.

"I'm not sure whether I should feel flattered or insulted," I said dryly, even though my heart was still pounding and pounding away. He was, after all, still holding onto my hand!

"Hey, Jason." *Dennis.* I'd almost forgotten he even existed. Jason stepped back to let Dennis move in between us with his two cups of punch. I quickly slipped my hand out of Jason's, thanked Dennis for the punch, and made the necessary brief intros. Jason raised an eyebrow at Dennis and looked him up and down in a measuring way that almost made me giggle. *Jealous, Jason? Surely not a big, popular football player like you!* Although Dennis wasn't my type, and I knew I wasn't his, he definitely was still fine eye candy. And a junior, besides! I glanced back at Jason after my own look-see at Dennis and had to catch my breath. Jason was looking at me again. *Really* looking. My hands were so trembly while I took a quick, nervous sip of punch that I was amazed I didn't drop the cup and splash punch all over the three of us.

Jason turned back to Dennis casually and said, "Hey, Dennis—my date, Angela, is busy messing with her hair, her face—I don't know. Mind if I dance with Kathy?"

*Dance? With Jason?* My heart irritatingly pounded faster.

Dennis shrugged. "If it's okay with Kathy."

Jason turned towards me with such a hopeful look on his face that it was impossible for me to say no.

I raised my eyebrows, trying my best to pretend I was Cool with this. "One dance."

The current song was fading out, to be replaced by another tune before there was even a second of silence—a tune with a softer volume.

And a definitely slower beat. *Not a slow song—please!* I wanted to tell Jason I didn't mind waiting for a fast song, but he'd already put his hand on my lower back and before I knew it, I was out on the dance floor, both of us in a slow-dance position: my hands on his shoulders, and his arms around my waist, both of us swaying and turning a slow circle to the slow beat of the song. It would be impossible to explain how strange—surreal—it felt to be slow dancing with Jason. Just the fact that he had his arms around my waist was—*unnerving.*

Neither of us said anything while I stared at his right shoulder, wondering if this was going to be a completely silent slow dance. I sneaked a look at Jason just as he turned to look down at me, and he smiled. A real smile.

"I've never seen you in a dress before. You look nice dressed up."

"Glad you think I clean up okay. And you look pretty nice yourself. For a big dumb jock."

Jason laughed. "Yeah, okay. Insult me. I guess it's better than being ignored."

"I suppose."

We lapsed back into silence for another thirty seconds before Jason spoke again.

"So, did you make it to the game last night?"

I raised my eyebrows at him again. "The game?"

Jason laughed. "Obviously not, I see."

"Oh, yeah. Homecoming. Of course. No, you're right. I didn't make it."

"I can't believe you didn't go!"

"I guess the idea of freezing my rear end on a hard, wooden bleacher for at least two solid hours watching people I don't know chase a ball around doesn't sound appealing to me."

Jason laughed again. "Where's your school spirit?"

I grinned back at him. "I guess I don't have any. Darn."

"Have you even been to any of the football games?"

"Can't say that I have."

"I can't believe that—I think I'm actually offended!"

"You shouldn't be. You've got plenty of fans to cheer you on. You wouldn't even notice if I was there. And obviously you haven't, if you had to ask if I've been to a game."

Jason sighed and rolled his eyes before grinning down at me. "Well, I think you need to come see a game. Next weekend. If only so you can at least say you experienced one high school football game during your sophomore year. Who knows? You may actually have *fun!*"

Jason wasn't going to get me to commit. I was going to stand firm. "I don't know—"

"Come on, say you'll go. You know you want to!" Jason teased. "Don't you want to see me play? Even just a little bit? Just once? I thought you'd jump at the chance to get some ammunition for making fun of me later."

I laughed. "We'll see. Maybe." That was all the commitment he was getting out of me.

Jason nodded, obviously satisfied. "Okay, then."

We lapsed back into silence. Not as uncomfortable as before, but I wasn't relaxed, either, and I wondered if he was as acutely aware of me as I was of him. When Jason decided to speak again, he spoke so softly I had to strain to hear him. "Kathy, I don't know if I did that great of a job yesterday, but you need to know—I've been wanting to tell you all week how sorry I am about this whole mess. Homecoming and everything else."

I nodded without looking at him. "So am I."

Jason looked down at me, his face serious now. "I miss studying with you."

I raised my eyebrows. "You mean, you missed getting an 'A' on your paper this week."

Jason laughed softly. "Torturing me, as usual."

"Only because you deserve it. And need it."

Jason looked down at me earnestly. "So, do you think you might decide to forgive me?"

I shrugged. "I don't know yet. Maybe. Eventually."

"Does this mean you'd consider being my . . . tutor again?"

I sighed and looked straight into his way-too-beautiful blue eyes. Eyes that were pleading with me. With *me!* "No. I'm sorry, Jason, but I can't. I have a lot to do to get my drama scenes ready for the Shakespeare festival. I just can't help you right now."

The song faded out to its end, so Jason mumbled that he understood, thanked me for the dance, and walked me off the floor back to Dennis. And to Angela, who glared at me before dragging Jason away. Dennis and I danced together, and I proved myself to be a better actor than I thought possible. I smiled, laughed, joked, and flirted as if I was having the time of my life. But all I had to do was catch a glimpse of Jason with Angela, and I knew that all I was doing was acting.

"Want to get our pictures taken? The line's probably slowed down by now."

"Yeah, sure. That sounds great, Dennis." My beautiful high heels weren't feeling so beautiful anymore, so I gratefully left the dance floor with Dennis and went through the whole dance-picture-taking ritual, as had every couple in line before us, each one posed in the exact same position for the photographer.

We made it back to the dance floor just in time to see Jason and Angela crowned homecoming king and queen. Everyone cheered while silly looking crowns were placed on their heads, and then everyone gawked while they had their royal slow dance. But I'd seen enough. It was late anyway, so with a word to Dennis, we left the homecoming dance behind.

———

I was all partied out, danced out, smiled out, and small talked out by the time I said good night to Dennis and locked the front door. I had just collapsed onto my bed when I heard a soft rap on my bedroom door.

"Yes? I mean—come in," I mumbled, already more asleep than awake.

Mom stood in the doorway, one hand toying with the gold locket around her neck, looking like she was about to burst.

"Mom? What is it?" If I thought I'd almost been asleep before, I was wide awake now.

"Nothing. Nothing, dear." She smiled and dropped a letter into my hands. The envelope was a faded white, almost yellow color, with the name "Kitty" printed on it in bold, black capitals with a line drawn firmly below it—handwriting that was unfamiliar to me.

"I've kept my promise for over fourteen years and haven't opened it. Even though I was tempted to more times than I care to admit."

I frowned at the envelope and moved out from under the covers to sit on the edge of my bed. *Kitty.* That had been an old family nickname for me when I'd been really little, but no one had called me that since I was about four years old.

Mom soundlessly moved across the floor to sit beside me on my bed. "And I haven't told a soul about it. Except your father, of course. But I did as he asked and didn't tell Alex or Sam."

I looked up from the envelope, truly bewildered. "Mom, what's— what is this?"

"Open it and find out." Mom smiled at me in a funny way before bumping my shoulder with hers. I looked back down at the envelope while Mom continued to sit by me, obviously waiting. "Well, aren't you going to open it?"

I didn't speak for a moment, and when I did, my voice sounded strange to me, all tight and strained. "Mom, whose name is on the envelope?" I didn't look up but kept my eyes focused on the unfamiliar handwriting before me.

"Why, it's your name, honey, of course." Mom put her arm around me and rubbed my arm, but after a few seconds of that, I couldn't help pulling away from her.

"Is anyone else's name on it?" I said flatly, still without looking up at her.

"Well, no, but—"

I took a deep breath. "Then I think it's safe to say the letter was meant for me. Just me."

It took less than a moment for Mom to get the hint. I knew she was shocked—hurt—but to her credit, she merely nodded and quietly stood and walked slowly to the door before turning to me again.

"Kathy, honey—if you want to—talk—"

I shook my head slowly before I looked up at Mom.

Mom nodded at me sadly. "Your father told me not to push, so I won't. But you know if you need someone—"

"I know where I can find you, so I'll let you know."

Mom nodded once more at me before quietly closing the door behind her.

I frowned at the envelope in my hands. It was heavy, obviously filled with more than just a single sheet of paper. I couldn't stop looking at the name "Kitty" suspiciously. *Who would have called me that?* After staring at it forever, I finally ripped it open. How else was I supposed to solve this mystery?

I pulled out several sheets of blank, unlined paper folded tightly together and found a key taped in the center. I gingerly removed the tape and examined the key's small silverness before I slipped out the single sheet of faded white lined paper and began to read.

Dear Kitty,

Ever since the day you figured out how to smile, you've saved your biggest smile for me. Knowing that, it's impossible to believe you'll never remember me. You see, I'm real sick, and I know I'm not going to be here much longer, so I won't see my beautiful baby sister grow up.

Two years ago, right before you were born, I found out I have leukemia. The fact made me want to give up and die. And then you came along, and the first time I held you and looked into those blue eyes of yours, I knew I had a reason to live.

We had a great start. I've spent more time with you these past amazing two years than anyone else. I know I wouldn't have had them if it wasn't for you. I've fought hard, but I know my time is short. It's been incredibly hard to say good-bye to everyone, but when it comes to you, I want you to know I'm not going to leave you. Not a chance! You helped me through the roughest two years of my life, so I've done something that I hope will help you as much as you've helped me. It's in the bottom of my gray strongbox. Your name's on it.

I love you,

Brett

I couldn't move. My heart had either stopped or was pounding too fast to count any of the beats. I read the letter through a couple more times in a daze. *This couldn't be real.*

I knew that most of Brett's things had been removed or gotten rid of a long time ago, which I'd always thought was strange, knowing how crazy my family was about him. I'd seen the box the letter referred to many times in our basement on the floor of the storage closet that also held our Christmas decorations. I'd never known the box was Brett's, though. I wasn't sure if Alex or Sam knew, either. To my knowledge, it'd never been opened.

I stared at the key in my palm. *And all along you were waiting for me.* Amazing.

Although it was late and I knew I should wait to open the box in the morning, I tiptoed downstairs to the storage closet. The box was small and a shiny gray. Even after all this time. After taking a deep breath, I carefully slipped the key into the lock and slowly opened the lid.

At first glance, I couldn't help feeling disappointed, because there were only a few things inside. A white football jersey with a big maroon number nine was neatly folded with a mass of get-well cards and letters and a couple of old videotapes on top. And underneath all of that—my heart pounded when I saw a package covered with faded wrapping paper with lots of once-colorful balloons. The package was addressed to "Kitty—for her sixteenth birthday. With love, Brett."

My hands trembled as I carefully locked the gray box. I quietly sneaked back to my room and then sat on my bed to stare at the package Brett had left for me. Questions oozed in circles in my brain. *Why the secrecy? Why now, on my sixteenth birthday? Why not sooner? Why hadn't anyone told me anything? Why, why . . . ?* Of course, none of my questions could be answered unless I opened the package. So I did.

I ripped off the paper almost frantically and carefully lifted the lid of the white box inside. A thick, dark maroon hardback book lay nestled in white tissue paper. I stared at it for I don't know how long before carefully, tentatively, opening the front cover.

The inside of the cover held more of the unfamiliar handwriting. All of the words were in small bold, capital letters, just like the words in the letter from Brett. I stared in disbelief at the two words, "Dear Kitty," before moving my eyes to read the inscription:

Although it seems strange to be saying this right now—Happy Sweet Sixteen. Someone turning sixteen needs a special surprise. I hope this was for you.

Love forever,
Brett

My hands trembled again as I turned the blank page opposite the cover and slowly read the title page: "This is the journal of Brett Bartholomew Colton."

---

*October 21*

Dr. Grenville gave me this journal after the shock of finding out what's wrong with me had worn off a little. He thinks keeping a journal's a good way to chart progress and will be therapeutic for me. At the time, I thought he was crazy. I didn't want to believe it, or have to live with it, much less write about it. But then, something happened to change my mind.

About five days ago, Mom went into the hospital because she was finally going to have the baby. I knew before anyone else in the family did—minus Dad—because I was there, too. I'd been in the hospital going through my first real chemotherapy treatment course—something I wouldn't wish on anybody. I was in the middle of one of my "discussions" with my shrink, who's been trying to help me deal with the fact that my body's messed up and that trying to off myself won't solve anything.

When I heard the baby was a girl, I was glad. Things would be even in the family now—two boys and two girls. Dad wheeled her up to my room so I could hold her. I don't know what shocked me more—the fact that Dad pulled strings and brought my new sister up to show me, or the fact that it was Dad who did it. Or maybe what shocked me most was his excitement. Very un-Dad-like. If I wasn't already flat on my back, the combo would've knocked me over easy. Usually nothing can make Dad crack a smile or squeeze out a tear.

The second Dad put her in my arms, I felt—something. There aren't any words to describe it, but it was powerful. I could feel that I knew her, and even crazier, that she knew me. When I looked into her little face and she gripped my finger, I knew—I knew that here was something that would make it all bearable.

Mom and Dad named her Kathryn Anne.

*October 22*

Now that my first grueling course of treatment is over and I'm home again and Kathryn Anne is finally home, too, from now on, I've decided that even though keeping a sickness/ progress journal is probably a great idea, I need to do something different with my book. Something that I hope will be worth reading. So from now on, this journal is for my baby sister.

Dear Kathryn Anne:

When Dr. Grenville first told me what was wrong with me, I was stunned. I wouldn't believe it—I couldn't let myself believe it. Stuff like this doesn't happen when you're only fifteen years old, for crying out loud! I'm only a sophomore, but I'm the number one quarterback on our high school's Varsity football team. And Alex— that's your other big brother—he's on the team, too. He's a split end, which means I throw the football to him a lot and pray he can take it to the goal posts. We've been throwing a football together practically all of our lives. When we were in Little League football, I met a kid named Kelly Baxter. We weren't in the same elementary school, but we met up again in junior high, and now we're in high school, still throwing the old pigskin around together and with Alex every chance we get. Kelly's a center, which means he's the guy whose position is right in front of mine on the field. He's the one who holds onto the football while I say, "Hut one, hut two."

A lot of times after football practice last summer and early this fall, I felt pretty tired, but everybody gets tired after doing something like playing football. Sometimes my joints would hurt, especially in my knees, so I'd wrap them tight. Our team was kicking you know what, and nothing else mattered. After every game, though, I'd get a nosebleed, and after a while, every practice session ended with one, too. Coach was worried and told me to see a doctor, so Mom took me to see our family doctor, Dr. Stanford. Dr. Stanford acted really serious when I told him what had been going on with me, so he took some blood samples and said he'd call back with the results.

In the meantime, I had to get ready for the next big game. Our team hadn't lost any of the preseason games, or our first game since school started. In fact, we had better than just a good chance of winning state championship this year. The only thing that could make the team even better would be if Kelly were on the Varsity team, too, instead of Junior Varsity.

Two days later was the night of our next game. I don't think I'll ever forget that night. Everyone was hyped. Before halftime I got a nosebleed, so our backup quarterback had to go in. I got the bleeding under control, so after about ten minutes, Coach let me back in the game. My knees hurt, but my adrenaline was pumping, so it was easy to ignore the pain. Nothing mattered to me but winning.

Then, the weird stuff started happening.

I'd been feeling a little tired since the beginning of the second quarter, but now I felt weak. Alex kept coming up to me between plays saying, "Are you okay, bud?" because I couldn't make the football reach him. Even my elbows hurt. And then, the fateful pass occurred. My knees hurt so bad I couldn't move my legs without feeling pain. After the snap, I jumped back a few steps—I saw Alex open and threw the ball as hard as I could, and after I let go of the ball, my knees couldn't take anymore, and I collapsed in a heap on the field. I tried to stand up, but my legs crumbled again. My knees ached and burned so bad I was afraid I was going to start bawling. And then, whistles were blowing and Coach and Alex were there with some of the guys on the team. Now, I'm not that big and neither is Alex, but Alex carried me most of the way to the bench where Mom and Dad now were, looking as freaked out as I felt, and faster than you can say "game over," I was at the hospital.

Dr. Stanford grabbed Dr. Grenville, an oncologist, who took a sample of my bone marrow. Definitely one of the worst experiences

I've ever had to go through, but the blood sample taken earlier was clear. I'll never forget his words or the pained, sad look on his face.

"Son, I'm so sorry. You have leukemia."

---

*October 23*

Dear Kitty,

I've christened you with the new name of "Kitty" for two reasons: First, Kathryn Anne is beautiful but pretty long; and second, while I was holding you today, I couldn't help thinking about cuddly things and "Kitty" seemed perfect, so that's the only name that comes to my head when I think of you now!

Even though it's not January yet, I've been making New Year's resolutions, because right now, both of us are at a starting point. I've known why I was sick for more than six weeks. At first, I tried to deny what was happening and pretend I was okay, but my first day of chemo and the immediate puking thereafter brought an end to that. So I tried getting angry and taking it out on everyone and everything around me, but making everyone else feel bad didn't make me feel better, and breaking stuff didn't, either (especially when it was my own stuff!), because no matter what I did or said, the sickness was still there. So then I tried feeling sorry for myself, but all that resulted in was my trying to do something stupid to myself, which resulted in lots of fun-filled visits with my shrink.

New years mean new hope, and seeing brand-new you has given me new hope. When everything first happened, my only goal was to be strong enough to play in more football games. But now, I have another reason—the best reason—to do everything I have to do to get better—and that would be you, Kitty! To start with, I want to be around to see you reach your first birthday. And I want to get into remission by Christmas. In the meantime, I want to show major improvement by next week for my next trip to Dr. Grenville, and see you learn to hold your head up by yourself . . .

*October 25*

Dear Kitty,

I wish the weather would clear up. I'm sick of being cooped up in the house all day. I had to start chemo within hours of being diagnosed, but I'm getting a break from treatments to see how my course of chemo's going to do, so it's nice not to be constantly puking anymore. Now that I'm done with the course, I don't have to stay in the hospital more than a few days at a time, so it's great to be back in my own bed and able to see you again. At least I haven't lost any of my hair yet. Dr. Grenville says I'm too stubborn to lose it. Plus, he's promised me that if the drug combo he's got me on shows signs of working, he's going to keep me in the hospital as little as possible.

The worst thing about chemo is that I'm getting out of shape fast. I can't hold food down, so nothing's sticking to me. I have to get better so I can get back into shape. Even though I haven't been able to play, the team's winning anyway. I can't decide if I like that fact or not. I only know that I have to get strong enough to play again next year. For the whole season this time. And I want you to be there to see me play. Even though I know you'll be too little to remember anything, just to be playing and to have you there—that would be amazing!

I can't believe I'm admitting this, but I miss school. I even miss going to the classes I hate! If I didn't feel so nauseated all the time, I think Dr. Grenville and Mom and Dad would let me go. I really need to get out of the house. I love Mom, but she's making me crazy. I feel like she's taking over my life, she's so overprotective sometimes. Whenever I want to blow up at her for treating me as if I'm either two or ninety-two, I think of that night after my last football game, after the trip to the hospital, and I remember looking into the rearview mirror from where I was sitting in the backseat and seeing tears streaming down her face. Dad just stared ahead and drove, but Mom was crying. That shook me up, because Mom is pretty strong . . .

*November 15*
Dear Kitty,

Today's been a good day. I haven't felt too sick at all. I even listened to the Beatles on my old record player. The *Rubber Soul* album, to be exact. One of my favorites. It's the perfect album for any mood—good, bad, or ugly. I haven't put it on since before I found out I'm sick. I didn't realize how much I'd missed it until the first song started to play. And you—wow, the way you reacted to it made me feel terrible for not introducing you to the Beatles sooner! You loved it almost more than me, and that's saying something!

And guess what else, Kitty? I have a tutor now. His name's Matt, and I like him. He's about 21 or so, and he's really smart. He was nervous at first to be tutoring a sick kid like me, but we've been having a good time ever since his second visit. His first visit, he wouldn't stop smiling and trying to act like it was perfectly normal to be tutoring a sick kid, but he sat tense and stiff in his chair, with his eyes bugging out from all the smiling, and he had this nervous cough thing going on. It had to come to a stop, so the second time he came, I snuck a whoopee cushion under his chair cushion. Only because something had to be done to loosen him up. The look on his face after he sat down almost made my liver erupt, I was laughing so hard. So we get along fine now. Sam always makes him treats and brings them into my room herself, so of course she has to stay and talk for a while.

I just realized I haven't written anything about Sam yet, have I? Well, Sam's the oldest. Every guy in school wants to go out with her, and believe me, she knows it! She thinks she's pretty special. She can come off as quite a snob, so I've had to pull a few whoopee cushions on her to bring her back to earth and all of us peons. For all that, though, she really can be human.

And Alex—your other big brother. He's not like Sam, but he's not like me, either. He's more on the serious side, so I know I've accomplished something if I can get him to laugh really hard. He's 16 going on 42. It's really nauseating, but that's just Alex.

And then there's Kelly. He's not as crazy and funny as me (well, who is?!), but he's not overly serious like Alex. There's something else about him, though—I can't explain it. This sounds really weird, but I was practically drawn to him when we met up again in junior high. Maybe not so much him but something about him— something he has that I don't. He's another reason I've got to be well enough to play football next year. He'll definitely make the Varsity team, and I want to be on it with both him and Alex. The three of us are going to have the greatest time together. When I first told Kelly about my sickness, he wasn't that surprised. He said he figured something had to be wrong with me from watching me in practice and at school. He said he's glad to know my "problem" isn't a big mystery anymore, so I can start doing something about it. Just like everyone else, Kelly doesn't want to admit that there isn't a cure for leukemia yet, even though he looks at me different now. Like he's afraid to let himself get too attached to me but also like he doesn't want to let go. Everyone in our family has the same look. Except for you, Kitty. You spit up and puke on me as much as you do on everyone else . . .

*November 18*
Dear Kitty,

The team's been winning all of its games, but just barely. I wish I could be playing instead of lounging around the house. I wish there was something I could do to just stop what's going on inside of me. I try to think it all away and concentrate on making all of the bad cells die. I think if I could just get a hold of these cells and crush them, I would get better for good.

I'm having bad dreams at night—dreams that always end with Dr. Grenville saying to me, "I'm sorry, son. You have leukemia." Last night I had a dream I was running down a long hallway. At the end of it was a door, and when my hand reached for the doorknob and turned it, Dr. Grenville was standing there, saying his wornout phrase to me again. I woke up in a cold sweat, and then I heard someone crying. The noises were so small and pitiful I knew they had to be coming from you. I snuck into Mom and Dad's room and picked you up and held you carefully in one arm and dragged your bassinet into my room with the other. You fell back to sleep with my finger held tightly in your fist.

Before I fell asleep, I put on the *Rubber Soul* album and watched you sleep. There's something about being told you're not going to be around forever that makes you think about everything in a totally different way. At first, I kept telling myself this sickness couldn't be happening to me. Not me! I'm in good shape. The best. I'm a football player, for crying out loud! I still have days when I scream inside my head: "This can't be real—my own body can't be killing me!"

But I'm not giving up. And I'm getting serious about my schoolwork. My next report card is going to have all "A's." So with that thought in my mind, and with you safe and cozy at my side, I fell asleep happy. When I woke up, you were already awake, and you smiled at me. At me! I'm the first person you've truly smiled at. I had to yell for everyone to come see. Of course, Sam wasn't thrilled about getting dragged out of bed so early. Still, you made my day . . .

*November 24*
Dear Kitty,

The team didn't do so well in the playoffs, so although we won region, there won't be any state championship title this year. Dr. Grenville started me on another course of chemotherapy, so I'm back in the hospital, which means I'm puking with regularity again. Kelly called me on the phone after the game and told me the team lost because our backup quarterback was too nervous to play with a straight head. It's hard to care much about anything when you're sick up to your eyeballs. I miss you, though—I miss you so much! I have a picture of you, framed, by my hospital bed, but it's not as good as having you by me. I have to be home by Christmas—that's the only goal I'm concentrating on. I have to be there for your first Christmas.

I can't believe it's Thanksgiving already. It feels so weird not to be home, stuffing my face with turkey. I never thought I'd miss being a part of our family's Thanksgiving, but I do. I hate being here with I.V.s dripping their puking potions into me, sucking more life out of me than they're putting in. So I've been lying in bed thinking about everything, missing everyone, especially you, and feeling sorry for myself. And then, I remembered today's Thanksgiving, and I thought of everything in my life that I'm thankful for, like my family and friends. Kelly comes and visits me all the time, except when I'm off limits from chemo. If he can't see me, he calls. He's the best. I'm trying to concentrate on the good stuff in my life and not to forget to notice everything. Even little things. Don't ever forget to notice the little good things in your life, because sometimes they're the most important things—the things that help you hold on and keep going . . .

# CHAPTER TWELVE

I'd wanted to keep myself cloistered in my bedroom all day Sunday, but when Sam, Stephen, and Curtis and then Alex and Julie showed up late in the day, Mom dragged me out, forcing me to join in all the family fun. I ignored Mom's questioning looks, since I was sure she was dying to ask about my letter from Brett, and from Dad's meaningful looks at her, I was just as sure he had told her to leave me alone. I had no idea whether she knew anything about Brett's journal. All I knew was that I wasn't about to discuss it with anyone right now. So instead, I curled up in one of the recliners in our living room and just let the conversation flow around me.

And then Brett's name was mentioned.

Sam told a story I'd heard a million times before about how hysterically funny Brett had been in Central High's performance of *Once upon a Mattress* and the stunts he'd pulled on stage to keep the other actors jumping and the audience roaring with laughter. Only this time, something was different. Something inside me felt different. It was hard to explain—

"What? No snide comments from Kathy? No eye-rolling?" Sam was watching me—studying me, really—her Brett Moment memory apparently finished.

I shrugged and ignored the looks everyone gave me. "Whatever," was all I had to offer.

"Well, well, well. Miracles *do* happen. Even in these nonbiblical times." Sam raised her eyebrows at me over Curtis's head while she bounced him around on her lap. I was going to say something clever back, but Alex cut me off before I could open my mouth.

"So how was the dance last night, Kathy? Did you have a good time?"

"I did."

Dad winked and grinned. "I'll bet you were definitely noticed at the dance!"

"Or at least that dress she wore certainly was." Mom gave me one of her disapproving looks that I chose to ignore.

"Speaking of—if I didn't say so before, Sam, thanks for helping me get ready." Sam looked up in surprise from babbling away at Curtis. "You know—doing my hair and makeup and all that. It was very un-Sam-like of you." Everyone had a good laugh at that. Even Sam laughed a little.

"Thanks. I guess." Sam raised her eyebrows.

I grinned. "You're welcome. I guess."

Everyone laughed again. Comfortable laughs. Mom smiled at me and twirled her gold locket around her fingers. I decided to shock everyone by staying in the living room for ice cream and cookies instead of hibernating in my room some more. And when Brett's name came up again, I didn't say anything. This time, I didn't even tune the memory out. In fact, I wouldn't be surprised if I let myself smile a little while Brett Moments were passed around for the rest of the evening.

---

*December 10*

Dear Kitty,

When I first got this journal from Dr. Grenville, I had no idea how grateful I'd eventually be for it. It's kind of like getting a sweater for Christmas. It doesn't seem like that amazing of a gift until there's a really cold, miserable day, and then, boy, you can't stop being glad someone thought to give you that sweater.

It is so great to be able to clear my head and just talk to you through this journal. You're the only person who doesn't treat me like I'm a piece of really thin glass, ready to break into a million pieces at the slightest nudge. When I'm with you, I can almost believe I'm not sick. Not only that, but I forget to feel sorry for myself. I've been trying to imagine what you're going to be like when you're older, but then I try to imagine you walking, and right now, that day seems incredibly far away. Still, you're really strong. I bet you'll learn how to do everything fast. I've been trying to teach you how to hold your bottle, but I guess you're not ready yet. Sam laughed in my face watching me try one afternoon. She was all, "Good grief, Brett, she's barely two months old!" Yeah, well. We'll show her.

The only thing I'm really having a hard time with is changing your diapers. My chemo medicine makes me feel sick enough without doing something that would make the healthiest person in the world puke, but I'm trying to get over it. When I do change you, my hands won't stop shaking. I know I'm going to harpoon you one of these days with the pins. But I'll get the hang of it. I'm just sorry money's so tight we can't buy disposables. Those look more comfortable than the cloth ones. But speaking of diapering, did we have fun with the baby powder today or what?! I thought for sure I had a good grip on the can—but then it slipped and powder was all over you and everything else! You smiled and waved your arms around as if you were having the time of your life, so I had to take a picture of you. The abominable snow baby.

Today was definitely a good day. One of those days when I almost forget I'm sick. But that's easy to do with you around. I always feel a hundred percent better when you're with me.

Even though I'm feeling a lot better lately, sometimes at night when I can't fall asleep, I start thinking about this sickness I have, and I get scared. For the most part, I try to ignore it and pretend it doesn't exist, but most of the time there's this little annoying part of me that's scared. If I dare say that to someone and talk about it, I'm afraid it will get so big it will take me over. I don't want anyone—especially the family—to know I'm scared. Besides, I can't talk to Dad. I've tried to joke with him to get a reaction out of him—something—anything—but I can never get more than one-word answers, nods, or grunts out of that stone face.

And then there's Mom. Total opposite. She explodes over everything I do, enough for two people. Most likely it's to make up for Dad. And she laughs—she loves to laugh at everything I say and do. I guess she thinks she needs to laugh for Dad, too. Since I got sick, though, she smothers me more than she ever did before. So where Dad's a statue, she's a mass of high-strung emotion, so I can't talk to her, either. I'd probably just send her over the edge. And I can't saddle Alex and Sam or Kelly with this. They have no clue what it's like to deal with what I'm dealing with every day. It'd freak them out too much if I turned to them for help. So it's only you I can really talk to, Kitty. But don't worry about anything. Everything's going to be fine. As long as I act like I'm okay, everyone else will be, too. If I don't, I know they'll all fall apart, and I don't think I could handle seeing that happen . . .

# CHAPTER THIRTEEN

N ow, Kathy, let's try your scene today without your script. Don't worry—I'll prompt you when necessary, but I think you'll be surprised at how much you already know."

As stressful as my private tutoring sessions with Miss Goforth were, it was actually a relief to have an hour a day when I didn't have to be me, and instead I had the rare privilege of stepping into another person's shoes for sixty whole minutes. I threw myself into the character with so much gusto that I almost scared myself into thinking I really *was* her. I was so into the moment that I'd been stretched out on a table for the dramatic ending of my scene, lying there for maybe a full minute, before I realized it'd been stone quiet for that entire minute.

"Hey." I sat up and swung my legs over the edge of the table. "Did I just get through the whole thing?"

Miss Goforth was studying me. "Yes, you did. I didn't have to prompt you once."

"Wow, I can't believe I've finally got all the lines memorized!" I was so excited I clapped my hands together and did my own little cheer for myself.

"Yes, you *do* have your lines memorized. Finally. But you've accomplished much more than that, Kathy."

I stopped congratulating myself to stare at Miss Goforth. "I have?"

Miss Goforth smiled. "Yes, you have. Indeed, I could almost believe you *were* the character today. Don't let your head inflate. You still need polishing, especially in your enunciation, but the emotion is there."

"Well, I guess I must have the Colton talent for drama after all!" I gloated.

"Yes, I suppose you do, but it's more than that. You definitely possess some natural talent for acting, which is satisfying to find in you after digging for results for so long." Miss Goforth walked across the floor and climbed the few stairs of the stage to stand directly in front of me. She looked hard into my eyes. "Keep going, Kathy. You're doing an amazing job already." Before I could beam for too long, she turned away abruptly and walked back down the stairs, casually throwing over her shoulder, "Now, if you could please put that same energy into poor Cordelia for your *King Lear* scene, I'm sure your classmates wouldn't indulge in the temptation to have you share Cordelia's sad fate."

———

I hadn't meant to end up standing at this particular spot after school, but Mom was late picking me up for my adventure at the DMV for my first, and hopefully last, attempt to get my driver's license. But here I was, where I seemed to find myself more and more often these days. I could've waited outside, but after I gave one casual glance over my shoulder, my feet refused to move on past the trophy case. Brett's trophy case. His picture was still there, as it always likely would be, still grinning away as if he was extremely pleased with himself. As he likely was. *Is—*

"I knew I'd find you here."

*Jason.* He had an incredibly annoying, uncanny ability to make me jump sky high and get my heart racing in a matter of about one second. Today was no exception, considering the fact that he'd practically put his lips against my ear to speak.

"You shouldn't sneak up on people like that!" I shoved him hard, but he only laughed.

"Hey, I wasn't sneaking!"

I folded my arms and tried to frown. "You made absolutely no noise whatsoever until you were practically standing on top of me. What would you call it?"

"I made the normal amount of noise I always do walking down a hall. A carpeted hall, by the way. You're just lost in space somewhere and didn't hear me. Like in English today."

"Whatever." Jason looked at me curiously, but I wasn't about to offer more. "Shouldn't you be outside with your little football friends? There *is* a game coming up in a few days. You don't want to be responsible for making the team lose, do you?"

Jason raised an eyebrow. "I'm amazed you even care! Does this mean you may actually show up to the game Friday night?"

"Only if there isn't anything good on TV."

Jason laughed, then I laughed, and then we both just looked at each other. The silence wasn't exactly awkward, but it wasn't comfortable, either. Considering that I wasn't even moving, it couldn't be good for my heart to be pounding so hard. And the way he looked at me was bringing back memories of Saturday night—a mere couple of days ago.

"So, what's going on?" Jason leaned against the wall by the trophy case and kept his gaze fixed on me. I lowered my eyes from his and made myself breathe.

"Just waiting for my mom. I'm going for my driver's license today."

"Really? That's great. I hope you pass."

"Yeah, me, too. But we'll see."

Jason lightly punched my shoulder. "Listen to you! You just need to have faith."

I shook my head firmly. "Faith. I don't need faith. I need more driving experience."

Jason looked as if I'd just announced I didn't need air anymore. "What? You always need faith!"

"Do I? Well, I don't know about that. In fact, I'm pretty sure I don't need it."

Jason raised his eyebrow again. "Oh, yeah? And why is that?"

I shrugged my shoulders. "I believe in what I can see. What I've got proof of."

Jason shook his head. "Faith is having a belief in something you *can't* see. Or in other words, 'Faith is not to have a perfect knowledge of things; therefore if ye have faith ye hope for things which are not seen, which are true.'"

I could sense a religious tangent coming. No one could stop him when he was having one of those. "Look who's being impressive! Did you make that up all on your own?"

"Something that good? Of course not. I'm quoting."

"Really? Who said it?"

"Alma. Alma the Younger, to be exact." Jason grinned.

"Never heard of him."

"Since you think you need to see to believe, I can show you his actual words. In fact—"

My mom had pulled up in front of the building in her car and was now honking the horn. I couldn't expose Jason to that for long. "I'm sorry—there's my ride. Wish me luck!" I threw my book bag over my shoulder and hustled out the door. But Jason wasn't finished yet.

"Luck? You don't need luck. You need faith!"

———

*December 20*

Dear Kitty,

Our family isn't exactly religious, but we're not atheists, either, so we do have a dust-covered Bible in the house. I've been feeling stronger, but I still have a bad day here and there, and on those days, staring at the TV helps to keep my mind off feeling sick so much.

There've been a lot of people on TV talking about the birth of Christ, since Christmas is almost here, so I snuck out our Bible so I could check up on what the TV was saying about Christ, just to make sure it was all on the level. Especially concerning hearing and answering prayers. That made me stand up and take notice, in a manner of speaking, since I was lying flat on my back on the couch feeling sick the first time it was pounded on by someone on TV. It was strange. As if I was remembering something I'd heard before. Not heard, exactly. Known before. Confusing, I know. I was confused myself.

So there I was, scouring through this old Bible of ours, trying to find passages on prayers, when the doorbell rang. I yelled "Come in," and in walks Kelly, scraping the snow off his sneakers and complaining about how cold it is. One look at me and the Bible, though, and he stopped in mid-sentence, staring at me as if he'd seen one of his dreams come true.

Like I told you before, there was something amazing about Kelly that made me want to be his friend. It's more than the fact that he's a great guy. I don't know what it is, but he has something—something I want, but I don't know what that something is. He's tried to tell me maybe it's got something to do with the church he goes to, but after bringing up religion and trying to "teach" me stuff a few times, I had to make him stop and promise he wouldn't talk about his beliefs unless I asked him to. I thought he'd be offended and hate me after that, but he was cool with it and didn't bring it up again, and we stayed best friends like always. That happened quite a while ago. Kelly's a Mormon, and although there's not a ton of them around where we live, there are enough of them that I've heard plenty about their church from people who aren't Mormons, as well as a few who are, to know all I really want to know. I know how much Mormons like to convert, and outside of celebrating Christmas and Easter, our family's never gotten into any sort of religious flow. And Kelly knew that, yet here I was, caught red-handed, reading out of the Bible.

So Kelly said, "I didn't know you were reading the Bible!" He looked too excited, so I knew I'd have to play this down quick. I tried to act like it was no big deal, but what I really wanted to do was to ask him something personal. He said it was okay to, so I went ahead and asked him if he believed in God. From the thrilled look on Kelly's face, I had a bad feeling I was going to regret asking, but it was too late now.

Of course, he said he believed in God. "Heavenly Father" was how he referred to Him. He said he believed in His son, Jesus Christ, too. I figured I might as well ask him some more questions and really make his day, so I asked him if he prays. Kelly said he did, and when I asked how often, he said, "Every day." When I asked if he thought God heard him, he said, "I know He does." So I asked him if I prayed, if he thought God would hear me, and maybe even listen to a heathen like me. Kelly smiled at me all reassuring-like and said that in his church, they believe God— Heavenly Father—does hear and listen to everyone, because he's our Father and He loves all of us. I didn't know what to say to that, so Kelly asked me if I was going to start praying to Him. I told him I thought it might help. Maybe.

Kelly showed me a bunch of stuff in the Bible about praying. I was impressed at how easily he found all the passages, but I guess if I went to church every week of my entire life like he does, I'd be able to find anything in the Bible, too. After Kelly gave me a few pointers on how to pray the way he does, I told him I was tired and ran him out. I actually did feel kind of tired after his lesson on the Art of Praying. I'll bet he rushed like some freak to buy me one of those Mormon Bibles. I'm going to have to be careful about what I say around him from now on.

So last night I prayed for the first time in my life. It felt strange to talk out loud, but then I remembered who I was supposed to be talking to, and do you know—I think He heard me . . .

## CHAPTER FOURTEEN

I hope everyone has read the assignment for this week, 'Seize the Day,' by Saul Bellow," said Mrs. Dubois. "In sum, this piece revolves around one sad, depressing day in the life of Tommy Wilhelm, a middle-class, middle-aged Everyman who has lost his sense of direction in life and attempts a quest for meaning in a turbulent, cruel world through an afternoon of stock market gambling and introspection. Some would call it a contemporary American treatise on greed, capitalism, and the complexity of relationships . . ." Mrs. Dubois and the rest of the class launched off into a deep, although somewhat boring, discussion concerning the obvious themes and points of the story. Although I usually loved throwing my two cents in, I couldn't get into the whole thing today.

"Mr. West. Tell us your thoughts on the piece." Mrs. Dubois had been slowly wandering up and down the aisles between our desks before stopping near Jason to look thoughtfully at him.

Jason's forehead was furrowed. I sat up from my slouched position, truly curious about what he might say. "Well, I guess my biggest question about the story is its title."

"Really? Explain."

"Well, 'seize the day,' or 'carpe diem,' means the 'enjoyment of the present without concern for the future,' but none of Tommy's 'seizing' gave him any happiness at all, and all he felt was stress about the future. And he definitely wasn't liking his present."

Mrs. Dubois nodded with her arms folded. "Yes, it *is* a sad, ironic title. The story does give the statement 'seize the day' an ironic twist, full of dark, bitter humor, rather than the exciting taking of a chance, as the phrase traditionally means. Poor Tommy's attempts to seize the day *are* miserably thwarted. Part of the risk one takes when one decides to seize the day."

"So what's worse? Seizing the day, knowing there's a chance your attempt could blow up in your face? Or not even trying at all, and always wondering whether or not something amazing would've happened if you *had* tried? Something that might change your life forever—for the better?" For a brief second, I was sure I'd just said those words to myself in my head, but Jason swiveled around in his seat to look in my direction, and everyone else in class felt the urge to turn and stare, too. And then Mrs. Dubois nodded, still keeping her arms folded.

"Excellent point, Miss Colton. One of life's intriguing questions we all must answer . . ."

I didn't mean to tune out Mrs. Dubois, but Jason was still staring at me. Not a typical stare, either. A stare as if he was debating something. Or making a decision. But then the bell rang, and everyone started filing out the door, making room to allow Angela to bounce into the classroom over to Jason, making sure to keep her back toward me.

———

*December 25*
Dear Kitty,

Christmas Day at the ol' Colton house. I've been feeling better, so I was able to join in ripping open presents in the morning. Mom kept saying that seeing me feeling good was the best present of all. I'm not sure what Mom and Dad would think about Kelly "teaching" me how to pray and everything, and reading from the Bible, so I told him if he wanted to talk religion with me again, he couldn't do it unless we were alone. Promising to keep our religious discussions a secret didn't stop Kelly from getting me a Mormon Bible for Christmas, though.

You're still too little to appreciate Christmas. You slept through most of it, so I know I have to stick around to watch you enjoy it next year. You did get a kick out of watching the lights on the tree blink on and off, so you're starting to get the idea.

Since I've been dragging your bassinet into my room every night, Mom finally agreed to let me move all of your stuff in here with me. So now we're going to be roommates!

You love to have me hold you as much as I love holding you. And you love it when I sing along to the Beatles. They're your favorite group, and I don't agree with Alex that it's only because they're the only group I've let you listen to. You can tell a classic when you hear one!

January 1st is almost here—which means it's time to make some New Year's resolutions. I didn't meet my goal to be in remission by Christmas, but Dr. Grenville says I'm coming along. In fact, he thinks I can try going back to school! That would be the best! I know, crazy that I'd actually like to go to school, but it beats lying around home puking all the time.

I've got to make it to remission. That's my number one resolution. It would also be great to play football again. It wouldn't matter to me anymore to win games or take titles. It'd just be great to really play with Kelly and Alex and the team.

Besides football, remission, and good grades, I have other goals, too. We've been working on one of those goals today, which is to get you rolling over and doing your baby pushups. If we work together, we can get you doing both things by your next doctor's visit . . .

# CHAPTER FIFTEEN

Friday after school, it finally happened. After three grueling tries, I had the long-awaited, coveted-for-years, most valuable possession of all teenagers across the United States: my driver's license. My happiness was nearly short-lived later on that evening, though, thanks to my overly cautious father, whom I'd been badgering since the second I arrived home from the DMV.

"Please, Dad—the football game's at Central, and the only other place I'm going is to pick up Mistie and Crystal. We won't even stop any-where after the game. I promise!"

Dad had a worried frown on his face that was downright offensive. "I don't know—you barely got your license today."

Definitely a hard point to argue. "But how else am I supposed to improve my driving skills if you won't let me drive? The longer I wait, the harder it will be and the worse I'll do. I need to keep driving while everything I've learned is still fresh in my head!"

Dad's frown only deepened at my speech. "What does your mother think about this?"

*Passing the buck?* Typical. "She said she didn't mind if I took the cruddy car." Which was the spare vehicle Mom and Dad had kept around for about a century or so. But of course, Dad had to continue being difficult.

"I don't know—I don't like this—"

So now I was forced to resort to begging. "Please! Oh please, Dad—I'll do anything—I'll pay for the gas, I'll wash the car—"

"Yes, but who'll have to pay for your insurance, and who'll have to pay if you get in an accident?"

Where was Jason and his views on faith when I needed him? "Let's think positively here. After all, I'm not even going to be five miles away!"

"Most accidents happen within twenty-five miles of a person's home. And you'll be driving at night, with lots of other teenagers all over the road—"

"Dad—" It was hopeless. Utterly.

But then, miracle of miracles, Dad sighed and rolled his eyes. "Oh, fine. Go ahead." Before I could go too ballistic, he quickly continued, "But you *are* taking the cruddy car. And you need to be home at a decent hour. That means no joy riding around after the game—"

But I was off and running with the car keys before I heard him say anything else.

———

Even though I was ecstatic to drive the cruddy car to the game, my heart pounded and my hands shook all the way to Central High's football stadium. I blamed my nerves on Dad and his negative comments. My heart wouldn't stop pounding even after successfully parking the car and making my entrance into the football stadium with Mistie and Crystal.

The stadium lights glared down onto the football field while the crowd whistled, cheered, and jeered in restless anticipation. The air was chilly and tangy with the smell of fall mixed with hot chocolate sold at the concession stand. *If I actually liked football, this could almost be fun!* We climbed over a dozen rows before settling into a section Mistie and Crystal picked out, and after zipping my jacket up to my chin and wishing I'd brought a blanket, Mistie nudged me with her shoulder and pointed towards the locker room doors of the school.

"Here they come!"

The school band blasted an ear-deafening pep song and within seconds, the home crowd was on their feet cheering as our team exited the locker room at a light jog, heading for the field. My ears were numb from the freezing cold air and the loud cheering and whistling while I scanned the players, each clutching a helmet under one arm. It would be my last chance to see Jason before the team would yank their helmets on, reducing them all to a clone-like state.

I bumped Crystal hard in the side. "Who are we playing again?" I screeched.

Crystal jumped and screeched back, "South High Panthers!"

I dug my hands deep into my pockets and bounced my legs hard, hoping to warm up, but as soon as I caught my first glance of Jason all decked out in his full football uniform glory, my heart jumped, and I forgot how cold I was and how hard the benches were. I might as well have been sitting in the stadium alone for all the notice I gave anything going on around me from that point on. My eyes followed Jason's number darting around the field, throwing the football impressive distances. Mistie and Crystal made fun of me if I let a gasp escape whenever he was slammed mercilessly to the ground.

And then, in the last minute before half-time, the unthinkable happened. Granted, everyone knows it can happen in a game like football, and certainly *does* happen, but that doesn't lessen the shock. At all.

One second, Jason was jumping and running around at the beginning of the last play before half-time, looking for someone to throw the football to—and the next, he was running with the football, trying to weave around the Panthers, towards the goal line. He did amazingly well for a few brief, shining moments—and then, two unnaturally large Panthers slammed him from the right and the left. Jason's legs twisted sharply at an awkward angle, and he was on the ground, getting piled on by the two giants and a few more Panthers.

This time, I wasn't the only one who gasped. Everyone jumped to their feet while the referees' whistles blew and the rest of the players ran to the pileup of Panthers and Jason. I remained on my feet with my heart in my mouth while the Panthers peeled off until finally Jason, lying on his side and clutching his right knee, appeared. Then our team's coaches were running over and talking to Jason and trying to help him up, and a minute later, an ambulance I hadn't even noticed in the school parking lot raced onto the field and EMT people jumped out of it to talk to Jason before carefully loading him onto a stretcher and carrying him off the field.

I couldn't believe what I was seeing. Watching the ambulance carry Jason off the field, I realized I was trembling. And it wasn't because of the cold. All I could think about and almost see was someone else who'd had to be carried off this same football field a long time ago.

# CHAPTER SIXTEEN

I must've woken up a hundred times Friday night from the nightmare of seeing Jason attacked and crumpling on the football field—and the horrifying pileup on top of him. It was impossible to care one iota about the game after seeing Jason carried off the field and watching the ambulance speed off, its lights flashing and sirens wailing.

After no sleep Friday night and a long weekend of pacing around my house, I was relieved to see Monday roll around, if only for my own peace of mind on the subject of Jason.

My relief didn't last long, unfortunately. And forget peace of mind. Shortly after the 8 A.M. bell rang, my heart sank when the familiar sound of Jason's sneakers screaming down the hall didn't happen. Long after the bell stopped ringing, I continued to stare worriedly, almost forlornly, at his empty desk in the front row.

Mrs. Dubois looked up from her desk when the bell rang and then moved her eyes to stare at Jason's desk, too. "Mr. West must have slept in this morning."

"No," the girl sitting in the seat directly to my right—Stacey—called out. "He's going in for knee surgery this morning."

"Knee surgery?" Mrs. Dubois frowned.

"Yeah. He blew his knee out at the game Friday night."

"How terrible. I didn't know. Well, I'm sure you all join me in wishing him well today."

I poked Stacey in the arm with my pen. "How do you know he's having surgery?"

"One of my sister's friends is going out with one of the guys on the football team."

"Do you know which hospital?" I couldn't believe I was being so brave and nosy, questioning a girl I'd never spoken with in class before.

"St. Mark's, I think. Most likely, anyway."

After that, I couldn't concentrate on anything Mrs. Dubois had to say about our assignment for the week. All I could focus on for the rest of Honors English was getting myself to the nearest bus stop as fast as I could move.

After class, I propelled myself out Central High's front doors, and now I was in St. Mark's, standing outside a room on the orthopedic floor with "Jason West" in big black letters on the door. I didn't know if it was okay to be visiting patients in the middle of the afternoon, but no official hospital personnel tried to stop me. My heart pounded as I knocked on the door.

"Come in." Jason's voice. Semi-groggy-sounding, but definitely Jason's.

I gave the door a nice, solid push and walked in, carefully closing it behind me, before hesitantly approaching him.

"Hey, you." I tried to smile, but I knew it had to look strained. It was just so strange to see Jason lying in a hospital room. And in a hospital gown, too. *Where's my camera when I need it?* I grinned to myself for a moment until I really looked at his right leg, all propped up on a pillow and looking pretty bruised, swollen, and gruesome.

Jason stared as if he was trying to make his eyes focus. "What are you doing here?"

Full of tact, as usual. "I had to find out why you weren't in English today. Oh, and you're welcome for coming all this way to visit you.

During class time, no less." My grin faded as Jason's leg twitched spasmodically while his face twisted into an unattractive grimace. "Is this a bad time? Because I could leave, maybe come back later—"

"No, it's okay." Jason breathed in and out a few times before closing his eyes and resting back against his pillows. I quietly edged a few steps closer.

"So—how's your knee?"

Jason opened one eye to grin weakly. "It'll stop hurting once the pain goes away."

I smiled back. "Have you had your surgery yet?"

"Couldn't—too much swelling. You should've seen how big my knee was."

"So—what exactly *did* happen?" I moved around to the other side of his bed and leaned my book bag against the wall.

"A major blowout. Ripped my medial collateral ligament, dislocated my knee really good in the process, and broke a part off my knee cap. It's floating around in my knee now."

Now *I* was the one grimacing. "Good grief—it sounds as bad as it looks! I guess I shouldn't be surprised after the way you were attacked out on the field."

Jason's eyes opened wide. "You were there? You saw it happen?"

I grinned. "Yes, I actually was. And did. I felt horrible watching the whole thing."

Jason grinned back. "Good."

*Good?* My smile faded fast. "What do you mean, 'good'?"

"Because it's *your* fault I'm lying here with a bum knee."

I was dumbfounded. Shocked, even. "*My* fault? How can any of this be *my* fault?"

"Well, I guess it's partly that Saul Bellow guy's fault, too."

"What in the world are you talking about?" Jason was making no sense. None at all. *Drugs,* I realized, shaking my head. Jason had to be on some major brain-addling painkillers.

"'Carpe diem.' I think I 'seized the day' a little too much." Jason rubbed awkwardly at his right leg for a second before continuing. "All of your talk about taking risks in class—you got me going out there on the field Friday night." Jason let out a ragged sigh and pointed towards his elevated, swollen right knee. "But, as you can see, my attempts back-fired." He leaned back wearily against his pillows. "I really hated that story."

Before I could respond, a female voice floated into the room. "Is it okay to come in?"

Before I knew what was happening, the room was filled to over-flowing. It was like watching clowns climb out of a tiny car at the circus. I was mentally kicking myself for allowing the idea of skipping class to spark in my head for even a second while I forced a smile and a "hi" back to the crowd of people now smashed into Jason's tiny hospital room. Jason smiled and returned the hugs and hellos from the horde while I planned my escape. A woman who had to have been Jason's mom hurried over to one side of his hospital bed to stroke his hair, as one of the men—likely his father—moved to stand by the other side. Everyone else grouped themselves at the foot of the bed near where I stood. I was sure I could find a way to gracefully exit without anyone noticing—

"Hey, everyone—this is Kathy. Kathy—this is my family."

I was forced to smile and pretend I was enjoying this moment of being caught in Jason's hospital room when I should be at school.

"This is my mom, and that's my dad." Jason pointed from one to the other before his father interjected, "Just in case you had us con-fused." Everyone had a nice laugh at Jason's expense over that. "And that's my brother Michael and my sis-in-law, Tracy. And that's Lance and Melinda. Michael and Lance are twins. And over there—that's Adam. He just got home from a mission."

My mind whirled from all the faces and names and introductions. I just prayed there wasn't going to be a quiz later, or that I would be expected to remember who anyone but Jason was once I was safely out of his hospital room.

"What about me?" a small, little girl's voice said. I hadn't even noticed a child had come with all the adults. She'd kept herself well hidden, but even before she finally surfaced from behind the forest of legs around her, I knew by the way Jason looked at her that this little girl with dark, wavy hair like Jason's had to be his eight-year-old sister, Emily.

"I was just saving the best for last." Jason smiled and patted the bed with his hand. "Come over here, sis." Emily quickly ran over and climbed on his bed while everyone yelled at her to watch for Jason's leg, which she carefully maneuvered herself around before landing on his chest to snuggle against his side. "Kathy—this is Emily. The one and only. You should see her on her bike riding around the neighborhood. She's a true speed racer, aren't you, kid?"

I said hello to Emily. She looked me over curiously before quickly turning her attention back to her brother. "Does your leg hurt really bad, Jason?"

I watched almost enviously while Jason kissed her cheek. "Well, Em, it doesn't exactly feel good, but it'll get better."

"I imagine you must be flying pretty high on painkillers right now, huh, bro?"

Jason gave a weak laugh. "Yeah, they've given me something pretty strong, although I can feel a lot of fire in my knee. Mostly the drugs I've been given just make me really sleepy."

*And loopy,* I almost chimed in.

"We wanted to come see you off before your surgery. And to give you a blessing, if you'd like that."

Jason nodded at his father. "Yes, I'd like that. Very much."

*Blessing?* I had no idea what Jason's father was talking about.

"You're going to need to climb down, Emily, dear." Jason's mom reached for Emily, who reluctantly let her mother pull her away from

Jason before scooting herself down to sit at the foot of the bed, being careful to avoid his right leg.

"Which one of your brothers do you want to have help me?"

"Since Adam's been doing this the most lately—Adam, would you mind?"

"Of course not."

While Adam stepped up to one side of Jason's bed and his dad positioned himself on the other, I was torn between guiltily wanting to observe this religious ritual, while the other half of me just wanted to get out. I made a stab at escaping, but I was trapped in the corner of Jason's room at the foot of his bed. I would either have to shove my way through the wall of family blocking my path, or climb over his bed and over Emily, since she'd planted herself cross-legged smack in the middle of the bottom of his bed. And there was the question of my book bag, which one of Jason's brothers was nearly standing on top of. *Stuck, stuck, stuck!* ran through my now-panicked mind. Surely they had to know I wasn't a member of their religion! Was it wrong—blasphemous—for me to be here listening in on this—blessing? And what if they all started doing something—anything—I didn't know a person was supposed to do and I ruined the whole moment? Since I was trapped beyond any form of escape, I tried to scrunch as deeply into the wall as I could, hoping no one would notice me or the absolute pain I was in, and while everyone else silently bowed their heads and folded their arms, I watched, spellbound, mechanically folding my own arms while Jason's father and his brother placed their hands on Jason's head and said a prayer—one that was just for Jason, to help heal his leg.

If someone had asked me later what words were spoken during that prayer, I couldn't have told them because of what washed over me, engulfing me completely. I honestly had never felt anything remotely like it before. Ever. The quiet, calm, peaceful *power* of it took me completely by surprise. I had no idea what I was feeling, but tears formed in my eyes and my heart pounded. The only feeling I could possibly relate it to was stepping from a cold room into bright sunlight, only instead of feeling warm on the outside, the warm, glowing sensation I felt was *inside* me. It was overwhelming. And now a few tears were creeping down my cheeks, and when Jason's father said amen, I watched while Jason thanked his father and brother and hugged them both, followed by everyone else in the room moving forward to do the same.

I meant to hurry and grab my book bag and excuse myself and leave, but I couldn't move my feet. The feeling was still there—it was so incredibly strong and so new to me. And then, no one was leaning over Jason anymore to hug him, and he was looking at me. I don't know what kind of an expression was on my face, but he was looking at me with an almost tender gaze that made me want to start bawling.

"Kathy—" he started, but before he or I could say or do anything, the brother standing practically in my book bag finally took a step forward. I quickly darted behind him, snatched up my bag, and weaved through the sea of Wests until I could bolt out the door to run down the hall as fast as I dared. And even after I arrived back at school, I couldn't stop trembling all over from everything I'd just seen and heard. And felt.

---

*January 13*
Dear Kitty,

The thirteenth. And a Friday. Dad had to work late tonight—like usual. We were all sitting around the table eating dinner while Mom opened bills. Bills are piling up, and since the cost of my treatments are a mile high and Dad's insurance only covers so much, don't think I don't feel guilty about all of the money being spent on me.

Watching Mom's face as she looked over the bills, dinner wasn't tasting so good to me anymore. I knew I had to get out for a while, so I asked if it was okay if I went over to Kelly's, but Mom said no because I looked tired. I got mad, but all she said was that I needed to start taking better care of myself and that I've been pushing myself too hard lately, going back to school and everything. So I yelled again and said I was doing fine, that I knew when I was too tired, and I wasn't, so I was going over to Kelly's. Mom got upset and said, "Brett, I said no! If you leave this house, I'll—I'll—" Before I knew what I was doing, I said, "You'll do what? I think I've got about the worst punishment I could ever ask for." That shook her up, but she held strong and told me not to dare speak to her in that tone of voice and to settle down and eat my dinner. I would've said more, but Mom got up and stormed into the kitchen, so after another minute of that wonderful silence, I got up and followed her. When she turned around to face me, she was crying. All she could say was "Why you?" before her voice broke. Then she said, "My Brett," and caught me in a fierce hug and really started to cry.

I tried to make Mom understand that just because I'm sick, it doesn't mean I'm not me anymore. I don't want to be treated like a baby, so I told her that I want to fight this thing. I don't want to lie around like I'm already beaten. Then I pinched her good under the ribs. That made her laugh, so I held onto that and told her I'm not out of here yet, so she better not make any plans to paint my room pink.

*February 3*
Dear Kitty,

Dr. Grenville said at my last appointment that I'm looking better. As much as I hate my chemo treatments, I guess they're doing something good for me. Instead of fighting against the treatments or just accepting them comatose style, I'm trying to think positively and work with the medicine. I think it's making a difference.

Kelly came over after school and asked me how my praying was coming along, so I told him—with my eyes closed, because I was tired—that I was still praying. Then he asked me if I'd been reading that Mormon Bible, and I was trying to figure out a nice way to tell him I hadn't when Mom came in and asked Kelly if she could talk to him alone in the kitchen. Once Kelly came back, he looked all uncomfortable and said he needed to get home and left. I called him later on the phone and made him tell me what Mom talked to him about. He tried to play it down, but I got him to admit that Mom told him to stop tiring me out with all of his religious talk. That was all he would say, but I'm sure Mom got into it more than that. I guess I wasn't giving her and Dad enough credit. They'd overheard us lots of times before, and after talking it over, they decided they're not crazy about Kelly trying to convert me. Poor Kelly—I could tell he felt really bad. I had a yelling session with Mom and Dad after I got off the phone about listening in on my private conversations, but they kept saying all of his religion talk is confusing and upsetting me and that I need to focus on getting well and not on the "weird" stuff Kelly's telling me. Mom kept harping on the fact that I've got enough to deal with without having Kelly trying to get me to join his religion. Which is funny, because Kelly hasn't asked me about joining. He's just told me stuff he believes in, and then he usually asks me what I think about it or what I believe. It's all been pretty interesting and harmless, so I think they're getting crazy over nothing. I just like talking with Kelly about more than just football. Besides—he's my friend, and he was my friend long before we ever started talking about religious stuff, so I know he's not just coming over to turn me into a Mormon. I had no idea it was driving Mom and Dad crazy—especially Mom. She says I get too worked up listening to Kelly talk Mormonism with me and that it worries her. If you ask me, she's the one who gets all worked up about Kelly and his talk—not me. But nothing I say can convince her of that.

And as if all that wasn't enough, Dad announced at dinner that Mom's going back to work. I felt sick—sicker than usual, since it's all because of me. Sam, thinking of herself—as usual—said, "Oh, great. So now I'm going to have to give up every semblance of a social life to get home and take care of Kitty." That made me mad, so I yelled that she wouldn't, because I'll be around to take care of you. I picked you up and left the table, slamming our bedroom door behind me, which I shouldn't have done, because the noise only scared you and made you cry.

Mom will go back to work. When I'm at home, I'll watch out for you, and when I'm at school, Mom will take you to the sitter's house until I get home. I know you're not going to be thrilled about that, and I'm sorry—I'm sorry for messing up your life, too . . .

# CHAPTER SEVENTEEN

I half-expected to get cornered by my parents for cutting class. I was sure that some annoying executive assistant at Central would've called Mom or Dad or both, but neither appeared to be wise to my hospital adventure. Or, it was possible they *had* been contacted but didn't want to bring it up in front of Alex and Julie and Sam and Stephen while they were over for dinner. Either way, it really didn't matter. That issue paled to almost nil in comparison to what I'd experienced. I couldn't get the scene out of my mind, watching Jason get blessed by his father and brother. And the feeling I'd had during Jason's blessing—it'd been too powerful and real.

"You've been awfully quiet tonight, Kathy. Is everything okay?" Mom said worriedly.

Had I been overly quiet? "I'm fine, Mom. Everything's fine."

"She's been hiding in her room since she came home from school. She's only just emerged since you all arrived," Dad said, looking at Alex and Sam.

"I've got homework and lots of reading to do," I said, stabbing quickly at my salad.

"You're sure you're okay?" Mom continued to dissect me with her eyes.

"Really, Mom." I felt bad about the look Mom was giving me—the one that said she didn't believe me, but I knew I couldn't offer more.

"So—Halloween's coming up. Any big plans, Kathy?"

I glanced at Alex and shrugged.

"She's probably been too busy worrying and fussing over Jason after the mangling he went through on Friday." Sam grinned at my surprised, open-mouthed face.

"What—How do you know about Jason's knee surgery?"

Samantha laughed. "Jason's pounding and his ambulance ride were in the high school sports news on TV last Friday, but they didn't say that he had to have knee surgery. The reporters should've come to you for full details. You probably know more than his parents do."

Before I could respond to that, Mom looked at me questioningly. "How did you know he had to have knee surgery, Kathy?"

"A girl in my English class said so today." Which was completely true.

"Yeah, right," Sam grinned.

I stared hard at Sam. "It's true!"

Alex rolled his eyes at Julie and Stephen in his "here we go again" way. And I knew Mom and Dad were tensing up, getting ready to tell me to stop fighting with Sam. None of them needed to worry, though. Something inside of me wanted to hold onto what I'd seen and felt, and somehow I knew fighting with Sam would make it disappear. So instead, I turned and googled at Curtis sitting across the table from me on Stephen's lap until I made him laugh before turning to Sam's surprised face with a real smile of my own. "Boy, he's getting bigger and bigger. And cuter and cuter! What are you going to dress him as for Halloween?"

Now it was Sam's turn to look slack-jawed. "I—I haven't decided yet. I don't really know—" Try as she might to recover, Sam looked surprised that I didn't have my dukes up for her.

"I think he'd make a really cute little ghost. That'd be a simple costume to put together."

Sam allowed herself to give me a little smile. "Yeah—that could be really cute. And I'd only need a pillowcase . . ." Sam babbled on about the details of the costume while I smiled and nodded and pretended to be oblivious to everyone else's now slack-jawed faces.

---

*February 14*
Dear Kitty,

Happy First Valentine's Day! Sam had a date, Alex asked some girl to the Valentine's Dance, and Mom and Dad needed a night out together, so I opted to be your valentine here at home. I put our Beatles tunes on the stereo, and we tired ourselves out tonight dancing before Kelly showed up. He didn't have the nerve to ask anyone to the dance. I thought Kelly would try talking religion with me, but he didn't. Something about respecting Mom and Dad's wishes to leave it alone—for now. You know what that means—Mom and Dad may have told him to stop talking religion with me, but he's not going to give up. I know I can count on him to find a way to work it back into our chats again. He just needs to figure out a way to suck back up to Mom and Dad again first. Anyway—we had a great time tonight, Kitty. Thanks for making my Valentine's Day . . .

*February 18*
Dear Kitty,

I had a dream the other night that really shook me up. In the dream, I was my old self again with the football team, playing for the state championship. I was in my usual quarterback position and playing better than I ever had before. No one could touch me or keep up with me. Then we were down to the final play of the game. No one was open for me to throw to, so I ran with the ball gripped tight in my hands. I dodged everyone with a precision that was magical. Guys from the other team flew at me, jumping for me right and left, but they always fell behind me. I ran and ran, and then— there was no one around me anymore, and I couldn't hear anything. No grunts or intense swearing. No cheers from the crowds. And instead of that forked goal post ahead, there was nothing—only an empty field.

I slowed down to a walk so I could look around before I just stood still. It was quiet, and there wasn't a soul in sight. I wasn't even on the football field anymore. I was in the middle of a huge meadow type place, and there were mountains all around me. I tried to run again, but I couldn't. It was like trying to run in water. I heard crying, and way ahead of me, I could see a little girl, just bawling her eyes out. My heart stopped, because I knew it was you. I tried to yell to you, but not even a whisper would come out of my throat. I tried to jump up and down and wave at you, but my knees hurt too much to get off the ground. When I looked at you again, you weren't a little girl anymore. Now you looked like you were my age, and you looked so lost and confused that I lunged for you— but I still couldn't run. I stumbled towards you, trying to yell some more, but I fell down hard. You were crying and calling for help, but I couldn't get to you. I tried to crawl, but it took forever to move an inch. I got as close as I could to you, but you acted as if you didn't know I was there. Wind whipped all around us, and I screamed through it for you to take my hand, but you couldn't hear anything I said. And then Dr. Grenville was behind me, saying, "I'm sorry, son. You have leukemia." I couldn't take it anymore, so I forced myself to wake up. That was definitely the weirdest dream I've ever had in my whole entire life. It seemed so real that it's been on my mind all day.

I'm still praying. No one else knows but you and Kelly . . .

*March 1*

Dear Kitty,

I just heard the most beautiful word in the whole world: REMISSION!

"You've worked hard and you deserve it. You are most definitely in remission." Those were Dr. Grenville's exact words. I don't think anyone's ever said anything nicer to me. I was so excited I almost kissed him.

In case you don't know what that magical word *remission* means, it means that my chemo treatments have sent the bad cells in my body on the run. Dr. Grenville stressed to me over and over again that I'm not cured—and I know that—but this is the first, positive step towards it. If a person can stay in remission for about five years, any doctor will say that person is basically cured. Since I've finally reached this major goal of mine, my next long-range goal is to hang on and hold out for those five years and beat this sickness. I know I can do it—I've got to!

I was so excited after I left Dr. Grenville's office, I did a stupid, spastic dance down the hall, and while I was coming around a corner, I tackled some poor girl in a pink and white striped skirt to the ground. And not just any girl. A gorgeous blonde. The candy striper of my dreams. I was feeling too good to be embarrassed, so I quickly stood up, pulled her to her feet, and apologized. She laughed and said she could tell I was in a good mood. Her eyes are really blue—and she has a smile that belongs on a magazine cover. I tried not to look at her legs too much while she fixed her skirt. I made sure to check her name tag—Jennifer—before I said, "Yeah, well, today's been a good day, Jennifer." She looked confused— surprised—for a second until I pointed at her name tag. And then she smiled at me—in an interested sort of a way—and said I had her at a disadvantage, because I knew her name, but she didn't know mine. I'd barely said, "Brett Colton" when some nurse with rotten timing called her, so she had to say good-bye. She sure is beautiful, Kitty . . .

*March 8*
Dear Kitty,

Sam and Alex both have parts in our school's musical, *Once upon a Mattress.* I missed the tryouts because I've been sick, but the guy who was supposed to be the king broke his leg and there's no understudy for him, so I thought, what the heck, and tried out for the part. I can play the piano a little by ear, so during lunch break at school, I put together a fancy piano part to a stupid campfire song. When it was my turn to try out, I acted all serious and said: "This is a song we've sung in my family for years. I think it's helped to bring us a lot closer." I sat down and played this fancy, sad, slow intro-duction, swaying dramatically like some professional at the piano, then I stopped and changed to a "Chopsticks" style of playing and sang:

> *Oh, it's $H_2O$, that makes you want to go*
> *On the farm (on the farm), on the farm (on the farm),*
> *Oh, it's $H_2O$, that makes you want to go*
> *On the Leland Stanford Junior Farm.*
> *My-eyes-are-dim-I-cannot-see-I-have-not-got-my-specs-with-me,*
> *I have not got my specs with me!*

I ended with a few dramatic chords, and at first, no one even breathed. Then a girl started to giggle, and a guy in the back of the room chuckled, then everyone laughed and clapped. I bowed while our drama teacher, Miss Goforth, shook her head and said, "Leave it to you, Brett!"

As of today, I am now King Sextimus the Silent. I don't think it will take me very long to learn my lines.

And then there's the football side of my life—Coach was pretty excited when I told him my remission news. It won't take me long to get back in shape, and football clinics this summer will get me back in the game. I know I'll make the team—I'm going to make myself play better than I ever have before. This time, we will take state!

Of course, Alex has to be a negative worrywort. He thinks I'm getting ahead of myself and trying to get back into everything too fast. How can you get back into life too fast? Good grief—I've missed too much as it is! Alex can frown at me until that scowl on his face sticks for good. I feel great, and that's all that matters.

At least everyone else is excited. Mom and Dad were ecstatic. Especially Mom. She cried and laughed at the same time and hugged me too much. And Kelly—he made up for Alex. He's psyched about my remission. He kept saying there's power in prayer. He asked me if I was still praying, so I had to admit that I thought I'd done enough praying for now, since I don't really need His help anymore. You should've seen the look on Kelly's face. He got all upset, telling me I can't stop praying now, just because I've finally made it to remission, and that you need to always pray, because we need His help all the time, and need to thank Him for everything He gives us every day, so I promised him I'd try to remember to keep praying.

And then there's you. When I told you the news, you just smiled as if you knew all along that my remission was going to happen . . .

## CHAPTER EIGHTEEN

*on't be such a wimp, Kathy—just do it!*

D I'd originally felt wonderful about my decision, but now that it was Saturday afternoon and I was standing on the doorstep of Jason's gigantic house, staring at the huge oak door in front of me, it took all of my courage to knock on it. It didn't help that I'd fought about the whole thing with Mom. The fact that she was completely against what I'd decided to do had been eating at my resolve all morning long.

I shifted my book bag nervously onto my shoulder before the sound of feet running to the door could be heard. A second later, the door was carefully opened a few inches. I had to look down to make eye contact with the little face framed with dark, wavy hair. I forced a bright smile onto my face. "Hi, Emily. Is your brother Jason home?"

Emily looked at me as if she thought I was an idiot. "He's lying on the couch. He can't go anywhere 'cause his knee is hurt."

"Yes, I know. Do you think I could come in and see him?"

Emily frowned and refused to open the door any wider. "How do you know my name?"

"I met you and your family at the hospital on Monday."

Emily thought this over for a moment before giving me a smile of her own. "Oh, yeah, I remember you now. You're Kathy."

I smiled back, impressed that she'd remembered my name. "Yes, I am."

The door swung open wide. "Come on in. I'll show you where Jason is."

I followed Emily nervously down the hall, freaking out a little inside, wondering what Jason's reaction would be to see me. In his house, of all places! But Emily shrieked my arrival to him before I could catch up with her down the hall and around a few corners to where Jason was lounging on a couch in a comfortable family room. A mean-looking brace was wrapped around his right leg, and a pair of metal crutches was propped conveniently near his head. Jason himself was wearing a price-less look of total surprise on his face.

Before either Jason or I could say a word, Emily plopped herself down on the couch near Jason. "Can I go ride my bike now?"

Jason turned from me to his sister. "Not until someone who can walk without crutches comes home."

"Why?"

"Because you're a speed racer, so someone needs to be around in case you crash!"

"I don't crash!"

"Well, you don't watch for cars very well."

"Yes I do! I'll be careful—I promise!"

"Tell your story to Adam when he gets home. I can't chase you down if something happens. Besides—you need to practice your piano lesson. So—why don't you go down the hall and wow us with your expertise."

Emily glumly stood up from the couch and walked slowly out of the room with her head down. I couldn't help smiling at her melodramatics as I watched her sad retreat down the hall.

"So—Kathy—what are you doing here?"

I turned back to face Jason and plowed straight ahead before my nerves caused me to turn tail and run for the front door. "Bringing your Honors English homework assignment, what else?" I casually reached into my book bag for a copy of our textbook and tossed it lightly into his hands. "Lucky for you, Mrs. Dubois had a couple extra copies in her classroom."

Jason looked stunned. "Thanks—I guess."

I grinned. "You're welcome—'I guess.'"

"Sorry—I guess I'm just surprised you'd go out of your way to bring me my homework."

I shrugged my book bag off my shoulder and welcomed myself to a chair near the couch. "I didn't bring your homework. I only brought your Honors English assignment. It's what an English tutor is supposed to do." I did my best to act casual, but the way Jason stared at me made my heart drum again.

"An English tutor?"

"Yeah. That's what you signed up for me to do, isn't it? Tutor you in English?"

"But I thought—"

"Yeah, well, whatever you thought isn't the case anymore."

Jason raised an eyebrow. "Don't tell me you feel sorry for me?"

I laughed. "Sorry for you? Of course I feel sorry for you. Anyone who sees that knee of yours is bound to feel sorry for you. However, I happen to feel more than just sorry for you."

Jason raised both eyebrows in an interested sort of way while a grin spread all over his face, and he leaned forward on the couch. "Really? What else do you feel about me?"

I raised my own eyebrows in response. "Guilt, actually."

His grin disappeared. "Guilt?"

"Yeah. I agreed to be your tutor, and then I flaked out on you. Then, thanks to me, you nearly destroyed your knee." I grinned and shrugged. "I figure the least I can do is finish my term as your tutor, and the least you can do is let me tutor you so I can get rid of my guilty conscience."

Jason rolled his eyes and sat back against the couch. "You know that was the drugs talking—that day in the hospital. It's not your fault at all."

"I don't know about that. I think I jinxed you for sure."

"Nah—not even." Jason sighed before looking my way again. "Don't get me wrong—I appreciate what you're trying to do for me here, but it's pointless now."

"Pointless?"

Jason nodded and ran his hand through his hair. "Yeah—I asked you to tutor me so I'd be able to stay on the football team. Well, I'm obviously out for the rest of the season, so what does it matter what my grade is now?"

*Jason—quit and give up?* I snatched the nearest decorative couch pillow and threw it at his startled face. "What does it matter? Don't pull a dumb jock move on me here! You know your knee will eventually get better—your grades need to be on top so once you make the team, you'll have no trouble staying on through the whole season!"

Jason laughed and tossed the pillow back at me. "I didn't think you cared about football."

I caught the pillow before it hit my face. "I don't, but I know *you* do. Your knee isn't the only thing that's going to need to be in shape for you to make the team." I did my best to act and sound as professionally tutorish as possible. "Besides—I thought you wanted a shot at the AP English test. And there's my teaching reputation to consider. You're the first person I've ever tutored. I'm not about to stand by and watch my first student fail. Not when you've been doing so well."

"You really think I'm doing okay in English?"

"More than okay. Honors English hasn't been the same without you."

"Really!"

I shrugged and tried to make my voice light. "I admit the class has been pretty stale this week. And I'd be lying if I said I didn't miss your always interesting remarks in class."

"That's me. Always full of interesting remarks." Jason folded his arms with a much too pleased look on his face.

"Careful or your head will get as big as your knee was."

Jason laughed and tried to reach for the pillow, but I quickly snatched it myself before he turned serious again. "Look, Kathy, thanks for wanting to help me, but it's not going to work."

I frowned. "Why not?" Then as I looked at his serious face, a horrifying thought slashed into my brain. *Good grief—how stupid could I be?* "Oh, wait—I see—" My words tripped all over my tongue, and I was wishing I was anywhere but here. "You don't *want* my help—?"

Jason's eyes grew a few sizes. "No—no! It's not that—It's just that I have physical therapy during study hour now."

I was glad he couldn't feel my relief or hear my heart beating faster again. "Then I'll just come over after school. What time would work for you?"

Jason raised an eyebrow again. "After school? Are you sure?"

"I wouldn't have suggested it if I wasn't."

Jason nodded and thought for a moment. "Well, since I can't practice with the team anymore, that frees up my afternoon, so I guess maybe around four, if that works for you?"

"That should be fine." Jason nodded again and then winced and grunted as he moved his right leg to position his knee better. I couldn't help wincing along with him.

"I'm sorry—you're probably not up to having people come barging over uninvited into your house. And I didn't even ask you how your surgery went—how rude can I be!"

"No big deal. I'm fine. And the surgery went great, of course. I knew it would."

I raised my eyebrows. "You knew? How did you know?"

Jason smiled. "Because I have faith."

I sighed. "Faith again, huh?"

"Yes, faith," Jason insisted, nodding his head. "I had faith that everything was going to go great. Especially after I had a blessing. That was pretty amazing." Jason looked at me intently. "You were there. Do you remember that?"

I nodded and looked down at my hands. "Yeah, I remember," I said softly.

Jason replied just as softly. "I felt really calm and peaceful about everything—I just knew everything would go okay. And it did." Silence reigned before he ventured to speak again. "You felt something that day, Kathy, didn't you?"

I looked up and tried to pretend I had no idea what he was talking about. "Felt something? What do you mean?"

Jason shook his head. "I saw it in your face that you felt something. Will you—I mean, would you *like* to—tell me about what you felt?"

I wasn't sure what to say, but there was something about the look on Jason's face that made me believe I *could* tell him. Although I could only manage a few hesitant words at first, before long, I was trying to explain the powerful experience I'd had that day. When I finished, I felt true relief that I could finally talk about it with someone. And I knew beyond a doubt that wanting to help Jason in Honors English again wasn't the only reason I'd had to see him and talk to him.

When I finished, Jason quietly said, "That's how I feel, too, whenever I feel the Spirit."

I frowned. "I—I don't know—I don't know what you mean by 'the Spirit.'"

Jason sighed and leaned back against the couch. "It's hard to explain something you feel." Jason frowned for a moment before turning to me again. "The Spirit is one of the ways God—our Heavenly Father—uses to communicate with us. Spirit to spirit. By the power and witness of the Spirit, we feel when something is true in our hearts, and then we can understand it in our minds. Feeling is a much more powerful, pure way of reaching a person's soul than words could ever be."

I was stunned. I truly could not think of anything to say. But there was one question his words had brought to my mind. I decided to dare voice it now. "Why do you believe that God wants to talk to us?"

Jason smiled. "Because we're His children and He loves us. He wants us to come back to live with Him forever. The Spirit testifies of truth to our spirits—truths that can lead us back to Him." Jason paused to look at me seriously. "But it's up to us to choose to follow."

---

*April 18*

Dear Kitty,

I love being back in school, but at the same time, I miss you. Alex caught me worrying at play rehearsal after school the other day and said, "What's wrong? Don't you trust Mom to take good care of her?" I can't help it—I worry about you!

The play's coming along great. I think it's going to be one of the best shows this school has ever done. Sam's doing an awesome job as Princess Winnifred (she has no problem at all "pretending" to be royalty), and Alex makes a great Sir Harry. He loves being a knight. As for me, since my character is under a curse that keeps him from talking, I get to do crazy things like pinching all of the ladies-in-waiting when I walk by them, so I'm happy.

You can roll around all over the place now—I almost regret helping you learn so fast! And you smile all the time—basically for anyone who makes you happy, but Mom says you smile the biggest when I get home from play rehearsal, so I look forward to that smile when I'm on my way home.

Kelly came over today after play rehearsal thinking he was the hottest guy on earth, because he got his driver's license. I called Mom at work and asked her if it'd be okay if Kelly drove us to the park, and of course, she said no. She asked if Kelly's been tiring me with his religion talk, and I told her no, which is true. Talking with Kelly about religion doesn't tire me out at all. Besides—what she doesn't know won't hurt her, right? You loved the park, and although Kelly wasn't thrilled about taking a baby along, I think he had fun, too. He even took our picture while we sat under a tree together.

You've been crying and fussing a lot lately. Mom thinks you may be cutting a tooth, and she was right. Kelly called later on that night while I was trying to get some homework done and keep you happy at the same time. You were gnawing away on my finger while I held you on my lap, and I don't know who jumped the highest out of the three of us when I felt your tooth bite my finger. So now you have your first tooth. We might even be able to see it in the picture Kelly took today at the park . . .

*April 22*

Dear Kitty,

This is definitely my month. My birthday's coming up, so I've been practicing my driving a ton. I know I'm a better driver than Kelly. No question there. School's going great, too. I've been studying my brains out. Matt still checks up on me and proofs my papers, so I've got to get a decent report card at the end of term.

I went with Mom today to the hospital for your six-month checkup and my own checkup. She let me drive the car, so that fact and my "thumbs up" checkup made it a good day, but once we got inside, my day went from good to great. Rounding the last corner to your doctor's office, there she was—Jennifer. Every time I see her I go crazy inside. She smiled when she saw me. Us, I should say. I didn't realize what a magnet babies are to girls. She hurried right over and made a big deal over you. I was worried you might freak out over a stranger, but you were happy to smile at all of her baby talking and googling. Mom couldn't stop grinning while I did the intros between her and Jennifer. I know I'm in for some major teasing now, but Jennifer's worth it. She was about to take a break, so I handed you over to Mom for your appointment, and then Jennifer and I headed to the cafeteria and had some colas and talked. I told her all about the play, and she asked when it was going to be performed. I don't know if I can explain what it's like talking with someone you like a lot. Maybe too much. Nerve wracking. She didn't seem nervous to be talking to me, though. Lucky for me, I actually made her laugh, and the conversation flowed between us pretty easily.

I can't believe I'm writing all of this down. I'm going to stop now before I make a bigger fool of myself. Try not to laugh too much at your whacked big brother . . .

———————

I hadn't listened to the *Rubber Soul* album since my birthday. I was almost afraid to listen to it now, but in spite of that, I put it on last night and realized why I'd been afraid to listen for so long. The music—it wasn't the same. All of the songs sounded different to me now. Completely different feelings and thoughts swirled inside me, and before I knew what was happening, I was bawling like a baby. I couldn't stop crying long after the last song had finished.

I blamed the dream I had that night—the night before Halloween— on the Beatles. And my crying fit. It was definitely the strangest dream I've ever had. And likely ever *would* have. The whole thing probably lasted a mere minute, but it drilled its way into my consciousness and seemed far too real to be just a dream.

In the dream, I saw a young man with dark black hair, dressed all in white. His back was towards me, his attention taken with something he held in his hands. Slowly, the young man turned around to look at me. One look at those eyes, that face, and I knew—it was *Brett!* My heart leapt, but as he looked at me, even though he wore a small attempt at a smile, there were tears in his eyes. And then, he looked at the object in his hands again, and he looked at me with a heart-wrenching, pleading look on his face that made me start to cry, too. It was all too strange—I couldn't handle more. Brett seemed to know because he disappeared in a flash, and I was awake, crying real tears of my own into my pillow.

# CHAPTER NINETEEN

I'd been standing in front of the trophy case after school staring at Brett's impishly grinning face, mulling over my dream. I finally pulled myself away from Brett's eyes to glance at my watch.

"Jason's going to kill me!" I said out loud. I snatched up my book bag and raced out the school doors. At Jason's request, even though Halloween fell on a Thursday and our weekly English papers were due on Friday, I'd agreed to come over and tutor him as usual.

"Come over to your house and study on Halloween? Are you kidding?"

"I just want you to take one final look at my paper before I hand it in."

"But surely you of all people have big party plans for Halloween!"

"With this leg? Not even. My dad has to work late, so my mom's driving Emily to go trick-or-treating with cousins. Adam won't be here, so that leaves me to hand out candy."

Although I'd rolled my eyes, the hopeful look on his face when he'd asked had me shamelessly looking forward to spending Halloween with him.

I was full of apologies after I'd screeched the cruddy car to a stop in front of Jason's house and sprinted for the front door. "It's already five

o'clock—I'm so sorry—I was studying at school and lost track of time—
If I'm too late and you want to forget it, I totally understand—"

"Stop!" Jason grinned and hobbled on his crutches back to where
he'd been languishing in the front fancy living room by a big bowl full
of candy. "It's no problem. Really. I've just been finishing up my own
paper here."

"Well, then," I took a seat on a recliner. "Let's take a look."

Ever since our conversation about the Spirit, Jason had become
more confident in bringing up religious subjects. Every day this week,
he'd found a way to work a story from his Book of Mormon into our
conversation. Rather than feeling annoyed over it, though, I was
impressed at how skillfully he was able to find something religious to
say that truly *did* relate to our assignment. He definitely knew his Book
of Mormon, and his enthusiasm in spouting off chapters and verses
made me smile. Even laugh out loud. Which happened tonight while he
excitedly told me about yet another adventure of a man named Nephi.

"And no one knew it was him instead of Laban—not even his own
brothers! Truly amazing story. One of my favorites." I was trying not to
smile, but Jason had been watching me too closely and narrowed his
eyes at me. "Hey, what's so funny?"

"You are."

Jason raised an eyebrow. "Me?"

"Yes—you. Don't be offended. I'm not laughing at your Bible story."

"No? Then what is it about me that's so hilarious?"

"You talk about this book as if it's the latest action movie instead of
an old Bible book!"

"'Old Bible book'? Just because it wasn't written yesterday doesn't
mean it's not exciting. And for your information, it *is* pretty action-
packed. Remind me to tell you about the stripling warriors some time."

I grinned. "I'll try to remember."

Jason laughed. "Sorry—I get excited over things that are important
to me."

"Don't apologize. It's one of the more appealing qualities about you."

"More appealing? You mean *all* of them aren't?"

Before I could say something fitting, the doorbell rang, and I watched while Jason struggled up onto his crutches and tried to clutch the bowl of trick or treat candy and hobble to the door before I hurried and snatched the bowl from him, saving it from crashing to the floor.

"I can do this—really," Jason protested.

"No, you can't. Really. You'll hurt yourself. So just sit down and let me do this, okay?"

Jason reluctantly gave in, but even he had to agree it was easier to let me take care of the little ghosts and witches that came pounding at the front door. Somehow in between all of the doorbell ringing and door knocking and kids laughing and screeching, we made it through Jason's paper. I'd barely finished reading the last sentence when some really loud pounding on the front door could be heard. I sighed and reached for the candy bowl and opened the door.

Frozen in place, I stared at Brad and Jeff, who wore the same surprised look on their faces I knew I had on mine. Jeff finally grunted, "Is Jason around?" I numbly stepped back to let them enter, and seconds later, they were loudly talking and laughing with Jason, and I was wishing I was anywhere in the world but here.

"Hey, what's up?" Jason finally said.

"Angela's party. She asked us to come get you." Jeff glanced my way briefly, but I only stared stonily back.

"Oh, yeah—I forgot. Kathy's been helping me with my English paper—"

Which was my cue to make my escape. "But we're done, so I think I'll take off."

Jason at least had the decency to look concerned. "Kathy—"

"You're coming, aren't you, Jason?" Brad interrupted as he grabbed

Jason's crutches and tried to balance on them, nearly toppling all over Jason in the process.

"Well, no one else is here to hand out candy." I almost felt sorry for Jason. He looked so torn and helpless and uncomfortable. His attempt to be Cool on top of it all would've been amusing, except that I didn't feel like smiling anymore.

Both Jeff and Brad had a good guffaw over Jason's pitiful excuse. Neither felt the urge to notice I was still in the room and wasn't a plant or a piece of furniture, but I knew hoping for that was asking for too much. I inched my way to the door and forced a big smile on my face. "Have fun at the party, Jason. I'll see you in class tomorrow." And then I quickly slipped out the front door, ran to the cruddy car, and drove for home as fast as I legally could.

---

*May 3*
Dear Kitty,

Happy Birthday to me, Happy Birthday to me,
Happy Birthday to ME—EE!! (yeah, it's my birthday today!)
Happy Birthday to ME!!

Yep, today's the big day! Your Big Brother Brett is now the Big Sixteen! The only thing I wanted to do for my birthday was go to the DMV, so Mom and Dad let me take a day off from school in honor of my birthday. Just like I knew I would, I passed the written test with flying colors, and I passed the driver's test my first try. Mom even let me drive the car home. Kelly's head will deflate once he's forced to deal with the truth that I'm truly the better driver!

Since today's my Big Sixteenth Birthday, we had cake and ice cream and presents, but you gave me the best present of all. It took a lot of practicing, but now you can sit up all by yourself, which you showed off on my birthday! I've sat you down on the floor so many times, only to have you nose dive into the carpet, that I got all excited and clapped my hands. You laughed and clapped your hands, too. Everyone was excited, because no one thought you could sit up by yourself yet. I knew you'd get the hang of it soon, but I never thought you'd catch on and do it perfectly on my birthday. You must have been doing some practicing on your own behind my back, little sneak that you are! Thanks for giving me such an awesome present . . .

*May 7*

Dear Kitty,

Well, all of my hard work—and, okay, everyone else's hard work, too—has really paid off. The musical was sold out every night. We had to extend it a few more nights, which has never happened at our school before. We were great, thanks mostly to the professional acting done by yours truly! Miss Goforth was so happy she cried.

Both football and drama give me a rush that nothing else can, but the thing that really got my adrenaline pumping was the night Jennifer came to the play. I couldn't believe it when I saw her standing in line to buy a ticket. I barely had time to say, "Come backstage after the show," before I had to hurry back down the hall to finish getting ready. After the play was over, having Jennifer walk into the drama room and then seeing her face light up when she saw me—wow. Kitty, that was something. And before I could do or say anything, she threw her arms around me and said, "Congratulations—that was so good—you were so funny—you're amazing!" I hugged her back and enjoyed the jealous looks I got from all my cohorts who were watching me with this incredibly gorgeous blonde who's Jennifer.

Now that the musical is over and it's time to tear down the scenery, I'm going to miss seeing and working with everyone in the play. Kitty, you've got to get involved in drama when you go to high school. Considering the amazing acting genes in this family, I know you'll come by this naturally. I'll bet you'll be the best actress the school has ever seen . . .

# CHAPTER TWENTY

I had the dream again on Halloween night. Again, Brett turned to me, holding something tight against his chest with a small, wistful smile on his face. I still couldn't tell what he was holding, and again, he quickly disappeared. I woke up fast when I could feel tears threatening to break loose.

I couldn't stop thinking about the dream—both dreams—until the sight of a certain someone sitting in his front row seat in Honors English brought my feet to a surprised halt.

"Hey, Kathy!"

*Jason!* "So—you're back. And on a Friday, no less!"

Jason grinned and shrugged. "I was getting sick of lying on the couch all the time. And I wanted to hand in my English paper personally."

"You're even early to class! How did you make that miracle happen?"

Jason laughed. "My seminary teacher took pity on me and let me out early so I'd make it safely over to the school."

I nodded. "Nice."

Students started to file in, mostly to exclaim "hello" and "welcome back" and "how's your knee" to Jason, so I quickly eased out of the crowd and moved to my own desk.

Even though having Jason in the room was distracting, another boy with dark hair disturbed my thoughts far more. I couldn't get those *visions*, as Jason would likely call them, out of my head. For once, I didn't venture one comment during the entire class period. Jason sneaked a look in my direction once or twice, surprising me with the worried frown he gave me, but we didn't have a chance to speak after class due to the onslaught of more well-wishers who wanted to welcome Jason back.

---

*May 10*

Dear Kitty,

The last dance of school—the senior ball—is coming up. Kelly thinks I should ask Jennifer. I ran into her on my way out of the hospital the other day when I was there for a checkup. I was in such a good mood that I stopped and joked with her for a minute. For all of my big talk about how I love being on stage and how I'm not intimidated by anyone, I guess I've found the one thing that turns my backbone into spaghetti. Crazy. I've faced some bad looking guys on the football field, and I've stood on stage a million times in front of tons of people doing plays, but ask Jennifer to the dance—this is harder than anything I've ever had to do before. Believe me, Kitty. Liking someone is the most nerve-wracking thing you'll ever do. Believe me . . .

*July 10*

Dear Kitty,

Summer is just zooming by—Kelly and Alex have been lifting weights with me every day, and summer football clinics have been going great, too. I'm determined to make up for lost time. I'm definitely back on the team, with both Alex and Kelly playing Varsity, too, and this time, we're taking state! I'm going to play better than I ever have before. Alex never stops worrying about me, but that's fine. I feel great, and that's all that matters to me right now.

And you—you're amazing! Every day you find a way to surprise me. I can't decide if it's just a girl thing or if it's your own unique gift. One thing's for sure that proves you're definitely a girl, and have some of Sam in you, is that you love hanging out in the bathroom too much. Kelly and I were supposed to be watching you today, but we got too involved zoning out in front of the TV. We were dead tired from football practice, and somehow we got off on another one of our religious tangents—something we haven't done much lately. I know Kelly's missed it, but the scary part is that I'm actually listening.

Midway into our discussion, we heard squeals and laughter coming from the bathroom, so we scrambled over each other to get down the hall—and there you were, sitting in the middle of the floor practically hidden in pink toilet paper. You just sat there grinning and blowing raspberries at us while we both yelled "Kitty!" I ran for my camera and snapped your picture before Kelly could snatch you up. I did my best to reroll the paper, but it didn't look too great. I'm definitely going to have to watch you a lot more closely now. Still, you'd make a great baby model. Advertising toilet paper, of course!

Even though I'm having a blast this summer, I do have one regret. I didn't ask Jennifer to the senior ball. I've been hanging out with her when I'm not with Kelly and Alex, so now I realize how stupid I was not to ask her. Don't be stupid like me, Kitty. When amazing opportunities come your way, you have to grab them, because you never know if they'll come again.

Anyway—Jennifer. I'll take her to every dance this year, starting with homecoming. We've been having an awesome time together. It's incredible—the power a girl can have over you. You have no idea what a powerful thing a smile can be. I don't know—you may say that a guy's smile can have the same powerful effect. I just hope whoever the guy is who has the privilege to be liked by you realizes how lucky he is . . .

# CHAPTER TWENTY-ONE

*August 25*

Dear Kitty,

We just played the first two games of the football season—preseason games, actually—and we won both! Even though winning was awesome, for the first time in my life, everything else to do with the game was more important and amazing than winning. Just being in the locker room, suiting up with the rest of the team—pulling my Number 9 jersey over my shoulder pads—was incredible. And stepping out onto our high school's football field as the home team with Alex and Kelly and everyone else, hearing the crowd cheer—it was the best! I'll never forget it. Just being there out on the field, playing the game—I loved it all! Even getting a good quarterback sack was fun—beats lying around in a hospital with tubes stuck all over me any day! In our last game, I ran with the ball and scored the first goal of the game. Standing at the goal posts, holding the ball over my head and listening to everyone scream and cheer—it was awesome! I just wish you were old enough to really see it and remember it. At least you were there both times, so now another goal of mine has come true: I've been able to play strong with you there in the stands. It gave me an extra shot of adrenaline to know you were there watching me . . .

*August 29*

Dear Kitty,

School started today, and Dr. Grenville said at my last checkup I'm good to go! Not only have I put weight and muscle back on, but I actually have a tan! Sam and Alex think I'm more proud of that than anything else. I feel so good lately that it feels almost as strange as feeling sick did at first. Of course, all summer long, Alex stalked me through football clinics and practices and especially during our two preseason games. He was so busy worrying about me he messed up a few plays and missed some key passes. Sometimes it really bugs me how closely he watches me. When he's really annoying me, I call him Sherlock. I think I'll get him a spy glass and a pipe for Christmas this year.

You weren't too happy about being shuffled off to your new sitter's house today. I hated leaving you there, but we had a long talk the night before about being brave, so I hope you were okay. Mom and Dad let me take you to the sitter's, so I reminded you of our talk on the way over. You stared at me real solemn-like, and today there weren't any raspberries for me. I wish you'd thrown me at least one so I'd know you were going to be okay. Even though you were crying, you were able to wave good bye to me as I drove away. Nearly broke my heart, but the fact that you were able to wave proved to me that you're tough.

It feels good to be back at school and hanging around with Kelly again. Today, my life almost felt like it did when I started school last year, before all of the madness really began . . .

*August 31*

Dear Kitty,

Sam's gone now. Mom cried pretty hard all the way home after we dropped her off at school down south. The rest of us were quiet the whole way back. It's weird to have someone leave. It's been Mom, Dad, Sam, Alex, and me (and now you, of course!) for so long I guess I took it for granted it would always be that way. I of all people should know nothing stays the same long enough. Just when you start getting used to something, everything changes. Why does that always have to happen? Dad says it's part of growing up and becoming an adult. Mom says it's part of life. I say it stinks, no matter how you look at it . . .

*September 5*
Dear Kitty,

We played our first real season football game today. Having Alex and now Kelly on the Varsity team with me is the best. The game was challenging, but so dang much fun! Usually when I play football, things will happen during the game to make me mad—like receivers who don't catch my passes—but like in preseason, nothing could make me angry. It almost seems like a crime to get so happy over playing football. We won this game, too. Our team is so incredible, smart, and fast that Coach feels good about teaching us more complicated plays. We're all so psyched and determined to take state this year that we're working as hard as we can, and it's paying off. We've already had a few write-ups in the paper about our team. They're saying we're the team to watch this year and that we have the best chance of going to state!

Everyone's amazed at how well and smart I can play this game. Believe me—the real game of football is played between the ears, not out on the field. Coach says that all the time, and it's true. You, of course, were—and are!—my inspiration to keep going and keep trying. I'm always going to be grateful to you for that . . .

# CHAPTER TWENTY-TWO

S o, Kathy, which study question are you doing your paper on this week?"

"Mmm—I think I'm going to do the one on Bartleby as a Christ figure."

Jason and I had been calmly reviewing Melville's short story together while Emily practiced her piano lesson. After the first time I'd come to Jason's to tutor him, I'd made it a point to tell Emily how much I loved hearing her play the piano. As a result, every afternoon at four o'clock, Emily made sure she was the one who scrambled to the door to let me in. After hurrying me to Jason, she'd scoot off to the piano and play and play—which as Jason had pointed out, made it a win-win situation for all of us: Emily got her practicing done, and we were able to study in peace.

"You've *got* to be kidding!"

I jumped at Jason's loud reaction and laughed. "Wow, Jason—you scared me!"

Jason shook his head incredulously. "So did you! But you're just messing with me, right? I mean—because of all the religious stuff we've talked about. You're not seriously going to write on Bartleby as a Christ figure, are you?"

I raised my eyebrows. "Actually, yes, I *am* seriously going to write a paper on Bartleby as a Christ figure."

"How—*why?* Especially after all the stuff we've talked about—"

"Exactly, Jason," I interrupted, much to Jason's annoyance. "Actually, *because* of all the stuff we've talked about. Considering all of your amazing knowledge on Christ, I'm surprised you didn't decide to write on this study question yourself."

Jason almost snorted in disgust. "I'm not writing on that stupid question because if there's one thing I know for sure, it's that Bartleby is not at *all* like Christ. I'd feel sacrilegious writing a paper on Bartleby as a Christ figure!"

"If that's how you feel, maybe you need to read the story again," I said evenly.

"I don't need to read the story again—I *know* he's nothing like Christ! I'm just sorry that *you* seem to think he is. Disappointed, actually."

"Hey, Jason—what's going on?"

I'd been so into our debate that I hadn't heard anyone come into the room. Jason didn't look like he'd heard anything, either, but none of that changed the harsh reality of Angela's presence bouncing toward us. I didn't know what to say. Jason wore a dumbfounded look on his face and, surprisingly, didn't seem to know what to say, either, but that was fine, because Angela had plenty to say, enough to make up for both of us.

"I made some cookies for you, Jas. Chocolate chip—your favorite! *Just* the way you like them—extra gooey." I groaned in pain while Angela planted herself so close to Jason she practically sat on him.

Jason finally found his voice. "Oh—wow—you didn't need to do that." Once again he had the decency to look uncomfortable and even a little embarrassed.

Angela smiled her biggest and did her best to pretend I wasn't there. "I wanted to."

Being turned into a piece of furniture by Jason's football buddies was one thing, but having to deal with it from Angela—I took a deep breath, closed my book, and reached for my book bag. "Well, I think I'll take off now, Jason."

Jason leaned down and snatched my book bag before I could touch it. "No—we're not done studying." Jason turned back to Angela. "You know Kathy's my English tutor, Angela—"

Angela quickly cut him off. "Brad and Jeff told me at my party on Halloween. All about Kathy tutoring you in your home. *Privately.*" Now that Angela was pointedly glaring at me, I decided that maybe being ignored by Angela was okay after all.

Jason tried to smile. "Oh—good. Well, Kathy's still tutoring me right now, so—"

"Oh, I know. Don't mind me! I'll just wait until you're done." Angela settled herself snugly on the couch next to Jason, clearly not intending to budge an inch.

"Is that okay with you, Kathy?" Jason tried to smile, but I knew his real smiles, and this one was too tight, tense, and painful looking.

"Good grief, Jason!" Angela interrupted. "I'm sure she doesn't mind if your *girlfriend* wants to wait around until you're done! I'll be quiet as a mouse. Quieter! You won't even know I'm here."

With an encouraging nod from Jason, I opened my literature book again while Angela grabbed a magazine and watched us over the top of its pages. I was seething inside, watching her gloat with an evil grin on her face, but of course whenever Jason looked up, she had nothing but innocent, flirty smiles for him. I was determined to grit my teeth and get through the session, hoping to bore her into leaving. Unfortunately, Angela was just as determined to get rid of me. After five minutes, she tossed the magazine aside and made Jason eat a cookie. Then she brought him a glass of milk and snuggled back beside him to lace her fingers into his and play with his hand. *This was mouse-like?* The only thing that got me through the rest of the hour was Jason's discomfort over our interesting triangle and every little flirty thing Angela inflicted upon him. I worked through my pain until the bitter end and drove home, sticking my tongue out at Angela's baby blue Volkswagen, hating that final, smug smile on Angela's face as she grinned her good-bye, still clinging to Jason's hand and feeding him her stupid cookies.

---

*October 1*

Dear Kitty,

While I've been busy winning football games, you've been busy scoring some touchdowns of your own! You crawl around everywhere now. You can crawl faster than I can run, and don't you know it! It's dangerous to leave you alone at all, because quick as lightning, you're off to some unknown destination that's sure to be trouble. You squeal all the way while I chase you at a dead run. I have no idea how you can move so fast. We need to suit you up and put you out on the field—you'd score us more touchdowns than Alex or I ever could!

We're all going to have to watch out, though, because you've figured out how to pull yourself up by holding onto just about anything. You'd think that would be enough to keep you satisfied, but no—you've barely figured out how to pull yourself up, and once you're there, you're cruising around the room, hanging onto furniture as you go.

And then there's dinnertime. That's become a whole new adventure. You prefer to feed yourself, but I've learned to keep a close eye on you, since you insist on having your highchair set up by me. If I ignore you at all, I get a blob of something thrown in my hair or face. If I try to get mad at you, you laugh and babble at me as if it's just a new game we're playing. I can't stay mad. Who could, after looking into those blue eyes of yours and seeing you smile?

I've just been in the best mood lately—there aren't any words to describe how awesome it's been to play football again, but as great as that's been, the greatest thing was having Jennifer say yes to going to homecoming with me. I sent her roses, and she drove me crazy making me wait before she answered with a huge mass of balloons. I had to pop every one before I found the Y, E, and S in the last three. You jumped a mile each time I popped a balloon, and then you stared in shock at all the dead balloons after I'd finished massacring them. It took a quick drive to the store for a few helium balloons to get you to even look at me again!

Jennifer gave me a piece of the dress she's making for the dance so I can make sure her corsage matches. I don't think I've ever been so excited and nervous at the same time.

Kelly came over later on and unfortunately got caught by Mom comparing some Bible stuff with similar stuff from his Book of Mormon with me. Mom looked like she was ready to get medieval about it, but I told her that I'd brought the religion thing up, not Kelly, which was true. This time, anyway. Kelly apologized for upsetting her, though. I thought that was pretty funny. He didn't apologize for talking Book of Mormon stuff with me—just for upsetting her.

Once Mom calmed down and was convinced Kelly wasn't going to baptize me on the spot, you woke up from your nap, so I got you out of your crib, and Kelly and I figured out the best way to help you learn to walk. Kelly brought a bag of M&Ms, and after he slipped one in your mouth, you were hooked and begged for more. He was pretty excited and said, "Hey, look—she really does like me!" but I told him, "Toss the bag to me, and we'll see who she's really in love with." Once he did, it was obvious who—or what—your first love was! Your head flipped around, and with your eyes glued to that M&M bag, you cruised your way over to me, and soon we had a great game of catch going between us with the M&M bag. Of course, we made sure you got a few M&Ms each time you crossed over to either of us. A couple more times of the old M&M

game and you'll be ready for your first marathon! So after we'd fed you enough M&Ms to make you sick for a week, I had to show Kelly our latest trick. If I say, "Kitty, where's your eyes?" you put your finger in your eye. If I say, "Where's your chin?" you put your finger on your chin. You can find your nose, your mouth—even your tongue and your knees. But I have to admit, I love to mess with your mind. If I say, "Kitty, where's your thighs?" you stick a finger in your eye. If I say, "where's your shin?" you, of course, touch your chin.

You're so much fun—I never imagined how much fun a little sister could be. You still love the Beatles as much as I do, so we listen to *Rubber Soul* every night. Hanging out with you in our room listening to music before going to sleep is always the best way to end the day . . .

# CHAPTER TWENTY-THREE

So explain to me again why you're doing your paper on Bartleby as a Christ figure."

I'd been listening to Emily practice her piano lesson with one ear while I'd reviewed the story with Jason when he blasted me with my paper choice again. I'd tried to keep the conversation away from that particular topic, considering how weird he had gotten over it yesterday, but Jason was giving me a determined look that pinned me into my chair.

"Well, the story's overflowing with similarities," I began carefully. "I can't believe you haven't noticed."

"Well, clue me in, because it's been bugging me. Show me what you're going to try and use for your paper."

I sighed and turned to my literature book. "Well, to begin with, the story's tone screams that not only is Bartleby misunderstood—or simply *not* understood—by everyone he has to deal with, but what he does and says is just plain confusing to everyone as well. Wasn't that true of Christ, too? That the things He did and said were misunderstood, or not understood at all, and usually confusing to those around Him? Then of course, there's the fact that like Christ, Bartleby has lawyers around him bugging him, asking questions, and trying to trip him up and confound him. However, again like Christ, *he* always ends up being the one who does the tripping and confounding! Plus, Bartleby responds calmly to every-one and refuses to freak out when people try to provoke him. Christ never lost control, either. And Bartleby's unjustly dumped into prison among thieves, like Christ was unjustly crucified between two thieves. And—why are you smiling?"

Jason folded his arms smugly. "It's just good to know you've been listening to me."

I raised both eyebrows back. "You mean, to your religious sermons?" Before Jason could retaliate, I grudgingly added, "Well, I admit some of the time I have. But I've been doing my usual amount of research for this paper, which just so happens to require opening a Bible." Jason's annoy-ing grin had returned to his face. "I know. Me reading a Bible. Hard to imagine, isn't it?"

Jason shook his head. "Nah—not really. But, hey, since you're will-ing to read the Bible for an English paper, what would it take for me to get you to read the Book of Mormon?"

"Haven't you practically quoted the entire book to me yourself?"

Jason beaned me in the head with one of the couch throw pillows. "Very funny!"

I grabbed the pillow off the floor and chucked it back at Jason's face as hard as I could. He neatly and easily caught it. I rolled my eyes and made a big show of picking up my book and settling it into my lap before motioning for Jason to do the same. Then I pointed out every-thing in the story that to me clearly showed the similarities between Bartleby and Christ.

"Well, I'll give you a few points," Jason said grudgingly when I was through. "But still, for every point about Bartleby that's like Christ, I can find two that show he's totally the opposite of Christ. All of that 'I prefer not to' stuff just bugs me. That's not Christlike at all."

"Then maybe you should compare and contrast him to Christ, explaining why you *don't* think he's a Christ figure. Just be sure to write something you feel strongly about. It'll show in your writing and make your paper more solid. And interesting. And Mrs. Dubois will have no choice but to give you an A."

Jason nodded slowly. "Yeah, maybe."

"That's part of literature, Jason—comparing two unlikely characters and finding not only their differences but their similarities as well. Any two people have at least one thing in common."

Jason nodded slowly before he looked at me carefully. Thoughtfully. "I guess that would explain why any two people can be friends. Even the two most unlikely people in the whole world, huh, Kathy?" He was looking at me so intently I had to fight not to squirm.

"Hey, Jason! Still studying?"

Both Jason and I jumped. *Angela.* Again! And once again, she looked through me as if I wasn't even there.

Jason sighed and leaned back into the pillows cushioning his back, the intense look now gone. "It's not five o'clock yet. Kathy tutors me for an hour."

Angela shrugged and bounced her way over to the couch, settling herself snugly against Jason's side. "Oh, sorry. Well, since I'm here, and it's going to be five soon, mind if I stay?"

"I guess not." Jason looked to me as if for an okay, but since I'd become a plant again as far as Angela was concerned, I couldn't imagine anything I might say would've made any difference.

———

*October 16*
Dear Kitty,

Happy birthday to you, happy birthday to you,

Happy birthday, dear Kitty (yeah, now it's finally YOUR birthday!!)

Happy birthday to You!!!

I can't believe you're a year old! Wow! My Kitty's a whole year old!!

What a fantastic day we've had—Mom made a big cake just for you that looks like a kitten. I had to videotape you plowing your hands and face into it. Even Sam, who came home for the weekend, got a kick out of it, though she wouldn't touch you while you had all that icing all over your face and hands. It didn't bother me any, though. I didn't even mind that you rubbed your hands in my hair when I lifted you out of your highchair. I thought it was pretty funny and made sure Alex took a picture of us covered in chocolate icing!

The greatest part of the whole party happened after we sang to you. You looked at me and pointed, then clapped your hands and said, "Bet!" I really freaked out, because although I've secretly been trying to get you to say my name, you've never let on that you were paying any attention. You'd either stare at me like I was an idiot, or you'd ignore me. You haven't even attempted "Mama" or "Dada" yet, so I'm pretty honored that the first word you've attempted to say is my name! I'll bet you did it on purpose—waiting until a big moment to let loose on something you'd been planning all along— like a true Colton! I got all choked up, because it's your birthday. You're the one who's supposed to be getting gifts, not giving out awesome gifts like the one you gave me . . .

## CHAPTER TWENTY-FOUR

I'd stopped vacuuming in the living room to stare at Brett's picture on the bookshelf, but after a few moments, my gaze moved to the three football heroes picture. I was still thinking about the three in the picture as I entered the kitchen to perch on one of the bar stools while Mom emptied the dishwasher, her locket swinging from its gold chain around her neck. I hadn't been listening to her while she attempted to ask me questions until she walked over to me and folded her arms.

"Hmmm. I don't know what to think about you these days, Kathy."

"What do you mean?"

Mom raised her eyebrow. "I haven't seen your friends around in weeks. You keep yourself locked in your room for hours at a time, yet when the family's around, I haven't had to drag you out to say hello. In fact, you've been unusually pleasant to everyone lately, especially to Sam. Mind you, I'm not complaining, but I *have* noticed. Everyone has. And now, this Jason West—the mere fact that you decided to resume tutoring him concerns me."

I could feel every defensive nerve in my body twitching. "I see Mistie and Crystal at school every day! And I *do* have my own studying to do in the evenings, and crazy as it may sound, I *do* like some peace and quiet while I do my homework. Most parents would be *thrilled* to see all their kids getting along instead of getting suspicious over it." I stopped for a breath before finishing my indignant speech. "And as for Jason, I'm just finishing what I agreed to do, Mom. It's no big deal. So don't make it one, okay?"

But Mom wasn't about to give up. "I worry about you helping a football player. I don't know—there must be other students who could help him—"

"Other students didn't agree to tutor him. I did." Unfortunately for Mom, I didn't give up easily, either.

Mom continued to frown. "I just worry that he spends your tutoring time trying to indoctrinate you with Mormonism and upsetting you instead of letting you tutor him."

I shook my head incredulously. "What? Indoctrinating? Upsetting me? Mom, please—"

"Don't 'Mom, please' me. I know how Mormon kids can be!"

I sat up straight in my stool and stared at her angry face. "You do?"

"Yes, I do." Mom wouldn't say more than that but turned away from me to stare past the kitchen wall. I waited for her to say more, but she didn't offer anything else.

"Mom, Jason's not forcing his religion on me. Really. Besides—give me a little credit. He doesn't do or say anything I can't deal with. I can hold my own just fine."

Mom whirled around to face me again. "So he *is* talking about his religion with you!"

*Exasperating.* Absolutely. I wasn't going to talk about this. Not when Mom was obviously going to be negative about everything. "So what else about me is bothering you?" I said stonily, matching her glare for glare.

Mom sighed and took a step back. "All right, fine. I give up." We were both quiet for a moment before Mom came around the counter to sit on a bar stool beside me. "Actually, there *is* something else I've wanted to talk about with you, Kathy."

I looked up at Mom suspiciously. "What?"

"I've seen you looking at Brett's pictures in the living room nearly every day." Mom reached out with her hand and smoothed my hair. She looked into my eyes, and although I looked back, I didn't speak. We both jumped when the phone rang.

Mom sighed and reached for the phone. "Oh, hello, June." One of Mom's friends. I didn't realize I'd been holding my breath until it came out in a rush while I made my getaway, escaping to my room as fast as I could.

---

*October 21*

Dear Kitty,

Well, it's official. I've got some hellish flu that's ripped me apart all night and all morning. Mom's already laid down the law against me going to the dance. Besides the fact that it would probably kill me to get out of this bed even if I could get up, I'd run the risk of getting Jennifer sick, so when Kelly showed up at noon, I wasn't in the greatest of moods. Being sick is bad enough, but trying to figure out a way to tell Jennifer I wasn't going to be able to take her to the dance was worse than having ten flus at once, believe me.

By the time Kelly came over, Mom had already told him I was sick with the flu, so he ignored all of my snotty, depressing comments. Of course, Kelly wasn't thinking about the dance. He didn't have a date. I have no idea why he didn't ask anybody. I know he wouldn't have a problem getting someone to go with him. I think we were both relieved to hear a soft knock on my bedroom door. Kelly's one-sided conversation was getting pretty stale.

I couldn't believe it when I heard, "Hey, Brett." Jennifer. She stood there smiling at me in the doorway for a second before she looked over at Kelly and smiled at him, too. Curiously. And then she said, looking at Kelly more than me, "I'm sorry—I didn't know you had a visitor."

I know Jennifer's pretty, but Kelly was looking at her as if he was starving and she was Thanksgiving dinner. And then he said something dumb like, "Don't mind me," and scooted over on my bed so Jennifer could sit down. Then he looked at me, and then at Jennifer, and then back at me expectantly, so I had to give in and said, "Jennifer, this is my friend Kelly." He was all, "Yeah, hi, I'm Kelly." I wanted to ask Kelly why he was acting like an idiot, but then Jennifer started talking to him, and when she said his whole name, he was all, "Yeah, that's me!" You should have seen how excited he got, just because she knew his stupid name. Just like a dog being offered a cookie.

Jennifer kept on smiling at Kelly while she said, "You play football, too, like Brett. I've seen your name in the football programs at Central." And then Kelly said, "Yeah—I'm a center." As if she had any idea what that meant. I rolled my eyes before I looked at Jennifer again. And guess what, Kitty? She was blushing! And then she looked at me, as if she all of a sudden remembered where she was and why she was sitting on my bed. She almost looked concerned when she asked me how I was feeling. I was wishing by then that they'd both just leave, but they didn't. Kelly kept talking to her, and she talked back and tried to get me into their stupid conversation, but I only answered in as few syllables as possible. I'd accidentally left that Mormon Bible Kelly gave me for Christmas on my nightstand last night, and when the conversation lulled, Jennifer picked it up and said to me, all grinning, "You've been holding out on me, Brett. Why didn't you tell me you're a Mormon, too?" I laughed in my most cynical way and said I most certainly was not a Mormon, but before I could say more, Kelly bored us all with, "But he's looking into it—I gave him that Book of Mormon last Christmas." So then the two of them had to go into ecstatics over the fact that both of them are Mormons, as if they're the only two

Mormons in the world! They were both starting to get on my nerves, and I guess they must have noticed, because Jennifer finally said, "Are you getting tired, Brett?" I could tell she wanted to ask me if I was going to be well enough to go to the dance, but she didn't, so I told her, "Yeah, I think I could stand some sleep right about now."

I stayed being mad and annoyed until Kelly called me fifteen minutes later, all worried that he'd "trespassed against me," or something. I wasn't up to discussing it, because by then I was feeling extremely lousy, and I told Kelly so. But an hour later, I called him back, because I'd had to be sick in the bathroom again, and I finally got it through my thick skull that there was no way I was going to the dance. So I had no choice but to go through the painful agony of asking Kelly if he'd take Jennifer to the dance for me. I just couldn't let her down after she and her mom made her dress and everything and she was so excited to go. I was hoping Kelly would be amazed that I'd want Jennifer to go to the dance without me, but that as my best friend, he'd say he just couldn't take the girl of my dreams to the dance I'd been so psyched about. And I was hoping Jennifer would feel the same way. But no. Do you know what Kelly had the nerve to say? He actually said he'd be "honored"—his exact stupid words—to take her. Probably too "honored." So I hurried and told him I needed to talk to Jennifer first. I was sure she'd say no and tell me how great I was for suggesting she go with Kelly instead, but she shocked me worse than Kelly did. Not only did she say she'd go with him, but she said she was "touched"—her actual words—that I would go out of my way to find another date for her. She kept saying I was "so sweet." I don't think I like being told anything I've done is "so sweet." I can't deny this sinking feeling that I've just done something incredibly stupid . . .

*October 26*

Dear Kitty,

Jennifer gave me a wallet-sized photo of her and Kelly's dance picture. She looked incredible, just like I knew she would. I'm going to find a picture of me so I can cut my head out of the picture and paste it over Kelly's face.

I'm basically well again, but I had to miss a game to get better. I'll be playing in the last game for October, though, so that'll be good . . .

## CHAPTER TWENTY-FIVE

I had my dream of Brett again last night. I hadn't been able to see what was in his hands the last time I'd had the dream, and as I looked down to see, he simply held out the object to me—a book— with that pleading look on his face. I could feel tears welling up in my eyes, and as if on cue, Brett quickly disappeared and I was awake, my heart pounding loudly in my chest.

I hadn't told anyone about my dreams of Brett. The whole experience had been too—strange. Thinking about the dreams had me sleep-walking my way through school all week long. Somehow—on automatic pilot, I guess—I made it through Honors English with the correct responses whenever Mrs. Dubois called my name. And drama—during class and my tutor sessions, as long as I let myself become my character and gave my memorization skills free reign, I made it through okay. Miss Goforth raised her eyebrow at me a few times, and Jason had a concerned frown that he directed at me during English when he caught me spacing off, but other than that, I did just fine. The end of each school day found me staring at the trophy case, searching Brett's grinning face for—everything. Anything.

It wasn't until I was alone in my room at night that I was able to focus on my dreams and wonder about the book Brett had tried to offer me. To relax, I slipped the *Rubber Soul* album onto the old turntable and pulled out Brett's journal hidden in my top bureau drawer to read while the Beatles softly sang to me.

I was sprawled on my stomach on my bed, Brett's journal in both hands, ready to read the opened page before me, but I could feel my eyes widening as I stared past the words—at the book itself—and a moment later, I'd slammed the book shut and flipped myself into a sitting position. *The book—Brett's book.*

"Of course—it has to be!" I said out loud, staring at the dark maroon cover of Brett's journal now gripped tightly in my hands. I hugged the journal and laughed softly over being excited to fall asleep that night. I even hoped I'd dream.

---

*October 31*

Dear Kitty,

Halloween. You looked so cute dressed like a little black kitten. The costume was my idea. What else would be appropriate for you to be? It was great to feel well enough to tote you all over the neighborhood trick-or-treating. I think your favorite part was refusing to talk and making me look like a dork while I said "trick or treat" at every house myself!

Now that my flu is over and I was able to help the team win another game, I'm basically back to my old self again. We're definitely in the quarter finals, which start next month. The whole school's pretty excited. It's been great, but it'd be even better if everything was going just as great with Jennifer. Now that the homecoming dance fiasco is over, we're basically okay again, but— I don't know. Things are different now. She asks about Kelly too much and always wants to set one of her friends up with him so we can double. And Alex—he's always telling me I'm pushing myself too hard in practice and when we work out after school. I'm okay now—why can't he get that through his thick skull? If only he'd get off my back . . .

# CHAPTER TWENTY-SIX

Since I'd been going out of my way to compliment Emily on her piano playing, she'd been drawing me pictures, all of which were religious. She was as sneaky as Jason, drawing pictures she knew would require me to ask her to explain, and in doing so, I usually received some religious instruction. Jason, of course, enjoyed the whole exchange.

When Emily opened the door for me that afternoon, she gave me a picture consisting of two young women and one young man, all in white and holding hands with musical notes around their heads. When I asked her to explain her picture to me, she calmly stated that it was herself and Jason and I singing together in heaven, "Before we were born, when we were all friends together." I thanked her for her very interesting drawing and carefully tucked it inside one of my notebooks, thankful she'd given me this one when I first came in, rather than after I'd joined Jason for tutoring.

We were studying Langston Hughes's poetry this week, and in particular, both Jason and I had been focusing on his poem "Harlem" for our papers. I tried to keep my mind on my paper, but one line of the poem kept repeating like a broken record, over and over in my head:

*"What happens to a dream deferred?"*

I didn't realize how long I'd been thinking about that line until Jason looked up at me.

"What?"

"Nothing." I quickly looked down at my paper. Jason was silent until I dared to look up again. I wasn't surprised to see he was still looking at me. And obviously waiting.

"What?" I said, as innocently as possible.

"Since you've been staring at my leg now for, oh, at least five, ten minutes straight, I know the right answer isn't 'nothing.'"

I wasn't sure how to say what I'd been thinking—what I'd been thinking for a long time and had been neatly and strongly summed up in Langston Hughes's poem. What *had* happened to Jason's dream deferred? It'd been weeks since his injury. Central's football team had been winning games like crazy and was now ready for the playoff finals. Without Jason. I didn't know how he could stand going to the games, but go he did. And it wasn't just at the games that he seemed to be in a good mood. It was *all* the time. I never saw him in a bad mood. Not at school and not during tutoring, either. I couldn't believe he could stay so—happy.

I voiced my thoughts as well as I could, stumbling along as he continued to watch me. "Knowing you, I guess you're going to tell me it's because of your religion, huh?" I tried to laugh and lighten the mood, but Jason was looking at me too seriously. He finally set his book and paper aside and leaned towards me.

"First of all, Kathy, believe me when I say that I'm not in a good mood every second over this." Jason pointed at his knee. "This knee injury is the hardest thing I've ever had to go through. Yeah, I guess my football dream *is* being deferred. Who knows—maybe I'll never live my dream of playing professional football someday. I've messed my knee up before, and as bad as this injury is, it's hard to say if I'll ever play again. I hate thinking about it, but that doesn't make the question go away. I could let myself get really bitter, but I can't shake the feeling I've had from day one that there's a reason this injury happened to me. That I'm supposed to learn something from all of this."

"And what *have* you learned?" I asked, setting my own book aside.

Jason smiled. "How to deal with disappointment. Patience, for another. And I think maybe God has a different plan in mind for me than the one I'm following."

A different plan. From God, no less. That was definitely interesting.

"Besides—all these things shall give me experience, and shall be for my good." Jason smiled then as if he was sharing a private "ah ha" with himself that I didn't understand.

"Amazing. Did you think that up yourself?"

Jason laughed. "Hardly. That's from the Doctrine and Covenants."

"Oh. Book of Mormon stuff."

"No, Doctrine and Covenants is a different book of scripture."

"There's more?"

Jason grinned. "There's always more, Kathy. That's what's so great."

"Hmmm." I sat back in my chair and folded my arms while Jason continued to smile at me in a way that was making me feel uncomfortable. Pleasantly uncomfortable.

"Hey, Jason!"

As if on cue, Angela bounced her way into the room, crashing and destroying the moment. Our time was about up anyway, so I quickly scrambled my books and papers together and made a hasty departure. I was busy fumbling with my car keys outside—

"Kathy! Hey, Kathy! Wait up a second!"

*Angela.* I slowly turned to face her, pasting a nice fake smile on my face.

"You were in such a hurry, you dropped this."

I looked at the paper she was waving in her hand as she bounced over to me. A crayon drawing. Emily's crayon drawing. Of Jason, Emily, and me holding hands and singing together.

"Oh, yeah. Emily made that for me. Thanks." I reached to snatch it from her, but she neatly pulled it away from my grasp to study it.

"It's an interesting picture. Did she tell you what it's about?"

"Oh, she said something about it being a picture of me and her and . . . Jason . . . in heaven. Before we were born."

"Oh, cute." But I could tell she didn't think it was cute at all.

"You know, it's just a drawing. By a kid. I mean—if you're worried about me coming over here to help Jason, nothing's going on or anything like that—"

Before I could continue, Angela laughed. "Oh, I know! I know you're *just* Jason's tutor! He's told me. I know how much he needs your help to get through English. He'd do practically *anything* to get your help." Angela continued to babble, hardly stopping for a breath. "And I know he's been teaching you stuff, too. Jason just *loves* sharing the gospel with anyone who'll listen! And he's good at getting just about anyone *to* listen! I think it's really cool that he's teaching you about our church. He's going to be such a great missionary someday."

I felt my insides go colder than ice while my own fake smile froze on my face. Angela turned with a quick "See ya!" and bounced triumphantly back into Jason's house, shutting the door firmly behind her.

———

I couldn't stop fuming over my thirty-second conversation with Angela the rest of the evening and into the night. But far worse than having to deal with Angela face to face was thinking about what she'd said. Or, more important, what she'd insinuated. And even more amazing, that I even cared. *Just Jason's tutor.* Well, I supposed she was right. After all, Jason had come to me looking for a tutor, not a friend. Certainly not a girlfriend. In fact, I'd known he and Angela had a *thing* before I'd ever agreed to tutor him. Plus, he hadn't made any real move towards me since the homecoming dance fiasco. And it wasn't that shocking that he liked talking about his religion with me. I knew Mormons were encouraged to share their religion with others. I'd seen the commercials on TV.

In the end, though, after raging and mulling everything over since I'd come home, I was forced to acknowledge that for all of my sarcasm and joking and acting like Jason was a real pain in my behind, the awful truth was that I didn't want to believe that all I was to Jason was just a tutor and someone to preach his religion to. I didn't want to believe that beyond the obvious and necessary tutoring, everything else was only because Jason wanted to convert me to his religion. I wouldn't believe it. I couldn't!

And then I wondered what Jason would do if I told him I wasn't interested in his religion, and that I would never be baptized in a million years, and for him to please stop telling me everything about it. Would he drop me as a tutor? I shook my head at that thought. Probably not. He wanted that final A too much. But would he treat me the same? Or would he turn cold and drop me flat on my behind to go hunt down another victim to preach to? Or would he still be friends with me? Would he even want to be?

I sat up straight in bed at that thought. *Friends?* Were Jason and I even friends? To be truthful, I didn't know *what* we really were. I was his tutor—he was a more than willing student. He'd worked hard and done his best. Truly. And he'd improved. Not just in his paper scores, but in other ways, too. He didn't talk like a jock so much anymore and was getting used to using words with more than one or two syllables. He'd even discovered there were other descriptive words besides *cool* and *awesome*. It was definitely gratifying to see that stuff I was teaching him was rubbing off on him as much as what he was trying to teach me was sticking to my brain. And the way he teased me and grinned at me and just looked at me—I was sure it added up to more than just flirting.

But none of that changed the fact that Angela's words had stung. Hurt, even. And I hated that they did, because I shouldn't care what a jock thought of me. Not even if the jock was Jason.

*But I did care.* The tears that were now on my pillowcase bore silent witness to that fact.

---

*November 15*

Dear Kitty,

Tomorrow's the semifinals. I had a fever a few days ago that had Mom driving me in a panic to the hospital, but I've really rested up, so I'm fine now. Kelly and I threw the football around today for a while before my elbow started to ache, and then after running to catch Kelly's passes to me, my knees started to hurt. I didn't want Kelly to know, so I said I was hungry, and why didn't we go get something to eat? I forced myself to choke down every bite of food. I wasn't feeling too good, so it took all of my energy to eat like a horse. I was sick to my stomach and wiped out by the time Kelly left, so I crashed for the rest of the day. Don't worry, though, Kitty. Your big brother will do you proud at the game tomorrow . . .

*November 22*

Dear Kitty,

This past week has gone by in a total blur. I'm still in shock—I can't tell you how amazing it feels to have a major dream come true. We won, Kitty! We won! Not just semifinals last week, but as of tonight, our school's the state high school football champions—I still can't believe it! I mean, I know I've worked hard—really hard—and so has the rest of the team, so I know we deserve this, but to finally reach this goal—it's an amazing feeling. It's incredible to make it to a place you've been dreaming about your whole life. So now I've accomplished another goal—and in front of the school, Jennifer, you, Mom, and Dad—and tons of university talent scouts too! They're saying I'm the one to watch next year! I tell you, Kitty, if it all ended tonight, I've had so much I could die happy.

Although the game was exciting, it was grueling. The other

team—South High Panthers—was incredibly good. They were just as determined to win as we were. We'd set up for a play, and the Panthers' defensive line would set up in just the perfect formation to ruin our play, so I'd have to signal everyone to cancel out the play and run a backup plan. Adrenaline was running all over the field, and with the score tied and not much time remaining in the last quarter, I took a major chance by substituting an old play for the fancy new play we were supposed to run. The old play—something you hardly ever see anymore—was the ol' Statue of Liberty play. We set up in a single wing formation, and once the ball was snapped, we had the defensive line faked into thinking we were going to move down one side of the field, but as I lifted my arm as if to throw the ball, one of the flanker guys on my right who was out by himself made a huge sweep, running behind me just as I had my arm up in perfect position to throw, looking a little like the Statue of Liberty. The Panthers were hounding Alex, who looked like he was in the perfect position to catch my pass—and then my flanker snuck up behind me and grabbed the football out of my hand. Before the Panthers realized what had happened, he'd already made his way through a lot of their defensive line, and seconds later, we made a touchdown! So without having to go into overtime, we won the game! Good thing, too, because Coach didn't want me to use an old play like that, but at the time, it felt right. Coach usually trusts my instincts, but he hates resorting to old stunts like that play. But it worked, so now we're big heroes! And having you there was incredible. My inspiration at all times! I'm so glad Mom and Dad brought you. I guess the reason I'm boring you with all of this football talk now is partly because I'm just way too excited to have won state, and partly so that you can experience a little of that day yourself now and know that you were there, and a part of it all. And that you played a major role in getting me here. Thank you for that, Kitty . . .

# CHAPTER TWENTY-SEVEN

I couldn't stop staring at the back of Jason's head during Honors English the next day. Angela's obnoxious remarks the day before still rankled. A lot. Jason must've felt my stare, because he turned around to look my way quite a few times during class. The first time he smiled, but after seeing my scowl, his smile faded, and each time he looked at me after that, he frowned questioningly instead.

After class, I dodged fast around Jason and his crutches with the rest of the herd of students as I hurried out the door. Final costume fittings for our Shakespeare festival were taking place after lunch, so after inhaling a sandwich, I hustled out of the cafeteria for the drama room. I'd made it to the end of the hall when Jason's voice stopped me.

"Kathy—hold up a second, will you?"

I waited until he'd limped over to me before speaking. "What do you want?"

"Nothing. Are you okay?" Jason's eyes were probing me—a habit of his I really hated.

"Me? I'm fine. Why?"

Jason shook his head, his eyes glued to my face. "You don't seem fine to me."

"Well, I am. Don't worry about me, okay?"

"Okay, fine." Jason gave me a baffled look before he turned to limp back down the hall. I pivoted to continue towards the drama room, but again, his voice had us both turning back around. "Hey, well—in case I don't see you again today, good luck on Monday."

Monday? I stared stupidly at Jason before saying the word myself.

"The Shakespeare festival. Remember? I can't believe *you* could've forgotten!"

His chuckling was irritating. My heart beating erratically as it always did around him was irritating. "I didn't forget. In fact, I'm heading for my last costume fitting right now."

Jason raised an eyebrow. "Oh yeah? Well—good luck. I know you'll do great."

"Thanks," I said grudgingly back.

"So, I guess I'll see you Monday?" He was still probing me with his eyes, so I took a deep breath and faced him squarely with my arms folded.

"Sure. During Honors English, of course. As far as after school goes, though, if you want to hang out with Angela at your house, fine, but don't expect me to come by for tutoring if she's going to be there." I turned sharp on my heel and walked fast and purposefully down the hall, a satisfied smirk on my face at the sight of Jason's mouth hanging open behind me.

---

*December 10*

Dear Kitty,

This morning I found some bruises on my legs. I tried to tell Mom they were just from playing state and all the games leading up to it, because I *had* been bashed around on the field pretty good. Besides, I feel fine, and I am in remission, so why is everyone starting to tiptoe around me again? Worst of all, Mom is making me go see Dr. Grenville this week . . .

*December 13*

Dear Kitty,

It's the thirteenth. It figures. I went to Dr. Grenville's for more tests, thanks to these stupid bruises not going away and the fact that my elbows and knees won't stop aching.

I'm out of remission.

# CHAPTER TWENTY-EIGHT

I couldn't sleep all Sunday night, just knowing Monday was the Big Day—the day I'd either make a fool of myself before the whole school and go from being invisible to being the school geek, famous for all the wrong reasons—or, possibly, maybe I *wouldn't*.

Honors English was among the first group of classes to see our Shakespeare festival. I'd hoped we'd have a chance to go over the whole show at least once before performing it in front of my class—and Jason—but that wasn't going to happen. At least both of my costumes were amazing, which helped. My Cordelia costume for the *King Lear* scene was a flowing, light, glowy white gown that whispered along the floor as I moved. Miss Goforth had put me in white with a gold circlet on my unbound and loosely-curled hair, while Goneril and Regan were dressed in heavy dark purple and blue gowns with their hair swept up in fancy do's topped by gold circlets, to visually illustrate I was the youngest of the three princess sisters, and the good, pure, truthful daughter with nothing to hide.

I wasn't one to wear very much makeup, but the girl posing as a makeup artist for the drama class insisted on putting some on my face. "So the lights on the stage don't wash you out completely," was her excuse. Once she'd finished painting and drawing all over my face, she stepped back with a grin. "Take a look, Kathy. Or should I say, 'Cordelia'?"

I turned in the dressing room to look at the whole effect in my portion of the wall-length mirror, and while Goneril, Regan, and the rest of the girls gasped, even *I* had to take a step back. *Was that really me?* It definitely didn't look like me. I looked too—*pretty.* And too royal. King Lear did a double take when he saw me and pursed his lips for a low wolf whistle. I arched an eyebrow back at him in my most ice princess way. "Now, is that appropriate for a royal father? We *are* doing *King Lear,* you know, not *Oedipus Rex!*"

Lear continued to, well, *leer* at me. "Yeah, well. You look amazing."

The Earl of Kent looked me up and down before folding his arms to rub his chin slowly with one hand and said, "Hey, aren't Kent and Cordelia supposed to kiss during this scene?"

I laughed. "I didn't see anything in the script about kissing."

Kent shrugged and grinned. "Well, it's all about interpretation. I'm sure during this scene while Kent stands up for Cordelia, Shakespeare *meant* to have Cordelia thank him—*really* thank him. I think it would add to the scene. In fact, I think we ought to practice right now—"

Kent grabbed me around the waist, but before he could completely swoop down on me, Miss Goforth opened the door to the backstage area and clapped her hands. "Enough—everyone quiet down! Students are already seating themselves, so we'll be starting in a few minutes. Those in the *King Lear* opening scene, come inside and take your places behind the curtain."

I hurried inside with the others in my scene to stand behind the curtain and wait for my moment to walk onto our little drama room stage while Miss Goforth gave a speech about our drama class's effort to introduce everyone to the Shakespeare plays that would be studied in English after Christmas.

The Earl of Gloucester's Bastard Son Edmund bumped me in the shoulder and winked at me. "You look awesome, Kathy. Really incredible. Good luck out there!"

"Yeah, you, too." I smiled shakily back and took a few deep breaths. I caught a final look at myself in the mirror backstage before I made my big entrance. One last glance at my transformation, and I knew I wasn't me anymore. I was Cordelia. When I heard Gloucester say, "The king is coming!" Cordelia, holding her head high as a princess should, walked slowly and calmly on stage with King Lear, Regan and Cornwall, and Goneril and Albany.

I listened intently to the others until I spoke my first line: "What shall Cordelia speak? Love, and be silent." I said the words as an aside to the audience, amazed that everyone was so quiet and actually paying attention, and in doing so, I caught a pair of wide, dark blue eyes fixing me with an intense, *captivated* look. It was Jason, who had seated himself firmly in the middle of the front row, looking at me—Cordelia—in a way I'd never imagined possible for him to ever look at *me*—Kathy. Ever.

But then it was my turn to respond. Again, as an aside to the audience: "Then poor Cordelia! And yet, not so, since I am sure my love's / More ponderous than my tongue." This time, I didn't let myself look at Jason, and as my next lines consisted of speaking back and forth with King Lear, I let Cordelia take over and allowed myself to believe we were all in Britain, that this long ago moment was reality and nothing else mattered.

The loud, sincere clapping when we finished made me jump. Jason pounded his hands together the loudest, grinning up at me with a look on his face that made me feel pretty, and self-conscious, and just a jumble of a lot of things at once. And then I was backstage changing into my second costume. I took my time, since my nearly-solo scene was to be the last one performed. I'd been shocked when Miss Goforth told me on Friday while I twirled in front of her in my costume.

"Perfect. Just perfect. Especially since you're going to be the big finale."

My mouth had dropped open. "I'm going to be *what?*"

Miss Goforth had answered me calmly. "Your scene will be the last one performed at our Shakespeare festival."

"*Me?* I can't—why—?"

Miss Goforth had waved her hand to shush me. "Yes, you. And yes, you can. And, quite honestly, because your scene is the best. I'd be foolish not to finish with the best scene."

"But—"

I knew when Miss Goforth made up her mind about something, there was no changing it. "Don't argue with me. You're doing your scene last, and that's final."

I smiled into the mirror in the dressing room. For this character, I'd plaited my hair into a loose braid with a dark red skull cap on the back of my head. The dress was dark red as well with tight sleeves that fanned out slightly at my wrists, and puffed a bit at my shoulders. The bodice was high and tight fitting with criss-crossing ribbons tying up the front. Tiny stripes of gold thread ran down the dress, sparkling in the light when I moved. It was a gorgeous gown, and again, I felt like I'd been transformed.

Although I was excited, congratulating everyone who entered and exited the stage, I couldn't stop my heart from hammering. But I knew my lines, and more important than that, I knew this character. I *knew* I could be her.

And then, the curtain opened on my scene, and I was Juliet. Romeo's Juliet.

"My dismal scene I must act alone. Come, vial. What if this mixture do not work at all? Shall I be married then tomorrow morning? No, no! This shall forbid it." As I spoke, I fell under the spell I was weaving and agonized aloud over what could happen. "What if it be poison which the friar subtly hath minist'red to have me dead?" Or worse, "How if, when I am laid into the tomb, I wake before the time that Romeo come to redeem me?" What if I were to "die strangled ere my Romeo comes?

Or, if I live, is it not very like," considering the horrible place I was in—a vault where the dead lie moldering and decaying, "is it not like that I, So early waking—what with loathsome smells," yes, shouldn't I be upset—go crazy, even, and "madly play with my forefathers' joints," and likely in a rage, "with some great kinsman's bone as with a club dash out my despr'rate brains?" Oh, the horror of it all! And look—"methinks I see cousin's ghost seeking out Romeo, that did spit his body upon a rapier's point. Stay, Tybalt, stay! Romeo, I come! This do I drink to thee." And as the potion slid down my throat, I sank upon my bed, my eyes closing to everything around me.

There was dead silence for a few seconds. I could almost believe I truly was drunk with the potion I'd ingested, fading slowly into unconsciousness. But then loud, fast clapping—even some whistling—erupted, and I slowly sat up to look out at the audience. Jason was staring at me as if he'd never seen me before, but he recovered fast and clapped and smiled broadly. A second later he'd grabbed his crutches and was on his feet.

I shakily jumped off the table draped with a large fancy blanket and pillows as my bed and curtsied to the incredibly kind audience of my peers before the curtains drew together. The loud clapping and cheering rang in my ears, and while the rest of the drama class who'd been watching backstage cheered and clapped me on the back and went nuts over how "incredible" I was, I was grinning like mad inside. *You're right, Brett—being on stage is an amazing rush!*

We did it all again before lunch—this time with fewer jitters and fewer mistakes—and had a blast. Word spread that our scenes were pretty spectacular, so each time we performed we did better and better, and the drama room became more and more crowded with spectators.

At lunch, we were allowed to go to the cafeteria and grab a quick bite before we had to hustle back into our costumes. I had my Cordelia hair and makeup on when I spotted Mistie and Crystal excitedly waving to me from a table near the back of the lunchroom. I smiled and moved forward with my lunch tray—but was brought up short. By some guy I didn't even know.

"Hey—Kathy, isn't it?"

I frowned at the stranger who stood in my path. "Yes, I'm Kathy."

The unknown but very cute blond guy in front of me grinned. "I'm Dallin."

"Hi." I smiled shyly back, wondering what he could possibly want to talk to me about.

Dallin continued to grin. "Hi. Hey, great job on the plays you did today."

*A compliment? From a stranger?* I stuttered out a "Thanks!" before he winked and left me standing there staring in shock at his nicely broad back as he walked out of the lunchroom.

I didn't have much time to be stunned over being stopped by a very cute someone I didn't even know, because it happened again. This time, a few girls called out, "Hey, Juliet—good job!" And then a few other guys stopped me before I could finally sit down with my friends.

"Being hounded by your public, Miss Superstar?" Mistie teased.

Crystal turned to Mistie and sighed dramatically. "Just think, Mistie, we'll be able to say we knew her when!"

"Yeah—don't forget us little people when you're rich and famous!"

"Oh, please—"

A second later, both King Lear and Kent had swooped down to squeeze in on either side of me at our table.

"Hey, Kath!" King Lear shocked me by casually draping an arm around my shoulders. "You were amazing as Cordelia, but I can't get over that *Romeo and Juliet* scene. That was incredible!"

"How come you didn't choose to do the balcony scene instead? I would've helped you out." Kent winked and grinned.

"I don't know—I just liked this scene better, I guess."

King Lear guffawed. "She'd rather 'die' than do an action scene with you!"

Kent gave Lear a hard smile back. "Good one. You were almost funny. For once."

King Lear still had his arm around me. "You're going to try out for the next play, aren't you, Kath? We might do *Barefoot in the Park*—or *Charlie's Aunt*. Something great, anyway."

I nodded at them both. "Yeah, I'll probably try out."

"Make sure that you do!" Kent grinned one more time into my eyes before leaning over to poke Lear. "Well, we've got to go get ready, so we better take off now. See you backstage, Kath!" Kent gave me a slug in the arm and winked again.

King Lear squeezed my shoulders before finally removing his arm from around my shoulders. And then both of them high-fived me before they left. After they were safely out of earshot, Mistie and Crystal leaned towards me, trying not to giggle out of control. Both had looked like they were about to explode from the moment Lear and Kent had sat down practically in my lap. I gave them each a kick under the table and leaned forward. "What is *wrong* with you guys?"

"Granted, the whole lunchroom has been sneaking looks at you— especially the guys—but *someone* in particular was watching you with your drama honeys." Crystal grinned.

"Someone who wasn't thrilled at *all* to see them hanging all over you!" Mistie added.

"Hold on—" Crystal gasped. "Angela's leaving the lunchroom. Alone! She doesn't look very happy." Her eyes grew larger as she gasped out, "Watch out—here he comes now!"

I quickly glanced behind me and saw Jason moving in easy, fast strides with his crutches towards our table. I hardly had a second to marvel at how well and fast he could move on those things before he was there, balanced in front of us.

"Hey, Kathy." Jason smiled at me, only this time, his smile was different. Definitely different.

"Hey, Jason." I could barely hear my words over my heart pounding loudly, but I managed a smile back and wondered if mine looked any different to him.

"Mind if I sit down?"

Sit down? By *me*? *Here*? "Yes! I mean—no! No, of course I don't mind—" Jason couldn't be sitting at my table. With me. A popular jock like him, with someone like *me*? Even if I *was* his tutor. It just wasn't *done*.

"So—I just wanted to tell you how great you were in those plays."

"Thanks—I'm glad it wasn't boring for you."

"Boring?" Jason shook his head in surprise. "No way. I liked it all. But your stuff was the best. How come you weren't in more of them?"

I decided not to mention my sordid drama past. "Just didn't want to overload myself, since this stuff is all new to me."

"Well, you were incredible. Absolutely."

I had to hide a grin behind my milk carton as I watched Jason stare down any guy who approached our table. It was both amusing and empowering to watch Jason try to hold a stiff smile on his face as I was congratulated again and again—and even received a few winks. Jason was sitting so close to me that I could see just how blue his eyes were, without any flecks of green or yellow or any other color. Solid blue. In fact, they almost looked violet, they were so dark. An uncomfortable yet pleasant feeling tumbled around in my stomach, and I knew I couldn't eat another mouthful.

Both Mistie and Crystal were standing now, reaching for their trays and wishing me good luck before giving me a thumbs up behind Jason's back.

I waved a firm good-bye to their giggling faces before pushing my chair back. "I better go, too—I've got to get back into costume."

"You're putting the plays on tonight, aren't you?"

"Yeah, at seven."

Jason nodded. "Then I guess you probably won't have time to tutor me tonight."

"No, not tonight," I agreed.

Jason nodded again. "That's cool. I understand. But—I hope you're planning on coming over tomorrow at four for tutoring."

I hesitated for a moment. "I don't know. Three's a crowd—"

"Then I'll make sure Emily leaves us alone," Jason finished firmly.

"I wasn't thinking of Emily."

"She's the only one you'd have to worry about."

*Only Emily?* I couldn't help staring at Jason's determined face. "You're sure about that?"

Jason nodded again. Firmly. "I'm sure. Absolutely."

I nodded slowly back. "If you can guarantee that, then I'll be there."

"Then I'll see you tomorrow at four."

"Okay, then." I waited for Jason to get his crutches in order before I smiled. "Well, wish me luck."

Jason smiled back. "You don't need luck. You've got talent. That's better than luck."

I wasn't sure if I believed I had that much talent, but I did know that I was liking getting up on that stage. It was hard to believe that I'd been so scared I was sick to my stomach that morning. Never mind the fact that I'd eaten my lunch with Jason in the school cafeteria in front of everyone, and at the same time, had been guaranteed our tutoring sessions wouldn't be crashed anymore. By anyone. *Amazing.*

———

The afternoon sets went even better than the morning ones. I couldn't wait to tell my family at dinner.

"So, Kathy, how'd your Shakespeare festival go today?" Dad brought up the subject seconds after Alex and Sam and their families had arrived and we'd all sat down to eat.

"Not only did it go great, but I had so much fun—I can't believe after tonight it's going to be all over."

"Didn't I tell you you'd love drama? I love it when I'm right!" Sam gloated while she fed spoonfuls of yogurt to Curtis. "Admit it, Kathy—I was right!"

Alex grinned and poked me with his butter knife. "Don't get too mad at her, Kathy. She's allowed to gloat a little, since she's hardly ever right about anything." Everyone laughed at that—except Sam, of course—and looked in my direction, obviously waiting for me to slam her with some cutting remark to ruin her moment of triumph, but I just smiled at them all seated in a circle around the table with me. Nothing could ruin my good mood today.

"I'm not mad. In fact, Sam, I guess I ought to thank you."

Sam's fork froze halfway to her mouth before she was able to choke out, "*Thank* me?"

I grinned. "For making me sign up for drama. I'm so glad I've had the chance to be a part of it—and whatever else will be happening for the rest of the year. All the plays, the musical—everything. So thank you." I didn't think that mini speech of mine was worthy of silence, but nobody moved or spoke for a few strange, electric seconds.

"Well, I guess congratulations are in order, Kathy." Everybody jumped at Mom's dry sounding voice, rising unusually loud out of the silence.

I turned and frowned at her. "Congratulations?"

Mom nodded back and grinned at everyone. "I think you're officially the first, and most likely the only, person who's ever been able to render Sam completely and utterly speechless!"

---

When I stepped into the girls' dressing room that night to get ready for our last performance, I wasn't surprised to find all the girls from my drama class giggling and talking excitedly and loudly. And running around like headless chickens. What I wasn't expecting, though, was to see what was resting on my dressing table. Smack in the middle and taking up a lot of space.

Flowers. A big bouquet of all kinds and colors, including several red roses. And they smelled absolutely incredible. I was sure they were just from my family as I slipped the tiny envelope out of the flowers—but that was before I actually opened it and read the card:

*For the best Cordelia or Juliet I've ever seen. Break a leg—just don't blow out your knee. Jason.*

---

I guess because we all knew this was our last chance to perform our Shakespeare festival, every scene went amazingly well. When the moment came for me to sink into unconsciousness as Juliet on my table bed, even with all the loud cheering and clapping, I felt sad knowing it was all over. After sweeping off the table to curtsy and bow for the applause, I was joined by the rest of the drama class for more bowing and curtsying before dragging Miss Goforth on stage to present her with roses. And then we were bombarded by our families and friends who rushed the stage to get to all of us.

Alex got to me first, grabbing me off my feet in a huge bear hug to sweep me around in a circle, laughing and babbling about how great an actress I was.

"Good grief! Put her down before you break one of her ribs!" Sam fought her way through the crowd and shoved Alex aside to hesitantly stand before me as if waiting for a cue.

"Well, are you going to hug her or just stand there?" Alex gave her a nudge, and a second later I was hugging my sister and she was hugging me back. Sam pulled away first to look at me, holding me at arm's length by the shoulders.

"So—did I embarrass the Colton family name too much?"

Sam gave me a little shake. "Really, Kathy! How can you say that?"

"You thought I did okay, then?"

"More than okay. When I think of where my acting talent was as a sophomore compared to you—I think I positively hate you!"

I laughed and hugged her again. From Sam, that was a true compliment.

While she was still hugging me, she whispered in my ear, "Is King Lear hot or what?!"

"Sam!" I gasped.

"I'm just looking—nothing more!" Sam insisted with a wide grin.

"Okay—enough—it's *our* turn now!" Mom and Dad finally made it to the stage, and after getting another huge, rib-cracking hug from Dad, I turned to Mom, who had teared up, blubbering about how proud she was of me, while she clutched me in a hug.

"Hey, Kathy! Congratulations—you were amazing!"

*Jason.* Jason's voice! I couldn't believe he was here—but of course, he'd brought the flowers. My heart pounded as I whirled to face him. He grinned at me while Emily clung to him around his crutches, looking up at me shyly. I gave Jason a brief smile and thanks before bending down to Emily's level.

"Hi, Emily! Did you enjoy the plays?"

Emily nodded, her eyes all big and round.

A moment later, Mom came up by my elbow and with a big, overly polite smile said, "Kathy, aren't you going to introduce us to your—friend?"

I turned from Jason to each family member in turn. "Mom—Dad—this is Jason. And his little sister, Emily." I quickly made the rounds of introducing him to the rest of my family, alternately impressed and disgruntled that he didn't seem as uncomfortable meeting them as I had been meeting his family that day in the hospital.

"So you're Jason, the student Kathy's been tutoring?" Mom hadn't stopped eyeing him as if she expected him to sprout horns and charge us all at any given moment.

Jason smiled and nodded. "I've been really lucky to have Kathy for my tutor."

Mom arched her eyebrows. "I hope you're allowing Kathy to truly tutor you in English during your hour together."

"Mom!" I gasped.

But Jason didn't let that fade his smile or his impressively polite behavior while Mom shushed me with a dark, hard look. "I really appreciate you and Mr. Colton allowing Kathy to come over to tutor me after school. I have physical therapy for my knee at one in the afternoons, so it's really helped me a lot that Kathy's been able to come over after school instead."

Mom relaxed slightly, but only slightly. "I see. Well, I'm glad Kathy's been of help to you. It was very nice meeting you. And your sister, of course."

I could tell Mom was trying to dismiss him, but to Jason's credit, he didn't slink away. I turned to the rest of my family, who were watching the two of us with way too much interest and excused myself from them for a minute to talk to Jason and Emily alone.

"Jason—I just wanted to say thank you for the flowers. You didn't have to do that!"

Jason smiled warmly at me. "I know, but I wanted to."

"Well—it was a wonderful surprise. Actually, more of a shock. But a good shock!"

Jason kept on smiling. "I'm glad you liked them."

And I kept babbling idiotically. "I did—I do! Very much."

Emily reached up then and tugged on my gown. "Are you coming over to help Jason tomorrow, Kathy? 'Cause you didn't come today."

I laughed and tugged her ponytail. "Yes, Emily. I'll be back on schedule tomorrow."

Emily smiled broadly. "Good!"

Jason nodded towards my family. "Your family's waiting, so I'll see you tomorrow."

"Okay—see you tomorrow, Jason. And thanks again—you know. For the flowers."

Jason smiled again. "You're welcome."

After Jason hobbled out of the drama room with Emily waving at me happily beside him, Dad was the first to recover.

"So that's the young man you've been tutoring." Dad poked me in the side with a teasing grin that I knew was just the beginning of my family's torture.

"He's also the one who's been filling Kathy's head with a bunch of religious nonsense—"

"Please, Mom—" I didn't have to beg for long, because Dad stepped in to cut her off.

"Honey, please. Let's not ruin Kathy's big moment, okay?" I don't know who was more shocked at Dad's interruption—Mom or me. Dad put his arm around Mom's shoulders. "He looks like a nice enough young man. He could be a lot worse. Let's just be grateful he isn't."

Mom clamped her lips shut tight in a firm line while Sam stepped forward, rubbing her hands together. With glee. "Well, well, well. No wonder you went back to tutoring him. And no wonder you said yes in the first place! Did I say King Lear was a hottie? Because he's cold compared to Jason the Studman!"

"Sam, please!"

"Just calling it as I see it. And believe me, there's plenty to see!"

"Stop!"

"Eye candy for me, and great eye *and* arm candy for you!"

I groaned. "I think I'm going to be sick—"

Sam laughed. "I don't know why you're getting so upset! I thought you'd be thrilled to have such a hot guy after you."

*After* me? "Jason isn't 'after' me. I'm just his English tutor."

Sam turned to Alex for support. "Oh, yeah? What do you think, Alex?"

Alex grinned. "Speaking from experience, Kathy, it's pretty obvious he thinks of you as more than just his English tutor."

*What?* This from Alex? "What makes you think that?"

Alex laughed. "Why else would he make the effort to come watch this again? And on crutches, no less! Besides—I saw the way he looked at you. A guy doesn't look at a girl who's just his English tutor the way he was looking at you."

"What do you mean?" I demanded.

Alex demonstrated how Jason had looked at me, horrifically exaggerated, making Jason out to be a wolf with his tongue lolling out to the side, ready to howl at the moon.

"See? I told you he likes you!" Sam gasped, exploding with laughter.

I decided to keep my mouth shut about the flowers. No need to upset Mom and wind up Alex and Sam higher than they already were. Especially since I knew I was nothing more than a tutor Jason enjoyed preaching religion to. A tutor he'd felt obligated to send flowers to in order to make sure she'd feel obligated to keep tutoring him. A tutor who'd just happened to impress him with her until now unknown acting talent. That was all. I couldn't let myself hope for anything more than that.

---

*December 14*

Dear Kitty,

I saw Jennifer on my way out of the exam room yesterday. I pretended not to hear her when she said, "Hi, Brett." I drove around town forever before I came home. Mom would've screamed if she'd seen how fast I was driving. It's kind of amazing I didn't get in a wreck, because the road and everything looked so blurry.

I feel like someone's slugged me really hard. Not in the stomach. In the heart. And whatever it is that's hit me hasn't taken its fist out of my chest yet. I've been lying here staring at the walls all day,

having all kinds of drugs pumped into me, but it hasn't made anything change, or lessened the force of anything. I think this time
was worse than hearing about it the first time around. Dr.
Grenville's face looked sad and old when he gave me the news.

"I'm so sorry . . ." I'm sick of sorrys.

I can be honest with you, Kitty. I don't want to face everything
again. I don't know if I can. When everything first happened, I'd
thought it was going to be tough to face death and dying, but
believe me, Kitty, it's equally as hard to try to face life and the living
when you know you're dying. And now, after kidding myself into
thinking I was basically cured, I have to face everything all over
again. The worst part is that I don't think I have the strength to do
this again.

Only Mom, Dad, Sam, and Alex know I'm sick again. I've made
them swear not to tell anyone. It's bad enough that my family's
Christmas is ruined—I don't want to ruin anyone else's.

Kelly would be disappointed. I haven't prayed since I found out
I was out of remission . . .

---

I'd fallen asleep with the Beatles album playing on the turntable,
and when my dreams began, I dreamed of Brett. This time, when he
turned around to pleadingly hold out the book he'd been hugging
tightly to his chest as he had before, I tried to answer him.

*The journal—your journal—*

But instead of getting the relieved, happy smile I'd been expecting
to see, he sadly shook his head, and again, he held the book out to me.

*I have your book, Brett—I do—*

Brett only shook his head again, his eyes asking me to please understand.

But I didn't. And the more he tried, the more frustrated I became,
until I could feel tears welling up in my eyes, and like he always did, he

quickly disappeared. I woke up just as quickly with wet eyes to the sound of the needle on the record player's arm softly whirring against the middle of the spinning record.

## CHAPTER TWENTY-NINE

No matter how much time passed, I hadn't been able to stop thinking about Angela's comments that all I was to Jason was a tutor and someone to preach his religion to. Not a real friend at all. Nothing more than a tutor. Ever. And then the Shakespeare festival happened—and Jason was looking at me so differently than he had before. Almost as if he might . . . But that was crazy, so I pushed that half-formed thought far into the back of my mind. And those flowers—obligation flowers. That's all they could be, even though the bouquet was huge and had roses in it. Roses! And they were red, too. Not white or yellow.

I had to give myself a mental shake for that thought. It was unlikely that Jason had the slightest inkling of the meaning of a red rose versus the other colors. But still—it had been really sweet of him to send the flowers. And infuriating. And confusing. And I was sure I was making far too big a deal over everything than I should.

I didn't know what to expect from Jason. Although the next two sessions of tutoring at his home were thankfully Angela-free, filled with a warmer, lighter form of teasing than usual, nothing else seemed to have changed. I'd been stewing over all of this on Thursday while Jason read his paper for our next English assignment on Nathaniel Hawthorne's

"The Birthmark" out loud, only half-realizing that although I'd been watching Jason's mouth move, I hadn't heard a word he'd said.

"So, Kathy—what do you think of my paper so far?"

"Well . . . I think—let's see. It's a good, solid three pages—that's good. And, well . . ." Jason frowned in confusion at my idiotic babbling as I snatched his paper from him and scanned it as fast as my eyes could go, trying to grab something I could respond to. For once, having Emily rush over to us and jump on the couch to snuggle against Jason was a welcome interruption.

"Are you guys done yet?"

Jason laughed before glancing at her badly skinned knees peeking out from underneath the edges of her cut-off jeans. Knees that looked like they'd been skinned and then bled and scabbed over only to be skinned again many times in a row, the last time likely being as recently as that very afternoon. Jason's forehead darkened into furrows. "Emily—look at those knees! Did you hurt yourself again today? On your bike, I'll bet!"

Emily shrugged and grinned, obviously enjoying Jason's worry and attention too much to be upset over her battle scars from her bouts with her bike. "Yeah—I crashed coming down the driveway. I turned too fast to miss a car coming up the road—"

I jumped along with Emily when Jason exploded. "*Em!* What are you doing, riding in the middle of the street again? How many times do I have to tell you to ride on the sidewalk!"

"You're not supposed to ride a bike on the sidewalk!" Emily protested.

"Who says?" Jason demanded.

"Everybody!" Emily folded her arms to stare darkly back at Jason.

"Well, I don't care what 'everybody' says! You're such a crazy speed racer, you need to stick to the sidewalks!" Jason gave Emily a little shake as he continued to stare her down. "You've got to watch where you're going or you're going to get yourself killed!"

"No, I won't—I won't!" Emily could be just as determined as Jason.

"I wish it would snow so you couldn't ride anymore. A good storm's the only thing that's going to keep you off the streets!"

Before Emily could retort or protest again, I broke in to add my two cents. "Your knees look like they really hurt, Emily. Do you need to put some medicine and Band-Aids on them?"

Emily turned to me with a big smile. Too big of a smile. "They'd get better faster if you stayed to have dinner with us!"

*Imp.* That's exactly what she was. A cute little imp, but still an imp. With both Emily and Jason working on me, I knew I had lost before I'd begun. A quick call home, and I was stuck. Dad wouldn't tell me no. All he had to say was, "You mean we don't have to feed you tonight? Great! I'll take your mother out to dinner instead"—and before you could say "Mormon funeral potatoes," I was seated around the West family dinner table with Jason, his parents, Emily, and Adam, Jason's recently returned missionary brother. Except for Adam's mission stories and the required interrogation of me by the family, the usual small talk in any household around a dinner table ensued. My mom would've been impressed at my ability to recall manners by remembering to tell Mrs. West how amazing her homemade stew was in between all of the semi-interesting mission stories being delivered to all by Adam.

I had to admit it—I was impressed with Jason's family. Truly. As I watched and listened to everyone, it was hard to believe they were real. No one had a rude or sarcastic comment for anyone. Sure, there was teasing and ribbing, but nothing malicious. Nothing was said that would cause anyone to need to storm from the table and stomp down the hall to slam a bedroom door shut.

I wondered if it was all for my non-Mormon benefit, but after spending so much time with Jason and after seeing how easily his family's conversation flowed back and forth to each other, I had to let go of the idea that it was all a big act being put on just for me. I'd never been in a Mormon household before, so I had no idea whether or not Jason's family was typical. All I knew was that I couldn't deny Jason's family simply had something—something that my family didn't. And whatever that missing piece was, I was wishing my family had it, too.

---

*December 24*
Dear Kitty,

I can't believe tomorrow's Christmas. Already. I wish I could've written more lately, but I've felt so tired and sick. Pretty weak, too. I'm just glad Dr. Grenville agreed to let me come home for today and tomorrow before heading back to the hospital for a few more days. It'll be a while before they'll let me come back home again, so I've got to really hold onto these two days.

You wanted me to swing you around like I used to, and like Alex does to you now, but just lifting you onto my bed made my arms ache and my body feel tired. You seemed to understand, though, so this morning we lay in bed and read Christmas stories. I held you for a long time. I don't want to forget how it feels to hold you.

It's been snowing every day. I wish I could get out and see the Christmas lights. No one's mentioned doing that yet. I hope the family doesn't miss out on everything because of me.

After lunch, I watched from my bedroom window while Alex and Sam helped you make a snowman. You looked so cute in your red snowsuit that I wanted to jump out of bed and run outside and pinch your rosy cheeks. You were all laughing and having a great time. I couldn't help feeling a little jealous of Alex as he swung you around so you could put a baseball cap on ol' Frosty. Well, okay. Maybe I was a lot jealous . . .

*December 25*
Dear Kitty,

Your first real Christmas. It's been quite a day. For both of us. You were a lot of fun to watch opening presents. I had Alex pick up a little tan teddy bear for me to give you for Christmas. You've been dragging it around behind you everywhere. I'm glad you like it so much. I almost forgot I was supposed to be depressed!

And then, Kelly came over.

Apparently, the whole entire school knows I'm out of remission. And even better—Kelly guiltily confessed that he and Jennifer have been "hanging out" and hoped I didn't mind. Mind? It's not like I can do anything about it. Some best friend—going out with my Jennifer while I'm stuck in bed. It's bad enough that Kelly and Jennifer went to homecoming together, but now they're hanging out, going out, and probably making out, too. Yeah, some best friend.

Kelly left a gift for me. I didn't open it . . .

*January 3*

Dear Kitty,

My chemo treatment course is finally over for now, so I've been allowed to come home to rest from the whole ordeal. I'm feeling better today, so at my request, Dad drove us around the neighborhood to see Christmas lights. At least, what's left of them on people's houses. You looked so cute all bundled up in your snowsuit, saying, "Ooo, ooo," over and over, pointing at all the lights you could see. I couldn't help feeling bad watching how excited you got, because you missed out on all of it this Christmas because of me. Mom and Dad have been at the hospital a lot with me, so they haven't felt the urge to go see the sights around town. They both look exhausted all the time. Don't think I don't notice, or that I don't feel guilty. Through some miracle, they've both held onto their jobs, done the family at home thing, taken care of you, and taken care of me, too. It's bad enough that Mom and Dad look like death warmed over and that Alex and Sam look stressed out, even when they're smiling, but what's really breaking my heart is everything you've had to miss out on. I don't think you even sat on

Santa's lap. I'm sorry about that, Kitty. I promise I'll find a way to make it up to you.

I was quiet all the way home while you sat in your car seat between me and Alex, my index finger held tight in your fist until you fell asleep.

I read a little in the Bible again tonight. I even took a look at that Mormon Bible Kelly gave me last year. And I prayed. It's the first time I have since I've been out of remission . . .

*January 17*
Dear Kitty,

I'm really starting the year off with a bang. I'm finally done with being quarantined from my chemo, and I'm feeling stronger, so Mom and Dad gave me the okay to go with Alex to a party at Mark's house—a huge lineman on the football team I've never especially liked, but since Mark's parents were out of town and he has a massive, fancy mansion of a home, the party was bound to be good.

By the time we made it to Mark's house, practically the whole school was there, too. I was having an okay time listening to the music and talking to people here and there until Mark walked over to me with a glass of some cloudy looking drink. I couldn't hear anything he was saying because of the blaring contest between his stereo and everyone else.

Mark shoved the glass he had in my hand with a "Here." I had to scream "What is it?" before Mark yelled "Coke" back. I took a big gulp and nearly blasted him in the face with it. I was gagging and coughing so bad I couldn't get any words out. Mark, the creep, just said, "Oh, yeah, I forgot. We mixed something with it." Mark laughed again at the look on my face and said, "Don't look so stressed. Just a little pick-you-up to start the New Year off with. You look like you could use it."

I was mad. Really mad. I shoved Mark as hard as I could, and since he was buzzing, he lost his balance pretty easily. After smacking into a bookcase behind him and sloshing the cola and whatever else was in it all down the front of his shirt, he fell in a heap on the floor. I stepped over him and stomped off into the kitchen.

And then I froze. I couldn't move or speak—I couldn't even feel my heart beating.

Kelly was in the kitchen. With Jennifer. And Kelly was kissing her. On the mouth. My Jennifer. Worst of all, I could tell she was liking it as much as he was enjoying slobbering all over her.

My heart was pounding fast and hard in my ears while I yelled at Kelly. I called him a pretty rotten name—the kind Mom would've fed me soap over for a month. Both of them jumped apart, so I took that moment to plow in as if I were on the football field and punched Kelly in the face as hard as I could. I heard Jennifer scream, and then I turned my back on both of them and stormed through the house looking for Alex before I grabbed him and demanded he take me home. Now. I was shaking all over. I thought my hand would hurt, but I guess the adrenaline was pumping too hard for me to feel any pain. In my hand, at least . . .

*January 20*

Dear Kitty,

Both Kelly and Jennifer have been driving me up a wall trying to call and come over every second. And I've been driving Mom, Dad, and Alex up a wall by refusing to see or talk to either of them.

I never opened the present Kelly gave me for Christmas. I threw that in a sack and asked Alex to take it back to Kelly. I even wrapped up the Book of Mormon he gave me last year in Santa paper with a note that said, "No thanks, 'friend,'" and threw that in the sack, too.

I'm having bad dreams again—the ones ending with seeing Dr. Grenville. And the dream with us stuck in the meadow. You still can't see me or hear me begging you to take my hand. I hate seeing you look so sad and lost—and afraid.

And then there's my sickness. I'd almost begun to believe I was immortal again. Since I'm only sixteen, it's hard to imagine dying or even getting old, but I guess in a way I have an advantage over some. Take the night of the party. Everyone else only cared about having a good time. No one was thinking about their life ending. No one else had to think twice about their health and dying and everything I have to worry about. They can go to a party and just relax and enjoy, but I can't go anywhere—not even a stupid party—without having to be on my guard. I've got to worry about what's in the drinks for a whole different reason than anyone else. Not to mention who I might find making out in the kitchen. The kitchen, of all places . . .

Sometimes I just want to run and never stop. Or else drive. I make Alex take me for long drives at night. It makes Mom crazy, but when I'm feeling okay and up to it, I just need to get away from my bed, the medicine—everything. I know I can't run away from my sickness, but it feels like I am when I'm in a car making Alex drive fast at the wheel. Sometimes I can even convince him to let me take the wheel on an extremely deserted road.

I haven't written it down before, but the true name of my sickness is acute myelogenous leukemia. The real kicker is that not only is there no cure, but there wasn't anything I could've done to prevent it. I wondered if I'd done something wrong, or if I hadn't done something I should've, but it just happened. I think Mom and Dad drove themselves crazy thinking the same thing. I've been asking God why He let it happen to me. I haven't gotten an answer yet . . .

# CHAPTER THIRTY

"Earth to Kathy. Come in, Kathy!"

I didn't know how long I'd been holding a glass of water almost to my lips, oblivious to the Thanksgiving dinner going on around me, but from the exasperation in Sam's voice, it must have been quite a while. "Sorry—sorry, Sam. What did you say?"

Sam rolled her eyes and said loudly and slowly, "I said, 'Could you please pass the stuffing?' If it's not completely ice cold by now, that is."

I quickly shoved the bowl into her hands. "Sorry. Here."

"From that grin you've had on your face all day, I think it's safe to say you've got something new to be thankful for this Thanksgiving." Thanks to Alex, now everyone was looking at me expectantly, as if they all thought I was going to tell them anything about where my smile had come from. And yes, Alex was right. I *did* have something new to be thankful for. Or shocked over. Definitely something to be analyzed and played out over and over in my brain.

Less than twenty-four hours ago, I'd been standing in front of Brett's trophy case, staring at Brett's laughing face and thinking about the broken-record dream I'd been having of him. I hadn't thought Jason would need me to tutor him this week, because the assignment was creative writing, but he insisted I come over on Tuesday to read what he'd written. "Just to see if it's completely worthless and stupid" were Jason's

214

exact words. So I'd left the trophy case behind, and at four o'clock as usual, Emily stampeded to the front door to let me in and handed me another crayon drawing. And as usual, Jason waited patiently while Emily taught me a story from the Book of Mormon via the crayon drawing and then scampered off to play the piano. Only this time, something was not usual at all. And it wasn't just the fact that I hadn't been ushered into the West family room as usual, due to a thorough carpet cleaning being performed, but instead, had been escorted by Emily down another hallway to a room with a small sofa in it that Jason was lounging on in his usual leg-propped-up position. It wasn't until I started to read Jason's attempt at creative writing that I finally put my finger on it.

Jason hadn't teased me. Or grinned. Not even once. And he seemed—*nervous*. He obviously had something on his mind. When he did speak again, I was in for a huge surprise.

"So, Kathy—the Christmas dance is coming up in a few weeks."

I kept my head down, busily scanning his creative writing piece for errors. "Yep—it is."

"Do you want to go?"

I frowned. "Mmmm—haven't thought about it."

"What?"

I lifted my head at the tone in Jason's voice and was surprised to see that his face looked—well, *surprised*—at my response. "Well, no one's asked me, and I don't know that anyone will, so there's really no point in thinking about it." Although Kent or Lear could possibly ask me. But I kept that thought to myself.

"Wait—no—Kathy, I don't think you understand—"

"Understand what?"

Jason took a deep breath and looked me straight in the eye. "When I asked—just now—if you wanted to go, I was wondering if—you know—you'd like to go. With me."

I could feel my insides tighten up into a knot as flashbacks of his last dance invitation and the painful results blazed their way through my brain. *How stupid did he think I was?* "You're joking, right?"

He actually looked baffled at my response. "Joking? What are you talking about?"

I shook my head and tossed his paper back to him. "This—dance invite. Did you think I'd be stupid enough to fall for that again?"

"Fall for what again?"

I laughed bitterly. "Like you don't know! I'm not about to agree to go to a dance with someone who'll change his mind and take someone else at the last second. I'm not going to be made to look like an idiot again—you can count on that!"

Jason's bafflement turned into an embarrassed scowl. "If I remember right, I *did* apologize for that. About a billion times—"

But I didn't want to talk about that. It was too embarrassing and—painful. "Just stop messing with my mind, Jason," I said irritably.

"What? All I wanted to do was ask you to the dance!"

"And why would you do that, when number one, you've already got a girlfriend—"

"*Girlfriend?*" Jason choked.

"—and number two—I don't believe you have the guts to seriously ask me and then follow through and actually *go* to the dance with me."

Jason's mouth gaped open. "What do you mean?"

"I mean, it's easy enough to ask me here in your house, with no one knowing but you and me, but what happens when your friends find out? Or your girlfriend? You'd probably just deny you were ever serious. That you were just messing around. Like you did before," I said hotly.

"First of all, I don't *have* a girlfriend—"

"Oh, really? Then what was Angela? One of your groupies?"

Jason scowled and looked away. "I'm not with her anymore."

*He wasn't?* This was definitely news to me. "Why not?" I demanded.

Jason looked at me resolutely. "You can't stay with someone when you're always thinking about someone else."

216

I couldn't say anything before I somehow stuttered out, "Does she know—"

Jason raked his fingers through his hair nervously. "She got the picture when I made it clear I wanted to take someone else to the Christmas dance."

I stared numbly at Jason, not sure whether I should dare to believe anything he was saying. And then, Jason slowly reached over and touched my fingers. I froze, staring at his hand against mine. In another second, he'd boldly taken hold of my entire hand.

"So, Kathy—how about it?" I almost didn't hear him, between his soft whispering and the roar of blood rushing to my ears. This couldn't be happening—things like this never happened to me—even though a lot of unreal things *had* been happening to me lately—

"I—I don't know—I—"

I was in that hot zone of being so freaked out I was dangerously close to tears. In a flash, I was out of my chair and blindly running down the hall in the direction that should've led me straight to the front door, had I been coming from the family room. Instead, the direction I'd flown ended abruptly above the stairs leading to the basement. I quickly grasped the banister to keep from plunging over the edge. I could hear Jason calling "Kathy!" before I heard grumbling mixed with the unmistakable sounds of his roughly getting himself off the couch and onto his crutches. I couldn't deal with him and more talk of the Christmas dance, so with no other form of escape available, I hurried down the stairs. I only turned when I heard him say "Kathy!" again. He was balanced on his crutches at the top of the stairs, looking at me in such an exasperated, bewildered manner that I could feel anger rising. How dare he look at me as if I had no reason to freak out!

"Kathy, please come back up here—"

"No!"

Jason looked at me in disbelief for a long second. "No? Why not?"

"Because I don't want to!"

Jason shook his head. "I can't believe this. You know, never in a million years would I have thought you'd react this way if I asked you out!"

I could feel the anger rising higher at that remark. "Oh, really? And what did you think I'd do? Cry tears of joy and kiss your feet in gratitude for asking me—again? Or better yet—that I'd faint dead away at having my ultimate dream come true?"

It took Jason a second to recover from my response before he shot back with, "I guess I'm just used to most girls being happy to get asked out by me—that's all!"

"Oh, I'm sure you are! I'm sorry to have to disappoint you, but I'm not most girls!"

Jason let out an exasperated gasp before yelling, "Kathy!"

"I don't want to talk anymore. And lucky for me, you can't crutch on down here, so just—leave me alone!"

Tell Jason there's something he can't do? Definitely the wrong thing for me to have said. Jason's look quickly hardened into that picking-up-the-gauntlet face he had—the one he wore under his football helmet before starting a play on the field. With an "oh, yeah?" he clenched his hands tightly around the crutches' handgrips on either side of him, and a second later, he'd carefully made it down the first stair. And then the next one, and the next—

I stepped backward a few paces, nervously watching his circus tightrope-type progress. "Jason—stop—you shouldn't be doing this! You're going to fall, I just know it!" Panic was rising from my stomach into my throat, snuffing out any remaining flickers of anger. Jason ignored me and continued to carefully make his way down the stairs. I could tell by his look of concentration that it wasn't easy, but by the time he had only a few stairs to go, his look changed to one of confidence and he lifted his head to grin at me. "See, Kathy? This is nothing"—right before his crutches became lodged awkwardly on the step. A second later, he was high-centered on them, and while he yelled "Whoa!" and I screamed, he fell face forward and crashed down the remaining few steps to land in a miserable heap at the bottom of the stairs.

"Jason!" I ran forward and quickly untangled his crutches from his legs and arms while he lay on his stomach groaning. My heart pounded while I frantically wondered how badly he'd hurt his knee. *And it's all my fault—all my stupid fault because of my dumb pride—*

I threw his crutches away from him while he slowly turned over onto his left side, leaning on his good leg with his head on his arm. His eyes were shut, and his face was twisted in pain. My heart leaped even higher. I fell to my knees, leaning over him.

"Jason—how bad does your knee hurt? Do you think anything ripped? I'll go get Adam—you need someone stronger than me to help you get up—" I was so scared I couldn't stop babbling, knowing he'd ruined his knee for good, thanks to me.

Jason didn't respond, but when I moved from crouching over him to get help, he reached out fast and grabbed my arm and yanked me back down on my knees beside him.

"No, I don't want their help." Jason's face relaxed into a smile. "You're worried about me, aren't you?"

"Worried? You're lying here in pain, thanks to me! Of course I'm worried!"

In another fast, fluid motion, Jason rolled onto his back, still clutching my arm, and in the next second, he had me by both upper arms, a few scant inches from his face.

Jason laughed softly. "I'm not in *that* much pain, Kathy."

My heart pounded even harder. And faster. "No?" I managed to gasp.

Jason drew me even closer to him. "You care about me, don't you?"

"How do you know that?" My lips were practically touching his now—

"Because I care about you, too."

A second later, his mouth had softly touched mine. I couldn't believe this was happening. My mind was spinning, and my heart was pounding. I quickly pulled away and scrambled to my feet, trembling all over, while Jason stared up at me with eyes so intense and dark blue they looked black. I tried to say I'd better go get some help and then ran up the stairs as if I was being chased. It wasn't until I got home that my shock began to wear off to let reality settle in. Jason had kissed me. *Jason had kissed me!* And then I'd realized something else. *I'd kissed him back.*

The whole afternoon marked the end and the beginning of something. I ran into the house and into my room after leaving Jason's. There I replayed everything that had led to the kiss. And then I relived that kiss a million times over and over in my brain. I hadn't seen Jason since. He'd had a doctor appointment for his knee the following morning, and then his family went out of town for Thanksgiving. I was alternately dreading and wishing for Monday to come. But during Thanksgiving dinner and after we all moved into the living room for pumpkin pie, I continued to replay Tuesday afternoon and that kiss, over and over. And apparently with a tiny smile that let everyone know I wasn't smiling at any of them.

"So, Kathy, what do you think?"

I walked slowly over to where a few new photos in gold frames had been added to our family collection. One frame held a picture of me dressed in white as Cordelia trying to reason with an angry King Lear. Another frame held a picture of just me dressed in my red Juliet dress and cap sitting on my table-bed, staring solemnly at my sleeping potion.

"Aren't they great? Sam took the photos. And picked the frames up yesterday," Mom said, giving my shoulders a squeeze.

I was stunned. The pictures were amazing. Anyone would think a professional photographer had taken them.

"Wow—Sam—" I turned to Sam to thank her, but she quickly caught me in a hug and whispered in my ear, "Wait 'til you see the one in your room!" The second I could sneak away, I casually walked down the hall before running into my room to find in a gold heart frame another picture from the Shakespeare festival. The photo was one of

Jason and me together, with me in my Juliet costume and Jason balanced on his crutches. If I felt embarrassed at how adoringly I was looking up at him, I was comforted by the fact that he was smiling down at me in a pretty enthralled way. Sam had put a stickie note on it with hearts that said, "You like?!" and although I was embarrassed she'd caught such a moment, I was happily and gratefully surprised that she'd chosen to leave it in my room for my eyes only. It was very un-Sam-like. But then, I'd become pretty un-Kathy-like myself.

---

*February 5*

Dear Kitty,

I definitely need to make some New Year's resolutions. You've inspired me more than you know, since you've already reached a few goals of your own, and it's only February! You have no problem walking at all anymore. In fact, you're running everywhere—I don't think I could keep up with you even if I wasn't sick and puking all the time! You're also learning more and more words. It's getting easier to figure out what you want, which is a plus! And you're showing an interest in moving on from diapers—another plus! So since you're already working on your goals for the year, I know I need to try and set a few of my own.

You still love the bear I gave you for Christmas. In fact, you sleep with it every night. I've been trying to teach you how to say "teddy" and "bear," but all you say back is "tiny." I can't believe how much you love that bear. Even though you have so many other toys, Tiny is it for you. I'm actually starting to get jealous of a stuffed animal!

Sometimes at night to make you fall asleep, I put you in bed with me and I read you stories. Usually with the Beatles playing in the background. Once you're asleep, I watch you for a while before I put you back in your crib. This is the kind of moment I wish could last forever . . .

## CHAPTER THIRTY-ONE

Decided to come up for air, I see."

I'd barely entered the living room the afternoon following Thanksgiving Day when Dad looked up from the book he'd been reading. "What's that supposed to mean?"

Dad shrugged and continued to study me over the top of his book. "Just that you've been hibernating in your room a lot lately."

"Lots of teenagers 'hibernate.' It's not unusual."

"True. But you've been spending a *lot* of time alone in your room. Even for a teenager."

I rolled my eyes. "I *do* get out once in a while. And I've been busy with drama and tutoring and everything."

Dad nodded again without showing any signs of retreat. "True again. But we haven't seen your friends around in a while. Don't you like spending time with them anymore?"

I shrugged and leaned against the bookshelves. "I've been busy."

"And when you *are* home and not in your room, you're off in some other world. Or you're being unusually nice to everyone."

I rolled my eyes again. "I've already had this conversation. With Mom."

Dad sighed and set his book aside. "Well, you can't blame us. We're your parents, so we worry about you." Then he sat up to lean towards me with his serious, concerned look. "Is there anything you'd like to talk about? Anything at all?"

I hesitated before raising an eyebrow at his overly hopeful face. "Well, there is one thing I've been wondering about lately."

"Yes?" Dad said hopefully.

I looked at him thoughtfully for a long moment before I blurted out, "Dad, whatever happened to my Tiny Bear?"

Dad raised his eyebrows in baffled surprise. "Tiny Bear? I can't believe you even remember him."

I grinned and plopped down near him on the couch. "Well, I don't know if I *do*. That's why I want to see him again."

Dad took off his reading glasses and rubbed his eyes. "Well, that's going to be difficult to do, since he was probably thrown out."

*My favorite toy when I was little?* "Thrown out? When?"

Dad looked uncomfortable as he reached to snatch up his book again and thumb quickly for his place in it. "Oh, I don't know. Years ago, I'm sure."

"Don't we have any pictures of him? Of Tiny Bear and me? Together?"

Dad glanced briefly at me before turning back to his book with a frown. "Not that I know of. Why all this interest in an old stuffed animal?"

I shrugged my shoulders and looked away. "I don't know. I guess I just miss him."

Dad studied me for a few moments over the top of his book. "Yeah, you really did love that funny old bear." He waited for me to say more, but I couldn't. Especially when I realized I hadn't been thinking about an old stuffed animal at all.

---

*March 5*

Dear Kitty,

Spring term just started, and Dr. Grenville said I'm strong enough to go back to school. Mom and Dad didn't want to let me go, but I won them over with my amazing charm. I kept out of Kelly's way, and although he stayed out of mine, I could feel his stare all day. It was almost creepy. Now I think I'm going to have to get him a Sherlock Holmes spy glass and pipe for Christmas this year.

I had to crash after school. Pretending you're fine and that everything's okay is hard work. Later, I had to go see Dr. Grenville. I don't think things are looking too good for me. I wouldn't let him talk too much about my slim chance of going into a second remission, though. Since I can't decide much for myself lately, I've definitely decided that I'll be the one to say when I'm going to die . . .

*April 8*

Dear Kitty,

You've now experienced your first real Easter, and for the first time in my life, I think I did, too. I felt sick on Easter Sunday, so I took it easy and stayed in bed most of the day. Sam's home for Easter break, so later that afternoon, Alex and Sam took you outside to find Easter eggs. I watched you trotting around with your Easter basket looking for eggs, holding Tiny Bear by one leg as you dragged him around the yard, while the scary-looking pink rabbit the good ol' Easter bunny brought for you lay ignored on the living room floor.

While I was lounging on the couch, I kept myself busy watching TV and listened to some preacher talking all about Christ and how He died to save us all. I caught a few of the verses he was talking about and looked them up like I've done before and ended up reading more than I meant to. I bored Alex with a bunch of stuff I'd read and told him that if what the Bible says is true, then because of Him, we can be saved and we can live again, after we've died. I asked Alex what he thought about that. Of course, Alex just looked at me as if I had three heads and said something stupid and completely off the point. I guess he was surprised I was thinking religious thoughts at all, although he shouldn't have been. Even though I've never talked about religion with Alex, he's seen the Bible and Kelly's Mormon Bible in my room often enough. And considering the fact that I'm shaking hands with death on a regular basis these days, I don't think he should be surprised at all. I don't know—it's just hard not having anyone to talk with about it. Intelligently. Believe it or not, Kitty, I'm really missing being able to talk about this kind of stuff with Kelly.

No, you're right, Kitty. I just really miss having Kelly around. Period.

# CHAPTER THIRTY-TWO

A s Mom and Dad both continued to notice, I *had* been spending a lot of time alone, and I knew it. Since my birthday, to be exact. Especially on Saturdays. Reading, mostly. And listening to the Beatles. Thanksgiving break was no exception. That is, until Mom dragged me out of my room, thrust a dust rag into my hand, and pointed me towards the living room.

"If you're just going to hang around here, you might as well do something useful."

I'd been mindlessly picking up picture after picture, giving each the once-over with the dust rag. I was about to set the one in my hand back on the bookshelf, but I couldn't stop staring at the three in the picture with their arms around each other's shoulders in sweaty football uniforms, their faces frozen into laughing smiles forever.

"Kelly," I said out loud. I tapped the handsome blond's face with the tip of one finger over and over. He was gorgeous like Jason. Only a different, blond sort of gorgeous. I'd looked at this picture many times, never giving Kelly more than idle curiosity-type thoughts. But now— now I couldn't stop wondering about him. After a few more seconds of staring, I carefully replaced the picture on its shelf and casually approached Mom in the kitchen.

"Mom, whatever happened to Kelly Baxter?" I leaned on the counter and looked at her face out of the corner of my eye to catch her reaction. Mom was concentrating so deeply on the chicken she was cleaning that I jumped when her head jerked up sharply.

"Kelly Baxter?"

"Yeah. He was one of Alex and Brett's friends, wasn't he?"

Mom shrugged and dug back into the chicken's insides with a vicious fervor, causing her locket to bounce against her chest. "Yes, but he was more Brett's friend than Alex's."

"Is that why we never see him anymore? Because he was Brett's friend?" I persisted.

Mom shrugged again. "I guess that's part of it. And people grow apart as they get older. I don't know—" Mom stopped torturing the chicken to eye me curiously. "Why do you want to know about Kelly Baxter?"

I shrugged nervously. "I don't know. I was just wondering whatever happened to him."

"Well, I'm sorry, but I really don't know. Honey, will you wash your hands and come help me with dinner? I'm having the darndest time with this chicken."

Mom wasn't about to delve into the subject of Kelly any further. And not because of the chicken. That fact made questions run in circles in my head, but I bit my lip and walked over to the sink. I sighed and stared out the window while the warm tap water ran down my hands. It was strange to realize I'd never truly met Kelly, and yet, I knew things about him. At least, the teenage version of him. And I wondered if he knew we had a picture of him on our bookshelf—a picture that had sat there for years, even though no one wanted to talk about him. And I wondered if he ever thought about Brett anymore. Or about my family. Or even about me.

*April 20*

Dear Kitty,

I don't think Dad can handle my sickness. He's been working late at the office practically every night ever since I got sick, and when he is home, I feel like he's purposely trying to avoid me. I've tried to talk about it with Mom, but she only says I never see him anymore because he has to work so much so we can pay the bills—meaning my hospital bills, of course—and that once he does get home, it's late, and he's too tired to do anything but go to bed. The funny thing is, I thought that was why Mom went back to work—to help pay for the bills so Dad wouldn't have to work more hours. I guess leukemia is more expensive than I thought. It's hard enough missing someone like Kelly—a good friend who doesn't live in the same house with me—but I think it's harder to miss someone who lives in the same house with you but might as well live on the whole other side of the world, for all the closeness you have with that person.

I'd been trying to talk to Mom about Dad and everything again today and at one point asked why Dad didn't at least just come in and say good night to me when he got home. Mom could only say that he was afraid of saying the wrong thing. So instead, he says nothing at all to me. Isn't that great, Kitty? Just great.

I had the dream again last night. You know the one. You were sixteen in the dream, like I am now. I yelled and yelled, trying to get you to look at me—hear me—but you stubbornly kept your back to me. Just when I was about to give up, you jumped—as if you'd felt something poke you in the back. And then you cautiously, carefully turned your head to look behind you, where I was! As if you'd heard me, somehow—finally! I guess the excitement was too much for me, because a second later I was awake yelling, "Kitty! Kitty!" out loud.

A second after that, a deep voice near my ear said, "Brett?" I nearly shot out of my skin. It was Dad—sitting in the dark in a chair pulled up close by my bed. His hand was in my hair, and he kept saying, "Kitty's asleep—she's fine—she's okay." I was so exhausted that I fell asleep before the strangeness of the moment—Dad being in my room and all—could fully sink in. You know how dreams are. Weird things seem perfectly normal. Having Dad in my room sitting by me, his hand in my hair and everything was so unreal that I convinced myself that that had just been a dream, too. I told Mom about it the next day while we gave you a bath. I don't know what I expected Mom to say, but what she did say—really quietly, like she was admitting a secret—nearly knocked me over. She said, "Sometimes, once you've fallen asleep, I've caught him sitting by your bed just watching you—watching over you—while you sleep. I think he does that a lot more often than we know . . ."

*May 3*
Dear Kitty,

I'm not doing so good. After my last checkup and blood tests, Dr. Grenville put me back in the hospital. He told me about some other types of meds he wants to try me on, so now I'm doing a course of some new drugs, which means I'm out flat when I'm not puking up a storm.

And today I turned seventeen. I never would have believed I would ever spend a birthday in the hospital, but fate and life have a sick sense of humor. At least Mom, Dad, and Alex came and brought you with them. I was afraid you'd be scared to come near me, being laid out in this hospital bed with a ton of tubes sticking out all over me, but when you saw me, you said, "Up, up!" to Alex, and once he lifted you up, you reached your little arms out to me and hugged me and kissed me, saying, "Bet! Bet!" And then you snuggled down by me and wouldn't move from my side. That made my birthday, Kitty. You'll never know how much that made my whole day.

I've been thinking about you a lot. Even though I know I'm

getting worse, I have to hang on to see you turn two. Dr. Grenville keeps telling me about what these amazing new drugs can do. Last ditch efforts, if you ask me.

I hope that somehow you know how much I love you. Those are three words that aren't said very often in our family. Not near enough. I hope you won't be like me and let much time go between saying those words to the important people in your life . . .

# CHAPTER THIRTY-THREE

*May 31*

Dear Kitty,

I've been doing a lot of serious thinking, and after talking my decision over with Dr. Grenville, he's finally decided to let me go through with it—and to let me go home! Yes! I can't wait to be home! I miss you and everyone else so much. Except for on my birthday, the hospital gestapo hasn't let you in to come see me. But I plastered my walls with your drawings. They've helped to make my days bearable. You've done about a million or so since I've been incarcerated in here! I've got a picture of us together in a frame by my bed—the one Kelly took of us in the park a while back. That's helped me get through this craziness, and it's given me something awesome to look forward to when I get the heck out of here! Those first few days in the hospital, I felt incredibly lonely, like there was only me and my sickness. But when I pray, I don't feel so alone. I feel like God or Jesus or someone is with me all of the time . . .

—

I'd read a ton of Brett's journal over Thanksgiving break, mostly to give my brain a rest from thinking about Jason, and as a result, I wasn't surprised at all that I dreamt about Brett again Sunday night. In the dream, Brett again held his precious book out to me, pleading with me to understand and accept it. All I could convey back to him was that I had his journal—and I was reading it—every day! But his reaction remained the same, which was to shake his head and then to disappear when my tears of frustration surfaced. And like I had done before, I woke up crying—and continued to cry until I couldn't cry anymore.

## CHAPTER THIRTY-FOUR

By Monday morning, I couldn't decide if I was nervous or excited to go to school again. I had no idea how I should act around Jason. I mean, we'd *kissed.* Did that mean I should sit on his lap in English and insist that he hold my hand? Or pretend I was Cool and act as if nothing had happened at all? I had no idea. I'd never kissed anyone before, much less someone like Jason.

After picking up Mistie and Crystal for school in the cruddy car, I felt my heart hammering fast as we rounded the last corner and Central High flared into view. I was busy making sure I didn't hit all the jaywalkers as I fought my way into the school parking lot, so when Mistie and Crystal screamed in unison, I was sure I'd run over something.

"What? What?!"

"The sign! Did you see it?!" Mistie shrieked in my ear.

"Sign? What sign?"

Crystal smacked me in the back of the head. "The school marquee in front of the building! Straight ahead, you dope! *Look* at it!"

When I did, my jaw crashed to the floor of the car—right onto the brakes, in fact, causing the car to screech and jerk enough to almost send poor Mistie flying through the windshield.

In big, bold, capital letters, the marquee had one message and one message only:

"Kathy Colton: Will U go 2 the X-mas Dance w/Jason West?"

"Can you believe it?! Kathy—can you believe it?" Mistie and Crystal both screamed.

I couldn't. I honestly couldn't. But the surprises didn't end there. The next surprise occurred when Jason walked into Honors English. Actually *walked*. With just a sturdy-looking walking leg brace on his right leg. And without crutches. And early, no less. I was the only one in class when Jason casually made his entrance minus crutches into the classroom, beaming a huge smile as he walked over to sit on the desk in front of me.

"So—what do you think?"

"Congratulations! This is so great!"

Jason's smile faded as he raised a confused eyebrow. "'Congratulations'?"

I pointed at his brace before Jason grinned. "Oh yeah—that."

"Yes, that! What did you think I meant?"

Jason's grin fell again as he stared at me. "You haven't seen it?"

I could feel myself blushing. "Oh—that. Yes, I've seen it. As I'm sure the whole school has by now!"

"And?" Jason persisted, leaning towards me with his hands braced on his knees.

"And, if these are the results I get for telling you that you don't have the guts to do something, then I think I should tell you you're gutless more often!" I laughed.

"Yeah, yeah. Laugh it up, Kathy—"

Students began filing in with Mrs. Dubois on their heels, and with everyone fussing over Jason and his newly uncrutched leg, Jason was forced to take his seat so class could begin.

My happy surprises didn't end there, though. In front of everyone, Jason joined Mistie and Crystal and me for lunch in the cafeteria. Mistie and Crystal had considerately, if not exactly discreetly, gathered up their stuff with huge grins on their faces once Jason sat down beside me and left us alone to eat lunch. And just because I was enjoying messing with Jason's mind so much, I kept him in suspense about whether I would accept his amazingly public invitation to the dance—for which both of us had received a lot of attention and comments. I only hoped his had been as congratulatory as mine were, even though the fact that mine *were* congratulatory was somewhat insulting and offensive.

I was on a roll of the Midas Touch level when I went whistling into the house, which caused Mom to raise her eyebrows and ask questions about my day. Before I knew what I was doing, I blabbed the best part of my news to her in one excited breath. "Jason asked me to the Christmas dance—twice! On Wednesday during tutoring and then again at school today!"

Mom's mouth dropped open. "What?!"

"I know!" I gushed excitedly. "I totally didn't think he meant it Wednesday at his house, even after we—" Mom stopped to put her hands on her hips and gave me her full, unsmiling attention while I reconsidered just how much I should blab. "Well, anyway—he obviously was serious, because he asked me at school—big as life on the marquee!"

"I can't believe it!" I hardly noticed Mom still wasn't smiling.

"Neither can I! I can't believe I'm really going with Jason!"

To my utter amazement, Mom pointed a finger at me threateningly and completely exploded. "You most certainly are *not* going with that boy! I strictly forbid it!"

I knew Mom wasn't thrilled about my—whatever it was that I had with Jason, mostly due to the religion factor, but I didn't think going to a dance with him would send her into orbit. But no matter how much I begged, she refused to give me the permission I needed to go to the dance.

"I can't believe you can't see this is just another proselytizing effort of his!" Mom yelled in frustration.

I could've handled it if she'd said he was only asking me because he thought he'd get more than dancing out of me. Or that he felt sorry for me. Or asked me on a dare. Anything but what she'd just said. I shut my mouth and looked stonily at her before calmly stating, "Of course. Everything's all about him looking for a convert. Honest attraction towards me clearly isn't believable to you. Or friendship. Why else would he want to go to a dance with me, right?"

"Kathy, honey—"

I grabbed my book bag and stalked out of the living room, slamming the front door behind me, before I could hear anything else she might say.

---

"Kathy—what's going on?"

One look at my unsuccessful efforts to act like everything was fine the second I'd sat down to begin tutoring, and Jason wouldn't stop bugging me until I was close to tears.

"My mom won't let me go to the dance with you," I finally said.

"She won't? Why not?"

"She thinks you're trying to turn me into a Mormon."

I was strangely relieved to see unfeigned shock on Jason's face. "*What?* I'm not trying to 'turn' you into anything! You know that, don't you?"

"Yes, I know."

"I just want to go to the dance with you!" Jason said exasperatedly.

"I know."

We both fell silent until Jason reassuringly squeezed my hand and smiled determinedly into my eyes. "Well, then I guess there's only one way to fix this."

Jason wouldn't elaborate on whatever scheme he was scheming, but I found out later that evening after I sulked through dinner and locked myself in my room. I'd had my music on so loud I couldn't hear anything but the Beatles screaming at me until Dad pounded on my bedroom door. I gave the door a yank and glared at Dad. "What is it?"

Dad made an attempt to shout over the music. "You have a visitor!"

"A visitor?"

"Just come on!" Dad walked away, so I had no choice but to switch off the record player and follow him back to the living room.

I stopped abruptly when I saw him. Jason. *Jason* was in my house, standing in the living room, looking over the pictures on our bookshelves. He turned around as quickly as he could with his leg brace and smiled. "Hey, Kathy!"

I hurried over to where he stood. "What are you doing here?"

"I actually came to see your parents, but your dad went looking for you before I could explain I really wasn't here to see you. I'm sorry, but I wasn't."

I wondered if I looked as confused as I sounded. "How did you get here?"

Jason grinned. "Adam gave me a ride. He's waiting outside in the car."

I gaped in disbelief through the window at the unfamiliar car in the driveway. "I can't believe it!"

"Yeah, well, it's amazing what twenty bucks can buy." Jason and I grinned at each other until his grin faded into his game face. "Can I talk to your mom and dad for a second?"

I nodded slowly at him. "I guess."

After rounding up my two baffled parents, it was my turn to be baffled as Jason politely but firmly asked me to please leave so he could talk to them alone. I walked in a daze back into my room, where I sat stiffly on my bed until I heard a soft rap on my door and found Dad standing there. Smiling.

"Okay, Cinderella. Go buy yourself a dress for the ball."

I could only stare at him dumbfoundedly. "What—but Mom said—"

Dad smiled and reached out to give a lock of my hair a tug. "I know what your mom said. And your friend's dramatics haven't changed her mind concerning how she feels about him. But she *was* impressed with his little show of bravado. And so was I. He must know you're someone special to go to this much effort to take you to a dance. I think that's what won your mother over, albeit grudgingly." Before I could answer, Dad hustled me out of my room. "He didn't want to leave without saying good-bye, so go get him out of my house."

Jason was studying the bookshelf pictures again when I entered the room. He turned, grinning the grin of the victorious. "So—everything's cool now?"

There was something about the look on his way-too-triumphant face that tempted me to torture him some more. "I don't remember ever saying I'd go with you. In fact, I haven't had a chance to give you my answer. I've never said yes or no yet."

"What the—but I thought—"

I had a horrible time keeping a straight face at the look on Jason's dumbfounded face. "I know what you thought. But just because my parents said yes doesn't mean I will!"

Jason stared in disbelief before speaking again. "Okay, well, will you tell me now? Finally? Will you go to the dance with me?"

I grinned back at him. "You're just going to have to wait to get my answer." And with that, I successfully kicked him out of the house, whistling as I skip-danced back down the hall to my room.

———

After everything Jason had gone through to ask me to the dance, I couldn't make him wait for my answer for long, so after a few phone calls to find out which student body officer would be willing to help me, by the next morning Jason received my "Jason West—Kathy Colton says yes!" answer back. By way of the school marquee, of course.

*June 5*

Dear Kitty,

It feels so good to be home! And to actually be feeling good. I hope this high lasts for a while, because it is so great to feel so much stronger right now.

I'd forgotten how tight Mom hugs. That always irritated me as a kid, but now it feels nice. Makes me feel like I'm truly home. Dad—I wasn't sure what to expect from him, but I took one step towards him and he grabbed me up in a bear hug and wouldn't let go. I didn't mind, though. Not at all.

You're so big—and you can say so many words! You were so proud of yourself, bringing me things like magazines and cinnamon rolls. If someone tried to help you, you'd yell, "Me do—me do! Myself!" Mom says you say that all the time—you have to do everything yourself—you're hardly a baby anymore! And you jabbered at me all day. I'm glad you haven't forgotten me and that you're happy I'm back.

We watched the sunset together on the porch again tonight with the Beatles as background music. There won't be many nice summer days left, and I don't want to miss any opportunity I have to watch sunsets with you.

I've been thinking a lot about God and Jesus, and all the things Kelly used to tell me about his religion. When I see something as beautiful as a sunset, I can believe in God. I can't accept the idea that this world just happened by chance—that you or I just happened, like some strange accident. Someone had to be in charge of making everything. Something as beautiful as a sunset couldn't just happen by chance. Someone had to be there to figure out how to make the sun and sky create such beautiful colors together—like still fire spread all across the sky.

While I was in the hospital, I made the decision not to take any more chemo meds. Dr. Grenville and I talked about my condition and the hard, cold, mean fact that I'm not getting better and that most likely, I'm not going to get better. My sickness is getting out of control, and now that I've accepted the fact that I don't have a lot of time left, I refuse to spend that time drugged up, lying in a hospital bed for who knows how many more months—or even years. That's just not a life to me, Kitty. I'd rather stay sane for what-ever time I have left and be able to enjoy everything around me with a clear head. Dr. Grenville prescribed some powerful painkillers for my worst days, but other than that, I just want to live my life the best I can for as long as I have. I've even prayed about this decision, and I feel good about it. Mom and Dad took it pretty hard, though. So did Sam and Alex. I hope in time they'll realize it's not only the best for me but for everyone else in the family, too. The only hard part about this decision is you. I hate the idea of not being able to watch you grow up, but Kitty, I also don't want your memories of me to be of some comatose guy lying around in a hos-pital bed. I hope that you'll have some memory of your own of me—a healthy me—but if that's not going to happen, then I want the me I've tried to record in this book be the me you think of instead . . .

*June 20*

Dear Kitty,

I'm glad to be home, but at the same time, I can't stand the way Alex and Sam treat me now. You'd think I was going to drop dead this second. Alex was bugging me so much today, fussing over me like he was Mom, that I finally just let it all out and yelled at him.

Alex got quiet, and when he finally looked up at me, he had tears running all down his face. I've never seen Alex cry like that before. And then he said, "I'm sorry, Brett, but I've never had to deal with having my brother die." All I could say to that was if he expected me to feel sorry for him, to just forget it. I'm the one who's dying here—not him.

What Alex did next shocked me. He'd been holding a glass of orange juice, but he turned and threw it as hard as he could, smashing it into millions of little pieces. We both stared at the sticky streaks of orange dripping down my wall before Alex faced me. He was still crying, and his voice shook when he said, "This illness of yours isn't just yours, you know. You're not the only one who's dying." His voice shook even harder when he said, "Some of me is dying, too."

We were both quiet for a while before I told him that I'm the one who's going to have to be without all of you, but he came back with, "But we're going to have to be without you! I'm going to have to try to learn to live my life without you. And I have no idea how I'm going to do that, Brett." He paced my room, running his fingers through his hair, while he said, "I don't know what to say, I don't know how to act—I can't even begin to understand what you're going through. I only know what I'm going through, and believe me, it's incredibly hard to watch you go through this." So I shouted back, "Do you think it's easy for me? I'm the one who's had to deal with the chemotherapy, the puking, the weakness, being in a stinking bed all day—"

But Alex cut me off with, "But I have to be the one to stand here helplessly watching all of it, because no matter what I do, I can't make it go away. I can't even take a millionth of it away. Maybe I can't understand your illness, but you can't understand what it's like not knowing what you're really going through, wondering how much you're keeping to yourself and wondering if there's something I could have done—something I'm not doing—" He had to stop and wipe his nose and eyes with his shirtsleeve before he could say, "Here I am, nothing wrong with me, and there you are, sick, and I can't give you any of my 'healthiness.' The only thing I can do is stand here and watch you . . ." He stopped and looked at me with those tears frozen on his face and said, "I don't want you to die."

I had to say something, so I said, "Think I do?" I tried to smile, but it didn't turn out quite right. Then Alex asked me real softly if I was scared, so I admitted, "Sometimes." But that felt like a lie, so I said, "No—I guess I'd have to say, a lot of the time I am," which was one of the most honest things I've said in a long time.

Then Alex grabbed me up in one of his fierce bear hugs and said, "So am I."

## CHAPTER THIRTY-FIVE

G ood grief—even *I* never got this much fuss made over me when I was asked to dances!" I decided to take Sam's reaction to Jason's little visit to Mom and Dad as a compliment when she called on the phone to demand details.

"Yeah, well, Mom's still not thrilled."

"I know, but she's letting you go. That's pretty amazing. So—have you got a dress yet?"

"Not yet."

Sam's shriek forced me to hold the phone away from my ear. "Not yet? Kathy—the dance is next week!"

"I know, but I want to get something amazing. But in a modest type of a way."

There was definite confusion in Sam's voice. "A 'modest type of a way'?"

"Yeah. I want to look hot without having to show a ton of skin."

Sam was silent for a moment. "You mean, you want to look classy and elegant."

*Yes!* "Exactly. And there's only one person I know who can help me find just the right, amazing dress. That is, of course, if she'll go with me."

I could hear the smile in Sam's voice. "I'll bet she'd love to go if you'd ask her."

"You really think she'd say yes?"

"I'd bet that amazing dress on it."

Now I was smiling into the phone. "Are you free Saturday?"

"For you? I'll make sure I am, Kathy. How about I pick you up at ten?"

"Sounds good. And hey—Sam—"

"Yes?"

"Thanks."

"Thanks yourself. For inviting me. It means a lot to me."

"To me, too." I could feel my throat tightening up in a weird way I wasn't used to having happen when I talked to Sam.

I never knew shopping with my sister could be so much fun. I had a tough time deciding because Sam's practiced eye and style guaranteed that every dress not only fit like magic but looked smashing, too. But when Sam handed me a velvet gown, I couldn't help groaning.

"What?" Sam demanded, peering over the dressing room door at me.

I shook the dress at her. "Velvet?"

Sam only gave me one of her determined looks. "It *is* winter, you know. Velvet is definitely acceptable during wintertime. And it's a Christmas color for a Christmas dance."

"But there's no snow outside, and it isn't even cold! I'll bake in this thing!"

"Just try it on!"

I knew there was no leaving the dressing room until I tried on the dress, so I sighed and yanked the gown down over my head and turned to face the mirror—

"Well? What do you think?" I stepped out of the dressing room and saw in Sam's eyes what I already knew.

"Wow—that's the amazing dress you've been looking for, isn't it?"

I smiled happily into the dressing room mirror. "Most definitely."

The gown really was amazing. The velvet was lightweight and

incredibly soft. It had a high, empire waist with a green satin ribbon that matched the velvet running the circumference of the dress over the high waist seam, ending in the back as a thin sash. The square neckline was a bit rounded, it was so softly squared, and the cap sleeves caused the dress to dip slightly off my shoulders. The dress pulled in snug at the waist to flare out softly from my hips in A-line fashion. I loved the soft rustling noise it made as I moved, and I loved how beautiful I felt in it.

Sam grinned and winked at me. "We just need to pick out some pumps to go with this baby, and then let's eat!"

Picking out shoes turned out to be easy enough. I found a pair as simple and elegant as the dress itself, and soon we were stuffing our faces on Chinese food at Sam's favorite restaurant. We'd hardly started in on our spicy meal, though, when Sam went in for the kill.

"So—Kathy. Has he kissed you yet? Jason, I mean, of course."

I definitely was not prepared for this kind of discussion. Dresses and shoes, yes. Kissing Jason—*no!*

Sam laughed. "Don't choke—and don't tell me you two haven't kissed! Not after all of those private lessons you've been giving him!"

"I've—we've—been completely professional. I agreed to tutor him in English, and that's what I've done."

Sam stared at me before leaning back in her chair. "Wow. You've definitely got more willpower than me. I would've been all over him the first time I had him alone."

I didn't want to talk with Sam about kissing Jason, so of course, I changed the subject. "Sam, will you come do my hair and makeup? Like you did before?"

Sam smiled and thankfully forgot all about kissing. "I'd love to. Besides, you couldn't keep me away. I've got to see how you look in that dress!" Sam winked. "And more importantly, I want to see that hot Jason of yours in a tux!"

*June 25*

Dear Kitty,

I've been happy to see that you still take Tiny Bear with you wherever you go. You even have to have him with you during our story time. It's become more of an athletic adventure trying to read you stories. You make it clear when the story's boring, because in mid-sentence while I'm trying to read to you, you'll grab the page and turn it before roughly turning lots of pages. Then you slam the back cover to close the book and turn to me proudly and say, "All done!" I'm learning which books not to choose anymore. I've also learned it's better to let you choose a story, only it usually works out that if I leave it to you to decide, you pick a stack! But of course, I don't mind. I'd read to you all day if you wanted me to.

Sam came into our room to fuss over me again today. She tries to talk cheerfully about the weather, but her hands shake while she dusts everything she can get her hands on. I must look worse than I think. Today I couldn't stand it anymore, so I interrupted her by saying "Sam." She was caught off guard, and when she finally looked at me, I smiled and said, "I feel lonely." She tried to laugh and said, "Oh, Brett—you're not going to get all mushy on me, are you?" I told her to just shut up and give me a hug. We were still hugging when she said, "Brett—I—I don't know what to say—" so I quickly said, "Then don't say anything." I told her if you don't know what to say, then don't waste time with talking. Just listen. And I told her you do that really well and that I bet she could learn to be almost as good at it as you are. That really made her laugh, because everyone knows how much Sam likes to talk. "Who put a quarter in her?" is a common phrase around here whenever Sam gets her mouth going.

But you do listen well, Kitty. I hope that's a quality—a talent—you never lose . . .

*July 5*

Dear Kitty,

Sam's decided to go to school here at home instead of back down south with all her friends. She cried all day the day they left to go back to school. I feel sick—well, sicker—that she's chosen to sacrifice so much for me.

And then Alex shocked me when he announced he's decided to hold off going to college. Instead, he's going to live at home and get a job somewhere doing who knows what. Just thinking of Alex doing something like bagging groceries or saying, "Do you want fries with that?" when he should be working out, practicing with a college football team, and studying for freshman exams makes me feel sick to my stomach, because now Alex is making sacrifices, too.

We watched the sunset outside again today, Kitty. I thought about God, and how He gives us every day, and then, He gives us a beautiful sunset to end each day with. Only someone who really cares about us all would do something as nice as that. Sometimes Alex and Sam watch the sunset with us. We talk about everything but what's happening now. I know they're scared, too. Every night, they both come into our room to hug me and say, "I love you." That's a phrase you don't hear much in our family, but everything's different now.

I hope when I die that I take all of my memories with me. If nothing else, I hope I'm at least allowed to remember what Mom and Dad, and Alex and Sam's faces look like. And yours, too, of course. But I don't think I could ever forget you, Kitty . . .

*August 7*

Dear Kitty,

I can tell I'm getting weaker. It seems like everything makes me tired. I still have my painkillers. They help some, but not much. But they're better than nothing.

I know I don't have a lot of time left, but I want you to know that I'm not afraid of death. I thought I was, but that's not what I'm worried about. It's dying—the actual process—that bothers me. I remember how much you slept just after you were born, and I wonder if dying is just as tiring. Maybe that's why they refer to dead people as being asleep. You know, "Rest in Peace," and all that. Since death will be the next adventure for me, I wonder what it will be like. Like whether or not it's a painful process. Or a hard one. Or maybe it's as easy as walking from one room into the next. And then I just wonder what it will be like for me. Is it going to be slow—or fast? Am I going to get a lot sicker—feel a lot more pain? I guess I'm just going to have to wait and find out for myself. I'm glad that at least I'll be at home. The idea of dying in a hospital is horrific. I want my last sights to be familiar, not cold and sterile.

I wonder what God is truly like. I have an idea of what Jesus must be like because of the Bible, but God—"Heavenly Father," like Kelly calls Him—if He is a different person from Jesus, what does He think of me? One thing I do know for sure now is that I believe there's something more after death. There has to be more. I've got to count for something more than just seventeen years here. Seasons come and go, over and over again, so to me, it's crazy to think that I, Brett Bartholomew Colton, will just—end. I've got to be going somewhere to do something more with myself. Nothing comes from nothing, as we've all heard Julie Andrews belt out in *The Sound of Music* a million times. I had to come from somewhere—so I must be going somewhere after this, too.

There has to be a reason why I had to get sick—why I have to deal with this, and why our whole family has to deal with it, too. There has to be some deeper, hidden meaning in and for everything that happens. Clouds come around because we need rain. They aren't just there to be there. There has to be a reason why I had to get sick . . .

249

# CHAPTER THIRTY-SIX

*August 28*

Dear Kitty,

School started this week. Big shock I can't be there. I try not to let myself think too much about not being on the team. It's strange. In a way, thinking about school and being disappointed about not playing football anymore is a good thing, because it keeps me from freaking out about dying. But at the same time, thinking about school and football makes me realize that although these are the things that used to be the main things I cared about, now I know there are a lot more important things in life. Like you, and everyone in the family, and making sure you guys know how much I love you all. And noticing and appreciating and being grateful for everything. I don't think I'd feel the way I do if I wasn't sick, and I don't know if I'd want to give up all of those "aha's" for a trade to be well again. It'd be a tough decision to make. More time would be great, but if I've figured out in two years what it takes healthy people their whole lives to figure out, then I feel lucky I've been given a way to figure it all out pretty fast.

Which brings me to my main regret. Another huge realization I've had is that I let my stupid pride take me over. What's left of me, anyway. Which means I haven't talked to Kelly or Jennifer. Don't be stupid like me and let pride get in the way of great friendships in your life.

Anyway—Kelly knows I'm home. I think he's tried to call and come over more than I know. I think Mom and Dad won't let him in because they're afraid he'll make me freak out because of Jennifer. Or maybe they think he'd try talking religion with me and don't want him to "upset" me that way, but I don't know. I don't know what to say to him, so I just keep avoiding calling him so I don't have to say anything. I guess I must get that from Dad . . .

*August 30*

Dear Kitty,

Today has been pretty amazing. I'm still in shock over everything. I didn't feel too sick this morning, and I had a little more energy. I could tell Mom was happy about that, but I knew something was up when she grabbed a pair of scissors and messed with my hair after she helped me wash it this morning—and when Dad insisted on helping me into jeans and an ironed shirt. And when Alex and Sam hung around all day as if they thought Santa was going to show up early this year. And I was right—something major was going on. Maybe Santa didn't show up, but someone—actually, some people—did. Believe it or not, the whole football team showed up, and so did this year's student body officers! Even Kelly made an appearance, looking scared and nervous. To say the least, I was surprised and in shock.

Once everyone was in the house, someone asked if it was okay to watch a video, so Alex shoved a videotape into the VCR that Mike, the student body pres, handed to him. And then I finally figured out what everyone was freaking out about.

The video was a taping of an assembly in the school's auditorium that happened at school today. It had the usual "welcome back to school" skits that weren't very funny, a slide show to some pop music of school scenes and events, then a dance by the drill team, and then a major pep rally by the cheerleaders. After the cheerleaders jogged off the stage, Mike got up on the stage and talked about somebody who'd been a great student, a great friend, and a great addition to the school, etc. and etc.—someone who'd shown true courage and hope. Imagine my surprise to discover the person he was babbling about was me!

The team had the award with them that Mike held up on the video: a big, shiny plaque with my name on it and some fancy words about how wonderful I was. They're planning on putting the plaque with my picture in the trophy case by the trophy we got for winning state last year. Pretty big deal type of thing. Once all the clapping and cheering on the tape quieted down, Mike went on about how amazing I was as a football player and stunned me by announcing the school's going to retire my number. More cheering and clapping happened after that. My home team jersey's going to be hung in the trophy case, too. I'm still in shock.

Mom was crying. Sam and Alex were crying. Even Dad cried. Everyone in our living room cheered and clapped like crazy. On the video, Mike asked Alex if he would come forward to accept the award plaque for me, and while Alex was still on stage with Mike and my award, Kelly joined them. He put his two cents in and said some more fancy words about me before announcing that the team had unanimously agreed to dedicate the football season to—me.

Everyone on the video and in the living room with me cheered again. Even you squealed and clapped. I wanted to say something, but I couldn't. And Kelly—he was staring at me in an embarrassed, hopeful, and sad sort of way. That really got to me. Kelly's the most amazing friend I've ever had, Kitty. I can't deny that. I was doing a lot of bawling, so after a while, everything was too blurry for me to see anything very clearly anymore . . .

252

*August 31*

Dear Kitty,

Yesterday was quite a day. My mind is still numb from it all. Once I was able to make my mouth work, I had Alex borrow a video camera from a neighbor and taped a thank-you from me to the school and the team. I tried to make the video amusing, so of course, everyone said I did great. I saved up my strength so I could give everyone who came a slug in the arm or a hug for bringing about all of that school attention. It really wasn't necessary. Still, it's always nice to know you're cared about and missed . . .

# CHAPTER THIRTY-SEVEN

I'd arrived at school early and spent the minutes before home room started by staring at Brett's face grinning at me from the trophy case. I could feel that strange connection I'd felt so many times before and took a step closer and reached towards him—

"Hey, you."

I jumped when I heard Jason's voice whisper near my ear and felt his hand slip around my waist. For a great big football player with a leg brace on, he had the most uncanny and unique ability to sneak up on me. "Hey, yourself." I grinned back and quickly hoisted my book bag from the floor and onto my shoulder before letting him take my hand. "Ready for class?"

Jason looked from me to Brett's picture. "Is everything okay?"

I smiled. "If you're still planning on taking me to the dance tomorrow night, then everything's more than okay. Unless you're planning on flaking on me. In which case I'd have to hunt you down like a dog and hurt your other leg."

Jason laughed as we walked away from the trophy case towards Honors English. "I didn't realize you had such a violent streak in you, Kathy."

I grinned. "Just consider it extra incentive to get yourself to my house tomorrow night."

———

*September 10*

Dear Kitty,

My head and heart are full of so many things. Memories keep flooding my mind. Like winning state—last Christmas—the day you were born—the first day of school—learning to ride a bike—all kinds of moments keep coming to me as clear as if they happened yesterday. And hugging—I can't seem to get enough of it lately. I've been hugging everyone like crazy.

I'm not leaving the planet this close to Christmas without giving everyone a little something, so with help from my good ol' tutor, Matt, I ordered a gold heart locket for Mom. I'm giving my music collection to Alex, but I saved the Beatles for you. I can't decide whether or not I should give everyone my Christmas gifts now while I'm still around. I wish I could be here for Christmas. I'm really going to miss being with everyone this year.

I have to apologize for scaring you and making you cry last night, Kitty. It was a bad night for me—one of the worst I've had in a long time, filled with lots of bad dreams that had me thrashing around in bed like a fish out of water. And I was sick—so sick—and something or someone was pressing down hard on my arms. I woke up blinded by the lamp on my nightstand, puking all over the place. Mostly all over Dad, who'd been watching me sleep again and was trying to keep me from falling out of bed. Even though I'd puked all over his shirt, he wouldn't leave my side until I'd calmed down and stopped crying and saying, "I'm sorry." He kept saying that it was okay while he held me and rocked me. You sat up in your crib and watched with big, scared eyes, whimpering softly and clutching Tiny Bear. After all three of us calmed down, Dad got rid of his shirt and helped me change into clean sweats. He even changed my sheets with me in the bed. I have no idea how he figured out how to do that. I asked him to stay with me until I fell asleep, so he sat back down in his chair by my bed and held my hand, and even though I was pretty exhausted and weak, I talked his ear off, telling him I was sorry I hadn't been a better son, and that I was sorry I hadn't been more like Alex so we could've been closer. That choked him up, and he told me I had nothing to be sorry for, and that he was sorry for not being a better father to me. I told him—begged him—to make sure he had a great relationship with you—the kind I'd always wished I'd had with him. And to make sure you were happy and would always know that you were loved. I made him promise again and again. And then he told me he loved me, and I told him I loved him. I honestly don't remember us ever doing that before. I'm truly sorry it's taken me getting sick to get everyone saying the words "I love you." It shouldn't be like that, Kitty. You should tell your family all the time that you love them. Everyone should know they're loved by everyone else all the time. It may seem crazy and uncool to go around saying, "I love you," but if there's yet another thing I've learned from my sickness, it's that it's even more uncool not to make sure your family knows you love them.

We talked for a long time. It was all highly emotional, personal stuff. I wish we'd talked like this a long time ago. We're barely starting to get to know each other—and like each other—and I won't be around to enjoy it. I really hate that . . .

# CHAPTER THIRTY-EIGHT

K nock, knock—anybody home?"

I'd been home alone and in my room most of the evening, but at the sound of a voice in the house, I quickly slid Brett's journal under my bed and hurried down the hall to find Alex standing in the living room studying a picture in his hands from the bookshelves.

"So, what are you doing here? Where's Julie?"

Alex jumped and quickly shoved the picture back on the shelf. "At home. Dad said I could borrow that folding table downstairs." But instead of heading downstairs, Alex headed straight for the kitchen and the refrigerator.

I walked over to the pictures to see which one Alex had been holding and had to catch my breath. *Alex, Brett—and Kelly.* The Football Heroes picture. My mind raced as I stared at the picture, and with my heart pounding faster and faster, I took a deep breath and followed Alex into the kitchen. *This was it.* I knew it could possibly be my one and only chance to talk to Alex alone, and I needed to ask him—to talk to him.

Everyone thought that since Alex and I never fought, we must have had a great relationship. Compared to Sam and me, I guess we did, but we never talked about anything serious. Ever. I didn't know if that really counted as a relationship. Right at that moment, for the first time in my life, I was wishing that we had something more solid. More of a real brother-sister-slash-friend relationship. It would've made everything I needed to talk with him about so much easier.

I waited until we'd both filled our glasses with water from the faucet before asking. "Alex, whatever happened to your friend Kelly Baxter from high school?"

Alex was quiet for a second. He wouldn't even look at me but studied his glass of water instead. "I don't have a friend named Kelly Baxter."

I sighed. "Well, then—*Brett's* friend."

Alex took a swallow of his water. "Why do you want to know anything about him?"

"I'm curious. That's all," I said lamely. "I mean—it's just strange to me. You and Brett were friends with him, and yet I've never even seen a Christmas card from him. He's never come for a visit, and he's never called. Unless he's called or visited just you at your house."

"No, he hasn't done either." Alex's voice was flat and cold.

I moved a step closer to him. "Why is that? Doesn't that seem strange to you, too? Why doesn't anyone know what happened to him after high school? After Brett—died?"

Alex set his glass down firmly and turned to face me without a smile on his face, and with a look that made me feel like I'd done something wrong. "What's strange to *me* is that you're asking about Kelly, of all people. Why do you even care?"

*Why did I care?!* "This whole family has acted like I ought to be stoned to death because I didn't feel like hearing about Brett every second of my life! But now that I actually care to ask a few questions, everyone's all suspicious and acts like I'm asking for top secret information!"

Alex shook his head and pointed at me accusingly. "You're not asking questions about Brett, though—you're asking questions about Kelly Baxter. Why do you think you need to know anything about him?"

"Why won't you tell me?" I shot back.

"Because there's no reason for you to be worrying about him!"

I couldn't believe Alex and I were actually yelling at each other. It was as strange as the fact that Sam and I were getting along. But Alex wasn't the only person who could give me answers. "Fine! If you won't talk to me, then I'll ask Kelly instead!" I turned sharp on my heel to run out of the kitchen, but Alex reached out fast, and in one quick swipe he had my arm in his grip, yanking me back to where I'd been standing in front of him.

"Kathy—stop!" Alex and I stared at each other for a moment before he loosened his hold on me and took a deep breath of his own. "Look—it's not as big a deal as you think. Kelly got a football scholarship out of state, and we just sort of—fell out of touch. That's all, okay?"

I folded my arms. "'That's all?' I don't believe 'that's all.' That may explain why you're not as close anymore, but it doesn't explain why no one wants to talk about him. I've tried asking Mom, but all she does is act as weird as you're acting right now."

Alex shook his head. "I don't know what else to tell you, Kathy. Kelly went away to school, and I got busy, too. And like I said, he was Brett's friend, not mine. Your life just gets crazier and busier after high school, and you don't have time for every person you've ever known in your life, let alone your brother's life. You'll see for yourself in a couple of years."

"There's more you're not telling me—I just know it—"

But Alex didn't want to talk anymore and cut me off firmly. Almost angrily. "Believe what you want to believe, Kathy, but I need to get that table and get back home."

*So much for answers.* I mutely followed Alex down to the basement and helped him lug the table up and into his car. Alex practically ran to slide behind the wheel and slam the door shut, but while he revved up the engine, I wrenched open the passenger door before he could lock it and climbed in, slamming the car door shut before facing his angry scowl. I tried again to get him to talk about Kelly—I hated to have to do it to him, but I didn't know when I'd get a chance to talk to him alone again. And it was important—so important to me. I only wished I could make Alex understand. And so, after I laid all of this on him, Alex sighed long and deep—almost painfully—before he glanced at me, and then he turned to squint out the windshield with his hands resting lightly on the steering wheel.

"When you're a teenager—a kid—you do a lot of dumb, stupid things, not realizing that those few seconds can affect the rest of your life for good." His voice was soft and had a sad, far away texture to it that matched the look in his eyes. "When Brett died, I needed someone to blame for—everything. I hated hurting, and I guess I thought blaming Kelly for some of that pain would make it all go away. I thought forcing Kelly out of all of our lives would help, but it didn't. The pain is still there. Even after all of this time."

We sat in silence for a long moment before I dared to speak. "What happened?" Alex remained unmoving, staring silently ahead for so long that I wasn't sure he'd heard me.

"Kelly didn't come around much towards the end—mostly because Brett wouldn't see him, I guess. I couldn't understand that, since he was Brett's best friend, but I guess it must've been hard for him to watch Brett die, too." Alex stopped for a moment and sighed. "And then, there was the mess with that girl Brett liked."

*Jennifer!* "A girl?" I whispered.

Alex nodded. "Yeah. Brett really liked this girl in high school. And she liked him for a while, until she met Kelly. It made me angry to see Brett hurting over the whole mess." Alex laughed bitterly. "It all seems so stupid now, but like I said, teenagers can let little things become big things and get melodramatic over just about anything." Alex turned and glanced briefly at me. "No offense, of course."

I nodded dully. "So you hate Kelly because of a girl he and Brett both liked?"

"I never said I hated Kelly," Alex said firmly. "But it was more than just the girl. I couldn't stand the fact that Kelly was filling Brett's head with a bunch of mumbo-jumbo about his crazy religion. It really drove Mom and Dad crazy, too. Especially Mom."

"Why?" I whispered.

"It was hard enough having to watch her son die a little bit more every day, but it was adding insult to injury to have her son's best friend taking what little time he had left and getting him all wound up about his religion and reading his Mormon Bible instead of helping him to relax and feel calm and loved and ready to let go when the time came. He had Brett thinking he needed to convert, which scared us all. The painkillers he was on would've made him a little crazy anyway, but those last couple of weeks especially, he was constantly freaking out—babbling about finding the truth and needing to be baptized before he died, and needing to talk to Kelly about it. It really upset Mom and Dad. All of us, actually. I knew he was probably just hallucinating big time, since he was so close to the end, but he never stopped talking about wanting to be baptized. He used to beg me to help him—to talk to Mom and Dad. He also begged me to read that crazy Mormon Bible—"

Alex stopped and I waited for him to go on, not daring to move a muscle. His voice was so low and quiet when he spoke again that I had to strain my ears to catch each word. "The day after Brett's funeral, I was home alone when Kelly came over. I'd been in Brett's room and found that Book of Mormon of his. Just looking at Kelly, thinking about the stuff Brett raved about at the end, and missing Brett so bad like I did, and knowing he wasn't coming back—I don't know—something inside me snapped. The next thing I knew I was yelling and screaming and swearing at Kelly about everything, including the girl and the religious stuff he'd filled Brett's head with. I told him I wanted him to get out and stay away forever. And I shoved the Book of Mormon at him and told him to take his crazy religion with him, since all it had done was to make Brett freak out, and so the rest of us had suffered, too, having to watch him suffer. As if having leukemia wasn't enough." Alex stopped, his voice catching in the back of his throat. "No matter how long I live,

I'll never be able to forget the look on Kelly's face—the hurt—all of that sadness and pain. Tears were all welled up in his eyes—I couldn't stand it, so I turned away and told him not to come around our house anymore. And I shut the door in his face. So he left." Alex's hands were trembling as he gripped the steering wheel. I blinked hard over and over while Alex wiped his eyes with the back of his hand.

"Mom and Dad wondered at first why Kelly never came around after Brett died, but then he left for college, and Sam was getting back into school, and soon they stopped asking about him. But I never told anybody what happened that day. Until now. Until you," he whispered, his voice shaking. He tried to give me a weak smile. "When I finally started college, I thought about trying out for football. Got really close to almost doing it, but the idea of playing without Brett—I don't know—I just couldn't do it. It wouldn't be the same without him there."

I sat back, dumbfounded, wiping my eyes. I was sorry I'd upset Alex so badly, but even worse was the part of me that was guiltily glad I'd asked him and that we'd talked. More awful still was the realization that instead of feeling sated, I was curious and hungry for more.

---

*September 20*
Dear Kitty,

I've been doing a lot of thinking since I got that award. When I first realized I was sick, I thought fifteen or sixteen years wasn't enough time to live—that I really hadn't had much of a life, but you can live seventy or eighty years and still not have much of a life if you don't take control of your time and spend it wisely. I've tried to make the most of the time I have left—not just let it be eaten away by dumb, unimportant things.

Kelly and I haven't had any of our old talks in a long time. I wish I could see him again. I've got so many questions no one else can answer. I try to casually talk about his religion with the family, but no one's interested in listening. Mom—she just gets upset and starts crying if I bring up "Kelly's crazy religion." Dad's never happy to hear about it, either. Neither of them have been from the start, but now that I'm at the end of my road, they think my religious thoughts and questions are doing me more harm than good and that I shouldn't be letting "things like that" get me all upset. They think my "seeing the light" is just an act of desperation because I'm dying. But it's more than that. I'm seeing things differently than I ever did before—probably than I ever would have if this disease had never happened to me.

To me, living and dying without leaving anything behind—as if you never existed—is the worst thing that could happen. I don't want to be forgotten. I hope that at least I'll live forever in memory and that I've done enough good things that people who knew me will be glad they did.

I found a poem in one of my English textbooks. It's by Walker Percy, and it's called "The Second Coming." It pretty much sums up what I've been thinking and feeling lately. Especially where the poem asks the question about whether people can miss their lives, in the same way a person can miss a plane. And then the lines,

> *And how is it that death, the nearness*
> *of death, can restore a missed life?*

Those two lines have echoed over and over in my head ever since I first read them.

I'm much better at expressing myself on paper than in spoken words, as you can probably tell by now, Kitty. The me I am in my head is a whole different person from the guy the world sees. I think being sick has helped me—the real me—show my face more often.

We watched the sunset from our bedroom window tonight until the first star came out. The one wish I have is that somehow you'll save in your mind some little memory of me . . .

*September 25*

Dear Kitty,

I know I'm getting closer to the end of the line. Mom, Dad, Alex, and Sam won't leave me alone anymore. One or two of them are always with me. You refuse to leave my side at all. Thank you for that, Kitty—you'll never know how much that means to me.

I tried one more time to talk to Mom when she came into my room today. I was trying to help her understand how I feel about "Kelly's religion," if only to get her to calm down and relax about everything, but she just got even more upset. More stuff about how I'm sick and don't need Kelly adding more stress in my life and that I shouldn't be concentrating on anything but relaxing and getting some rest so I can feel better. I wish she would let herself see that Kelly's faith has really helped me see and understand so much, but she's got a major mind wall against the whole religion issue, and nothing I can say or do is going to bring it down. Maybe someday, something will help her and Dad to change their minds, but it's not going to happen while I'm still on this planet. All I can do at this point is agree to disagree and make sure she knows I love her and always will, no matter what happens here or beyond this life.

I made Mom open her Christmas present from me today. She cried when she opened the locket. Sam put a recent, before-my-illness picture of me on one side of the heart. When I tried to joke and tell Mom I was giving her the locket so she wouldn't forget me, she cried even more and said she didn't need a locket, because she'd already locked me safe inside her heart forever. That really got me, Kitty, so we bawled and hugged and talked. Believe me, Kitty—the hardest part about dying is saying good-bye and letting go . . .

# CHAPTER THIRTY-NINE

O kay—I think I'm about done here. Take a look and tell me what you think."

I turned around to survey myself in my bedroom's full-length mirror—and couldn't stop staring. The velvet dress Sam helped me pick out for the dance had looked amazing at the store, but now that it was pressed and I had it on with my new heels, along with the benefit of Sam's expert makeup-applying skills, the whole look was incredible. Sam had even created a fancy hairstyle on me with a wavy ringlet framing each side of my face and an up-do of curls formed into what she called a "clytie knot," wound Grecian-style with a thin, forest green ribbon to match my dress.

"I can't believe it's me! Thanks for making me look so gorgeous, Sam!" I reached out to give her a hug, but Sam dodged, laughing, and blew me an air kiss instead.

"Watch the hair and makeup, Kathy—besides, I'm not quite finished with you yet."

I raised my eyebrows. "I don't think there's an inch left of me that hasn't been curled, powdered, painted, or dressed up! What could possibly be missing?"

"Just this." Sam had turned to her purse and now held up something that glistened as it dangled from her fingers. My eyes nearly popped out of my head, but even as I protested, Sam shushed me and firmly turned me around so she could secure the choker-style strand of pearls Stephen had given to her for their last anniversary.

"Sam! I can't—really—"

"Yes, you can, and yes, you will." While I stared at the glistening pearls around my neck, Sam dug into the bag she'd packed everything in for fancying me up tonight and pulled out an elegant short black evening coat that she draped around my shoulders.

"Sam!"

"Just stick your arms in the sleeves and see if it fits okay."

It did fit. More than okay. "But really, Sam, it's not that cold outside!"

"Maybe not right now, but it *is* December, even if there isn't any snow yet. And it'll be colder when the dance is over. Besides—it has pockets in case you want to take your lip gloss."

I dug my hands into the coat's soft, warm pockets—and gasped again.

Sam grinned and folded her arms. "Don't say no. Smart girls carry some cash on a date, no matter *who* the date is." Sam walked a circle around me, checking for any wayward bit of anything. "Now all you need is your corsage, and you'll be all set!"

Sam and I both grinned at my reflection in the mirror, and after I laid the jacket on my bed, this time Sam couldn't stop me from hugging her.

"You've got Jason's boutonniere?" Sam reminded me.

I nodded. "Yeah—it's in the fridge."

My stomach tightened into a knot, and nerves and worry took over as horrible thoughts I'd been shoving down all day began to plague me. Now that I had nothing else to do but wait for Jason to arrive, the time had come to freak out over whether or not he really *would* show up—or if I'd get an apology call at the last second. It was horrible of me to have such little faith in him—I knew that—but I couldn't help feeling wary, bracing myself for possible disappointment, even at this late hour—

"Kathy, your date's here!"

Dad's voice had my heart jumping and me racing for the door after snatching Sam's evening jacket off my bed. Before I could set one high heel into the hallway, Sam rushed to block my way.

"Good grief! You don't need to run—he's not ringing a dinner bell! Besides—you're in heels and a dress, not shorts and sneakers. Keep that in mind tonight and walk accordingly."

I did my best to sweep elegantly down the hall and into the living room for my grand entrance, expecting to see Jason nervously squirming in front of my parents, but what I *did* see brought me to a quick halt with my mouth hanging open.

Jason was standing, smiling, and talking to my parents. And looking incredibly, heart-stoppingly handsome. I definitely hadn't expected Jason to go to the effort of renting a tuxedo, and yet there he was in black tie, his eyes sparkling as he looked me up and down. I felt so fish-out-of-water-y that I stuttered and mumbled like an idiot about needing to get his boutonniere, but Sam quickly volunteered to grab that out of the fridge for me. While I stood in the living room doorway gawking at Jason in his tux, Sam thrust the boutonniere in my hand and quickly whispered, "He knew to get a dance tuxedo and not one with tails—I'm impressed!" before shoving me forward with a huge smile while she introduced herself to Jason.

Jason carefully tied my corsage of three tiny red rosebuds surrounded by white lace and pearls to my wrist. My hands wouldn't stop trembling while I awkwardly tried to pin on his boutonniere, but somehow even with Sam, Mom, and Dad gathered too closely around us, scrutinizing my progress, I successfully harpooned the red rose onto his tuxedo jacket.

"Okay, kids, let's take a few pictures!" Dad grabbed his camera, and even though I begged him not to, he insisted on taking some shots of

Jason and me outside. "Those dance pictures are always so posed and stiff. Don't be afraid to look like you're having some fun here!"

Jason laughed when I tried to thank him after Dad finally finished taking an entire roll of film. "No big deal, Kathy. I just hope one of these turns out okay."

Once we were safely back inside, Dad took a few more pictures before Jason promised to bring me home safe at a decent hour. Even Mom smiled and waved good-bye and seemed to have warmed up to Jason a little. And then, I was in for another surprise. This time I couldn't stop the shriek that burst out of my mouth. Parked in front of my house was a huge, shiny black limousine. Complete with a driver in a black uniform and hat.

Jason laughed. "Like it?"

"Like it?" I laughed. "I can't believe you did this!"

Jason's eyes wouldn't stop sparkling at me the whole time we were in the limousine. "If I didn't tell you already, Kathy, you look—wow. Beautiful."

I laughed nervously while he squeezed my hand. "You look pretty amazing yourself. I can't believe you rented a tuxedo! You didn't have to do that, you know."

"I wanted to. And seeing how incredible you look, I'm glad I did."

We were both silent while Jason continued to just *look* at me with those beautiful dark blue eyes of his. I looked away and cleared my throat nervously and with my free hand smoothed my dress before turning back to him. "So—where are we going for dinner?"

"I made reservations at a French restaurant in the city."

I giggled at Jason's attempt to pronounce the name. "A French restaurant? Wow—I'm impressed."

Jason smiled back. "You are, huh? Good."

Jason's pleased smile didn't last once our plates of food were finally placed in front of us, even though he'd been careful not to order snails or cow brains. "Tell me this is just the first course!"

"First course? No, I don't think so. I'm pretty sure this is the main course."

Jason raised an eyebrow. "Main course?"

"Yeah. You know—our 'entrees.'"

"You mean—this is *it?*"

"Unless you're planning on dessert." I picked up my fork and knife to start in on my own meal and smiled as I chewed and swallowed my first bite. *Heavenly.* But after his first bite, Jason only frowned. "What's wrong now? Does it taste funny?"

Jason shook his head. "No—it's not that—I'm just used to eating more food for dinner."

"I don't think the French are familiar with the term 'super size,'" I laughed.

"Maybe someone ought to fill them in," Jason grumbled. The food was excellent, though, which Jason couldn't deny, even if he didn't think the portions were massive enough.

"It'll keep you from wanting to loosen your belt and take a nap. We'll both be ready to dance once we get to the Grand America hotel." It was unbelievable that a place as ritzy as the Grand America would condescend to allow a high school dance to invade it. I had to say "wow" when the limo pulled up to the hotel, and again once we stepped through the revolving doors into the hotel's palatial lobby. And again when we arrived at the ballroom, complete with huge, sparkling chandeliers, a live band, and fancy tables for eating fancy treats.

Jason spotted the treat table area right away. "Do you want anything?"

"No, but I'm sure *you* do. Let's go." Jason took my hand and quickly maneuvered us around suits and fluffy skirts before releasing my hand to happily devour a cookie.

I laughed, watching him reach for another. "I guess I ought to grab us some punch—"

"Jason—is that you?"

*Angela.* I shouldn't have been surprised. In fact, I should've been surprised if she *wasn't* at the dance. And of course, she looked stunning. Angela wouldn't know how to look anything *but.* She wore a huge, model-perfect smile on her face while she clung to the arm of a tall, broad-shouldered senior—one I'd seen strutting down the halls in a letterman's jacket. Although she was clinging to him—whatever his name was—her eyes and smile were set squarely on Jason. My stomach turned into a tense ball of knots while I forced my mouth into a smile.

Jason swallowed a mouthful of cookie before speaking. "Hey, Rob—Angela."

Rob grinned and pointed at Jason's brace. "How's the knee?"

"It's getting there."

Rob nodded. "Good to hear." And then, Rob's eyes moved to me. And stayed. "Hey—you're the girl from the Shakespeare festival!"

"Yes, that would be me." A senior athlete acknowledging my presence *and* speaking to me? I was truly amazed.

"Kathy—this is Rob. Rob—Kathy." I felt Jason's hand glide around my waist and pull me closer against his side. I glanced up at him, and although he smiled directly at Rob, the smile didn't reach his eyes. I grinned as I felt his arm around me tighten. Sam had done a better makeover on me than I'd thought!

"Jas! What's up?"

Jeff and his date, followed by Brad and his date, hurried over from across the ballroom and crowded around on the other side of Jason and me—and immediately ignored me to talk to Jason.

"Hi, girls!" Angela stepped in closer to speak to Brad and Jeff's dates, practically squeezing me out of our wonderful little circle. But Rob was still looking at me and moving in closer by the second, even though Jason kept his arm firmly around my waist.

"You came with Jason?" Rob asked, leaning in even closer.

"Yes, I did."

"Lucky him." I knew I was blushing at Rob's flirting grin and wink.

Even better—now Brad and Jeff were looking at us. Their dates were watching, too, clearly not interested anymore in what Angela had to say.

"Hey, didn't you play Juliet in the Shakespeare festival a few weeks ago?" Brad's date was looking at me curiously.

"Yes, that was me."

"You were in another one, too, weren't you?" Jeff's date was now speaking to me, too! Miracles truly never ceased.

"*King Lear.* I was Cordelia."

"Oh yeah—in that fabulous white dress!" Jeff's date was actually gushing. Her comment was quickly followed by, "I loved that dress!" from Brad's date.

Both Brad and Jeff were as shocked as I was that their dates were speaking to me. Of their own free will and choice! At that point, I dared to throw a glance Angela's way. The model-perfect smile she'd been wearing was gone. Her eyes narrowed slightly at me before she quickly pasted on her trademark fake smile and gave Rob's arm a healthy tug before loudly announcing, "Hey—I just *love* this song. Come on, Rob— let's go dance, okay?" And with a purposeful glare at Brad and Jeff's dates, she quickly steered Rob away from me. Brad and Jeff's dates hurried to follow her, pushing Brad and Jeff in front of them towards the dance floor.

Jason leaned down and moved his lips near my ear. "I thought they'd never leave!"

I couldn't help laughing. "That sounds like something I should be saying—not you!"

"Yeah, well, they were starting to get on my nerves," Jason grumbled.

"But they're your friends!"

Jason almost snorted. "Some friend! Moving in on you when he's got his own date."

"You mean Rob?"

Jason rolled his eyes. "Of course I mean Rob. Who else would I mean?"

I laughed again. "I'm sure he was just being nice."

"Nice? Don't even! Like you didn't notice he was all over you!" I laughed again, which Jason didn't like at all. "You didn't have to look like you were enjoying talking to him so much."

"I didn't realize having a hot guy in a tux flirt with me was supposed to equal torture!"

"Well, it was torture for *me!*"

I grinned up at Jason's unhappy face and bumped his hip with mine. "Good!"

Jason rolled his eyes and grinned back. "Come on—let's go dance!"

Jason took my hand and led me out onto the dance floor before I could tease him more. The song was a slow one, and for that brief second when we turned to face each other, there was a moment of awkwardness. I actually felt shy—and self-conscious—about putting my arms around his neck. The first and last time I'd danced with Jason had been at the homecoming dance, which seemed like a million years ago. So much had changed since then. I never would've believed I'd ever dance with Jason again. Certainly not at a fancy dance as his date. For just that brief moment, I thought I saw some of the awkwardness I was feeling reflected in Jason's eyes. The idea of his being nervous about anything to do with *me* was both strange and heartening. I smiled, he smiled back, and then Jason reached for my hand just as I held it out to him, and slid his other hand behind my waist as I placed my other hand on his shoulder.

I raised my eyebrows. "I wasn't sure if you knew how to slow dance like this."

"I don't. I'm sure you'll be able to tell pretty quick."

I laughed. "Don't worry. I'm not expecting anything fancy. This easy side-to-side, shifting from one foot to the other thing we've got going works for me." I had to choke back a scream when a second later, Jason dipped me low and brought me up smoothly again in front of him with a grin. "What—what was that for?" I gasped.

Jason laughed. "Just because you weren't expecting anything fancy doesn't mean something fancy isn't going to happen. I can be spontaneous and surprise you, you know!"

"Well, I definitely know now!"

Jason pulled me in closer to him and looked down at me with a satisfied, pleased-with-himself smile. I smiled back, and as I moved in closer, he rested his cheek against my head. We stayed liked that for the rest of the song. And for the next song. And the next. And for the first time in my life, I didn't mind having several slow songs in a row played at a dance.

———

When a fast song did present itself, Jason reluctantly let go of me and shook his braced leg for a second. "Is it okay with you if we skip this one? My leg's screaming for a break."

The leg brace. *And his knee!* I couldn't believe I could've been so self-absorbed that I'd forgotten. This was probably the longest he'd stood on his leg since the blowout. "Your leg! Of course—I'm sorry! We should've sat down a long time ago!"

Jason sighed. "It's only my leg that wants a break, believe me. I'm just glad that I don't have to mess around with crutches anymore."

I hadn't thought about that. Going to a dance with his crutches in tow would have been interesting—and not in a good way. "I'm glad you're through with your crutches, too."

"Not half as glad as I am. A brace is better than crutches any day."

While Jason carefully lowered himself into a chair, I craned my neck to see if I could locate where dance pictures were being taken. "This might be a good time to get our dance pictures out of the way. I'll go see how long the line is while you rest your leg, okay?" I moved along behind the chairs to one of the ballroom exits and glimpsed a Dance Pictures This Way sign pointing down a narrow hall. The line wasn't too horrific, and since the picture-taking area was located by the restrooms,

I took advantage of the vanity opportunity before me to see if my water-proof mascara was doing its job and also to see how my fancy hairdo was holding up.

The restroom was as incredible as the rest of the hotel. The room I'd entered had couches and fancy golden dressing tables with huge, gold framed mirrors above them. Plush red carpeting shushed my footsteps as I moved toward one wall that was a solid mirror from top to bottom and side to side. The room was an unbelievably fabulous place—fit for royalty.

The door to the sinks and toilets opened, and the three who had been talking together immediately fell silent when I locked eyes with all three of them through the mirror's reflection.

Brad and Jeff's dates. And Angela. I decided to be brave and turned to face them with a smile. "Hello."

Angela recovered first and put a big, fake smile on her face before walking slowly over while Brad and Jeff's dates followed along behind. "Hello, Kathy. Having fun with Jason?"

"Yes, I am. Are you having a good time with Rob?"

Angela's big, fake smile got even bigger as she gushed, "I'm having an incredible time—it's amazing what a difference it is to date a *senior* instead of a *sophomore*. I was *majorly* wasting my time before."

I folded my arms. "Really? Well, I guess I'll find out for myself when Jason's a senior." Brad and Jeff's dates erupted in surprised laughter, and while Angela whirled around to glare at them, I figured now was a great time to make my getaway.

"See you later." I pushed open the main door and walked out, but not before I heard Angela angrily and loudly whisper, "I can't believe you guys *laughed!* As if there's any chance Jason will be with *her* a *month* from now, much less two *years!* . . ." The bathroom door thankfully finished closing on those delightful last words from Angela. I didn't want to let her ruin tonight for me, but I needed a few minutes to walk off the feeling I'd just been slapped before I could face Jason with a smile again.

Unfortunately, I was able to move only a few steps down the hall before I heard him calling my name.

"Kathy!" Jason was standing at the end of the line for the dance pictures, waving me over. "You were gone so long I thought maybe you got lost. Everything okay?"

I glanced briefly at him before looking down to smooth my dress. "I'm fine."

"You don't look fine. In one sense of the word only, of course," Jason tried to tease.

"Mmmm." Jason wouldn't stop scrutinizing me as if I were under a microscope while we stepped up to the end of the picture-taking line. Before I could say anything else, I could tell something had caught his attention over my shoulder. Turning, I saw Angela and Brad and Jeff's dates exit the fancy bathroom and move down the hall away from us.

"What happened?" Jason demanded.

I shrugged. "Nothing. She was just being Angela."

"That can't be good."

"It wasn't," I agreed as flippantly as possible.

Jason elbowed me in the ribs. "Forget about her. She's just jealous."

I could feel my jaw drop. "Of *me?*"

Jason rolled his eyes. "Yes, *you.* Just try not to let her get to you, okay?" Jason smiled and squeezed my hand as we moved to take our turn in front of the camera. The pose was every bit as stiff as my dad had warned us it would be. Afterwards, we slow danced on the ballroom floor until I could almost believe nothing mattered or existed but that night and the two of us.

---

The last song of the night was ending when Jason moved his mouth near my ear and whispered, "You ready to blow this hot dog stand?"

I laughed and nodded while Jason led me off the dance floor and helped me on with Sam's jacket. "Handsome *and* romantic. Lucky me!"

We snuggled together in the backseat of the limo and rode in silence until curiosity took over. "So—where are you taking me now?"

Jason tapped at the window by him with the back of his hand. "I thought you might like to drive around the city. You know, look at all the Christmas lights."

I smiled and peered out Jason's window. "Sounds nice, but tell the driver to stop at this next corner for a second."

Jason turned to look out the window himself. "At that fast food place?"

"Exactly."

Jason grinned. "Was my stomach growling that loudly?"

"I don't know whose was louder—yours or mine."

Jason laughed but didn't protest, and once we were inside, he happily ordered disgustingly huge hamburgers, fries, and drinks for both of us. "It's going to be a few minutes—let's sit." Jason moved to sit at a table near the food-ordering line, but I'd spotted a picture-taking booth, which had me pulling on Jason to follow me. I dug my hand into one of the jacket's pockets for the dollars Sam had sneaked inside and then quickly fed the money into the booth. I slipped behind the curtain and sat on the little stool inside before peeking out to find Jason watching me.

"Well, aren't you coming in?"

Jason grinned, and scrunched together on the tiny seat inside, we took picture after picture—getting progressively sillier and sillier until all of Sam's money was gone.

"Number seventy-three? Number seventy-three? Last call, number seventy-three!" We'd both been laughing so hard looking at the photos that I'd forgotten we'd ordered anything at all.

"That's us—be right back!"

I gathered up the photos and carefully put them in Sam's jacket pocket while Jason picked up our order. After we climbed back into the limo, we happily gorged ourselves on the food and oohed and ahhed over the lights we could see as we were chauffeured through the city.

"I can't believe tonight is almost over." Jason fumbled with the radio controls while I held his hand and leaned against his shoulder, mumbling an "mm hmm" in agreement, until Paul McCartney's voice racing by made me jump.

"Wait—turn it back—"

Jason jumped himself before flipping the dial back to Paul McCartney. "Sorry—I forgot. You like the Beatles, don't you?"

I smiled and leaned back into the car seat. "This song's from the record album I have."

"The one you told me about? The one that was your brother's?"

I nodded and looked back out the window again. "Yeah—the U.S. release of the *Rubber Soul* album. I don't think you can buy anything but the U.K. version on CD now."

Jason leaned back against the seat and put his arm around my shoulders and listened along with me. The limo had wound its way to the top of the hill where the capitol building overlooked the city. The view was absolutely incredible. We both stared in silence at the lights glittering below us and all the stars winking above us.

"In case I forgot to tell you, I had a wonderful time tonight. Thank you." Jason reached out to smooth a strand of hair back behind my ear, and as his hand slowly moved to my neck, his eyes lowered to my lips. My heart raced as he leaned his face towards mine and softly kissed me. Before he could pull away, I slipped my arms around his neck and kissed him back. My heart pounded faster as Jason pulled me closer to him while we kissed.

———

*September 27*

Dear Kitty,

I wish I could see Kelly one more time. I haven't seen him since the day he was here with the football team. I can't tell you how much I miss him. I wish I'd never said all of those crazy, mean things to him. Kelly's been a brother to me—he's helped to make me who I am. He has no idea how much he's done for me. The hope he's given me with his belief in God is only one of a billion things he's given me. Best of all was his true friendship. I wish I could talk to Kelly, but I'm so weak and tired all the time—Mom won't let anyone who's not family come in to see me. If he has tried to come by, no one's clueing me in. I wish I could walk over to his house and tell him I'm sorry and I love him. And thank him for being the best friend I could ever have. But somewhere in the back of my mind, I know that no matter what happens, we'll always be friends.

Even though it's hard for me to talk very long to anyone, you seem to understand. You lie by me in bed with Tiny and listen to music with me a lot. I think we've nearly worn out that Beatles album. And I've told you I love you a thousand times. Today you put your little hands on my face and whispered back, "Love Bet— Love Bet." I'll hold onto that forever, Kitty.

I've taken a lot of things for granted. I never realized how lucky I was before just to be able to run. It's hard for me now to just think about doing a lot of things without getting tired.

They say that life's greatest hell is wondering what might have been and regretting not seizing onto every opportunity that comes your way. If I can leave you only one piece of advice, it would be to do just that with your life—seize every opportunity that comes. Not just big ones, like trying out for the lead in the school play or becoming a doctor someday, but the "little" ones, too, like telling someone "I love you," and "thanks for being my friend." Most of the time, those turn out to be the biggest moments and opportunities in your life. I don't want you to have to live with regrets. Believe me, nothing is worse than having to live with regret.

When I first accepted I was sick, I knew I'd reached a turning point, because I knew my life would never be the same again. I wasn't able to choose to have leukemia any more than I was allowed to prepare for it. I knew I could either give up or else I could try to make sense of it and make the most of the time I had left. You were the one who pointed me in the right direction, who made me want to change my mind and choose to make the most of the time I had left. I'm grateful that at least I'd been given some time. People in fatal car accidents aren't given any warning at all. At least I've been warned. I've been given the chance to say good-bye . . .

## CHAPTER FORTY

When I finally woke up on Saturday, the house was quiet. I lay in bed, happily reliving the highlights of Friday night in my mind before reaching for Brett's journal. I was nearing the end, and while part of me wanted to finish it, another part didn't want to turn the last page. So I carefully set Brett's journal back in my top dresser drawer, and finding the house to be empty with no one around to ask me about the big dance, I decided to take Sam's jacket back to her house. She, of course, would ask for details, which would give me the wonderful opportunity of reliving every minute detail aloud.

After throwing myself together, I reached for the jacket and checked the pockets before smiling as my fingers closed around all of the strips of black-and-white photos. I giggled looking at the silly ones and blushed while I looked at the ones of Jason holding me on his lap. They weren't silly at all. I carefully put the photos inside the front cover of Brett's journal, reached into the other jacket pocket—and pulled out Jason's tuxedo tie.

I grinned as I examined the tie in my hand. I'd forgotten Jason had unstrangled himself from it the second the dance was over. I'd played with the tie in the limo and stuffed it into my jacket pocket when we pulled up to the fast food restaurant, and then I'd forgotten to remember to give it back when Jason kissed me one last time—a few "last times," actually—before saying good night on my doorstep. My grin deepened as I relived that moment again. Tuxedo ties had been the last thing on my mind. "Lucky, lucky accident," I said out loud to nobody but myself. And the tie. "Time to return you to Jason." With my excuse in place, I happily jogged out of my bedroom to the kitchen for the car keys. And after refixing my hair and changing into a nicer pair of jeans, I jumped into the cruddy car and headed for Jason's house.

———

I'd been singing along with the radio the whole way to Jason's until blaring sirens had me not only reaching quickly to turn down the volume but pulling over to let a police car with lights flashing rush by as well. *Good grief!* My heart raced as the police car zoomed down the road. It wasn't until I signaled to get back onto the road that I realized the sirens—lots of sirens—were getting louder and louder the closer I got to Jason's street.

When I finally rounded the last bend that caused Jason's house to come into view, I caught back a hard gasp. My foot responded at the same time, grinding my brakes to a halt. My heart pounded and my hands shook as I clutched the steering wheel. I froze, sitting in the cruddy car in the middle of the road with my foot glued to the brake. But as my body reacted in its way, my mind and my wide eyes strangely, calmly, unbelievingly—almost as if both were trying to pretend it was a movie screen in front of me instead of real life—numbly took in the scene before me.

There was an ambulance—a big white one with red lights flashing— directly in front of Jason's home. And a car—a dark blue car on the other side of the road—with a mangled front bumper. And a bike—a small, pink bike—just as mangled—lying in the middle of the road—

I couldn't look anymore at that bike, because I didn't want to know—I didn't want to know for sure whether or not it was Emily's, even though I knew—I knew.

I jerked my eyes away from the bike and looked towards the other side of the road. There was a boy—a boy probably not much older than me—sitting on the curb with his head in his hands. A police officer was crouched by him with a clipboard, talking to him with a concerned but focused and determined look on his face.

There was a small group of people—EMTs, mostly—and Jason's parents, too—all kneeling on the road behind the ambulance, looking down at something. At someone. Jason's mother was crying, and Jason's father had his arms around her, holding her back while the EMTs continued to concentrate with smooth, orchestrated, practiced movements on the one in the middle of their circle. Jason's parents drew away as the EMTs lifted the stretcher before rolling it into the ambulance, so for a brief moment, I was able to catch a glimpse of a small, still figure with dark curls.

"Emily—" My throat closed tightly as I continued to stare at the unbelievable scene before me. The ambulance—the car—the bike—and Emily, lying so still. So horribly still.

A car honking behind me jerked me back to myself. My body didn't seem to belong to me as I turned the car away from the driveway I was blocking. I pulled over to the side of the road before shakily turning off the engine. And with the car now closer to Jason's home, I could see something I'd missed before.

*Jason*—sitting on the grass by the sidewalk right by the ambulance, with his good left knee drawn up tight to his chest, his arms clutched around it, and his head buried against it. And he was rocking slowly back and forth.

I couldn't stay where I was anymore—not after seeing Jason like that on top of the other unreal scenes around me. I was shaking all over, but somehow I forced myself out of the car. No one tried to stop me as I slowly walked towards Jason.

He didn't look up when I finally stood beside him. I doubt he even knew I was there, so I carefully, slowly sat down close to him while he continued to rock back and forth. I was afraid to touch him as I softly said his name.

"Jason?"

The rocking stopped, and after a moment, he lifted his red-eyed, tear-stained face to me. He'd been crying. Crying hard. And there was blood on his shirt.

I stifled a gasp. I'd never seen so much pain etched onto a person's face before, and for a brief moment, I could see Alex—Sam—even Kelly—and I felt ashamed of myself for ever thinking lightly and uncaringly of such pain. Or for thinking that my pain could've been more. But knowing it was Jason's face before me now, and knowing it was *his* pain that was fresh and real broke my heart. "Jason!" I said again, reaching out tentatively with trembling fingers to touch his hair.

Jason stared at me for a moment while time—everything—seemed to stand still—even the wind—and all sound around us fell silent while I stared back at him. Then with a cry, he dived into my chest and clutched me while he cried, and I held him just as tightly. Jason tried to speak between his sobs. "She wasn't wearing her helmet—I should've made her—I should've been watching her—no one else was home but me—it's my fault—"

I stroked his hair with my hand and shushed him softly, telling him over and over that none of it was his fault and to stop saying such things—that he shouldn't even *think* something like that. I'd never held someone so close before in my entire life. Jason was holding me so tightly I could hardly breathe, but I didn't move. I wouldn't have moved if my life depended on it. And as horrible and strange as this moment was, my eyes were drawn over Jason's head to the ambulance. With my hand moving softly through Jason's hair as I held him, I watched while the EMTs helped Jason's mother into the ambulance, and then I saw Jason's father do something that would amaze me for the rest of my life.

Jason's father turned and looked across the street at the boy sitting on the curb with his head in his hands. The police officer was still talking to him, and after a brief moment, Jason's father walked slowly across the street until he was standing in front of the boy. The boy looked up, and I held my breath, tensely waiting for—I didn't know, but something that would likely be terrible. I could see tears streaming down the boy's face. I couldn't see Jason's father's face, but a moment later, the boy was on his feet, and I watched in amazement as Jason's father gathered the boy in his arms and held him while the boy and Jason's father cried. I could hear the boy sobbing, "I'm so sorry!" over and over.

Watching Jason's father put his arms around the boy while the two cried together was the most incredible thing I'd ever seen in my life, and at that moment, I began to understand why Jason was such an amazing person. Having a father like that—and the family he had—it would be hard *not* to turn out to be the kind of person Jason was. I could feel tears sliding down my own cheeks, and I cried. I'd never cried like that before. I cried for Jason—his parents—Emily—the boy across the street— everyone but myself. I'd never cried for anyone *but* myself before, but at that moment, I was the last person on my mind.

# CHAPTER FORTY-ONE

I couldn't sleep that night. Or the next few nights. Jason was basically living up at the children's hospital with his parents. On Sunday evening, I was finally able to reach him by phone at home and tentatively ask about Emily.

"She's got a concussion. Grade three."

"Is that bad?"

"It isn't good."

"Is she awake?"

"No—" Jason's voice broke, so I didn't ask any more questions.

I was able to catch him at home in the evenings again by phone over the next few days, but his message each day regarding Emily didn't change. The only thing that did seem to be changing was Jason. The sadness in his voice deepened every day, and I could feel that he was pulling in and away. The whole thing scared me. Other than calling him late in the evening each night to see how he was and if Emily had awakened yet, I hadn't seen or really spoken with him since the accident. When I asked if he wanted me to come over, he always claimed he was too tired. After three days had gone by with only a minute's worth of empty, blank telephone conversation each night, I jumped into the cruddy car to drive over to Jason's, determined to wait at his home until he arrived. Jason, of course, wasn't home, nor were his parents. His twin brothers' wives, Tracy and Melinda, were there, though, and smiled and invited me in.

Before I could do more than offer sympathy and ask for any news of Emily—of which, sadly, there was none—the house was invaded by an army of women who bustled in with wonderful smelling dishes covered in tin foil, bowls of salad, and even a couple of pies. Tracy introduced me to the women as "Jason's girlfriend," which caused all of the women to smile broadly at me with eye-sparkling interest and an avalanche of excited comments, like "Jason's such a nice boy!" "So kind and helpful!" and "I wish my own boys were more like him!"

I watched, dumbfounded, while the army followed Tracy into the dining room, waiting until all were out of earshot before whispering to Melinda, "Who were they?"

Melinda laughed. "Women from Mom and Dad's ward. Relief Society sisters. They're taking turns bringing meals in to help Mom out."

I watched Melinda hurry into the kitchen to help Tracy and the other women set up the food. Bringing over food—it was a great idea. I felt the guilts hit then, wishing I'd thought to do something so thoughtful instead of showing up empty-handed. I walked slowly towards the kitchen and peeked my head in to watch the women and the sisters-in-law set the food out on the table and eavesdropped on their conversation about the accident.

"Jason is taking it pretty hard. He saw the accident happen and called 911."

"Oh, my."

"Sister West told me that he held Emily's hand until the ambulance arrived."

My heart stopped as I fought back tears. As horrific and tender as that scene was to picture, what tugged on my heart the most was the third woman's comment.

"It's always delighted me to see the wonderful relationship Jason has with Emily. I don't know of another teenage boy who takes time out for a little sister the way Jason has."

I had to blink back tears and swallow a large lump that had formed in my throat as another boy's face easily formed in my mind.

---

*September 30*

Dear Kitty,

You're almost two years old. Two years. You've grown up way too fast. The whole world is still new to you, and because of you, everything became new to me, too. I'd thought my world would turn dull and gray once I became sick, but you brought life, hope, color, and laughter back into it, and I'll always be grateful to you for that.

I am going to miss you so much. Too much. I don't know how I'm going to handle not having you around me all the time. I've held you and cried so much at night that I can't believe I can still cry at all. Now that I can't pick you up at all, you've been climbing up onto my bed to snuggle in my arms for hours at a time. Holding you as tight as I can now, it's impossible for me to face the fact that I'm going to have to miss out on everything else to come in your life.

I love you so much, Kitty. Tonight, my wish on the first star we're seeing is that you'll have a happy life filled with more laughter and love than you can imagine. If there's anything I can do to make it happen, you can be sure I will.

Happy Second Birthday next month. I hope all your birthdays are happy.

> With all of my love,
> Your brother Brett

P.S. I dreamed the dream again last night, only this time, when I called you, you stopped crying and looked at me. I reached out my hand, and while you stared hard at me, I pressed my hand against my lips and blew you a kiss. Your face lit up, and you quickly lifted your hand to catch it—and then you pressed it to your heart. It was amazing. Wonderful. There aren't any words to describe the whole experience. I woke up crying, it was so real.

No matter where I am when you read this, please remember that I'll never, never forget you. And that I'll always love you . . .

# CHAPTER FORTY-TWO

I'd spent many late nights reading the entries in Brett's journal. Now that I'd read the last few words and turned the final page, I couldn't begin to describe how I felt. Was I happy to have the journal? Or sad? Glad to have finished it? Maybe relieved? Or wishing there was more? I didn't know—I didn't know. It was all still incredibly overwhelming. The stunned amazement I'd felt the night of my sixteenth birthday had never disappeared. After all, Brett *had* done an amazing thing for me. I knew the journal had affected me in more than just a few ways. I wasn't the same Kathy I was before the night of my sixteenth birthday.

At first, I didn't—and couldn't—read more than a few entries a day. My mind usually needed time to digest it all, and then to connect it with what I'd read yesterday, and the day before, and the day before that, until I'd worked my way back to the beginning. And then, I'd ponder all I'd learned and sift through the answers and the remaining questions.

I gripped the book tightly with both hands and read the final lines again with dry eyes. I finally shut the book and stared at the front cover for a moment before carefully replacing the journal in my top dresser drawer. After a moment, I drew out Brett's letter to me from the drawer and removed the small silver key inside. I hadn't touched Brett's strongbox since my sixteenth birthday. I stared at the key in my palm

289

before retracing the steps I'd made that night downstairs to the storage closet.

Most of the Christmas decorations had been removed from the closet and now invaded every inch of free space in our house. Besides Brett's box, only some old, scraggly tinsel that needed to be tossed and a twelve-inch-high Christmas tree decorated with tiny colored ball ornaments remained. I carefully picked up the box and carried it into the family room downstairs to sit on the couch in front of the television. Mom and Dad had left early in the morning to do some massive Christmas shopping and hadn't returned home yet. I was glad. I needed to have the house to myself today. My heart pounded as I turned the key and opened the lid. I hadn't missed the fact that there was more inside Brett's strongbox than just his journal, but my birthday night—that night had been too unbelievable for words. Receiving a gift from a brother who'd died had been all I could handle at the time. I stared inside the box before carefully removing the two videotapes inside and Brett's football jersey. I gently shook the jersey open to look at our name— "Colton"—proudly arched in maroon letters above Brett's number nine.

I took a deep breath before getting up off the couch to stick one of the videos into the VCR. After my hard push on the "play" button, the videotape began.

There was a rough, messy "snowstorm" until a blur of color was visible, which soon focused into something familiar. My school's auditorium. The inner sanctum of Central High.

The camera was focused on the stage, and within moments, I was watching the "welcome back to school" assembly with the audience from over a decade ago. Strangely enough, besides the hair, clothing styles, and the type of music being played, the actual "welcome back" assembly hadn't really changed over the years. I could almost hear Brett's words from one of his last journal entries echoing in my head as I watched the footage before me. It had the usual skits that weren't very funny, a slide show to some pop music of school scenes and events, then

290

a dance by the drill team, and then a big pep rally by the cheerleaders. Once the cheerleaders left the stage, a guy in a letterman's jacket—Mike, the student body president of that year—moved to stand behind a microphone hooked to a podium on the stage and began speaking about somebody who'd been a great student, a great friend, and a great addition to the school. My heart pounded faster as I listened to his words.

" . . . we've really missed having him around, but his spirit is here, and he's been a great inspiration to all of us. This year, all the students have joined together to present this award to the one student who's not only been an amazing athlete, student, and friend during his two years here, but he's shown true courage and hope while fighting something much worse than any opposing team, and that's been his every day battle with leukemia. Brett—this is for you."

Another guy joined Mike on the stage carrying a large plaque. A slide projector in the back of the auditorium threw a huge, smiling picture of Brett in his football uniform onto a screen to the right of the speaker. Huge cheers, screams, and claps came from the audience, who was now on its feet, while Mike held up a big, shiny plaque with Brett's name on it. I squinted as the camera zoomed in and focused on it—the plaque in the trophy case above Brett's picture, voting him the most courageous student in the school and the one with the most school spirit.

As soon as the audience quieted down, Mike spoke more about Brett—about how amazing he was as a football player—before saying, "Therefore, in honor of Brett's accomplishments in the game of football at Central High, we're retiring his number." More cheering and clapping erupted over that announcement. Mike then asked Alex if he would come forward to accept the award for Brett. In a few moments, a much younger, yet familiar figure of my brother Alex climbed the stairs leading to the stage to accept the award for Brett. He only said a few words and kept wiping his eyes before he shook Mike's hand. While Alex was still up at the podium with Mike, Kelly joined them and spoke a few words.

" . . . almost two years ago, when we all learned Brett had leukemia and wouldn't be able to finish out the year, I don't think anyone on the Varsity team had it in them to keep playing. So we lost state. And then last year, Brett showed us what a true champion is by coming back stronger than ever to lead our team to state finals and a victory none of us will ever forget. When word got out that his fight with leukemia hadn't ended and that he would again have to play the worst opponent he's ever faced, we as a team unanimously agreed to dedicate the season to the one person who had always united us together with more school spirit than anyone else. That's you, Brett. We're going to state this year, and we're going to win it for you . . ." More screams and cheers erupted in the auditorium that lasted an incredibly long time.

The next few film clips showed Brett in his football uniform, scrambling around the school's football field with the rest of the team. Ear-deafening cheers reverberated in the stadium while Brett did his magic and made touchdown after touchdown happen—sometimes weaving amazingly fast through tangles of players before sprinting for the goal line. This was followed by big moments from the school plays he'd been in, including the infamous *Once upon a Mattress.* Next came a look down the familiar halls of Central High, minus the wall-to-wall carpeting the school now sported, with Brett joking and clowning in the halls and classrooms, followed by footage of students wishing Brett well and hoping to see him at school again soon.

But all I could see in my mind was an auditorium full of students on their feet cheering for Brett. I wiped my eyes with my pajama sleeve before pressing the "stop" button and switching to the other videotape.

Green grass and blue sky. Our backyard. The boy on the screen was running around so much that it took me a minute to figure out that the nicely muscled, dark-haired boy with the wide grin was my brother Brett. Brett laughed, and chills ran up my spine because I *knew* that laugh—that infectious, wonderful, happy laugh. Then all I could see was Kelly's blond head and familiar, handsome face sticking his tongue out at the camera once Brett had wrenched it from him. Alex or someone else must've come outside, because now I could see both Brett and Kelly with their arms around each other's shoulders. It was hard for me to believe that one of them was even a little bit sick.

Another rough scene change happened again moments later. It took me another minute before I realized the tiny girl with hardly any hair and big, blue eyes Brett carried around everywhere was me. There was tape of him feeding me, dancing with me, and reading and singing with me. There was even footage of Brett tossing an M&M bag back and forth from him to Kelly while I tottered between the two, begging for candy.

In the next section of the tape, I was older, with more hair and a more confident toddler's walk. I caught my breath at the sight of Brett. He was so thin—so horribly thin—with large black circles around his eyes and skin that was pale. Too pale. And yet, his smile was still there. That same beautiful, wide grin he never lost.

In the footage before me now, Brett and I were playing together on the back lawn. He was holding me and pointing at the camera, but I wouldn't take my eyes off of his face. He finally gave up and tickled me until we both laughed. And then he kissed me and hugged me.

At some point, I had picked up Brett's football jersey, and with my legs pulled up against me with my chin on my knees, Brett's jersey was tight in my arms while tears quietly slipped down my cheeks. I stopped the tape, and with Brett's jersey close to my heart, I finally let go and cried and cried until there were no more tears left to cry.

———

It was a long time later, still clutching Brett's jersey, before I reached for Brett's strongbox again. When I looked inside, I was stunned at what I could now see had been hidden under the football jersey. A shoebox—a baby-feet-sized shoebox—was tucked into the corner. I had to clap a hand over my mouth at what was carefully nestled inside.

Pictures. Many, many pictures. A baby in a bassinet. A tiny baby with baby powder all over her body, laughing up at the camera. A baby girl sitting in clouds of pink toilet paper blowing raspberries. A little toddler in a red snowsuit, building a snowman with Alex and Sam. Me, covered in chocolate icing, held by a dark-haired boy equally covered in icing. And me, sitting on Brett's lap—and in another picture, sitting on Kelly's lap—

My hands trembled as my eyes hungrily devoured each moment from my early childhood while tears threatened to break free again. At the bottom of the stack was a larger picture of a tiny girl in a pink sundress sitting on the lap of a grinning, dark-haired teenaged boy resting against a tree. The picture Kelly had taken. I stared at that picture for a long time before wiping at my face and eyes again.

And then I thought of the journal. And Kelly. A second later, I'd raced upstairs to bring the journal back downstairs to thumb through the end again and was sad to discover I hadn't missed anything. There weren't any more entries about Kelly. Brett hadn't written anything about seeing Kelly again before he died, and the fact made me cry again. And as I rewatched the video with pieces of Kelly and Brett clowning around together in our house and with me, I knew what I had to do. If not for me, then for Brett. Definitely.

# CHAPTER FORTY-THREE

The house was white brick with French window shutters painted green. A small red wagon and a couple of yellow Tonka trucks were strewn about the front lawn. I checked the address on my crumpled slip of paper for the millionth time before I got out of the cruddy car, grabbed my book bag, and slowly walked up the brick path leading to the house. My legs were shaking, but somehow I made it to the front door and rang the bell.

No answer. I sighed shakily. It'd been a long shot anyway, fueled by a people search on the Internet that was probably old—or wrong—information. I turned to leave—and then the pounding of feet—small feet—scrambled to the door, and as someone struggled to open it, my heart hurt as Emily's face flashed into my mind, but the little boy with blond hair and big blue eyes who opened the door wasn't Emily. We stared at each other before I finally made myself smile and say, "Hi. Is your dad—or mom—home?"

The little boy scampered off, leaving the door open a little, screaming, "Mommy—someone's at the door!"

I could hear more footsteps approaching—adult ones—before the front door swung open, and a woman's voice said, "Yes?" I thought I was going to faint. A beautiful, slim, blue-eyed blonde stood before me. The face was older—more mature—but it was Jennifer.

"Mmm—Mrs. Baxter?"

"Yes?" She looked at me questioningly and smiled.

"I—I came to see Kelly. Your husband, Kelly. Is he home?"

"He is." She held the door open wider for me. "Won't you come in?"

I was actually walking into Kelly's home. *Amazing.* I clutched my book bag tighter. Jennifer motioned for me to sit before she disappeared down the hall.

The room was beautiful. It was done all in blues and whites, and although there were toys scattered around, the room was clean. A big family portrait hung on the wall above the fireplace. There was no question that the handsome man with the amazing smile that could still even now turn a girl into a glob of Jell-O was Kelly. Both he and Jennifer were holding little blond, blue-eyed boys on their laps. Two more blond, blue-eyed boys were gathered around them.

"Four kids—four boys!" I whispered aloud, shaking my head. There were single pictures of each miniature Kelly on the fireplace mantel as well, although two of the boys looked more like Jennifer than Kelly. But what really caught my eye and wouldn't let go was a framed 5 x 7 photo on one of the lamp tables. The photo was of a young Kelly on Central High's football field, his helmet off and dangling from his fingertips at his side, while in the background were crowds of students and football uniforms blurred together, obviously going crazy because of the win. But to look at Kelly's unsmiling face, anyone looking at the photo would have been shocked to know he'd been on the winning team. There was a sad quality in his eyes and hard-set mouth that was both heartbreaking and puzzling.

"That was taken my senior year. By my wife, Jennifer, actually. Right after my high school football team won the state championship."

I jumped and swung around. I couldn't help it, but I gasped. *Kelly.* Like Jennifer, he looked just like his picture, only older. More mature. He was still a handsome blond, but his eyes had that sad quality to them that was missing in Brett's old photographs but easily seen in the photo I had clutched in my hand.

"I'm—I'm—"

"Why don't we all sit down?" Jennifer offered kindly. It was clear I'd sparked their curiosity, but that was better than having their suspicion sparked. *Definitely.*

I couldn't talk. And because pictures are said to be worth a thousand words, I figured letting something else talk for me might be the best way to start. So after we were all seated, I set the photo of Kelly next to me on the couch and reached into my book bag. With fingers that trembled a little, I handed Kelly a snapshot. He frowned at it for a second while Jennifer looked over his shoulder, and then he broke into a smile.

"Hey, that's me! And the baby—"

"Is me," I said simply.

He looked up quickly, his eyes big and round. "You're—you're *Brett's* little sister—"

"Kitty!" Jennifer said excitedly.

Before either could begin to shoot questions at me, I finally found my voice and started talking. And pretty fast, too. "I—I had to come. Brett gave me this—" I pulled the maroon journal out of my book bag with trembling fingers. I was nervous and I was babbling, but I couldn't stop now—I'd come too far. "It was a present saved for my sixteenth birthday." I handed it to Kelly. He carefully opened the front cover and read Brett's name in it.

"I recognize his handwriting," he said softly with a smile that was sad like his eyes.

"I know you never got much of a chance to see Brett again before he died. He wrote about you at the end of the journal a lot, so I thought maybe you'd like to read it."

Kelly looked up at me questioningly with amazement. "I can't believe you're doing this. Why are you?"

I sighed. "I just need to. For Brett. It's something I can do for him."

Kelly shook his head. "You already did a lot for him, Kitty. I wish you could've seen how he was with you. It was like someone turned on a light switch inside him when you were around. I know he wouldn't have gotten through everything without having you there with him."

I hungrily listened, blinking hard to keep from crying while Kelly shared moments he'd had with Brett—even moments I'd been a part of. I turned away to quickly wipe away tears and then picked up the framed photo of Kelly beside me on the couch. I handed it back to Kelly and tried to smile. "For someone who just won state, you don't look very happy."

Kelly nodded, looking down at the photo in his hands. "We dedicated the football season to Brett my senior year. I just wish he'd been able to hang on long enough to be a part of that day. It was hard going through the season without him." We all fell silent before Kelly spoke again. "You know," he said in a low voice, "I never meant to hurt anyone. Least of all, Alex and Brett. They were like brothers to me. Especially Brett—"

Jennifer took hold of Kelly's hand then, and at her request, I filled them in on the details of my family, all about what Alex and Sam were up to now, and what I'd been doing, and he in turn updated me on his life. How he'd played football in college out of state before going on to graduate school and becoming an engineer. And how he'd served an LDS mission in the Netherlands and married Jennifer when he came home. And then I was introduced to all four of his boys—ranging from age two to age ten—all of them full of giggles and questions and smiles.

I knew I needed to be getting back, but when it was time to say our good-byes, Kelly stopped me before I could get up off the couch.

"You know, Kitty, I have something for you, too."

*A gift? From Kelly?* I watched him leave the room to return in a minute with a small, old blue book in his hands. He gave it to me almost reverently. The cover was a faded blue with gold letters on the front. My breath caught as I read the title that stared solemnly, calmly, and irresistibly up at me. The Book of Mormon.

---

"I gave a Book of Mormon to Brett after he was diagnosed with leukemia," Kelly explained. "He had so many questions about what I believed that I thought this might help." He looked down briefly. "Brett gave that copy back to me. On the day of his funeral, I went to your home, and Alex—he was really upset. He gave me this copy and told me—" Kelly sighed and shook his head. "That's not important. The important thing is that Brett had gotten another copy somewhere along the line. I knew it was pointless to try and give it back, since it would probably be thrown away, and I didn't want that to happen to it. I was happy to see Brett had been reading it and marking it, but it made me sad, too, so I put it away. And then when we moved back here, Jennifer found it and showed me the inside of the front cover. I can't believe I never noticed it before, but now I know why I couldn't throw it away, or even give it away, because it was meant for you. It's yours." Kelly motioned for me to open the front cover, and when I did and saw Brett's strangely familiar handwriting, I couldn't stop myself from crying.

---

After thanking me for coming to his house and lending him Brett's journal, and after I promised to call Kelly if I had any questions—any questions at all—regarding Brett's book, I finally drove home. It was early evening by then, but my parents still hadn't made it home yet.

Once I was safely back in my bedroom, my fingers trembled as I carefully opened the book's cover and turned its pages. The stories were all there—all of those strange, amazing stories both Jason and Emily had told me about. Stories they insisted weren't really stories at all, but true events that were part of the history of the American continents. Nephi and his brothers returning to Jerusalem for brass plates—a record like the Bible. The young stripling warriors and their amazing victory without the loss of even one life in battle. Captain Moroni and his Title of Liberty. Christ's visit to the American continent after His crucifixion and resurrection in Jerusalem. The last, huge battle between the two warring sides—Lamanites and Nephites. And the burying of the book of metal plates that had been passed down from generation to generation, each person adding his people's history before being written in last of all by Moroni, who then buried the book, which remained hidden for centuries.

There was something incredibly personal and private about turning the pages of a book of scripture that once belonged to someone else. Brett had highlighted portions and scribbled so many notes in the margins that I almost felt he'd given me yet another journal. Even though Brett had often mentioned in his journal towards the end how much he was starting to believe in the Mormon church, actually seeing for myself how worn his copy of the book was and all the marking up and highlighting of scriptures was serious proof.

I flipped through the pages and felt my eyes well up with tears again as one of the themes Brett highlighted the most began to stand out. "Repent all ye ends of the earth, and come unto me, and be baptized in my name, and have faith in me, that ye may be saved." " . . . that ye may be washed from your sins, that ye may have faith on the Lamb of God, who taketh away the sins of the world, who is mighty to save and to cleanse from all unrighteousness."

I couldn't believe I had any tears left as I read the other main theme that stood out, marked in bold red: "This mortal body is raised to an immortal body, that is from death, even from the first death unto life, that they can die no more; . . ." "The soul shall be restored to the body, . . . yea, even a hair of the head shall not be lost; but all things shall be restored to their proper and perfect frame." " . . . there is a resurrection, therefore the grave hath no victory, and the sting of death is swallowed up in Christ."

## CHAPTER FORTY-FOUR

I'd brought Brett's football jersey along with the pictures and videos upstairs to keep in my room. It was lightly snowing outside, so I snuggled back into my bed and kept reading Brett's Book of Mormon. Considering how strangely the sentences were put together, I was surprised at how many pages I'd made my way through that evening, but after stopping to eat dinner with my parents once they finally did return home, with Brett's jersey clutched against my chest and his book on my pillow, I fell asleep while the snow continued to fall.

I hadn't dreamed of Brett in a while, but that night I dreamed of him again. He pleadingly held out his blue book to me as he'd done so many times in the past, urging me to take it. I begged him to help me understand, but all he did was continue to hold out the book, disappearing with a sigh when my tears of frustration came and woke me. I turned my face to my pillow and cried until I was too exhausted to cry anymore. Finally I slept until late in the morning.

---

I didn't know how it was with other people who weren't part of the LDS faith when they read the Book of Mormon. All I knew was what it was like for me. I didn't know if it was normal to sit and read huge chunks of it at a time, but the book held my attention in a way I never would've thought possible a couple of months ago. But then, a lot of things had happened in the last few months.

I read more after breakfast the next day once I'd checked out the three inches of snow outside that Mom and Dad were all excited about. Not enough to do any damage but enough to prove that Christmas truly was around the corner. I always slid the blue book under my bed whenever Mom came knocking. I felt bad about hiding it, but I knew this would take even more explaining than Brett's journal, and I didn't want to have to explain or defend any of it right now.

For such a deceptively small book, it was packed with a million things. New ideas, and yet somehow not so new. And principles that made sense. To me, at least. I set the book aside for a moment to rub my eyes and lie back on my bed so I could just absorb everything I'd been reading. Liken all scriptures unto us—opposition in all things—we're all free to choose—endure to the end—seek Christ—feast on the words of Christ—whatever persuades to do good is from God—pray always—counsel with the Lord and He will direct your path—by small and simple things are great things brought to pass—

I sat up in bed and stared at the book. By small and simple things, great things really *did* come to pass. I shook my head and ran my hands through my hair. There was no denying it—I was curious about Jason's religion. For better or worse. I couldn't help wondering why I, of all people, felt this strange need to understand and learn more. And yet, at the same time, I *knew* I'd learned it all somewhere before. It was as if I was remembering something I'd known and believed long ago.

I shook my head again and set the book down in front of me. Even if it really *was* all true, there was still a confused war going on inside of me. Maybe it was what Jason called "the adversary"—I didn't know. Maybe it was my own fears—of the idea of even thinking about changing more of my life. Maybe it was a combination of both. I didn't know—I didn't know what to think. I sighed before reaching down to idly flip through the book until I came to the end, where Brett had high-lighted in yellow yet another scripture:

"And when ye shall receive these things, I would exhort you that ye would ask God, the Eternal Father, in the name of Christ, if these things are not true; and if ye shall ask with a sincere heart, with real intent, hav-ing faith in Christ, he will manifest the truth of it unto you, by the power of the Holy Ghost."

I stared at the page, my mind racing. *Yes*—Jason had said something to that effect once.

"You have to read the book with the sincere desire to know if it *is* true." And then, he'd shown me a scripture—one that Brett had marked as well: "'Ask, and it shall be given unto you; seek, and ye shall find; knock, and it shall be opened unto you. For every one that asketh, receiveth; and he that seeketh, findeth; and to him that knocketh, it shall be opened.' If you're willing to be receptive to the Spirit and *listen,* you'll get your answer. I promise."

I shut the book and sighed again, rubbing my eyes with both hands. There was just so much to take in and think about. And then there was that dream of Brett—Brett and his strange, blue mystery book that only frustrated me to tears again and again.

I stared at the book on my bed, and as I did, my heart started to pound. And pound. As I picked up the book again with trembling fin-gers and looked at its very blue cover—as blue as the book in my dream of Brett—as blue as it had *always* been—why hadn't I paid attention and really noticed before?—the tears really started to flow, and I realized—*finally*—that the book Brett had felt was important enough to hold out to me over and over in my dreams—pleadingly offering it to me—had never been his journal at all.

# CHAPTER FORTY-FIVE

That afternoon, it struck me that I hadn't made my usual call to Jason the night before. I didn't want to call Jason on the phone, but I knew I needed to talk to him. And that I needed to see him. And Emily, too, but I didn't want to go to the hospital empty-handed.

An idea formed in my mind while I pulled myself together, and with the first real Christmasy feeling I'd had that season, I made one more trip to the storage closet before carefully packing up a few things and heading for the hospital. On the drive over, I couldn't help grinning, just thinking of how disappointed Jason would be to find out Brett had beat him to the Book of Mormon punch.

When I finally arrived on the ICU floor of the children's hospital, I saw Jason before he saw me. He was sitting in the waiting area, hunched over with his head down and his braced leg stretched in front of him. He looked like he hadn't slept in days, which he likely hadn't.

My feet made no sound as I walked quietly over to him. I stood by him for a second before tossing a small sack in his lap, which made him jump and jerk his head up. My grin faded when I saw the dark circles around his eyes.

"Hey, you," I said softly.

"Kathy." Jason tried to smile as he looked from me to the sack in his lap. "What's this?"

"Just call me the Junior Relief Society." Jason gave me a dull, confused look. "It's a hamburger and fries. I thought you could use some food." It was good to see Jason laugh—even though the laugh didn't last long—before he thanked me and actually took a bite of the hamburger. I sat down beside him and watched him force a few more bites down before speaking. "So are your parents in with Emily?"

"Nah—the doctor's checking her."

We were both quiet before I ventured to speak again. "Do you think I could see her when the doctor's done?"

Jason shrugged. "They let me go in to see her. I'll just tell them you're family."

When we finally did make it in to Emily's room, I was shaken by how still Emily was. Lying there in her hospital bed, it was hard to believe this was the same little girl who raced to greet me when I came to tutor Jason—the little girl who loved playing the piano, drawing pictures, and chattering. And who loved her brother so much and knew how much he loved her. *No.* This girl who lay so still and unmoving wasn't Emily—not the Emily I had grown to love.

Jason moved to the chair at the side of the bed to take Emily's hand. I watched him for a moment and then determinedly took from my bag something for Emily and placed it on the table near the head of her bed.

"What's that?"

I moved back so Jason could see the tiny tree I'd brought from home. "A Christmas tree, of course. She'll want to see this when she wakes up, since it's so close to Christmas now."

Jason's voice was low. "I hope she *does* get to see it."

I frowned and dragged a chair over from the foot of Emily's bed to sit by Jason. "Hope? You don't have to just 'hope.' She's got more on her side than that."

Jason sighed and turned his sad, purple-ringed eyes to me. "I know. I mean, I know the doctors are doing everything they can, but it's been quite a few days since the accident—"

I frowned and shook my head. "I don't mean medicine. You guys just need to give her one of those fancy, amazing blessings. Like the one you got when you were in the hospital."

Jason ran his hand through his hair. "We *did* give her a blessing. The second we could, actually."

"Well, then, everything's going to be okay."

Jason shook his head. "You don't know that."

I shook my head back, amazed at what I was hearing. From *Jason*, of all people! "What I *do* know is that everything's going to work out. I have faith. You just need to have faith, too. You can't have miracles without faith first—"

I couldn't believe I was actually seeing *despair* in Jason's face. I knew it was scaring me, because I was babbling now. My heart pounded as I snatched my book bag from off the floor and grabbed Brett's Book of Mormon I'd brought along. I'd meant to make a big production out of amazing Jason with the fact that I was reading his scripture book, but he was frustrating me with his lack of faith, and so in desperation, I started flipping madly through its pages.

"Hold on—I know it's in here somewhere. Brett marked it in red." I continued flipping without looking at Jason before I finally found the passage I wanted in the book of Ether. "Here we go. Ether 12:6: 'Faith is things which are hoped for and not seen; wherefore, dispute not because ye see not, for ye receive no witness until after the trial of your faith.' See? You have to have faith, but it's going to be tried hard before any miracle happens. But you have to have the faith first." I looked up triumphantly and was surprised to see Jason looking at me as if I had two heads. "What?" I demanded.

"I just can't believe what I'm seeing and hearing. That's all."

"What do you mean?"

"I mean *you*. You've been reading—actually *reading* the Book of Mormon!" Jason shook his head in true wonderment. "I do believe I'm witnessing a miracle."

I closed the Book of Mormon on my lap and traced the gold letters on its blue cover with my finger. "It's Brett's book. I—I got it from one of his friends." Jason's eyes grew larger when I hesitantly looked up. "I—I found Kelly Baxter and went to see him the other day, and he gave it to me." I could feel tears forming in my eyes and threatening to close my throat. "He kept it for me. And Brett marked it up everywhere—how could I *not* read it when it meant so much to him?" I stopped and took a deep breath, not wanting to cry in front of Jason.

Jason carefully took the Book of Mormon out of my hands and slowly thumbed through its pages. "Wow. I don't know what else to say. This is pretty incredible."

I nodded and watched Jason reverently run his finger down passages Brett had marked before he looked at me with true tenderness in his eyes and squeezed my hand. "I'm so happy you're reading it. Really *reading* it."

I took a deep breath and looked in Jason's eyes with all the determination I had. "All I know for sure is that if a massive miracle like me not only finding this book but reading it, too, could happen, then *anything* can happen. Especially something like Emily getting better!" Jason tried to smile, but I could tell he wasn't convinced. "Besides—lots of faith and a blessing worked for you, so it has to work for Emily, too, right?"

Jason sighed and ran his hand through his hair again. "Well—it's definitely important to have faith, but blessings don't exactly work that way."

"But they *are* dependent on faith, aren't they? Isn't that what you've been trying to tell me for months now? That you need to have faith?"

"Yes, faith *is* a huge part of blessings—"

"Then that's all you need to do—have faith that her blessing is going to do the trick!"

"If that's what God has in mind for her."

I frowned. "'In mind for her?' What do you mean by that?"

"I mean, the whole 'not my will, but thine be done.'" He handed me Brett's Book of Mormon before continuing. "Faith is important, but putting it in God's hands and asking that His will be done, not mine, is important, too. Having faith in Him is more important than having faith in anything else. If it's God's will, then she'll pull through, but if her time on earth was always meant to be short, then she won't be here much longer."

I nodded, trying to digest what Jason had said before I carefully put Brett's Book of Mormon back in my book bag, walked to the other side of Emily's bed, and gently took her hand in both of mine. I turned and looked at Jason. "If it's all the same to you, I'm still going to have faith that she's going to be okay." Jason looked down and slowly nodded before taking Emily's other hand while I whispered softly near Emily's ear. My voice trembled as I told her how much I appreciated everything she'd done to help me learn about the Book of Mormon, and that I was reading it now. And that I missed hearing her play the piano. "You need to get better so you can play for me again." I squeezed her hand and stared at her unmoving face until tears blurred her small, perfect features.

"Kathy." I looked up to see tears in Jason's eyes, too. "I just wanted you to know that it means a lot to me that you came."

I carefully released Emily's hand before stepping around her hospital bed to put my arms around Jason's neck while he pulled me tightly to him and knew that for now, there was no need for words.

# CHAPTER FORTY-SIX

It was a nice change for me—doing nice things for others. And I was discovering I actually enjoyed doing them. It brought a whole new dimension to the Christmas spirit for me, yet at the same time, it was strange to have others like Emily and Jason—even Jason's entire family—even Brett and Kelly—on my mind instead of just myself all the time. I found my way over to Jason's home more often instead of calling on the phone. Mostly because I wanted to be there to help in any way possible, even if it was just to set the table with food the Relief Society sisters continued to bring. I also took turns with Tracy and Melinda delivering washed pots, casserole dishes, and plastic food containers back to all kinds of people in the neighborhood. It was incredible not only to see so many people wanting to rally around Jason's family and help but to be a part of it myself, too. Jason told me more than once how much I amazed him.

"What's so amazing about fixing a sandwich?" I'd been in the kitchen helping Melinda fix sandwiches while Jason couldn't seem to stop staring at me. He'd been doing a lot of that lately, and I knew it wasn't due to the clothes I was wearing, or how I'd fixed my hair.

"It's not the sandwich, and you know it. It's you."

"Me?"

Jason smiled. "You're changing."

I blushed and laughed. "For the better, I hope!"

Although Jason seemed to find my newfound ability to look beyond myself amazing, what he and his entire family were completely oblivious to was the fact that *they* were the ones who were truly amazing. Although there was still no change in Emily, instead of falling into their own separate pools of depression, Jason's whole family was truly there for each other. In fact, they all seemed to grow closer as a result of Emily's accident. And even more incredible to me was the family's forgiveness towards the boy who had hurt Emily. No harsh words or angry outbursts against him had happened. There was no tense, electric charge in their home. The only words that fit the atmosphere of their home was a comforting peace that seemed to blanket every inch of the place, which only served to heighten my belief that Emily was going to be fine.

Shortly before Christmas Eve, one evening I drove over to Jason's to get him out of the house for a walk around the neighborhood. More snow had fallen over the last couple of days, and with colored lights strung up everywhere sparkling against the snow, the effect was dazzling. Jason and I held hands, walking slowly together before Jason broke the silence.

"You know something, Kathy? I'm starting to figure out that it's easy to have all the faith and belief in the world when everything's going great, but it's when really bad things happen that you find out what you really believe, and how strong your faith is."

I stopped and faced Jason and took hold of his other hand in my free hand and looked up into his eyes determinedly. "So that's what you've got to do now, Jason. Just hold onto your faith. It's going to be okay. Everything is. You know that, don't you? You *have* to know that!" Jason silently nodded. "I've thought your parents—your family—being so strong and positive was so incredible. I still do. I couldn't believe your family could truly forgive that boy who hurt Emily—but I know why now. Your family can forgive, because you believe your family can last forever, don't you? I mean, no matter what happens, Emily will always be your sister, and she'll always be your parents' daughter. And you *will* be with her again. That's what pulls you through. That's what's going to get you through now. You just have to have *faith*, Jason!"

Jason had tears on his cheeks, but I didn't realize I was crying, too, until Jason pulled off his gloves to reach out and wipe my face with his hands before pulling me close to him.

I'd spent most of the day before I went to Jason's house reading more of the Book of Mormon, and as a result of that and talking with Jason, there was only one thing on my mind that I knew I had to do. Something I didn't want to put off for even one second longer once I'd driven back home that night from Jason's home.

Mom and Dad were both sitting on the couch watching television. Without even stopping to take off my coat, I walked up to both of them and stood in front of the TV.

"Mom—Dad—I want to see the missionaries. The Mormon church missionaries. I have to talk to them. I don't expect you to understand— I just need to know that it's okay to invite them over. Is it okay?" It all came out in a blurted rush, but at least it was finally out there and in the open. Just that much was a huge relief.

My parents looked at each other, stunned by my announcement, before turning back to face me again. I watched Mom shake her head and clutch the gold locket around her throat while Dad stated firmly, "I'm sorry, Kathy, but our answer has to be no."

———

Their answer didn't change over the next two days leading up to Christmas Eve. I asked, and begged, and pleaded—I got angry and yelled—even cried—but their response remained the same: "No, Kathy. We don't want them coming here. I'm sorry, but you're just going to have to accept that." The problem was, I couldn't accept that. And wouldn't.

Christmas Eve arrived a day later, and there was still no change in

Emily. And yet, somehow I still knew she was going to be okay. My faith hadn't been shaken at all. Hadn't even trembled yet.

I drove over to Jason's late Christmas Eve morning to give him his Christmas present. "Before you open it, you should know that I'm not big on gift giving. I mean, I don't believe in giving people something they can easily go buy for themselves. Things as gifts are only good if they remind you of an especially good time. Or if the thing in question reminds you of an incredible person in your life—the person you're giving the gift to. And sometimes, it can represent both . . ."

My babbled speech was inspired by the horrible thought that what I'd spent a good amount of time and love creating for Jason might be viewed by him as stupid. Jason's look of confusion only grew as I babbled on and on before sighing and telling him to just open the box, which he did while I held my breath. Only when I saw his mouth turn into one of his truly beatific smiles did I finally relax and smile myself. "Do you like it?"

"*Like* it? I don't just *like* it, Kathy—I love it!" Jason reached for me and kissed me and hugged me, and kissed me again, before turning to look marvelingly at my Christmas gift to him. Dad had been right. The Christmas dance pictures he'd taken had turned out much better than the one taken at the dance. I'd liked the one taken outside with me sitting on Jason's knee with his braced leg stretched out in front of him the best, so I'd bought a frame that was purposely too large for it, and surrounded the enlarged photo with the small black and white squares of pictures of us from the fast food restaurant's photo booth the night of the dance.

Jason continued to marvel over each picture in turn before finally holding a red and green package out to me. "Okay—now—here's yours."

He handed me a small, flat, square object. I ripped off the paper—and gasped.

Jason smiled. "I just thought you'd like listening to it in CD form for a change."

I stared at the CD with one hand over my mouth. It was Brett's *Rubber Soul* album. It had all the songs—all of them. "Jason—this is the U.S. release!"

"That's what you've wanted, isn't it?"

"Yes! I've never been able to find anything but the U.K. release in stores. That's why I've never bought a copy before." I looked up at Jason's smiling face wonderingly. "Where did you find it?"

Jason shrugged. "Actually, I didn't. I couldn't find anything but the U.K. version either in stores or on the Internet, but the U.K. *Help!* album has the missing songs from the U.S. *Rubber Soul*, so I bought that CD, too, and burned songs from both albums to make this *Rubber Soul* version for you."

I shook my head and stared at the CD again. He could've just given me the two Beatles CDs he'd bought. I shook my head again. All of that effort. For me. With everything that was going on with Emily. He'd even gone through the trouble of copying the *Rubber Soul* CD slip cover, as well as creating the song listing for the backside of the CD to match Brett's album.

Jason motioned for me to dig into the box again, but I couldn't stop looking at the CD in my hands, so Jason reached inside for the remaining two CDs in the box instead. "I thought you might like to have these two Beatles CDs, too. The *Help!* album has a lot of good songs on it, and the extra songs on *Rubber Soul* aren't bad, either—you're not crying again, are you, Kathy?"

"Yeah, well, it seems like that's all I ever do anymore." I reached up and hugged Jason and thanked him. Over and over. When he finally released me, I looked up at him hesitantly, almost shyly. "I actually have one more present for you. Sort of."

Jason raised an eyebrow but didn't move his arms from around my waist. "A 'sort of' present? Is it legal?"

I laughed. "I think it is. Even if my parents don't seem to think so."

"What is it?"

"It's not really an 'it.' I mean, it's more of an announcement, I guess."
I took a deep breath. "I asked my parents if I could see the missionaries." I didn't know how I thought Jason would react, but after staring in disbelief with bulging eyes, he let out a whoop and snatched me off my feet in a huge bear hug. I gasped and then laughed. "Careful—don't forget your knee! You've still got your brace on!"

Jason couldn't speak coherently for the next minute or so, even after he finally let my feet touch the floor again and released me from his bear hug. He was too busy doing the kind of thing I would've thought he'd only do on the football field after touchdowns.

"I wish my parents felt the way you do."

Jason's huge smile faded at my words as he turned to face me again. "They're not happy about this?"

"Not exactly." I looked down and sighed before looking at Jason again. "They said no."

Jason put his hands on my shoulders. "When did you ask them?"

"A few days ago."

"Well, maybe you need to ask them again!"

"I've asked them a million times every day, but the answer's still no."

Jason frowned and thought for a moment. "You could always have the missionaries come to my house and come over here to listen."

I shook my head firmly. "No. I don't want to sneak around behind my parents' backs. I don't want to have to lie about anything. Especially not something potentially life changing like this."

Even though it was Christmas Eve and I was thrilled with the CD Jason had given me, and even though his excitement was wonderful to see after the negative reaction from my parents, it was hard not to sulk through the Christmas Eve party with Sam and Stephen and Alex and Julie, even with Curtis tottering around and babbling excitedly to everyone. Mom and Dad filled them in on my big announcement of my wanting to meet with Mormon missionaries, but surprisingly, neither

Alex nor Sam tried to talk me out of it, which was probably the best Christmas gift I'd be getting this year.

———

I was exhausted Christmas Eve night by the time our family party ended, but even so, I was able to make it through the entire *Rubber Soul* album—on CD, this time—before I fell asleep. When I did fall asleep, I was in for another amazing Christmas present. This time when I dreamed of Brett, his hands were empty. No blue book was in sight. But his face—his face was lit up with his wide grin. I could hear him happily shouting, *Yes! Yes! Yes!* All I could do was smile and laugh back, but my smile faded when I thought of Mom and Dad and their unwillingness to budge even the slightest bit of an inch. Brett's grin faded, too, but his eyes continued to sparkle with determination.

*Don't give up!*

I nodded slowly back, and as we stood facing each other, I knew I would hold onto this moment forever.

*I love you, Brett.*

Brett reached out his hand to me and then took it back to press it against his lips before blowing a kiss off his fingertips to me. I quickly lifted my own hand to catch it and pressed his kiss firmly to my heart.

I could see tears in Brett's eyes, even though he was smiling.

*I love you, too, Kitty.*

# CHAPTER FORTY-SEVEN

It happened on Christmas morning, shortly after presents were exchanged and opened and after everyone had smiled and laughed at Curtis jumping and playing in masses of ripped-up Christmas wrapping paper. When the present-opening ritual was finally over and everyone was relaxed and talking calmly and normally again, having a third cinnamon roll and more juice, and Curtis had sacked out on top of the mound of wrapping paper with his thumb in his mouth, I knew the time had come. I had to seize the moment. *Carpe diem.* There was no going back. After all, it was Christmas—the perfect time for gift giving. Especially to your family. With my heart pounding so hard and fast I knew I had to go for it now, I made my trembling legs stand up, and I faced my family seated around me. I opened my mouth and took a deep breath to speak—

And someone rang the doorbell.

Dad frowned at the door. "Who in the world could that be?"

Alex didn't even look up from the book he was leafing through. "Get that, will you, Kathy? Since you're standing and everything."

I sighed and grumbled my way to the door with legs that were still shaking before wrenching the door open with an angry yank. And then—

"Merry Christmas!"

I could only stare back with my mouth hanging open at the handsome, blond-haired, blue-eyed man bundled up on the doorstep smiling at me.

*Kelly.*

———

There were no words to describe the shock my family went through when I led Kelly into the living room and said, "It's Kelly—Kelly Baxter."

It was a strange, surreal moment. Everyone just stared at Kelly, like I had. "We were visiting my parents for Christmas, and I needed to get this back to Kitty, so I thought I'd drop it by personally and wish everyone a Merry Christmas."

Alex was the first to speak. "Get what back to—'Kitty'?"

Kelly's smile faded a little. "Brett's journal. She loaned it to me so I could read it." Kelly turned to me and handed Brett's journal back. "Thank you, Kitty. So much—"

"Brett's journal?" Sam's voice was sharp.

Kelly looked from everyone back to me in confusion. "They don't know about this?"

Before I could lose my nerve, I shook my head silently at Kelly before turning to face my family's questioning faces with Brett's journal now in my hands. "Brett gave it to me for my birthday. My sixteenth birthday."

Everyone just stared. Again. Kelly was the first—again—to break the charged, electric silence filling every inch of space in the room. "I'm sorry—when Kitty came to see me a few days ago with the journal, I assumed you all knew about it—"

Dad's voice was as sharp as Sam's. "You went to Kelly's house? When did that happen?"

"When you were out Christmas shopping—I'm sorry I didn't ask permission to take the car, but I just had to find Kelly—Brett wrote so much about him—" I was babbling now, because nothing was turning out right. This was not the Christmas card moment I'd wanted it to be, even though part of me knew it likely never would have been anything like a Christmas card.

Kelly jumped in to the rescue. "Look, I'm sorry. This was obviously a bad idea. I shouldn't have come—not on Christmas Day, but it—it seemed like a good idea. It felt right." Kelly turned to me with a sad smile on his face that made my heart hurt. "I'm sorry, Kitty. I think I probably ought to leave. But thank you—thank you so much—for letting me read Brett's journal. It—it meant everything to me." There were tears in Kelly's voice. I tried to tell him to stay and not to leave—not now—not yet—

And then Alex quietly spoke. "I—I never even knew Brett kept a journal. Did you?"

Alex looked at Sam who quietly answered. "No—I never knew, either."

But what jerked my head away from Alex and Sam staring at the book in my hands, both of whom were looking at it as if they were afraid to touch it, was Mom's voice.

"Please, Kathy—may I see it?" Her pleading voice was soft and trembling, and with tears in her eyes, she carefully—reverently—took the book from me, staring at the cover in disbelief for a moment before slowly opening the journal to see my brother's printed name. Mom put a hand over her mouth before she whispered, "It's Brett's handwriting— it's his handwriting!"

Alex and Sam scrambled over to join Mom and Dad on the couch while I pleadingly motioned for Kelly to take a seat on one of the recliners. Kelly didn't move for a second before he finally nodded and sat down. I sat on the edge of the other recliner near Kelly and trembled, watching my family with Brett's journal.

Dad looked up at me with tears in his eyes after they'd reached the first entry addressed to "Dear Kitty." "Kathy, this isn't a traditional journal—these are Brett's thoughts, meant only for you."

"I know, but Brett wouldn't mind—I know he wouldn't. I want you to read it—all of you. That's why I had to find Kelly, so he could read it, too." Everyone passed the journal around to read entries out loud, laughing over some, and letting tears fall over others. And so many stories were shared—and their viewpoints over events Brett had written about, wondering and pondering over Brett's reactions. Even Kelly was brave enough to join in and share his viewpoints and amazement over how Brett had truly felt and thought about so many things. And my family actually listened.

And then came the best stories of all—stories I'd never heard before—from everyone—about how much I had meant to Brett, and the special connection that was between us from the start. How I always calmed down quickly, even as a tiny baby, when Brett held me. How I was the happiest with him and how I was always the best medicine for him throughout his entire sickness. Kelly even had stories about times he'd shared with Brett and me. Between all of us—even Julie and Stephen—we easily used up a box of tissues. There was a wonderful blanket of peace in our home—a true Christmasy feeling. It was definitely the best Christmas I had ever experienced. Definitely one I would never forget. One I doubt any of us would ever forget.

Kelly asked me then what time it was before he quickly stood up and pulled his coat back on. "I really should go—I'm sorry for staying so long, on Christmas and everything!"

Alex had the journal in his hands and raised his eyes to me, shaking his head. "I still can't believe you went to the trouble of hunting down Kelly to let him see this. I can't believe you'd do that much for Brett."

I shook my head slowly. "I didn't do it just for Brett, Alex." Not only was Alex looking at me questioningly, but Kelly and everyone else were, too. "I may not be able to give you the chance to play football with Brett again, but I *can* give you the chance to have a good friend back. A friend who loves Brett, too. And who always will."

Alex's stunned look lasted only a second before he nodded and stood up. Slowly, he walked over to Kelly and held out his hand. Kelly looked at it for a moment before quickly taking Alex's offering and gripping his hand in his. It was then I noticed the sad quality I'd seen in Kelly's eyes when I'd been in his home wasn't there anymore, and the fact made me smile.

Kelly hadn't let go of Alex's hand yet, and a second later the two gave each other a brief hug. A guy kind of hug, with a back slap given by both and tears trying to be hid by each. Then of course Mom came forward and hugged Kelly, and Sam and Dad did, too.

Before I could move away, Alex grabbed me up in his arms. "I can't believe you, Kathy! I just can't—" Alex couldn't talk anymore, but it was okay, because I couldn't get a word past the lump in my throat. Alex didn't let go for a long time. And neither did I.

---

I walked Kelly to the door once all the hugging had died down and thanked him for being brave enough to come over. "You could've just mailed Brett's journal. Or called me up, and I could've come over again. But you brought it yourself. Personally! That was—*is*—so amazing. Thank you—so much!"

Kelly reached out and wrapped me in his arms. "Thank *you*, Kitty, for being brave yourself. You're an incredible girl." Kelly asked me then if I'd had a chance to take a look at Brett's Book of Mormon yet.

"You mean, have I read about Nephi and the brass plates? Or Ammon's mission among the Lamanites? Or Christ's visit to the Americas? Or Captain Moroni and his javelin-throwing man Teancum?" Kelly's jaw dropped, but his eyes shone with excitement. I couldn't help laughing. "Yes, I'm 'looking' at it."

"If you have any questions, you know you can call me. Anytime. I'd love to help you, Kitty. You know that, don't you?"

I smiled. "Yes, I know that. And thank you, Kelly. For everything."

When my family asked me later on that day why I'd decided not to keep Brett's journal my secret and why I actually let them read it, too, I could feel my heart pounding, because there was more—so much more I needed to say and tell them. And show them.

Brett's journal had changed me. They could all see that, and had been seeing that for months now. But as much as Brett's journal had changed me, another book was starting to change me as well, and now I had other questions that needed to be answered. Questions that I still needed permission from my parents to ask before they could ever be answered.

Dad sighed. "Kathy, this isn't the time or place for you to be asking to see those missionaries again—"

"Why not?"

Dad's voice was rising. "Because it's Christmas, and Alex and Sam are here, and we've been having a wonderful day—"

"If you only knew how important this is to me!"

Now Mom's voice was rising as well. "Kathy, please give us a little credit. We know how much you like Jason West. We *know* you're just doing this for him—"

*Jason?* Doing this for Jason? "No—you're wrong—so wrong! I'm not doing this for Jason—I'm not! If you have to blame someone, then blame it on Brett—it's his 'fault' that I want to learn about this religion!" And with that, in frustration and not at all in the spirit I'd planned when I'd had my carpe diem moment only a few hours ago, I angrily marched out of the room and into my bedroom to grab Brett's Book of Mormon. I marched back into the living room to thrust it into Mom's surprised hands.

"This was Brett's copy. Look at it! Look at how he wrote in it—and look inside the front cover. You see? See? He wanted me to have it, because he believed in it! He wanted this in his life, and he wanted it for me, too." Mom's stunned look made me step back and lower my voice. "This was important to Brett—as important as it's always been to Jason. If you only knew how I feel when I read this book—you could feel the same way, if you'd read it, too."

Mom's voice had dropped to a whisper. "Brett—Brett gave this to you?"

"Yes—he did. He and Kelly." I moved to kneel in front of Mom while she stared at the book in her hands. "Brett's journal helped me find this book. I want to learn more. I *have* to. And not because of Jason or Brett, but because of *me*, and what I know now, and what I've felt. I can't go back—I have to move forward. Please let me have that chance. Please don't take that away."

I was pleading for all I was worth and waiting for Mom to answer me. When she finally did, there were tears in her eyes. And then, Mom did something I'd never seen her do before. Yes, I'd seen tears slip down her cheeks, but I'd never witnessed anything like this. With the book still tight in her hands, she broke down hard and cried and cried.

---

It was later on Christmas evening when another knock sounded at the front door. A frantic, excited knocking that didn't stop until I'd finally unlocked and opened the door.

"Jason!"

Jason looked like he was about to burst. "Kathy—she's awake! She's awake!" Before I could say anything else, he stepped inside and swung me around in one of his huge bear hugs.

"Awake? Who—"

"Emily! Emily's awake—she woke up this morning—"

The news had me shrieking, laughing, crying, and screaming, "I knew she'd be okay!" causing Mom and Dad to come running, and in seconds they were as excited as Jason and I.

After everyone had calmed down and Jason and I were left alone in the living room, Jason continued to go on and on about his amazement over Emily's awakening. "It's just like her—waiting until Christmas morning to finally wake up! She's definitely a drama queen!"

I smiled and leaned back against the couch where I was sitting by Jason. "I'm not surprised that she finally woke up, Jason. I just knew she'd be okay!"

Jason reached for my hand, then lifted it to his lips and kissed the back of it. "Yes—you never gave up. Not even for a second!"

"You know you didn't have to come all the way over. How did you get here?"

Jason's eyes grew large, as if remembering something he wasn't supposed to forget. "Adam! He's been circling the block waiting for me— probably about a hundred times by now!" We both burst out laughing, and then Jason smiled and squeezed my hand. "I had to come. I couldn't just tell you news like this over the phone! Besides, Emily wanted me to."

I had to raise both eyebrows at that. "Emily?"

Jason grinned. "Since she couldn't come herself, Emily wanted me to thank you personally for her. For the Christmas tree!"

## CHAPTER FORTY-EIGHT

My family spent the days up through New Year's looking over Brett's journal, reading and rereading, and talking about it together. I still hadn't gotten my answer about whether I could see the missionaries yet, but I had hope. Enough to equal a lot of faith.

For New Year's Eve, I agreed to watch Curtis while Sam and Stephen went to a party, and Sam in turn had agreed to let Jason come over and help tend.

"Although I'm worried not a lot of 'tending' is going to go on."

Sam's knowing look was hugely embarrassing. "Please! It's not going to be like that!"

"Well, he *is* still wearing that horrid old knee brace, so I guess that will keep things restricted to a certain degree."

"Sam!" I groaned, burying my red face in one of her couch pillows.

"And I made sure Curtis had a nice, long nap this afternoon, so he'll be ready and willing to ring in the new year with both of you, believe me!" Sam laughed and yanked the pillow off my face while I groaned some more. "I bought lots of treats for all of you, and there's plenty of movies for you to choose from, so you should still be able to have a good time!"

Curtis came running out from the bathroom with Stephen after him to finish dressing him. I laughed and held out my arms to him while he quickly and happily reached up to let me lift him onto my lap. Sam watched us hug and play together for a minute in silence.

"You know, watching the two of you together—reminds me of seeing you with Brett."

"Really?"

Sam nodded and smiled before sitting down beside us. "Really. You were the happiest with him. And he was happiest with you. I have to admit I was a little jealous at times of the relationship you two had. You wouldn't let me pick you up when Brett was around. No one could get your attention when he was in the room."

I shook my head slowly, dumbfounded. "No one ever told me that before."

Sam nodded again, and we were both quiet until she spoke. "When Brett died, Mom and Dad moved you into my room, but you hated being there. You cried and cried at night and wouldn't let me—or anyone—comfort you. So Mom and Dad decided to move you back into Brett's room, and you finally went back to sleeping through the night. And then, little by little, they got rid of Brett's things, and the room became your room only."

I raised my eyebrows. "They just got rid of his stuff? Why?"

"Brett asked them to. Insisted on it, actually. He didn't want a shrine to be left behind. He wanted it to be *your* room. He knew, somehow, that you'd want to keep that room."

I was quiet for a minute before turning to look at my sister. "I'm sorry, Sam."

Sam raised her eyebrows. "Sorry? For what?"

"I'm sorry—that I didn't sleep in your room. That we didn't have a chance to be—you know—closer."

Sam smiled and draped an arm around my shoulders. "We're closer now. That's what counts."

"You know, Sam, I can't guarantee I'm not going to fight with you ever again, but I *can* guarantee that underneath whatever is going on, I'm really glad you're my sister."

Sam squeezed my shoulders and kissed the top of my head. "The same goes double for me."

———

Jason was wonderful with Curtis and bonded with him in no time, mostly due to the M&Ms he'd brought with him. I was afraid hanging out with me and my nephew on New Year's Eve instead of going to a party with all of his usual friends would bore him to tears, but he insisted he was having a good time.

"I'd rather spend New Year's with you than anyone else."

And yet my parents still wondered why I liked having him for my boyfriend.

Jason was nearly as amazed as Kelly had been when I told him about Brett's journal, but he was ecstatic that I'd shown my family Brett's Book of Mormon and listened enthralled while I told him about the adventures of Christmas Day, complete with a surprise visit from Kelly and another pleading session to let me see the missionaries, which had ended with my mom in tears.

"Don't give up yet, Kathy. It sounds like you're getting close!"

While Jason bounced Curtis happily on his good knee, I tentatively asked about Emily.

"She's doing pretty good. It's going to take some time before she's back a hundred percent, since she was out for so long, but she's got a lot of fire in her, so she'll be okay."

"Any aftereffects?"

Jason sighed. "Well, she threw up a lot when she first woke up. And she's having a hard time walking, and she gets tired fast. She's had a few seizures, too, but the doctor says that's to be expected right now. And she's going to need physical therapy and other kinds of therapy to help her get her motor skills back and everything."

I mulled this over before asking my next question. "Does she remember what happened?"

Jason shook his head. "No—she has no memory at all of the accident. Which I'm actually happy about. I'm glad she won't ever remember that."

I thought about everything Emily now had before her and shook my head. "It doesn't seem fair that a little girl like Emily has to deal with this. It's bad enough she was hit by a car, but I had no idea she would have so much healing and rehabilitation to go through. She's too young to have to go through all of this. It's not fair!"

Jason shrugged. "My theory is that maybe Heavenly Father's giving Emily a challenge like this because she's stronger than we know and needs a bigger challenge in her life right now."

I raised my eyebrows. "Interesting." I didn't know quite what to think of Jason's theory, but it was wonderful to see that the old Jason was back, stronger than ever. And to get a New Year's kiss from him, too. New Year's kisses, that is.

Jason's words were definitely something to think about. But then, Jason was always giving me something new to think about. I hoped that with everything else that was changing in me and all around me, that was something that would never change.

## CHAPTER FORTY-NINE

When school started up again after New Year's Day, I knew Mistie and Crystal would have to pick their jaws up off the floor over everything that had happened to me. From the Christmas dance, to Brett's journal, to Emily's accident, to Christmas Day and Kelly, to the Book of Mormon and my wish to see the missionaries—I could hardly believe it all myself.

I sighed and reached for Brett's journal on my night stand and slowly turned its pages. This gift Brett had given to me—everything he'd given me—was still overwhelming. There were no words to describe everything that had happened to me. And the change that was taking place inside of me was truly indescribable.

I smiled as I looked down at the journal. *By small and simple things.* Who would've ever guessed what a small journal would put into motion? Brett probably never guessed that writing a few paragraphs each day to his little sister would result in such truly great things coming to pass. But then again, maybe he *did* know.

A soft rap on my bedroom door had me calling out, "Come in." A moment later, Dad opened the door carrying something wrapped in a small blanket.

"Mind if I interrupt you for a minute?"

"Of course not. Come on in."

Dad shut the door softly and sat down on the edge of my bed beside me, carefully resting the item beside him. "Your mother wants to come in and talk with you, too, but I wanted to talk with you first."

"Is something wrong?"

"No—nothing's wrong. We're just trying to come to grips with everything." A lot *had* happened. Kelly had returned with his family for another visit. And he'd had Alex and Julie over for dinner. And he'd even encouraged my parents to let me see the missionaries. "You know, Kathy, I've tried hard to be a good father to you—better than I was to Brett. I don't want you to ever doubt that I love you, the way I know Brett did."

I reached up and put my arms around him. "I know you love me, Dad. And I love you."

Dad gently released me after a moment. "There's something else I want you to know." He reached out a hand to smooth my hair. "Remember when you asked me what happened to your bear?"

"Tiny Bear?"

Dad nodded. "When Brett passed away, the day he died, here at home, I picked you up out of your crib to carry you out of the room before the ambulance arrived. You were holding your bear—and somehow, you seemed to know Brett was going away and wouldn't be coming back. You reached your arms out for him and said, 'Bet!' When I reached down to let you give him a final kiss, which you did, you placed Tiny in his arms. When Brett was taken away, at your insistence, the bear went with him."

I didn't know what to say. I watched the emotions play across Dad's face as he continued. "That look of determination you had on your little face, even though you were hardly two—I knew it was pointless to try and fight you. Ever since then, whenever I've seen that determined look, I've known it's going to be impossible to fight it." He smiled and shook his head. "You had that same look on your face the first time you asked if you could see the Mormon missionaries, and it hasn't left your face yet. I know better than to keep fighting it."

My heart stopped at his words, but before I could get my mouth moving again, Dad reached for the bundle resting beside him and handed it to me. I frowned in confusion, but he simply motioned to me to look inside, and when I did, I gasped.

"Is this—?"

Dad smiled. "The hospital returned your bear to us before Brett's funeral, and although we all tried to get you to take Tiny back, you only cried and turned away. I didn't know what your mother did with it after that. I thought somewhere along the line he'd gotten an invitation to the Teddy Bear Picnic but didn't have the heart to tell you that when you asked about him. When I talked to your mother about it, she told me Tiny had found his way back and showed me where she'd tucked him away in our closet."

I stared at the faded tan teddy bear in my lap, slowly touching its black felt eyes and worn but still soft ears while Dad continued. "We thought you'd like a little piece of Brett back, since you were so willing to give us such an incredible piece of Brett through his journal." He patted my leg before hugging me once more. I let the tears slide down my cheeks after he left my room and didn't move to wipe them away until another knock sounded on my door.

Mom stood hesitantly in the doorway until she saw Tiny Bear in my arms and smiled. I patted my bed, inviting her to sit. She didn't speak until she'd carefully sat down where Dad had been.

"It's good to see that old bear with you again. Brings back a lot of memories."

"Dad told me you kept Tiny for me. Thank you for saving him, Mom." She nodded, but I continued before she could speak. "Dad also told me—" I hesitated briefly at her questioning look and then moved forward with my words. "Dad said it's okay for me to see the missionaries. Is that true?"

Mom slowly nodded. "Yes."

"What made you change your mind?"

Mom sighed and looked away for a moment. "I never could face just how much Brett truly *was* interested in the Mormon faith. But I've read his journal, and I've seen his Book of Mormon, and now I know." She took a deep breath before continuing. "Sometimes I've wondered if Brett hadn't been sick when Kelly started to talk to him about his religion whether I would've felt differently." Mom shrugged and looked down at Tiny before looking at me again. "All I knew was that Brett was in enough pain. He didn't need to be put through more stress. It was hard not to take offense that Kelly, a teenaged friend, believed he had all the answers, when I, Brett's mother—" Mom shook her head. "It was taking all my strength just to live through one moment to the next." I hardly dared to breathe, waiting for her to continue. "But you know, Kathy, seeing you become interested in the same religion Brett was interested in has done more than stir up old memories. It's made me realize what I truly feared most of all."

I frowned. "What's that?"

Mom smiled sadly. "Anything that keeps life from staying the same. You expect and prepare for certain life changes, but terminal illnesses and joining a new religion—how could I prepare myself for such a possibility?" She stood up and walked slowly towards the window with her arms folded and stared outside for a moment before continuing softly. "Brett's illness was something I wasn't ready for. And then his interest in Kelly's faith—" Mom shook her head slowly. "I could only see such a thing as harmful. Something beyond his illness that was separating him from the rest of our family." She turned to face me. "Seeing you moving in that same direction—I didn't handle it very well. Too many sad memories went with it."

"But you're letting me see the missionaries anyway. Why?"

Mom walked back to sit next to me again and sighed. "Change can bring pain, but it can also be good. I'd forgotten about that." She stopped and looked at me thoughtfully. "I wouldn't let myself see the changes for good in Brett, even as he became more and more ill. I was so afraid of what such changes might do to our family, to me—" She sighed and reached out and touched a lock of my hair. "But I've seen the same changes in you over the past few months, and I've read Brett's journal, and I'm not so afraid anymore."

Mom took another deep, ragged breath before continuing. "I refused to acknowledge when Brett was alive just how important this religion was to him. But it was, and it's important to you, too." She'd been trying not to cry the whole time she'd been talking to me, and that was making it hard for me not to cry, too. "I'm sorry for trying to keep you from anything that's important to you." Mom held her arms out to me then and hugged me while we both cried. When we finally drew apart, Mom reached both hands up behind her neck and unclasped the golden necklace I'd never seen her without. She opened my hand, pressed the locket into my palm, and closed my fingers around it. "I want you to have this, Kathy."

I gasped. "No—I can't—Brett gave it to you—it has his pictures inside it!"

Mom frowned in confusion. "Brett's pictures?"

"Yes." I opened the locket and showed her. "A picture of him right before he got sick on one side, and his baby picture on the other."

Mom shook her head in amazement. "That's not Brett's baby picture, Kathy. It's *your* baby picture. The baby is *you.*"

I was stunned. I stared at the two tiny faces in the opened locket in my palm before shaking my head and looking at Mom again. "I can't— Brett gave it to you."

"And now I'm giving it you," Mom said firmly. "I want you to have this. Besides, like I told Brett when he gave it to me, I don't need a locket to keep him close. I have him locked safe in my heart forever." Mom cupped her hand under my chin and kissed me on the cheek. "Just like I have Alex and Sam—and you, Kathy—in my heart forever."

# EPILOGUE

I was staring at a picture again today, studying it for the hundredth time. In the picture was the image of a dark-haired boy sitting under a tree, smiling down at a tiny little girl snuggled on his lap. I smiled myself, just looking at it. I placed the picture Kelly had taken back in its spot on my dresser, right by Tiny Bear. I'd framed it some time ago and filled an empty space on my dresser with it. I opened the top drawer of my dresser and took out the journal, my special journal from Brett, and hugged it. It, too, had filled an empty space—in my heart—forever.

Mom poked her head around my opened bedroom door. "Well, your visitors are here. Are you ready?"

I nodded. "I'll be right there." I quickly returned the journal to its drawer and turned to pick up the book I'd also been reading and rereading a lot lately. My mind raced back a few months to my eventful— fateful—sixteenth birthday. Unlike the journal I'd received that life-changing night, this book had a midnight blue cover and one of the most peculiar titles I'd ever read. Brett had scrawled a message on the inside front cover in his now-familiar handwriting:

Dear Kitty—

This book was given to me by two amazing guys one day at the hospital during a particularly bad stay. It brought me a lot of comfort during my darkest hours, and now I'm not so scared to die anymore. If this book brought me comfort to face death, then surely it should give you strength to face life. According to what these two teach and what is found in this book, I *will* see you and everyone in our family again someday. So, although our time together on earth was short, we'll always have forever.

My heart was pounding after reading those words for about the millionth time. I still couldn't believe my parents had finally agreed to let me invite two special "visitors" to our house so I could learn more about this book. Jason had offered to come over today, but I'd thanked him and told him no—I wanted to do this on my own. My hands were shaking as I closed the cover, took a deep breath, and walked, clutching the book in my hands, down the hall to the living room.

The two young men in suits and ties stood up when I walked into the room. With huge smiles, they introduced themselves and shook my hand. My heart continued to pound as I nervously smiled back. We all sat down, and one of the young men asked if he could offer a prayer. I nodded, and as I did, my eyes found the laughing, smiling face in a framed picture resting where it always had, on the top shelf of the bookcase in our living room. Only this time, I could have sworn the smile was bigger and happier than it had ever looked before.